TIME FOR BATTLE

Han tugged at his bonds, but they held firm. "Nice fair fight, Thrackan," he said. "A Selonian against a human with his hands tied behind his back."

Thrackan laughed. "I'm interested in entertainment, Han, not fairness." He indicated the four guards, who, by this time, had positioned themselves in the four corners of the chamber's upper level. "Shoot," he ordered. All four of them aimed their blasters at the center of the chamber's floor and fired simultaneously.

The floor exploded in a gout of flame. Han flinched back from the blast, and felt stinging pains on his face and hands as he was peppered with micro-fragments of pulverized stresscrete.

Han staggered back, half-blinded and half-deafened. "If you do not acquit yourself well, my troopers will fire again. At both of you. I would suggest you make the fight convincing."

Han shook his head and blinked, trying to get over the effect of the blaster shots at close range. "How am I supposed to fight convincingly with my hands behind my back?" he asked.

Thrackan laughed again. "You can't expect me to give you all the answers," he said. "Show a little initiative."

Han's vision had cleared enough now for him to see Dracmus, and it was plain that the Selonian was more than prepared to give a good fight. She had her mouth open, putting her needle-sharp teeth on clear display.

Books by Roger MacBride Allen

ASSAULT AT SELONIA

Book Two of the Corellian Trilogy

Roger MacBride Allen

™
SPECTRA

BANTAM BOOKS
NEW YORK • TORONTO • LONDON • SYDNEY • AUCKLAND

ASSAULT AT SELONIA
A Bantam Spectra Book / July 1995

SPECTRA and the portrayal of a boxed "s" are trademarks of
Bantam Books, a division of Bantam Doubleday Dell Publishing Group, Inc.

ISBN 0-553-29805-4

Published simultaneously in the United States and Canada

PRINTED IN THE UNITED STATES OF AMERICA
RAD   0 9 8 7 6 5 4 3 2 1

To Beth and Mike,
who taught me to believe in
the innocence of Richard III,
the inevitable mortality of Bluebottle,
and the perils of an inside straight.

Author's Note

I would like, once again, to thank my editor, Tom Dupree, for all his kindness, encouragement, and determination. God knows he's earned thanks. Without him, there would be no book, and believe me, I know of what I speak.

I would likewise wish to thank my wife, Eleanore Fox, who whipped the manuscript into shape, and kept my nose to the grindstone while enduring a husband occupied in a galaxy far, far away for much of the last few months.

* * *

When I read a book, I always like to know what is behind the dedications, and I find the cryptic ones a trifle frustrating. For those readers who feel the same way, a quick word regarding the dedication of this book, and of the previous volume, might well be in order.

Taking it in order, Book One, *Ambush at Corellia,* was dedicated to Taylor Blanchard and Kathei Logue, on account of two things. First, I take at least half the credit for introducing them to each other. Second, by the time you read this, and assuming all goes well, I will have had the honor to serve as Taylor's best man at their wedding. If that's not worth a dedication, I don't know what is.

This book, *Assault at Selonia,* is dedicated to Mike and Beth Zipser. Beth was my eleventh-grade English teacher. Some lucky people can point to a teacher and say he or she was the one who made a difference, the one who set that person down the path that led to where they are. So with Beth. I can trace a lot of what I am back to her classroom.

Many years after high school and college and all that, more or less by chance, I was sitting on the floor at some party at a science-fiction convention, and who but that same person should quite literally crawl up to me and ask if I was the Roger Allen who went to Walt Whitman High School in Bethesda. I answered in the affirmative, and it wasn't long before we were both sitting in on the same monthly poker game. (And she's a much better player than I am.) Mike has proved to be as good and true a friend as his wife ever since. They are good people, though I question their taste in neckwear. (I'm allowed one cryptic reference.) For those curious about the lessons mentioned in this book's dedication, I invite you to study the novel *The Daughter of Time* by Josephine Tey, the 1950s BBC radio program *The Goon Show,* and a friendly neighborhood game of seven-stud high-low poker, nothing wild.

And don't forget to ante up.

ROGER MACBRIDE ALLEN
Arlington, Virginia
January 1995

What Has Gone Before

It is a time of uncertain peace in the Galaxy. Fourteen years have passed since the defeat of the Empire and the death of Darth Vader. **Leia Organa Solo,** her husband, **Han Solo,** and their three children, **Jaina, Jacen,** and **Anakin,** accompanied by **Chewbacca** the Wookiee, have planned a family trip to Corellia, Han's home world.

Meanwhile, a group known as the **Human League** is conspiring to overthrow the New Republic's government of the Corellian Sector. Some hints of the danger have reached New Republic Intelligence, and NRI agent **Belindi Kalenda** gives Han a cryptic warning about it. Kalenda herself travels to Corellia under cover, but her ship is promptly shot down by unknown assailants who plainly knew that she was coming. Kalenda survives the shoot-down.

Meantime, **Luke Skywalker** has agreed to accompany **Lando Calrissian** on his search for a suitable wife, a search that carries him through a series of misadventures. Lando at last meets the charming **Tendra Risant** of the planet **Sacorria.** However, heavy-handed local authorities force Luke and Lando to leave Sacorria almost as soon as they arrive.

Upon arrival at the Corellian System, the *Millennium Falcon* is subject to a staged attack. Once on the ground, Leia engages a tutor for the children, a Drall named **Ebrihim,** and the family attempts to settle in. During a tour of a large archaeological site, the three children, led by Anakin's power in the Force, locate a huge and strange installation of unknown age and purpose—an installation for which the Human League would seem to be searching.

Mara Jade arrives at Corellia just as the trade summit gets under way. She is the bearer of a coded message for Leia and Han. It contains uncertain evidence that the senders deliberately touched off a recent supernova, and intend to set off more, in populated star systems, if their unspecified demands are not met.

The Human League begins its long-planned revolt against the New Republic. The cities of Corellia erupt. Chewbacca, assisted by **Q9-X2,** Ebrihim's irascible droid, manages to take the children to safety aboard the *Millennium Falcon,* but the ship is damaged and cannot escape into hyperspace. Chewbacca is forced to fly to Drall, Ebrihim's home world.

Once the revolt has scored some initial successes, **Thrackan Sal-Solo,** Han's long-lost cousin and a man known for his guile and cruelty, reveals himself as the leader of the Human League. A powerful jamming system powers up, cutting off communications in the Corellian planetary system.

Han manages to establish contact with Kalenda just before the jamming begins. He provides a diversion for her as she steals an X-TIE "Ugly" fighter and flies toward Coruscant with news of the catastrophe. Han, however, is captured by the Human League.

Meanwhile, Luke and Lando fly into a huge interdiction field that surrounds all of the Corellian star system. The field, far larger than any in history, prevents travel through hyperspace anywhere in the system. Lando and

Luke turn back for Coruscant to bring word. Leia is held hostage with the rest of the trade delegates at Corona House, the Governor's residence. She does not know where the children, Chewbacca, Ebrihim, and Q9, aboard the *Falcon,* have gone, and Han Solo languishes in a Human League prison. . . .

CHAPTER ONE

Family Ties

Hands tied behind his back, Han Solo stumbled as the guards shoved him into the gloomy audience chamber. He realized a moment too late that the floor of the central area was a half meter below the level of the entrance. Moving too fast to stop, he fell over the edge. His shoulder slammed down onto the hard stone floor.

Han rolled over onto his side, then levered himself up into a sitting position. The guards who had shoved him into the chamber stepped back out and slammed the portal shut behind them. Han was alone in the echoing gloom.

He looked around, wondering what was next. At least he was out of that cell. That was something. Not much, maybe, but something. And of course, whatever came next was not likely to be an improvement. In his experience, it was reasonably safe to be filed away in a cell. It was when you were pulled *out* that the trouble began.

Han got himself up onto his feet and looked around. The walls and floors of the place were made of some sort of utilitarian dark gray stresscrete, and there was a dank scent to the air that suggested the windowless chamber was underground. The room was about twenty meters wide and thirty long, with the central floor set a

1

half meter below a two-meter-wide platform that ran around the chamber's perimeter. There were four heavy steel doors, one on each side of the chamber, each of them opening out onto the perimeter platform. Anyone who stood on the platform would be looking down at whoever was in the central area.

The door he had entered was at his back, and he was facing a not quite thronelike chair made of dark wood on the opposite side of the perimeter platform. The chair was large and grand enough that whoever got into it would probably be taller sitting than standing. Han would have an eye-level view of the occupant's knees. That chair told him a good deal about why he was here, and who was going to see him.

Han continued his survey of the chamber. Aside from the throne chair, the place was undecorated, and poorly lit. Nor was it that well made. There were cracks in the floor, and whatever sort of stresscrete they had used in the walls was crumbly-looking. A rush job.

Han had been in a lot of impressive places, and a lot of places that *tried* to be impressive. This place definitely fit into the second category. The Human League had clearly wanted a chamber that would overawe its prisoners as the Hidden Leader sat in judgment—or watched them die for the fun of it—but clearly the League hadn't had the time or resources for a first-class job. All very interesting, but it wasn't the sort of information that might help keep him alive.

Han turned his attention back to the chair. That was obviously where the Big Man would sit when he got here—and Han had a very good idea of who the Big Man was going to be.

There was really only one man it could be. His cousin, Thrackan Sal-Solo. Good old murderous, scheming, vindictive, paranoid Thrackan. That was the who, but what was the *why*? At a minimum, Thrackan wanted to get a look at Han. There was good news and bad news in that.

Obviously, they had been keeping him alive for this meeting. But would they have any reason to keep him alive *afterward*? Did Thrackan have any further use for him?

After all, Han *had* blown up half a squadron of Pocket Patrol Boats. That was offense enough to get a fellow executed most places, and this place was no better than most.

Nor would his relationship to Thrackan do him any good. Once Thrackan had indulged his curiosity, he would be quite capable of killing Han on the spot.

No, Han knew he wasn't going to live through this because of family feeling. He would have to make himself seem valuable to Thrackan if he wanted to survive. But he had no intention of being the slightest help to Thrackan's Human League.

So how to *seem* to be valuable without actually doing these thugs any good?

Han heard something moving on the other side of the doors behind the not-quite-throne. He had run out of time for thinking.

Han backed away a step or two from the door. If Thrackan the adult was anything like the Thrackan of Han's childhood, he was going to have to be careful, very careful, in the way he played this. Thrackan, as he recalled, had been quite young when he had started making a show of pulling the wings off insects and beating up smaller children. He had found out very early just how loudly a reputation for cruelty could speak. *Here's what I do to someone I'm not even mad at. What do you think will happen if I get mad at you?* There were those in the Galaxy for whom cruelty, threats, and intimidation were art forms. Not Thrackan. He used them as blunt instruments, weapons. Which was not to say that he did not enjoy his work.

The doors swung fully open and a double line of seedy-looking men in officers' uniforms came in. One column turned and marched around the corner of the platform to the left of the throne, the other to the right. The two columns lined up on the perimeter platform to either side of the big chair, turned, and faced forward, eyes straight ahead, staring at each other across the center of the room, right over Han's head.

Judging by the insignia, which seemed to follow the old Imperial pattern, these were some very senior officers indeed. But today's field marshals had, no doubt, been yesterday's malcontents. Fancy uniforms and a forest of shoulder pips did not make the wearer a seasoned officer worthy of respect. These fellows were no more the equals of the Imperial officers of the past than a child with a toy lightsaber would be a match for Luke Skywalker.

By the looks of their paunches, none of them had done any real training in years. Their bleary eyes, flushed faces, and unshaved jaws—and the smell of strong drink that wafted in with them—told Han that at least some of these very grand officers had been doing some fairly serious celebrating the night before. *That* was a bit premature. How could even the most drunken of fools think that the Human League had won already?

Plainly, this crowd was not made up of Galaxy-class minds. They were here as window dressing, and nothing more. Han paid them no more mind. He turned his attention back to the open door behind the big chair. There was a moment's delay, either because the Great Man was running late, or because someone thought it made for a more dramatic entrance. But then, Thrackan Sal-Solo, onetime Hidden Leader of the Human League, and now the self-declared Diktat of the Corellian Sector—came into the room. He walked with the brisk, steady confidence of a man who knew exactly what he was doing and where he was going, a man absolutely certain he could do the job at hand. Thrackan Sal-Solo stepped around the right-hand side of the big chair, came forward to the edge of the platform and paused there a moment. He stared long and hard at his long-lost cousin, and Han stared back.

Han felt as if he were staring into a strange, distorting mirror. Thrackan wore Han's face, or else Han wore his. Not that one could not be told from the other. Thrackan's hair was darker, a black-brown shot through with gray. He was a few kilos heavier, and he had a neatly trimmed beard. Thrackan was perhaps two or three centimeters taller than Han. There was a harshness, a ruthlessness, not just in Thrackan's expression, but in the set of his face, as if that look of anger and suspicion was the one his face fell into most naturally.

But even those differences did little more than emphasize how much they were alike. Han felt as if that imaginary mirror were showing him the man he might have been. He did not like the idea. Not one little bit. This first meeting was a lot more disconcerting than he had expected it to be.

It was not just Han who saw the resemblance. The uniformed types that lined the two sides of the room were obviously supposed to keep eyes ahead, but not one of them could resist the temptation to stare first at Han, and then at Thrackan. Small murmurs of astonishment filled the room.

Indeed, it seemed as if Thrackan were the only one who did not find it all off-putting. He looked down at Han with a calm and steady gaze.

Han decided he had better do his best to take it all in stride as well. Or at least pretend. "Hello, Thrackan," he said. "I sort of figured I'd be seeing you."

"And hello to you, Han," his cousin replied, in a voice that was startlingly similar to Han's. "Some things never change, do they?"

"I'm not exactly sure I know what you mean."

"Back in the old days, Han," Thrackan said. "Back in the old days. You were always the one who liked to play games. And I was always the one who had to come in and clean up after you."

"That's not exactly the way I remember it," Han said. Thrackan had never cleaned up after himself, let alone anyone else. But he had always been good at making it *seem* like he had. Most bullies were good at playing the victim. Thrackan had never had the slightest problem blaming others for his foul-ups, or taking all the credit for someone else's effort and success. "But you're right," Han went on. "Some things never change."

"This time there's rather a lot to clean up," Thrackan went on. "You shot up my spaceport, damaged or destroyed six of my Pocket Patrol Boats, and allowed that X-TIE Ugly fighter to escape," Thrackan said. "We believe that X-TIE managed to jump into hyperspace. If its pilot is able to get word to the New Republic, that could throw many of my plans into disarray."

"I thought the spaceport and the PPBs belonged to the Corellian government. I didn't think they were yours," Han said.

"They are now," Thrackan said. "For that matter, the government is mine as well. But just now the point is that the games you are playing have caused me a great deal of trouble."

"I'm real broken up about that," Han said.

"I doubt it," Thrackan said. "I wouldn't be, if I were you. But the question remains—what am I to do with you?"

"I have a suggestion." Han said, his voice light and casual. "Let me go and then let me accept your surrender. I might be able to get the New Republic to go easy on you."

"I don't suppose you'd be willing to explain why I should do that." Thrackan said, the trace of a smile on his face.

"Because you're going to lose, Thrackan," Han said. "Because that X-TIE got through, and even if it didn't, someone else will get the word out, somehow. And you're up against the same New Republic that beat the Empire. If they could take on the Emperor and Darth Vader and Admiral Thrawn and the Death Stars, what makes you think they should have any problems with the likes of *you*? Why not save everyone a lot of trouble and give up now?"

Thrackan smiled, but there was nothing warm or happy about his expression. Instead, the smile made him look colder, harsher. He shook his head sadly. "Still the same old Han. Beaten up, dirty, unshaved, a captive fresh from a night in his cell, and still full of the same old tired bluster and bluff." He hesitated a moment, and leaned back in his chair. "There's a very good reason I'm not going to lose," he said. "I've won already. It's all over. The New Republic might be able to cause me some limited trouble, but nothing more. Not unless they want a few inhabited star systems vaporized. Otherwise, they will leave me strictly alone."

Han hesitated a moment before replying. Was there anything behind that claim? There was no doubt that a star had gone supernova, a star that had no business doing any such thing. The League had claimed responsibility, but how could a bunch of ignorant malcontents and thugs manage to blow up a star? "That was a nice parlor trick," Han said. "But I'm not sure you can repeat it."

"Oh, we'll convince you," Thrackan said. "Have no doubt of that." His voice, his manner, were absolutely confident. If it was a bluff, it was an awfully convincing one.

"So why am I here, Thrackan?" Han asked, in a tone of voice that made it sound as if he were a busy man who had more important things to do. With most people, it would have been a suicidal display of arrogance. But Han knew his cousin. A show of politeness would

have won Han little more than a sneer of contempt
from Thrackan.

"In such a hurry to get back to your cell?" Thrackan
asked with a wicked smile.

Han resisted the temptation to let out a sigh of relief.
Until that moment he hadn't been sure if Thrackan intended him to live long enough to see his cell again.
"No," he said. "But I'm not much interested in trading
threats, either. Why am I here?"

"I *did* have the vague idea that you might be willing to
cooperate with me. Act like a patriotic Corellian, help
me get rid of these New Republic interlopers. But I
never did have much hope for that idea. It's not going to
happen, is it?"

"Not in a million years."

"All right, then," Thrackan said. "If you won't help
me, why should I keep you alive?"

That question would have terrified most people under
the circumstances, but Han knew Thrackan from way
back. Even a few moments' reacquaintance told him he
hadn't changed much since the old days. If Thrackan
had already decided to kill him, he wouldn't have
wasted his time with word games. Han would already
have had a blaster hole through his chest. Thrackan's
cruelty had never been capricious or pointless. Whenever he did something vicious—or indeed anything at all
—it was because doing it benefited him directly. Nor
had Thrackan ever been shy about letting others do his
dirty work, or been much interested in putting himself
to extra effort. There was no way to know for sure, but
at a guess, Thrackan had genuinely not yet decided
whether or not to let Han live. He could go either way.
And *that* meant the reasons for letting him live or die
were in the balance. The reasons for killing Han were
depressingly obvious, but why would Thrackan want him
alive?

"There are lots of good reasons for not killing me,"

Han said, trying to stall for time. He tried to sound calm and confident, but Han's tone of voice didn't seem very convincing, even in his own ears.

"Perhaps you could help me think of a few," Thrackan said coolly.

Think, Han told himself. *Work it out.* Why *would* Thrackan want him alive? Wait a second. Why were *any* of them alive? It was obvious that the Human League had deliberately timed its phony uprising to coincide with the trade summit, when lots of off-planet movers and shakers would be on Corellia. And all of those brass were staying in the Governor-General's residence, Corona House. If the League had wanted to, it could have blown the building to smithereens, killing everyone inside, decapitating the planetary government at a stroke, and killing the New Republic's Chief of State as well.

But they had done no such thing. Han had been at Corona House when the assault came. In his best judgment, it had been a clumsily executed surgical strike, not a bungled decapitation attempt. It was clear that the League had intended to bottle up the Governor-General and Leia and the rest of the higher-ups in Coronet House by sealing off all the exits and burying them in rubble. That Han had managed to escape was a testament to their incompetence, not their intent.

It was hard to escape the notion that Thrackan wanted Leia and the others for use as bargaining chips, hostages. Suddenly Han understood. His cousin was keeping him alive in hopes of using him to ensure Leia's cooperation in whatever plots he was hatching. But if he needed something from Leia, that meant Thrackan Sal-Solo was not the master of all he surveyed, all bluster to the contrary. Han grinned, and this time he wasn't trying to pretend. "There's no reason at all to keep me alive," Han said. "None whatsoever. At least there isn't if you don't care how upset the Chief of State gets. And she tends to get real angry when members of her family are murdered in cold blood."

Thrackan was suddenly angry. "I don't need your Chief of State," he snapped.

"Then why did you work so hard to capture her?" Han demanded. "Why was the revolt timed for the beginning of the trade summit?"

"Quiet!" Thrackan half shouted. "I'll ask the questions around here. One more word out of you about your wife and I swear I'll kill you myself, here and now, no matter how much I need you alive."

Han said nothing, but simply smiled, knowing that he had won and that Thrackan knew it. Han had called his bluff.

Thrackan glared at him and drummed his fingers on the arm of his chair. "I had forgotten just how much you used to drive me crazy," he said. "But I think I can at least remind you that it is not wise to try and score points off me. Besides," he said, gesturing to the men lining the two sides of the room, "my officers have been working very hard and they deserve some recreation." Thrackan smiled again, and, if anything, it was an even more unpleasant expression than it had been the last time. "Honor detail may stand at ease," Thrackan said, keeping his eyes squarely on Han. The thugs-in-uniform relaxed, shifted their feet, and smiled at each other with a certain nasty eagerness. "Captain Falco, instruct the keepers to send the ah—other—prisoner—in."

One of the greasier-looking officers saluted and said, "Yes, sir." He pulled a comlink out of his pocket and spoke into it. "Send it in, Sergeant."

There was a moment's pause, one that Han did not enjoy at all. Then, faintly at first, but gradually getting louder, Han could hear muffled footsteps coming from behind him, from beyond the door he had come through. Han turned to face the door, and backed away from it. Doing so put Thrackan directly behind him, but it seemed to Han that, all things considered, his cousin was dangerous no matter where he was. He was, at any rate, the danger Han knew. Best to concentrate on the danger he didn't know.

The doors swung open and a pair of heavily armed Human League troopers came in, their blasters at the ready. They immediately took up positions on either side of the door, with their backs to the wall. Han had rated no such precautions. It would seem the Leaguers regarded the whatever-it-was as far more of a threat than Han.

After a moment's pause, the "other prisoner" came in —and suddenly Han understood all the precautions. The "other prisoner" was a Selonian. Even thugs and fools knew to take Selonians very seriously indeed.

And this Selonian was a big and tough-looking female, though that was no surprise. All the Selonians ever seen in public were big, tough, and female.

Selonians tended to be a trifle taller and more slender than humans. They had somewhat longer bodies, and shorter arms and legs. Though normally bipedal, they could go on all fours when they wanted. Their hands and feet had retractable claws, good for climbing or digging—also very good in a fight. They were strong swimmers, with short, powerful tails that helped steer and propel them in the water, and served as a counterbalance while walking—and, not incidentally, as a fearsome club in a fight.

Theory had it that Selonians had evolved from some sort of predatory swimming mammal that lived in riverside burrows, a species that moved from riverside burrowing to sophisticated tunneling far from water. They had sleek, short fur, usually brown or black, and long pointed faces full of sharp teeth. They had bristly whiskers and equally bristly tempers if you didn't know how to handle them right. They lived in underground dens for the most part, and their social structure was unusual, to say the least.

But, interesting though it was, Han was not worried about how the Selonian society was controlled by sterile females just at the moment. He was more interested in this particular sterile female's very, very sharp teeth.

The big, lithe, graceful creature walked into the room calmly, casually, with such self-assurance she might have been the master of the place rather than a prisoner. Two more guards followed her into the chamber, but she paid no more mind to them than she had to the first pair.

There was one other thing that Han could not help but notice—the Selonian had her hands free. That could only mean that the Selonian had given her parole, promised not to disobey or attempt to escape. It would otherwise be absolute madness to let her go free. But if she had given her parole, then the guards were not only superfluous, they were a deadly insult. It was definitely not advisable to question a Selonian's honor. Arrogance or ignorance might explain such a lapse, but nothing could forgive it.

"Get down there, you," said one of the guards, pointing to the lower level of the chamber, where Han waited. They had shoved Han over the edge with his hands tied behind his back. The Selonian they allowed to use a small set of stairs set in the left rear corner of the chamber. She walked down the stairs with a calm grace, and came to stand in the center of the chamber. She turned toward Han and looked at him, her expression utterly neutral.

"Say hello to Dracmus," Thrackan said. "Quite an impressive specimen, don't you think? She was trying to do us a little damage in Coronet when we picked her up."

Han said nothing. Taunting Thrackan was one thing. He could know just how far to push things, know what the consequences might be. Not with a Selonian. Not with the way things were shaping up here.

Thrackan laughed. "Not taking any chances, I see. Dracmus, say hello to the family pirate and traitor, my dear cousin Han Solo."

"Bellorna-fa ecto mandaba-sa, despecto Han Solo!" said Dracmus. *"Pada ectal ferbraz bellorna-cra."* Her voice dripped with contempt, but the words did not match the tone. *"Speak you this language of mine, Honorable Han Solo? None of these fools do."*

Han thought fast. He had no way of knowing what Dracmus intended. All he knew was that she was the enemy of his enemy—if even that much was true. She could be some hired stooge of Thrackan's, playing a part in some convoluted plan of his. Could this be a trap? But what point to a trap when he was already a prisoner? And suppose Dracmus was wrong, and one of the Leaguers *did* speak Selonian?

But the universe never had given Han many sure answers, and it wasn't likely to start anytime soon. *"Belorna-sa mandaba-fa kurso-kurso,"* Han snarled back, trying to make his voice as abusive sounding as Dracmus's had been. *"Speak me it well enough."* Han backed to the corner and risked a glance at Thrackan. His cousin was grinning from ear to ear. Clearly he had no doubt the two of them were trading insults.

"Kurso! Sa kogna fos zul embaga. Persa chana-sa prognas els abta for dejed kurso," Dracmus growled the words, and snapped her jaws at him. *"Good! I think they will force us to fight. Allow me to win quickly and you will avoid being well injured."*

Han had been afraid of that. It would be just like Thrackan to force two prisoners to fight, especially in a combat as unequal as this one would be.

"I see there is great love between you," Thrackan said. "I think our Selonian friend has many pent-up feelings for her hosts. She cannot vent them on us, as she has given her parole, and must not break her oath. I must say that it is convenient to have an enemy of such strong principles. I think I shall reward her honorable behavior and let her take it all out on you."

Han tugged at his bonds, but they held firm. "Nice fair fight, Thrackan," he said. "A Selonian against a human with his hands tied behind his back."

Thrackan laughed. "I'm interested in entertainment, Han, not fairness." He indicated the four guards, who, by this time, had positioned themselves in the four corners of the chamber's upper level. "Shoot," he ordered. All four of them aimed their blasters at the center of the chamber's floor and fired simultaneously.

The floor exploded in a gout of flame. Han flinched back from the blast, and felt stinging pains on his face and hands as he was peppered with micro-fragments of pulverized stresscrete.

Han staggered back, half-blinded and half-deafened. "If you do not acquit yourself well, my troopers will fire again. At both of you. I would suggest you make the fight convincing."

Han shook his head and blinked, trying to get over the effect of the blaster shots at close range. "How am I supposed to fight convincingly with my hands behind my back?" he asked.

Thrackan laughed again. "You can't expect me to give you all the answers," he said. "Show a little initiative."

Han's vision had cleared enough now for him to see Dracmus, and it was plain that the Selonian was more than prepared to give a good fight. She had her mouth open, putting her needle-sharp teeth on clear display.

The only thing Han had going for him was surprise, and he decided to use it. He shouted at the top of his lungs and charged straight for Dracmus, his head down. He got under her guard, if just barely, and managed to give her a good solid head butt to the gut. He hit her hard enough to knock down a human, but she managed to use her tail to steady herself against the floor and stay upright. She took a swipe at his head with her left hand-paw. She didn't connect fully, but it was enough to send him sprawling.

He slammed his left shoulder into the side of the raised platform and almost fell. He recovered and spun to his right just in time to dodge another open-handed slap at his head.

And in that split second Han knew he could trust her, at least part of the way. He saw her claws retract in the split second before her hand-paw whipped past his face, and she had missed by less than the length of those claws.

No claws. She could have raked them across his face twice by now. She was playing fair, or would be until it came down to killing Han or Thrackan's goons killing them both. He would have to lose fast, and convincingly. *That* ought to be easy. He could do it with both hands tied behind his back. At least he'd better be able to do so. He pulled at the bindings on his wrists, but it was clear that they weren't going to give.

Han dodged another swing from the left, but ran straight into the sucker punch to his chest. The blow knocked him clean off his feet. He landed on the hard stresscrete floor, taking most of the fall across the top of his back, even though he managed to crush his hands and bounce the back of his head off the stresscrete.

Dracmus was lunging for him before he could even begin to recover, and it was either Han's dumb luck or Dracmus's superb reflexes that sent her diving left as he rolled right.

Han managed to roll to his feet one more time—and almost collapsed again. His ankle had somehow gotten twisted in that last fall. Just what he needed. A bad sprain. He swore under his breath and hobbled to the far side of the chamber as fast as he could. His right eye was beginning to swell, and he was pretty sure his nose was bleeding. If this was going easy on him, he'd hate to deal with Dracmus in a bad mood. But he was going to have to trust her. Either she was going to change her mind and kill him, or she wasn't.

She swung around and came toward him in the stalking, wide-stepping gait of a wrestler, her arms spread wide, her tail slashing back and forth. The men on either side of the chamber were hooting and cheering and cursing. The air was getting thick, and the lights in the room seemed to have dimmed. Han shook his head again to try to clear it, and instantly regretted it as his dizziness got worse. He was not going to last much longer.

Finish it. He would have to finish it quick, and go down fighting, satisfy Thrackan that he had gotten a good show. Han knew that Thrackan, at least the Thrackan of old, would only be satisfied if Han were knocked out by a blow from Dracmus. He'd feel cheated if Han simply passed out, collapsed in a heap, but that was going to happen if Han stayed in this thing much longer. And Han did not want Thrackan to be dissatisfied. Not when he had a blaster handy to vent his frustrations and Han available as a convenient target. Han *thought* that Thrackan wanted him alive, but he wasn't sure enough to bet his life on it. Besides, a well-aimed blaster bolt could maim him and still leave him perfectly alive.

Keep fighting. Han staggered to the right, circling around. Dracmus came no closer, but circled as well, watching for her chance. Han yanked once more at his wrist restraints, out of frustration as much as anything else, and was astonished to feel them snap.

Either the restraints' locks had been damaged in the fall or, more likely, Thrackan had put him in gimmicked restraints to start with, something that could released by remote control at whatever moment seemed most amusing to the operator. It didn't matter. He had his hands.

He spread his arms wide in a wrestler's stance and moved in on Dracmus.

Dracmus was at least as surprised as Han to realize her opponent suddenly had his hands free. She backpedaled a bit, putting a bit more distance between Han and herself. She snarled, a sound full of anger and frustration, and Han felt sure she meant it. She wasn't acting. She might or might not want to kill Han, but she had every intention of *beating* him.

Well, he was going to make her work for it. The advantages were all still with Dracmus, but maybe, now, he had a fighting chance. He feinted to the left, once, twice, and then to the right before diving straight in, grasping his hands together in a pile-driver punch to the gut, to knock the wind out of her. He remembered at the last possible moment to strike higher on her abdomen than he would on a human. He caught the right spot, but just barely. She staggered backward, and Han scrambled to regain his own balance and follow up. She had sagged down enough that Han could try for a punch in the snout, a delicate spot on the Selonian anatomy. He swung and connected cleanly—and then instantly wondered if doing so was such a good idea.

From the expression on Dracmus's face, it clearly hurt a lot—but it also got her good and mad. Those sharp jaws swung around and snapped down on thin air a centimeter from Han's arm, and even before he had stopped dodging, an iron-hard fist hit him square in the chest. If it had hit him in the stomach, he would have doubled over in pain, but Dracmus had placed her blow too high. As it was, Han was thrown onto the floor. He recovered and winced with pain as he got back to his feet. It seemed likely that either the blow or the landing had bruised or cracked a rib.

Dracmus's tail was lashing back and forth, and she had her fangs bared—but she did not dive in to get her teeth around his throat, or rake her claws across his eyes. She was still restraining herself, at least somewhat. Han realized that he had to throw this fight immediately, before she lost all control of her anger and moved in for the kill. *"Use your tail!"* he bellowed to her in Selonian. *"Batter me with that!"*

The mad, angry light in her eye seemed to dim for a moment, and she looked at him, as if she were surprised to see him there. Good. Maybe that meant the words were reaching her—though Han could not be altogether sure. She swung toward him and snapped her jaws at him again, and Han dodged back to his left. Even though he had urged her to make the move, he didn't even realize she was still swinging around, pivoting on one foot to bring her tail around. She had it raised high, and caught Han neatly in the head with it.

Han staggered one last time, and lurched backward, slumping over until he was facing his cousin on his throne. Han's vision was going, going black, but he could see Thrackan grinning at him, laughing, that face that was so similar to his own contorted by a cruel, sadistic leer.

Han was almost glad when the darkness closed over him.

CHAPTER TWO

The Fabric Torn

The *Lady Luck* cut her lightspeed engines and dropped into normal space in the Coruscant system. Lando Calrissian checked the navicomputer and nodded in satisfaction. "In the groove," he said. "We've got auto-clearance from Coruscant Control, all the way in."

"Good," Luke said. "The sooner we're there, the better."

"Shouldn't we try and contact the navy brass from here?" Lando asked. "We don't want to waste any time."

Luke shook his head. "No," he said. "We're up against something big and organized. We have to assume that an organization that can seal off the entire Corellian star system is capable of monitoring communications, even on secure links. I think we should play it safe and not say anything until we can talk to our people face-to-face."

"You might be right," Lando said. "At any rate, you're right that we're up against something big." Someone or something had placed an interdiction field around the entire Corellian system, produced by using a gravity-well generator to distort the mass lines of real-space. No hyperdrive could operate inside an interdiction field. No ship inside the field could make the jump to lightspeed, and any craft that passed through the field while in hyperspace would be forced out into normal space. Luke and Lando had discovered the interdiction field when the *Lady Luck* was abruptly decanted out of hyperspace on the outskirts of the Corellian system, far out enough that the journey in toward the planet of Corellia through realspace would take months at best.

No one had ever managed to generate an interdiction field a hundredth, a thousandth, as large as the Corellian field. Even if Lando and Luke had no other information beyond that, the mere fact of an interdiction field that size was more than enough to justify raising the alarm.

But there was more. Leia Organa Solo, Chief of State of the New Republic, was in the Corellian system, and the news out of Corellia had not been good for some time.

Something would have to be done, that much was clear—but what? The Corellian system was sealed off from the outside universe, and there was no fast way in. Whoever had done this thing would have plenty of time to work whatever mischief they pleased.

But Lando had other, more personal, worries. Tendra. Lady Tendra Risant of the planet Sacorria. Lando had met her for the first and only time just a few days before, but he already knew that she was someone special, someone who could be important in his life.

It was more than a trifle ironic that he had set off across the Galaxy in search of a bride with money, only to meet a woman who made him forget all about money. Well, at least made him stop thinking about it for a while.

What worried him at the moment was that when he had bid her farewell, he had been bound for Corellia, and she had known it. Sooner or later—probably sooner —Sacorria, along with the rest of the Galaxy, would learn that Corellia had cut itself off from the outside universe. Tendra would hear about it, and have every reason to think he was on Corellia. She would worry, and would likely do more than that. Tendra was not the sort of person to sit idly by. She would act. She would do something, though space alone knew what. And knowing that gave Lando plenty to worry about himself.

But even if she did just sit tight, Tendra had said that things were brewing on her home world of Sacorria. Sacorria was one of the "Outlier" planets, so called because it was on the fringes of the Corellian Sector, in both physical and political terms.

Sacorria was populated by the same three species as Corellia—human, Drall, and Selonian. It was ruled by the Triad, a mysterious triumvirate made of self-appointed representatives from each of the three species. That right there was enough to give Lando some concern. In his experience, oligarchies were not the most rational or stable forms of governments.

And there had been a very definite clamp-down in progress when Luke and Lando had been on Sacorria; enough of one to get them kicked off the planet.

Lando checked his system displays one more time, then looked over to Luke in the copilot's seat. "Luke," he said, "do you think that the trouble on Sacorria might have something to do with the Corellian interdiction field?"

Luke looked toward Lando and frowned. "What makes you think that?"

"Well, one place *threw* us out, and the other threw up an interdiction field like a wall to *keep* us out."

"Come on," Luke said. "The whole interdiction field just to keep *us* out? I knew you had a big ego, Lando, but let's not get carried away."

"I don't mean that the field was meant to keep *us* out," Lando said. "Just you. I'm not that important, but you are. You're the Jedi Master. That's why I brought you along on this trip—so you could impress everybody. Well, maybe the Corellians were impressed. There could be plenty of reasons for wanting to keep you out of the way. As a general rule, troublemakers don't want you around. It wouldn't be the first time someone went to extremes just to keep you at arm's length."

"Maybe," Luke said, not entirely convinced. "But it still seems to me like an awful lot of trouble. Besides, not many people knew we were going to Corellia. *I* didn't know I was going until the night before we left Coruscant."

"The folks who kicked us off Sacorria could have guessed that's where we were headed, and they could have found out for sure a half-dozen ways." Lando hooked a thumb toward the wardroom, where R2-D2 and C-3PO were. "All they'd have to do is set Golden Boy back there to talking, and they'd have our life stories in thirty seconds."

"I heard that, and I must deny it," said Threepio, his voice coming from the intercom. "I am always discreet in my dealings with outsiders—"

"Get off this feed and quit snooping, you blabbermouth collection of spare parts," Lando said.

"But I must protest—"

"There's no need for you to be listening in, Threepio," Luke said, cutting him off. "Just tell R2-D2 to get ready for final approach. We'll be home on Coruscant soon." He reached over and cut the power to the intercom.

Lando glared at the intercom. "I think Threepio just made my point for me," he said. "If the Sacorrians had wanted to find out where we were headed, they could have done it."

"No doubt about it," Luke said. "But that interdiction field is immense! Think how much power, how much planning and organization and engineering it must have taken to get it up and running. It's not the sort of thing you casually switch on just to keep out one unwanted visitor. There are easier ways to keep a person out of a star system, even a Jedi Knight. The Sacorrians could have simply locked us up, or had us shot, or put a bomb on the *Lady Luck*."

"I suppose," Lando said. "But even if the Corellian field wasn't activated just to keep us out of the picture, I still think there might be a connection between the clampdown on Sacorria and whatever has happened in the Corellian system."

"You might have something," Luke said. "But I've got a feeling we're not going to know, one way or the other, for quite a while yet."

The *Lady Luck* flew on.

* * *

Luke was more than a little surprised to see the reception committee that was waiting for them on Coruscant as they disembarked from the *Lady Luck*. The usual landing-bay crew was nowhere to be seen, and instead they were greeted by a distinctly closemouthed security team of two men and one woman in New Republic Intelligence uniforms.

"This doesn't exactly feel relaxed," Lando muttered as the senior NRI officer came forward. "Sort of reminds me of the way the customs agents did things the last time I was arrested for smuggling."

"Master Skywalker, Captain Calrissian, good day to you both," the officer said. He was a young man, a little pale-faced and on the beefy side. He looked as if he hadn't gotten much sleep in a while. "I am Captain Showolter of New Republic Intelligence," he said. "The two of you are wanted rather urgently at an important meeting. Would you be so kind as to come with us?"

"Suppose we *wouldn't* be so kind?" Lando asked. Changed circumstances or not, he still had the smug-

gler's instinctive distrust of police who told him where
to go.

Showolter sighed and gave Lando a look of tired ex-
asperation. "Then we bundle you up and take you along
anyway, to keep you quiet for a while, if nothing else.
We could decide later on if we were arresting you or
putting you into protective custody. Now will you come
along, or do we have to waste time with more nonsense?"

"What is it about?" Lando asked.

"I can't tell you that," Showolter said. "But I bet
you're smart enough to figure it out."

"Corellia," Luke said.

Showolter gave them a tired smile. "I have specific
orders not to tell you, but I have this feeling you might
be good guessers. Now, are you coming or aren't you?"

"We're coming," Luke said. "Mind if we bring the
droids? One of them has some important data stored in
him."

"The more the merrier," Showolter said in a deadpan
voice.

"Great," Lando muttered as they followed Showolter
to a waiting hovercar. "I was looking forward to getting
away from those two."

Luke laughed and slapped his friend on the back.
"Looks like you're stuck with all of us for a while
longer."

They got into the hovercar and it took off, Showolter
riding in the rear compartment with Luke and Lando
and the droids while the other two NRI officers rode up
front. The windows of the hovercar instantly went
opaque. Whether this was meant to conceal the passengers from passersby, or to keep Luke and Lando from
knowing where they were going, Luke had no idea. If it
was the latter, then the effort was, of course, wasted. A
Jedi Master had no need to look out a window to know
where he was going. Luke didn't even have to concen-

trate in order to know they were headed toward the towers of the palace, albeit by a circuitous route. Well, that was no surprise.

Luke sat back and took the time to think. It was obvious that at least someone on Coruscant already knew something was up. But Showolter clearly had no intention of telling them what that something was, or where they were being taken. They had not received any sort of invitation to this mysterious meeting until they arrived on planet. That convinced Luke that the leadership on Coruscant was at least as worried as Luke was that the opposition—whoever the opposition was—was capable of tapping secure communications.

And if they were worried about that back here, then something else must have already have gone wrong.

The car slowed, and there was a change in the sound of the air rushing past the aircar's exterior. Luke's sense of direction told him the same thing that the shift in sound had—the aircar had just flown directly *into* the palace, through one of the upper-level access ports. Not unheard of, but not the usual thing, either. Clearly, they were taking security seriously.

The car landed with a gentle bump. The door opened and Luke and Lando stepped out into a wholly anonymous shipping dock. Showolter was right behind them, and escorted them toward a waiting turbolift. The other two NRI officers stayed in the aircar, watching Luke, Lando, Showolter, and the droids cross to the lift doors.

The turbolift doors shut as soon as they were in, though none of them had activated any control. Much to Luke's surprise, the car began to descend. He exchanged a glance with Lando and saw that his friend was reading the same thing into the movement downward. *Up* meant status on Coruscant. Grand ceremonies, important meetings, and opulent receptions could only take place on the upper levels of the great city. *Down* was the low-status direction, and movers and shakers of Coruscant quite literally looked down at the lower above-surface levels, while the subterranean levels were beneath their contempt.

But if *down* was the unfashionable direction, it was also the high-security one. The lower depths were full of forgotten chambers and hidden places. No one outside could throw a grenade or fire a missile or listen in at a window when you were half a kilometer underground. But Luke knew the rich and powerful of Coruscant— and he also knew just how unsavory parts of the lower depths could be. Things were clearly dire if the powers-that-be were willing to go underground.

"Where to?" he asked.

"An NRI safe room," Showolter said. "And we're going in by the back door. Protocol requires that each party come by a separate route if at all possible. Makes it harder for the opposition to realize that people are getting together. But the bad news is that the two direct routes into this safe room have already been used."

"What would you call a direct route?" Lando asked.

"Well, one of them is a turbolift that opens out directly into the safe room. The other is a concealed side tunnel from a maintenance tunnel that's still in active use. But we have to use the back door. And let's just say this route will never be a tourist attraction."

Lando raised his eyebrows, but said no more.

Luke was trying to judge the descent of the turbolift car. As best he could estimate, they were at least eight hundred meters below their starting point when the turbolift car came to a halt. The door did not open. Instead, Showolter drew his sidearm, a New Republic standard-issue blaster. For a fleeting moment Luke wondered if they had just walked into a trap. But he sensed no malice or deception on Showolter's part, and the NRI officer's next words set him at ease. "Captain Calrissian, Master Skywalker, I believe you are both

armed. Might I suggest you draw your weapons before
we open the door?"

"Ah, sure," Lando said as he drew his own blaster.
"But mind if I ask why?"

"Local wildlife," Showolter said.

"Oh, my!" Threepio said. "Feral hunters? Here?"

"That's right," Showolter said.

"Ah," Luke said. "I guess I shouldn't be surprised."
The city of Coruscant had been where it was for a long,
long time, and any number of strange animals had been
brought to the planet for a variety of reasons—some of
them meant for pets, some for food, some for exhibi-
tion. Over the millennia a certain number of them had
escaped, and of those, a fair number had gone feral,
even evolved to adapt to their new circumstances.

The upper city was a source of resources—mostly in
the form of garbage. It was all but inevitable that a
warped sort of ecosystem would come into being as the
denizens of the depths adapted to their environment.
There were even stories—unsubstantiated, so far as
Luke knew—that some of the feral species in the lower
depths had, over time, devolved from their intelligent
ancestors. There were endless urban legends of un-
derlevel zombies, ferocious creatures descended from
hapless tourists or office workers who had gotten lost in
the subterranean levels thousands of years in the past.

"So what's the local nuisance in this part of the city?"
asked Lando.

"We call them corridor ghouls," Showolter said, "but
we're not quite sure what they are. However, they are
definitely hungry. Nasty little things, quadrupeds about
knee-high. They seem to be more or less mammalian,
but they don't have fur, just dead-white skin. They're
blind—totally eyeless, in fact. But they have big ears—
and big teeth. We think they navigate by echo location.
At least that would explain the high-pitched screams

they make. But however they get around, they are fast and precise when they go for you. So watch it."

"We're doomed!" Threepio moaned, and Artoo let out a dispirited moan.

"Take it easy, you two," Luke said.

"Yeah, relax. Sounds like they'd make perfect pets," Lando muttered. He checked the charge on his blaster. "Ready," he said.

Luke unclipped his lightsaber from his belt and held it at the ready, but did not switch it on. "Ready," he said.

"Good," Showolter said. "We have the lights on so we can see them. That evens things up a bit. I wouldn't want to meet them in the dark, that's for sure. Now, we're going to step out of the turbolift, go straight down the corridor for fifty meters, then take a left and another immediate left. We go another twenty meters, and then we have a steep ramp that leads down to another level about fifteen meters down. Can that droid on rollers handle a steep ramp?"

Artoo let out an indignant blurting noise.

"Sure," Luke said with a smile. "He can handle pretty much anything."

"Well, I hope so," Showolter said, clearly a bit dubious. "But everybody watch your step—or your wheels, or whatever. The corridor is *old,* and the footing is not all it could be. And watch it at the bottom of the ramp. The ghouls know that's a good place to lie in wait. Now, once we're at the base of the ramp, we'll be in front of a big blast-proof door, about ten meters away the base of the ramp. Beyond the door is the safe room where we're meeting. There's a keypad entrance system on the door, and if you could cover me while I'm punching in the code, that would be most helpful. The ghouls seem to like attacking while we're working the door."

"Ah—just a quick question," Lando said.

"Yes, what?" Showolter asked.

"If the corridor ghouls are as nasty as you say, why can't you just sweep them out of this part of the tunnels and then block all the entrances?"

Showolter laughed unpleasantly. "I see I haven't made myself clear. We *like* having them around. They're part of the security system. So if you don't *need* to shoot one, please don't."

"I don't get it," Lando said.

"Very simple," Showolter replied. "Once we're all inside the safe room, we turn out the lights in the corridors. Anyone who comes snooping around is going to get a *very* nasty surprise."

"*That* sounds like the NRI I've heard about. And you people wonder why you have trouble with recruiting," Lando said.

Showolter laughed. "Whatever. Just be ready." He turned, faced the front of the car, and held his weapon at the ready. "All right Berleman," he said to the open air. "Open door."

Obviously someone was running the turbolift by remote. The door slid open and Showolter stepped into a huge, grim-looking chamber cut out of the living rock. The chamber was dimly lit, its only illumination coming from the turbolift interior and from ceiling glowtube fixtures in a tunnel that opened out in the chamber wall directly opposite the turbolift door.

The turbolift door slid shut, instantly cutting off half the light in the chamber. It was clearly a large space, but the light from the tunnel glowtubes was nowhere near bright enough to illuminate all of it.

But there was little time to look around. Showolter was leading them toward the tunnel at a brisk pace, his blaster at the ready. The group entered the narrow tunnel single file, Showolter in the lead, followed by Lando, then the droids, with Luke in the rear.

The walls of the tunnel were raw, dark brown stone, moist and dank, with some sort of slimy fluid seeping down them. Luke could hear a steady *drip, drip, drip* in the distance. The air was cold enough that he could see his breath.

The light in the corridor was dim, coming from occasional glowtubes bolted to the low ceiling of the corridor, which was barely wide enough for two humans to walk abreast. Luke could see that the grimy stone floor of the corridor had been smooth and finished once, perhaps back when the Old Republic was a new idea. Now it was cracked and broken, with a vile, meandering stream of fluid flowing down it, off into the darkness. In most places the stone surface was covered with muddy dirt that had silted down from the upper levels of the city over the generations.

"Oh my goodness!" Threepio said. "What a perfectly dreadful place. We're all certain to be destroyed!"

"Take it easy, Threepio," Luke said. "We've been in worse places."

"Considering some of the places we *have* been, I hardly take that as a recommendation, Master Luke," Threepio replied. "I can't imagine why anyone would want to bring us to such awful surroundings."

Luke had to admit, if only to himself, that Threepio had a point. This fetid tunnel was not a good place to be. He reached out with his Force ability to see if he could sense any of Showolter's corridor ghouls in the area, but it was no use. The abandoned lower levels of Coruscant were home to myriad forms of life, and there was no way to know which of the minds he was sensing were ghouls and which were not.

But, then, suddenly, just as Showolter was nearing the first intersection in the tunnel and their first left turn, Luke had no trouble at all sensing the ghouls.

Because, at that moment, the ghouls started to scream—and the sound was coming from in *front* of them. Luke looked to Showolter and Lando, saw the fear in their eyes, and knew the same look had to be on

his own face. The screaming went on and on, voice over
voice, echoing through the corridor. Luke reminded
himself that it was a hunting cry, nothing more, a call
from one predator to another. But even so, the sound
made his blood run cold. He might know, in cold, logical
terms, that the ghoul screams had no more meaning
than a bird's song or a womp rat's chittering. And yet, to
human ears, it was a primordial shriek of terror, of ha-
tred, of loss, of pain.

Showolter pulled back from the intersection and
threw his back against the slimy wall. "Master
Skywalker!" he called out, trying to make himself heard
over the terrible noise. "If you could be so good as to
switch on that lightsaber of yours and watch our
back . . . They like to come from both—"

But then the screaming started from *behind* them,
and there was no need to give a further warning.

Luke switched on his lightsaber and took up a one-
handed position at guard. He ignored the screams from
ahead. Let Showolter and Lando worry about them. He
concentrated his full attention behind him, and tried to
see beyond the end of the lights, to the chamber with
the turbolift.

The screaming stopped as abruptly as it had begun,
and just then, Luke saw a flicker of movement, barely
discernible in the gloom. Then another, and another.
"Company coming for sure from back here," Luke
called out.

And suddenly, there they were; three of them, standing there at the tunnel entrance. Showolter's description
of them was right as far as it went. They were about a
meter high at the shoulder with a fairly conventional
quadrupedal body arrangement, their bodies long and
lean and wiry. They were long legged, and clearly made
for running and jumping. Their ears were huge and
pointed, and were constantly swiveling back and forth,
independent of each other, as if they were tuning in on

each sound in turn. Their eyeless heads had long muz-
zles, their noses twitching constantly. Luke guessed that
their sense of smell was as good as their hearing. The
three of them were just standing there with their mouths
open, making no sound at all that Luke could hear.
Luke called over his shoulder, "Threepio, Artoo—can
you hear anything in ultrasonic?"

"Why yes, of course, Master Luke. The sound appears to be coming from the ghouls directly ahead of
you. It is similar to the screams we just heard, but at a
far higher frequency." Artoo bleeped and blooped, and
Threepio translated. "Good heavens! Artoo reports
they are directing beamed ultrasonics at us. He suggests
—suggests they are probing our internal structures in
order to decide which of us might be good to eat!"

"Relax, then, Threepio," Luke said. "I doubt they'd
find much good eating on a metal android."

"Why, that's true," Threepio said, obviously relieved.
"That's quite a great comfort."

"Glad to hear it," Luke muttered. "Lando! Captain
Showolter," he called out. "Talk to me. What's going on
up there?"

"We can't see them, or hear them, but they're still
there, somewhere."

"Hold on a moment," Luke said. He reached out with
his power in the Force and felt for the minds of the
creatures in front of him. He found spirits full of hunger, and cunning, and eagerness. Now he knew what a
corridor ghoul's mind felt like. He reached out further,
into the darkness of the tunnel at his back, feeling for
the same sort of mind. There were an astonishing number of creature minds in the dark corridors, but now
Luke knew what to look for. "There are three more of
them," he said. The three hungry minds were close by,
but on a lower level. "If I've got the layout straight, then
they're at the bottom of that ramp you talked about. Let
me see what I can do."

"What are you talking about?" Showolter demanded.

"Quiet," Lando said. "Let the man work."

Luke reached out for the minds of the ghouls in front of him, searching for a way to send them away. Even without Showolter's admonition, he would have had no desire to kill them. They had clever little minds, sharp and quick and direct. No subtle tricks or indirection would work here. Well, sometimes the simplest ways were best. Luke found the proper spots in their minds and struck them with a jolt of pure terror.

They were gone almost before Luke was aware they had moved at all, and he relaxed his guard, if only a trifle. Even if they were easily scared, they would no doubt work up the nerve to come back again soon. "I've chased off our friends back here," Luke said. "Artoo, keep watch on the rear and give a shout if you spot anything. Lando, you watch the rear as well. I've got to go up to the front."

"Right, Luke," said Lando. Artoo acknowledged with a beep.

Luke cut the power on his lightsaber and shouldered past Lando and the droids to the first intersection, where Showolter was waiting, his back still to the wall. "All right," Luke said, "I need to know if that's a dead-end corridor down there."

"Yes," Showolter said. "At least so far as we know. The corridor ends in an area of rockfall. There are cracks and crevices all over the place. We *think* we've plugged all the ones that lead somewhere, but we can't be absolutely sure. And there's always the chance that the ghouls or some other animals managed to reopen a hole we thought we sealed. But for humans, yes, a dead end."

"But maybe not for the ghouls," Luke said. But even the possibility that the corridor *was* a dead end meant that he couldn't use the same trick of inducing terror. If creatures like the ghouls were terrified with their backs against the wall, they would almost certainly fight their way out. One look at the creatures had convinced him that they might well do a lot of damage if they wanted to. He would have to find another way. "You wait here and watch my back," he told Showolter. "I want to try something."

Showolter looked as if he wanted to protest, but he kept his mouth shut. Luke moved past him, took the left turn of the corridor, and then another immediate left. Here, the tunnel immediately started heading down at a pretty fair decline. He unclipped his lightsaber again and switched it on. It lit up with the familiar low thrum of power, its blade glowing eerily in the corridor.

Luke moved down the ramp into the gloomy depths. He was not entirely sure what he intended to do, except that he did not wish to kill needlessly. He reached out for the minds of the three waiting corridor ghouls. There they were, three bundles of nervous energy; eager, hungry, voracious, fearful minds already teetering on the edge of fight or flight. It would take but the slightest touch for them to run in terror—or attack with relentless savagery. Careful. He would have to be very careful.

He came to the bottom of the ramp, where it opened into a wide corridor that was even more decrepit than the one above.

And there they were, directly in front of the blastdoor Showolter had described, the rubble of collapsed tunneling just to Luke's left. Three of the eyeless creatures, ghost-white, pointed-eared hobgoblins, open-mouthed, their needle-sharp teeth at the ready. It was clear they "saw" Luke through their echo-location sense. They were alert, plainly watching him. The three of them backed up a bit as Luke entered the chamber, and one of them, the smallest and spindliest of them, let out a sort of nervous yelp. That set off the other two, and suddenly the chamber was echoing with a terrifying racket of yelps and squeals and screams.

"Easy, now," Luke said as he sidled off to the right of the ramp entrance, trying to put his back to the wall, trying to put as much of a soothing tone into his voice as he could manage. The ghouls whimpered and yelped, growing even more restive. Did they know that their companions by the turbolift shaft had vanished? Was that part of what was spooking them? Or were corridor ghouls always this nervous?

Luke reached a trifle deeper into their minds, trying to soothe them. But there was little in the minds of these creatures that was much interested in being soothed. How could there be, when they had evolved, somehow, to survive in the miserable, eat-or-be-eaten darkness of Coruscant's undercity?

Luke noticed a few scattered bones on the floor, and recognized one of them as teeth in a jawbone that looked as if it came from a ghoul. A corridor ghoul had died, right here, not so long ago. This place was dangerous to them. No, there was no hope of calming these creatures down.

At least Luke had gained one more bit of information from his mental probing and from their behavior. They had made no move toward the rubble of the collapsed tunnel on Luke's left, and had no thoughts concerning it. Perhaps smaller creatures could negotiate the rockfall, but so far as the ghouls were concerned, it was a dead end. The only way out for them was up the ramp Luke had just come down. Once on the upper level, they might choose to go down any of the corridors—and might well blunder into Showolter and Lando and the droids.

A Jedi did not meddle in any living being's mind capriciously, but only at need—and now there was need. He probed more deeply, and found what he sought. Most unwillingly, he took direct control of the ghouls' bodies. Their yipping and keening came to an abrupt halt, and suddenly they were standing stock-still. Luke *willed* the creatures to move away from the blastdoor, toward the rubble pile, and they moved that way, stiff-leggedly and awkwardly. He forced them toward the farthest corner of the lower chamber and held them there.

Luke knew he could hold them more or less indefinitely, but to do so was to risk terrible damage to the creatures and, likely enough, to Luke himself. The ghouls would fight against his will, and could easily do themselves harm. He already could feel them straining against him. He eased back just enough to allow them to shift their stance and move their ears, but instead of growing calmer, they only resisted the remaining constraint all the harder.

"Captain Showolter! Lando!" he called out. "I have the way open, but I need you down here on the double!"

"Coming!" Lando called, and Luke could hear the sounds of the two men and the droids moving down the corridor toward him.

The entrance from the ramp was just inside Luke's peripheral vision as he kept watch on the ghouls. After a moment he could see Showolter come in, spot the immobilized ghouls, and freeze up. "What in the—"

"Worry about it later," Luke said. "Just get the blastdoor open, and hurry."

"Of course—" Showolter said, and moved toward the blastdoor keypad—but at that moment the screaming began again, coming from up the ramp. The ghouls Luke had immobilized immediately began to strain all the harder at the invisible bonds that held them, and yelped and moaned and snapped their jaws.

Showolter seemed about to say something, but thought better of it, and hurried toward his task.

The two droids came down the ramp next, with Lando right behind them, doing his best to watch behind himself as he moved.

Luke could hear Showolter punching the code into the blastdoor keypad, and, a moment later, he heard the door start to swing open.

He risked a backward glance, and saw Showolter and the droids ducking inside before the door was fully open. Lando hesitated at the entrance and turned. "Come on, Luke," he said. "The others are headed back this way."

Luke didn't need any more prompting. Still holding his lightsaber at the ready, he looked back toward the frozen ghouls and backed toward the blastdoor.

Just as he stepped toward the entrance, the other pack of ghouls appeared at the base of the ramp, screaming, ululating, their ears pivoting and twitching as they divided their attention between their immobilized comrades and the open blastdoor. Luke did not wait to see the end of the drama, but backed through the door, his lightsaber still at the ready.

Lando hit the slapswitch, and the blastdoor slammed back shut. Luke released his control of the ghouls. In less time than he would have thought possible, he could hear them leaping for the blastdoor, howling and keening, their claws clattering and clicking on the door's durasteel exterior.

Luke let out a sigh of relief, shut off his lightsaber, and clipped it back on his belt. "Well, *that* wasn't exactly the sort of reception committee I was expecting."

"I quite agree," Threepio piped up. "Even for those of us not in danger of being eaten, I have not seen such unpleasant and unsanitary conditions in quite some time."

"Stow it, Golden Boy," Lando said. "And that's coming from *all* of us not in danger of being disassembled, if you take the hint." He holstered his blaster and leaned up against the wall of the blastdoor chamber. "Captain Showolter, with all due respect, to the devil with your security procedures about everyone using separate entrances. I am not leaving by that door."

Showolter nodded weakly. "I would say that you have a point. That's the most aggressive I've ever seen our little friends. But in the meantime there are some folks waiting to see you inside. Right now. Come on."

"That's what I like about spending time with you, Luke," Lando growled. "There's always plenty of time to catch my breath between bouts of excitement."

"Hey, remember, you're the one who asked *me* to come on this trip," Luke replied. "But let's go find out who's here."

The blastdoor did not open up directly into the safe room, but into a sort of airlock chamber about four meters long, with another blastdoor at the far end. Showolter used the keypad on the second door, and it swung open to reveal a well-appointed, perfectly conventional, L-shaped conference room. The inner blastdoor opened out on the short end of the L, and the three men and two droids went into the room.

"I might have known you'd be the one to get here the hard way," a familiar, gravelly voice said from around the corner.

Luke stepped into the long end of the L and looked down the long table that took up its center. The speaker was seated at the far end of the table.

"Admiral Ackbar!" he cried out. "Good to see you again!"

"It would be better if you were seeing him again under somewhat more pleasant circumstances," said another voice. It was Mon Mothma, standing behind the Mon Calamari Admiral. It looked as if she had been reading a report over his shoulder.

"Mon Mothma!" said Luke. "It is good to see you as well, under any circumstances."

"I see that you took my advice and went traveling with my good friend Lando Calrissian," Mon Mothma said, a slight smile on her lips. "Please, both of you, be seated. Captain Showolter, perhaps you could arrange for some refreshment?"

"Nothing for me, thanks," Lando said.

"I'm fine as well," Luke said. "Somehow going through those corridors didn't leave me with much of an appetite. Not the most appealing odors out there. My apologies if we brought any of it in with us."

"Not at all," Mon Mothma said. "But please, all of you, be seated." They all took chairs toward the same end of the table. "Tell me, Captain Calrissian," Mon Mothma went on, "was your trip profitable?"

"Very definitely yes, Mon Mothma, although in a personal sense, rather than a financial one," Lando said. "However, I'm afraid it was cut short somewhat abruptly before we got as far as Corellia."

"How so?" Admiral Ackbar asked, a bit eagerly. "Please, tell us everything."

"Well," said Lando, "we got as far as Sacorria, but we were there less than half a day before we were ordered off the planet. It was some sort of antiforeigner crackdown. We weren't there long enough to learn much, but Tendra—the local woman I—we—spoke with, seemed to think there was some sort of crisis coming to a head."

"Could that crisis have anything to do with Corellia?" Showolter asked.

"I suppose it's possible," Lando replied. "We never got a chance to find out. We were stopped by an interdiction field."

"An interdiction field near the Corellian planetary system?" Ackbar asked. "Why didn't one of you say so? How big and where?"

"I was *about* to say so, but we got a little sidetracked," Lando said evenly. "That's why we never got a chance to learn what was going on in the Corellian system. The field is what kept us from getting there."

"How could that be?" Ackbar demanded.

"The field isn't just *near* Corellia. It completely *surrounds* the Corellian planetary system," Luke explained.

"*What?* That's impossible!" Ackbar said. "No one has ever managed to generate a field that large."

"That's exactly what I thought," Lando replied. "But it's there, nevertheless. We were knocked out of hyperspace about twenty light-hours out from Corell, Corellia's star. And it's not just a big field. It's a powerful one. It nearly blew out the safeties on the *Lady Luck*'s hyperdrive."

Luke looked to Ackbar and Mon Mothma. "Wait a second. If you don't know about the interdiction field, why are we here?"

"It's very simple," Mon Mothma said. "We have lost all—and I repeat, *all*—communication with the Corellian planetary system."

"Communicator silence?" Lando asked. "Maybe, if there's some sort of military situation going on, Governor-General Micamberlecto decided to order a blackout."

"Things would have to be pretty grim for that to be plausible," Ackbar said, "but I'm afraid even *that* is a highly optimistic interpretation. It's not a blackout. It's jamming. System-wide jamming of *all* communications in and out of the Corellian planetary system."

Lando let out a low whistle. "Whoever is behind all this is not shy about thinking big."

"But you have something else that's got you worried," Luke said. "Otherwise we wouldn't be meeting underground."

"Quite right. Captain Showolter?"

"Thank you, ma'am." Showolter turned to Luke and Lando. "Even before the communications blackout, we were concerned that someone in the Corellian planetary system had managed to penetrate *our* communications. We kept sending agents in, and they kept vanishing. The more carefully we planned the penetration, the faster we lost the agent. There has to be some sort of leak outside the Corellian system. Even without the communications blackout, it was getting to be enough to raise a major ruckus back here. It would seem the last two or three agents we tried to insert were shot down or apprehended the moment they entered the system."

"Therefore," said Mon Mothma, "we have decided that all business related to this situation must be dealt with in top-secret, face-to-face meetings, in secure facilities."

"We have also decided we're going to have to go in," Admiral Ackbar said in a voice that was gruff, even for him. "I don't see any real way around it. Unfortunately, I don't have any ships available for the job." Admiral Ackbar swiveled his goggle eyes from side to side and shook his head. "Readiness is at an all-time low. We have all the admirals anyone could want, but the fleet is a skeleton force at the moment. And I don't need to tell you *that* information is highly confidential.

"We must assume that whoever grabbed our agents and ordered the jamming—and created this interdiction field—did so to cover something we're not supposed to know about. And they managed to do it at exactly the moment nearly all of our ships were committed elsewhere, or in dry dock. I don't think that's a coincidence. But leave all that to one side for the moment. What more do you know about the interdiction field?" Ackbar said.

Luke turned to his astromech droid. "Artoo?" R2-D2 beeped twice and rolled over to stand next to Luke's chair. "Show the graphic images on the interdiction field."

Artoo blooped obediently and activated his internal holographic generator. An image started to form.

"We didn't stay around long enough to get much information, but we did pull what we could off the *Lady Luck*'s automatic data recorders and then enhanced it as best we could. And bear in mind that this data has been more than a little massaged. All sorts of errors could have crept into it."

Artoo projected a standard wire-frame schematic diagram of the Corellian planetary system, showing the star Corell, the planet Corellia, and the other inhabited planets—Selonia, Drall, and the Double Worlds of Tralus and Talus, along with the outer planets. After a few moments a hazy gray cloud appeared around all of it, a sphere that extended far beyond the outermost planet of the system.

"It's not centered on the star," Ackbar said at once.

"Very good, Admiral. It took us the better part of a day to notice that. But you're right, it isn't. As best we can tell, it *seems* to be centered somewhere in the vicinity of Talus and Tralus, the Double Worlds."

"The Double Worlds?" Mon Mothma asked. "I'm sorry, I'm not as familiar with the Corellian system as I ought to be."

"Don't feel bad about it," said Luke. "I had to look them up myself. They're the least populous and least important of the inhabited Corellian worlds. They're called the Double Worlds because they are in a co-orbital relationship. They orbit about each other, or more accurately about their common center of gravity, or barycenter. And, of course, the system of two planets is in orbit around Corell as well."

"There's some sort of big space station in the barycenter point, isn't there?" Ackbar asked. "One that might make a base of operations?"

Luke smiled at his old friend. "So there is. Already thinking tactics?"

"Of course," Ackbar replied. "That's my job, after all. And I might add that our imagery of the jamming looks very similar to this display of the interdiction field."

"So we've got the infiltration of NRI, the jamming,

and the giant interdiction field," said Luke. "What in the Corellian system is worth going to all this effort?"

"I should think that was obvious," Mon Mothma said. "The Corellian system itself. Someone in there, one of the rebel groups, has seized power, and has done everything possible to keep the outside universe from interfering while it consolidates its position."

"Quite right," Admiral Ackbar said, "but I am less interested in their political plans than their military capabilities and intentions. What they have done suggests that our mysterious enemies have technology far superior to ours."

"I agree, sir," Captain Showolter said. "But that brings up another question—*where did they get it?* Corellia used to be known as a trading center, not a hotbed of high-technology research and development. I'd be much less surprised if this sort of capability showed up on your own world of Mons Calamari. And yes, obviously, if someone was going to try and sell a superweapon like this to the highest bidder, a trading planet would be the place to go. But Corellia hasn't been one of the preeminent trade centers since before the war. If I were trying to auction off a wonder weapon, I wouldn't sell it to a planet that's strapped for cash."

"Unless you consider that the better-off planets might not be interested in buying such a device," Mon Mothma said. "High-power jamming and interdiction systems aren't of much use unless you want to keep the outside universe—and the New Republic—from interfering with your plans. Plans for a rebellion, for example. And what is to stop the sellers from offering their wares elsewhere?"

There was a moment's dead silence. "*That* is a most disturbing thought, Captain Calrissian," Ackbar said at last. "If this super-interdiction system is for sale, then we might be in very serious trouble indeed."

"We're *already* in very serious trouble," Mon Mothma

replied. "You're off on about three hypotheticals at the
moment. Let's not go borrowing extra worries until we
have to. The Corellian crisis is quite enough to keep us
busy for the moment."

"But we must bear in mind that a successful revolt on
Corellia might well inspire others to rebel against the
New Republic. The name Corellia has influence, even if
the Corellian Sector has been little heard of in recent
years. A successful Corellian rebellion could be the beginning of the end for the New Republic. It would rep-
resent not some minor fraying at the edge, but a huge
tear right in the center of the fabric. If others chose to
pull on that tear, it could only get wider."

Mon Mothma frowned. "As unhappy as I am to admit
it, Admiral Ackbar is quite right. We *must* get the situation under control. We *must* get into the Corellian system and find out what is going on. And we must get in
there with a force capable of setting things right. A battle fleet, at the very minimum."

"But with the interdiction field in place, you can't use
hyperdrive in the Corellian planetary system," Lando
said. "It could take months to travel from the edge of
the field to the inner planets via normal space."

"Then it will take months," Ackbar said. "I don't have
to tell you all the tactical and logistical disadvantages we
will have if we can't fly in hyperspace, but if we have no
choice, then we have no choice. There is, of course, the
trifling matter of *finding* a battle fleet. To put it very
bluntly, we don't have one at the moment, and it could
easily take us months to assemble one. But that is the
very point we wished to discuss with you, the reason we
called you here."

"You mean you didn't call us in here because we had
just come from Corellia?" Lando asked.

"We thought it *possible* that you might have made it
that far," Admiral Ackbar said, "but we had no way of
knowing. Your information about the interdiction field

is invaluable, of course, but we had another reason to bring you in here—or at least, another reason to bring Master Skywalker in. We could certainly make use of your services as well, Captain Calrissian, but—how shall I put this delicately? Master Skywalker has a, ah, certain *contact* that we need him to cultivate."

Admiral Ackbar was a Mon Calamari, and it was far from easy for a human to read his expression. Even so, there was something about the way he spoke, the way he held his head, that gave Luke a funny feeling. "What sort of contact?" Luke asked.

"An old one," Mon Mothma said. "A personal one. I might even say—a romantic one."

"Wait a minute," Luke said. "I don't know what you're getting at, but—"

"The thing of it is," Captain Showolter said, "there's a lady of your acquaintance, by the name of Gaeriel Captison, out in the Bakuran system. She seems to have a battle fleet in her possession. We were hoping you might ask her if you could borrow it."

CHAPTER THREE

Coming In, Going Out

The X-TIE fighter lumbered along through hyperspace, and Lieutenant Belindi Kalenda of New Republic Intelligence knew she should be grateful for even that much performance. The thing had barely made it into hyperspace at the beginning of the flight, and she was more than a bit nervous about how it would handle when the time came to jump back out. But for the moment, at any rate, she was all right, and that had to count for something.

The X-TIE was an Ugly, a chop job made up out of salvaged parts of an X-wing and an early-model TIE fighter. As best Kalenda could tell, it combined all the worst handling characteristics of the two old adversaries, with maybe a few of its own nasty surprises thrown in.

But say what you might, the thing flew, and it had gotten her this far. Given the way the flight had started, with her stealing the ship on Corellia while Han Solo provided a diversion by blowing up what seemed like half the spaceport, it was a miracle she had a ship at all, let alone one that flew. By all rights she should have crashed or been shot down thirty seconds after launch.

But none of that mattered now. She was on her way to Coruscant—nearly there, in fact—and she had information no one outside the Corellian system was likely to have. She *had* to get through. Nothing else mattered.

Belindi Kalenda was all of twenty-five standard years old. She was a slightly odd-looking young woman even at the best of times, and she had not been at her best in a long time. Her hair was jet-black, and would have hung nearly down to her waist if she did not normally wear it in an elaborate braid at the back of her head. Right now, of course, she had her hair jammed up under her flight helmet, and had for some time. Combing out her hair was not going to be any great joy. She couldn't remember the last time she had been really clean and presentable. If only the need for a shower was the worst of her worries.

Her eyes were set a bit wide apart and were a trifle glassy, her gaze a bit off-kilter, almost, but not quite, cross-eyed. It was disconcerting to many people, and gave them the feeling that she was looking not at them but past them, at something hovering just behind them. That was not too far wrong, in point of fact. She had never worked to develop it, or had all that much faith in it, but Kalenda had long felt she had just the slightest of skill in the Force, just enough to give her a warning now and then, make her intuitions a bit stronger, more reliable.

Unfortunately, all her intuition was telling her at the moment was what she would have known anyway: she was in over her head. The survival of who knew how many planets, how many intelligent beings, had been dumped in her lap. *She* was the only one with the information. Her thoughts never strayed far from that point. It was all there, in the datachip she had tucked into the pocket of her flight suit. It didn't take much imagination for her to feel as if the tiny chip in her pocket were huge and heavy, a massive burden pulling her down.

She *had* to get the message out. And she did not feel up to it. She felt strung out, tired, scared.

However, aside from being responsible for the fate of millions, she had the un-minor task of jollying this monstrosity of a spacecraft long enough to get her to Coruscant. At least that part of it was almost over. Assuming the X-TIE didn't blow up or melt down in the next few minutes, she ought to be dropping out of hyperspace in the Coruscant system very soon now.

Of course, there was the question of what sort of reception she would receive. The capital had been attacked, bombed, besieged, and who knows what else over the years. The New Republic Navy therefore took its job of defending the place very seriously, and the years of peace hadn't taken the edge off Coruscant Command. If she had learned anything in NRI, she had learned that much. She also knew how suspicious they were of unknown ship types—such as the X-TIE she was riding in. It might be unfortunate, but it would be understandable if they blasted her out of the sky first and asked questions later.

Kalenda smiled to herself. But why borrow trouble? The X-TIE's hyperspace systems might blow before she got there, and then the problem would never come up. For at least the dozenth time in the last hour, she checked her systems' status display. More than a few of the propulsion subsystems were in the amber, but so far at least, none of them had spiked up into the red. She double-checked her navigational settings and willed the X-TIE Ugly to fly a trifle more gracefully.

The Ugly refused to cooperate.

*   *   *

The *Lady Luck* lifted off from Coruscant with a smooth surge of power and moved gracefully toward orbit. Lando checked his instruments. "Everything in the green," he announced. He checked the central repeater boards. "Artoo's got your X-wing right in the groove behind us. I must admit I'm impressed. I wasn't quite sure our little friend was up to the job."

"I hope you've learned your lesson," Luke said. "Artoo knows what he's doing."

"Oh, I've learned it," Lando said. "Now I know the only incompetent droid on this trip is the one sitting behind you."

"Really, Captain Calrissian!"

"Quiet, Threepio, or I'll make you ride outside on the hull."

It had taken some fairly ingenious improvised engineering to hook up the X-wing and the *Lady Luck*. But now that it was done, the X-wing could fly up under the base of the *Lady* and dock itself to the space yacht's newly installed ventral docking clamps. The *Lady* could take Luke's refurbished and upgraded X-wing fighter in tow. Even if *had* taken a bit of doing, no one had minded. They were going to be flying into the unknown, more than likely a hostile part of it, and there was nothing like having an X-wing's firepower and maneuverability if things got sticky.

However, no one had been able to dream up a way to fly the two craft through atmosphere while they were docked together—and there was no real need to try too hard, as long as Artoo could fly the X-wing to orbit. Lando had been a bit worried by the idea, but not Luke. After all, the R2 series had been designed to serve as pilot assistants. The brief flight from the surface of Coruscant merely marked the first occasion in a long, long time that Artoo had done the job he had been designed for in the first place.

"That droid can do some tight formation flying," Lando said. "Maybe I ought to let *him* do the docking maneuver once we're in free space."

"If you like," Luke said, not really paying attention.

Lando looked over at his friend. He was plainly aware that Luke was not exactly fully engaged at the moment and was trying to cheer him up. "Yes, sir," he said, "we get all docked up, and next stop, Bakura."

"Yes," Luke said, in the same absent tone of voice. "Bakura. Bakura and Gaeriel Captison." Luke stared out the port of the *Lady Luck* without seeing anything, and remembered Gaeriel. *There* was a name out of the past, if ever there was one.

Luke had not so much as heard her name in years, but the thought of her had not lost its power to move him. He had met Gaeriel in the tumultuous days just after the destruction of the second Death Star and the deaths of Darth Vader and the Emperor. Her planet, Bakura, had been attacked by a hitherto unknown alien race, the Ssi-ruuk, which was intent on enslaving humanity. It had taken a joint force of Imperial and Republic forces to push the Ssi-ruuk back, and the Bakurans had kept a close watch on their borders ever since.

Luke and Gaeriel met during the time he was on Bakura. They had quickly gotten to know each other very well in a very short period of time—and then had been forced to part just as quickly. It would have been a gross exaggeration to say she had been one of the great loves of his life—or indeed a love at all—but she *might* have been. That was what gnawed at him. If Luke's path through life had been any different, if Gaeriel's religion and her duty to her home world had not called to her, if they had met in a Galaxy at peace instead of one not yet done with war . . . if, if, if.

Luke sighed and rubbed his eyes. But none of the ifs had come to be. And truth to tell, Luke knew that even if all the ifs *had* come true, there would have been no guarantees. Luke and Gaeriel might have meant something to each other. Or they might not have. The tragedy was that they had never had the chance to find out.

"It was a long time ago," Lando said gently. It seemed he had given up pretending that nothing was wrong. "Life moves on."

"Quite right, Master Luke," Threepio piped up from the temporary jump seat they had rigged for him behind Luke's copilot seat. "I doubt your brief encounter with her will be of the slightest consequence to our forthcoming meeting."

"Oh, great," Lando said. "Now we get to hear from the greatest living authority on missing the point." Luke and Lando had decided it might be smart to have Threepio in the control cabin, with a direct hyperwave comlink to Artoo, just in case there was any problem with the docking maneuver and the normal com systems couldn't cope. Lando was plainly beginning to regret the move, and Luke was inclined to agree.

"It is approximately fourteen standard years since you have had any contact with her," Threepio went on, in the relentlessly cheerful tone of voice he always seemed to use when he was putting his foot in it. "While the diplomatic phase of our mission will be quite delicate, I would not concern myself overmuch about how she reacts to seeing you. Why, given the unreliability of human psychology, it is quite possible that she will not even remember you."

"I remember *her,*" Luke said in a quiet voice.

"I see that you do," said Threepio. "But I do not believe that you have had the opportunity to review her career since your last contact."

"Let me guess," Lando growled. "You took it upon yourself to link yourself to the Upper Bloovatavian Historical Reference Data Bank and download her entire life story into that rusty tin head of yours."

"I am *not* familiar with Upper Bloovatavia, Captain Calrissian. However, the material on Gaeriel Captison was readily available in the Diplomatic Archives of Coruscant University. I might add that there was no tin at all used in the construction of my head, and, furthermore, tin does not rust."

"Luke, would it really bother you that much if I put just a *few* blaster holes in him?" Lando asked.

Luke managed a wan smile and glanced back at Threepio. "Don't be so hard on him, Lando. After all, he did save your life when you were about to marry the life witch on Leria Kersil."

"Yeah, but if it means I have to listen to him, I'm not sure it was worth it," Lando said.

"Well!" Threepio said. "I never! I don't know why I bother collecting information when it seems no one is the least bit interested in it."

"Go ahead," Luke said in a soothing tone of voice. "Tell me what you've got on Gaeriel."

"Would you care for a complete report, or just a summary?"

"Just the summary, thank you very much." Threepio's idea of complete report might take from here until the end of time to recite.

"Very good, Master Luke. Well, there is really not that much to tell. She continued in politics after the Ssi-ruuk were defeated and became a powerful figure in her faction of the senate. After holding various posts of increasing importance, she became the youngest person ever to hold the post of Prime Minister on Bakura."

"I didn't know she had become Prime Minister," Luke said, though there was no particular reason to be surprised. She was young and smart and ambitious. Why shouldn't she rise to the top?

"I am afraid she not only became Prime Minister, but then ceased to be Prime Minister. Her party was defeated in the last elections. Several press accounts attribute this to her being distracted from the campaign by the illness and death of her husband."

"Husband?" Luke said. "She had a husband?"

"Oh, yes, Master Luke. Did I neglect to mention that? She married about six years ago, to a man called Pter Thanas . . . a former Imperial officer. I believe you met him during our time in Bakura. They had a child, a girl, whom they named Malinza. She is now four and half standard years old. Thanas contracted a lingering ailment with which I am not familiar, something called Knowt's disease, just as the campaign was getting under way, and expired two days after Gaeriel's party was defeated. It would seem that she's out of active politics, at least for the moment."

That large a dose of news hit Luke hard. Strange to think that Gaeriel had gained and lost a husband, reached to and fallen from the heights of power on her world, and given birth to a daughter, all without Luke knowing a thing about it.

Somewhere in the back of his mind he had held a picture of Gaeriel. He realized with a shock just how unchanging that image had been. In his mind's eye, she had stayed the effervescent young woman he had known, all the drive and enthusiasm of youth eternally hers, frozen in time. But he should have known better. Life was not like that.

Luke felt he should say something, but he didn't know what. Somehow he did not much want to explain his feelings to Lando—and certainly not to Threepio. "I hadn't heard any news of her in a long time," he said. "I'm sorry to hear that Thanas died."

"But that was over a year ago, Master Luke. She is more than likely over it by now."

Somehow Luke doubted that. The Gaeriel he remembered was not the type to marry on a whim. She would have married a man she loved very deeply. She might well have gotten on with her life by now—but she would not have gotten over her husband.

And she had had a child, a daughter. . . .

Gaeriel. He thought of her, and all the *possibilities* that name had represented in his mind. He had always doubted that he would ever marry. Romantic love had never seemed to be part of his destiny. Even a Jedi Master could not see far into the future, but Luke needed little more than common sense to know that a life such as his had little room for the pleasures of ordinary people. There were times when his extraordinary gifts were compensation enough—and there were times when they were not.

Luke knew perfectly well that he treasured Leia's children in large part because they represented as much family as he was ever likely to have. He thought he had come to be at peace with that fact. Now he knew he was wrong.

"Given that you once knew her well, I have a good deal of additional information on her that might prove interesting. Much of it is from the less reliable segments of the press, and is somewhat speculative. However—"

"Look," said Lando, "I don't know the whole story, and I don't want to. But it seems to me that Luke might not want to have this discussion in front of me."

"Thank you, Lando," Luke said. "I appreciate that. We'll talk later, Threepio." He undid his seat restraint. "Actually, I think I could do with a bit of time to myself right now. Call me if you need me for anything. I'll be in my cabin."

"Sure thing, Luke," Lando said. "I don't think anything's going to come up."

Luke nodded absently and headed aft toward his cabin. When he got there, he slid the hatch open, shut it behind him, and flopped down on his back. He lay back so he could stare at the overhead bulkhead in comfort.

Amazing how a name from the past could affect someone.

*   *   *

Belindi Kalenda watched the navicomputer's count-down clock and took a deep breath. Thirty seconds. Thirty seconds until she dropped out of hyperspace into the Coruscant system. The moment she did so, she knew she was going to land in a world of trouble. The X-TIE had nothing she could cobble together into an interrogator that would send an approved identity code. On top of that, her craft was of an unknown type that carried a lot of ex-Imperial hardware.

Kalenda knew just how twitchy the automatic systems were on the subject of Imperial spacecraft. When the autodetectors spotted the TIE side shields welded to the X-wing body, every detector screen in the system would light up like a glitterdance projector.

Her only hope was that she could patch through to NRI headquarters, and do it fast, before half of Coruscant Command started blazing away at her. She would have to make a voice call to NRI HQ, use a one-shot word code, and convince them she was legitimate, while doing her best to stay alive.

Twenty seconds. Try not to think about the last time you dropped out of hyperspace, into Corellian space, she thought. The locals shot your ship out from under you almost before you knew what was happening. You don't want to try a crash landing onto Coruscant. No, indeed.

Eighteen seconds. Check that comlink one more time. Confirm the frequency setting on the thing. You don't want to send your SOS to the Bureau of Agronomic Policy Adjustment by accident. No, indeed.

Fifteen seconds. Check the navicomputer one last time. It would be just your luck if the brutalized thing scrammed up its programming and dropped you outside the authorized arrival zone—or locked up for good and all and never dropped you out of hyperspace. Ships vanished every once in a while. No doubt about that. Check it again. No desire to be one of them.

Ten seconds. Weapons systems powered up or powered down? If Coruscant Command spotted your turbo laser juiced up, they'd be just that more tempted to fire at once. But if they fired missiles at you, you might be able to shoot them down, *if* your weapons were at the ready on arrival. But suppose the power surge from switching them on was just enough to wonk out the navicomputer? And how likely were they to shoot missiles and not blaster fire? Leave the weapons systems off.

Seven seconds. Shields. Shields were a different matter. On, definitely on. But don't risk the power surge to the navicomputer. Slap the shield switch as soon as dropout is complete.

If dropout ever happened. Five seconds.

Four.

Three.

Two. Be ready for manual cutoff if the autos drop the ball.

One. Hand on manual cutoff switch.

Zero—

And the universe flared into existence around her, star lines blasting out from the center, flashing past her before they resolved down into the familiar stars and sky of Coruscant. She had made it. Now if she could just manage to stay alive long enough to enjoy it.

She powered up the X-TIE's shields—and saw the navicomputer flicker and wink out before it popped back on with zeroed-out coordinates. Kalenda congratulated herself on holding off the shields until after arrival, and then started worrying about other things.

Comlink. Activate the comlink. Pray that the NRI was still on that frequency. She keyed the switch and spoke. "Dartmakers out of luck with frequently iced manifolds. Dartmakers out of luck with frequently iced manifolds. Dartmakers out of luck with frequently iced manifolds."

The nonsense phrase was supposed to be stored in some NRI computer somewhere, keyed to her voice pattern. In theory, three repeats of the phrase would track the coordinates of whatever craft sent the signal, and send an emergency clearance to Coruscant Traffic Control, while sending an all-clear to Coruscant Command. A nice theory, all in all. Unless the computers were down, or some fogbrain had changed the procedure, or erased her phrase-voice match, or someone in Coruscant Command decided not to take NRI's word that the mystery ship was on their side.

Three repeats of the phrase. Wait two minutes, and send three more repeats. Wait another two minutes, and send the third and final set of repeats. That was the standard procedure, and Kalenda planned to follow it, if she lived long enough.

In the meantime she'd best get her ship's detectors—such as they were—powered up. She threw the appropriate switches and was more disappointed than surprised when nothing happened. Whoever had slapped this Ugly together out of spare parts had probably meant it for some sort of raider support job. It was supposed to follow the other ships in and start shooting when the enemy showed up. Keeping the detection system up to speed would be a real low-maintenance priority.

"Should have been more choosy about what ship I stole," Kalenda muttered to herself. She might be able to bring the detectors back on-line if she worked on it for half an hour. Then again, she might not—and besides, she definitely did not have half an hour.

In fact, it looked as if she did not have even half a minute. There. Coming in hard and fast from dead ahead—a full flight of six Y-wings, all of them looking very much as if they meant business.

Her hand was on the joystick and she was doing a hard roll to starboard before she had even consciously decided to take evasive action. A turbolaser blast sliced straight through the piece of space she occupied just a moment before. Still working on sheer reflex, she started powering up the weapons systems before she realized that the Y-wings were on her side. She didn't want to shoot them down. If it had been a choice between trading the life of one or two fighter pilots and the chance to get word of the plot to blow up the star of an inhabited planet, she would have gone to the attack without a moment's hesitation, although with a great deal of regret. But against six fighters—and whatever else Coruscant would throw at her if she acted hostile—she knew there was no chance at all of her information surviving.

Her only hope was to go evasive and stay that way long enough for the NRI to scramble a clearance. She checked her chronometer and realized it was time for her to repeat the message. Another laser blast nearly clipped her portside screen, and she flipped the X-TIE and jinked sideways.

She switched on the comlink and started talking. "Dartmakers out of luck with frequently iced manifolds. Dartmakers out of luck with frequently iced manifolds. Dartmakers out of luck with frequently iced manifolds." She chanted the words as if they were some sort of mantra, a magic spell that could save her life. And with any luck, that would be exactly right.

Speaking of communications, it might be that the Y-wings were trying to reach her. She hit the scan command on her com panel and sent it sniffing for all the standard frequencies. Nothing. Not that she expected it. Fighter pilots rarely tried to chat with the people they were attempting to kill.

The Y-wings were splitting wide, trying to get her in a spherical cross fire. If they managed that, it was going to be all over in short order. Well, if they couldn't talk to her, maybe she could talk to them. Kalenda punched in what had been the standard channel for the general fighter command link last time she had been briefed. "Y-wing fighters! This is the X-TIE you are pursuing. Please hold your fire! I am not hostile. I am on a courier mission." Another laser blast streaked out. This one caught her X-TIE amidships. The Ugly shuddered, bucked and swayed, and the interior lights dimmed, but the shields held—this time. A whole bunch of the lights that had been amber abruptly clicked over to red. The next hit was going to do plenty of damage. She twisted the X-TIE through a one-eighty and dove straight for the closest pair of Y-wings. She flew right between them and managed to get outside the formation—and then instantly wished she hadn't.

A Mon Calamari star cruiser had appeared from out of nowhere and was bearing down on her. If she had been inside the Y-wing cross fire, the cruiser wouldn't have dared fire on her. Now, however, the cruiser could blaze away as she liked. And there was the cruiser's forward turbolasers turning ponderously about, bearing down on her.

Kalenda went vertical, flipped her ship through ninety degrees, and punched for sky, trying to move faster than that gun turret could. Hopeless, of course, but she had to go down fighting. She punched back to the NRI frequency and spoke, perhaps for the last time. Strange that her last words were going to be a nonsense phrase. "Dartmakers out of luck with frequently iced manifolds. Dartmakers out of luck with frequently iced—"

Suddenly a giant, invisible hand grabbed at her X-TIE and grabbed at it hard. She was nearly thrown up against her restraint harness and banged her helmet against the inside of the canopy. Momentarily stunned, she needed a moment to regain her senses. A near miss. It must have been a near miss from the cruiser. She

slammed over the joystick, trying to heel the ship over
to port, trying to go evasive one last time. But the
X-TIE only shuddered and moaned, and the cabin was
suddenly full of the smell of something burning. Then
she got it. She cut the engines, pulled her hands off the
joystick, and breathed a sigh of relief.

A tractor beam. They had caught her with a tractor
beam.

She shut her eyes and slumped back against her seat
back. She started breathing again, not realizing she had
stopped for a little bit there. "Praise be to the
dartmakers," she said to no one at all. "Praise be to the
dartmakers, and may their manifolds never ice up
again."

*   *   *

Bakura.

Even in all the years of peace since the invasion crisis,
Bakura had maintained its powerful defense forces.
There had been no sign of a renewed attack from the
Ssi-ruuk, but on the other hand, there had been no
warning at all before the Ssi-ruuk's first attack. It would
be a long time before Bakura let down her guard again.

Which led to the inevitable question of why the New
Republic had let *its* guard down. Part of the answer was
that it hadn't. Though the fleet and the surface forces
were far smaller than they had been during the war
against the Empire, they were still formidable fighters.
They were simply committed elsewhere at the moment,
or else undergoing repairs. The Mons Calamari shipyards were doing big business these days. If the revolt in
Corellia had happened six months earlier or three
months later, the New Republic could have sent a massive fleet.

And, truth be told, Luke had a hunch that Mon
Mothma *could* have raised a New Republic force if ab-

solutely necessary. It would have been risky and expensive, and would have left this outpost or that with minimal defenses for a while, but it could have been done.

But Mon Mothma was not just a strategist. She was a politician, and a good one. Good politicians know how to make use of a crisis, how to use one problem to solve several others. By sending Luke and Lando to call on the Bakurans, she was killing a multiplicity of birds with one stone. She was indeed conserving Republic resources, so that she could deal with other potential crises that might erupt. But she was also appealing to the Bakuran psychology. Bakura was near the borders of the New Republic, and its citizens were often fearful of being forgotten, left out of the equation. If Mon Mothma's guesses were correct, asking them for help would encourage Bakurans to retain close ties to the Republic, making them feel needed, committed to the cause.

And there was another matter. She had, not so very long ago, told Luke that it was only a matter of time before he entered the political arena, and she was perfectly capable of using this opportunity to give him a hearty shove in that direction. Going to Bakura was not a job for a hero who charged in with his lightsaber at the ready. It was a job for a negotiator. Mon Mothma was forcing Luke to act not like a lone swashbuckler, but like a leader, a representative—a politician. Mon Mothma was very good. There was no doubting that.

Luke sat up. Enough of this. It was ridiculous for him to be moping around this way. There was too much to do, too much to get ready for. He needed to know more. It was high time to get that briefing from Threepio.

He was on the verge of pushing the intercom button to summon Threepio when the intercom came on all by itself—with Threepio on the line. "Master Luke—

please come to the cockpit. Artoo is passing us a feed from the military sensor net. There's some sort of intercept taking place. A flight of Y-wing fighters are attacking some peculiar combination of an X-wing and an old-style TIE fighter."

Lando's voice came on, very excited. "It's an X-TIE Ugly, Luke! And the only shipyards that can put those together—"

"—are in Corellia," Luke said, finishing Lando's thought as he ran out of his cabin toward the cockpit. The cockpit hatch was open and he dove through it. "Tell Artoo to contact the intercept fighters!" he said. "Tell them to call off—"

"No need," Lando interrupted. "Whoever is on that thing must have done some fast talking for himself. The Y-wings ceased fire and the cruiser *Naritus* slapped a tractor beam on her. They're taking her aboard. And before you can tell me to do it, yeah, we're changing course. That's *got* to be someone with news."

Luke dropped back into the copilot's seat and punched up the audio com channel to his X-wing. "Artoo—contact the cruiser and request permission for us to come aboard."

Artoo replied with an affirmative-sounding triple beep. Luke leaned forward and peered eagerly through the viewport of the *Lady Luck*. The *Naritus* was nowhere near, of course, and it was going to take some time to get there, but maybe now they were going to get some information.

"Turn this thing around, Lando. Let's get moving."

*   *   *

Kalenda knew her problems weren't over, not by a long shot. Not when she was sitting in a cell in the cruiser's detention block, rather than at a table in its briefing center. Not that she could blame the captain of the

Naritus for viewing her with more than a little suspicion. She was, after all, traveling without any papers or proof of her identity; the NRI did not send its agents out on undercover missions with photo ID. Even if she *had* carried ID, it would have been phony from top to bottom, matching her cover story from the time of her entry into the Corellian system. But she had ditched *that* long ago, of course. That identity was blown, and blown big.

So all they had was a frazzled-looking young woman in a rumpled jumpsuit, both woman and jumpsuit badly in need of cleaning. But Kalenda was not about to ask for a shower or a fresh set of clothes. Not yet. So far they had just given her a quick pat-down, checking for weapons. They hadn't thought to search her clothing all that carefully, and she didn't want this crowd finding that datachip. No. She had her orders regarding that.

But there was another worry. That X-TIE she had stolen. *That* they were going over with a fine-tooth comb, and she couldn't blame them. The trouble was, she had no real idea what was aboard it. It took very little imagination to think of things that could be aboard the Ugly, things that could get her into very, very big trouble. But, she told herself once again, no point at all in borrowing trouble when there was so much currently available.

She could hear the outer hatch of the detention block opening, and, a few minutes later, the door of her own cell opened. The hard-bitten rating who had taken charge of her came into the room. "Still checking your story," she said. "The NRI confirms that's a legitimate one-shot word code you used, but they point out that those things aren't foolproof."

Kalenda nodded. She knew at least three ways to get around the word codes—but that was why the NRI didn't take word-code recognition signals on faith, even with a positive voice-pattern match. "So they've sent you to get fingerprint and retinal patterns and a DNA sample," she said.

The rating cocked her head and gave a sort of half smile. "At least you know your NRI procedures. If you're a plant, they did a good job briefing you."

There didn't seem to be much to say to that, so Kalenda said nothing.

"I don't suppose you've changed your mind about making a statement," the rating said.

"Sorry," Kalenda said. "I have orders from the other side. Direct from the Chief of State." Well, not quite *direct.* But surely the Chief of State's husband was close enough, even if it didn't sound quite as authoritative. "I am to talk only to Admiral Ackbar, Mon Mothma, or Luke Skywalker." And *that* wasn't quite accurate, either, but it was close enough. Han Solo had told her to hand the datachip over to one of those three, and no one else. She couldn't pull the datachip and tell her captor she wasn't allowed to hand it over to her. Not unless she wanted the chip being played back by the captain of the *Naritus* five minutes from now. There had been too many leaks already. The story of the starbuster plot would have to be tightly held, in order to avoid a panic, if for no other reason.

The rating shook her head. "You don't ask for much, do you?"

"I don't write the orders, friend. I just follow them." *After I've rewritten them,* she thought.

"Wish to burning stars I could get the same folks to write *my* orders," the rating said. "Yours seem to get results."

"What?" Kalenda asked. "What do you mean?"

"Be back in a second," the rating said. With that she left the cell. Kalenda could not help but notice that she had left the door open. Was that a test? Did they figure if she wasn't who she said she was, she'd try to make a break for it? Or *should* she try to make a break for it?

What did the rating mean about getting results? Were they about to bring in some sort of interrogation specialist? Whatever the rating had meant, it didn't sound very pleasant. But no. Stop being foolish. They could interrogate her all they wanted. All they'd get was the truth.

Still, that didn't make the thought of someone using all the latest hardware to perform science experiments on her mind seem all that comforting an idea.

When the rating returned, with a tall, grim-faced stranger, the idea seemed even less pleasant. Was he an interrogator? He was a tall, lean man, sandy haired and blue eyed, wearing a New Republic Navy fighter pilot's undress uniform, with no insignia. He didn't *look* like an interrogator. In fact, his face seemed familiar. She had never seen him face to face, of course, but still . . .

"My name is Skywalker," the stranger said. "You wanted to talk with me?"

CHAPTER FOUR

The Flowers of Home

The *Millennium Falcon* eased cautiously out of its parking orbit around Drall and headed down toward the planet's surface. Chewbacca, in his accustomed seat in the copilot's right-hand chair, made a nervous little moaning roar as they headed in. "Don't worry," said Q9-X2, who was clamped to the floor behind Chewbacca. "We are now well inside the Drallish defenses. Our slow approach strategy has paid off."

"I wish I shared your confidence, Q9," said Ebrihim. The Drall was distinctly too short for the pilot's seat, and was reduced to the indignity of standing on the seat in order to see out the forward viewscreen. He was more or less strapped in, but he knew perfectly well he was not all that likely to stay in one place if the going got difficult.

Ebrihim was tall for a Drall, though he was well aware that was not saying a great deal. He was about a meter and a quarter in height. He had short, thick gray fur, with a sprinkling of lighter gray on his face and throat. Like all Drall, he was short-limbed, with clawed, fur-covered feet and hands. Like nearly all Drall, he was a bit on the roly-poly side by human standards. While normal for a Drall, being short and pudgy and furry was often a nuisance for a dignified creature, especially when dealing with humans. Too many of them seemed ready to regard a Drall as a sort of living stuffed-animal toy. Perhaps that was why Drall tended to stand so much on their dignity.

Q9 turned toward Chewbacca. "My master is often extremely overcautious," he said. "I am glad to see you do not share this trait."

"I am *not* overcautious, but neither am I not madly overconfident, as some are. Drall's defenses are not elaborate, and are intended to detect fast-moving, aggressive craft. I am sure we have gotten past all the defenses I *know* about, and those this ship can detect, but that's a far cry from saying there will be no further surprises."

Chewbacca moaned again and shook his head.

"Assuming I understand you properly, I quite agree," said Ebrihim. "I, too, have had my share and more of surprises on this trip." He glanced up toward the interior monitor screen, which was showing a view of the three children in their cabin, strapped down on their beds, which were doing double duty as acceleration couches.

At least the children were behaving for the moment. When *those* three got going, there was no way to stop them. Why in the blue sun he had volunteered to become their tutor, he would never know. He had thought a temporary job teaching a few basics of Corellian life to the children of an extremely powerful and influential human might prove entertaining, and provide him with some opportunities he would not otherwise have had, perhaps improving his prospects in the job market as well. But the entertaining temporary assignment had ended up with him being shot at and chased off the planet.

"All will be well," Ebrihim said in his most reassuring voice. "We will be able to set down quietly on my family lands. There you will be able to effect repairs on this— ah—ship." He had been about to refer to the *Millennium Falcon* by a less respectful term, until he had noticed the Wookiee's expression. Chewbacca seemed to have a complicated love-hate relationship with the old rattletrap of a spacecraft. One minute he prized it above all things, and the next he cursed it most impressively.

"Little good repairing the ship will do while the entire system is under this interdiction field," Q9 said. Q9-X2 bore a vague family resemblance to the R2 series of astromech droids. More accurately, the Q9 series was an experimental design, based on the later-model R7 chassis. Opinion was still split on the outcome of the experiment. Some argued it was a flat-out failure, while the optimists argued it was still too early to know for sure.

Q9-X2's behavior did not always make him the best argument for success. He was nothing more or less than a nuisance most of the time. He seemed to have a knack for driving his master—and everyone else—to distraction, and then demonstrating his own indispensability. Q9 had saved Ebrihim's life in the Corona House attack, a fact that had reminded the tutor just how useful it was to have an overintelligent droid with too much initiative. But even so, Q9 could *still* be most aggravating.

For one thing, Q9 was forever modifying himself, installing new equipment. He had installed his own repulsor units, allowing him to move far more freely over terrain where his wheels would not take him. He had also installed his own voder unit, rendering him capable of speech, rather than being forced to rely on the boops and bleeps of the average astromech. Ebrihim was not certain that Q9 with a voice was an improvement. Ever since he had plugged the voder in, he had talked too

much. "Once the ship is repaired, what will we do?" Q9
asked, demonstrating that very tendency.

"Once we are on the ground, we will plan our next
move," Ebrihim said, attempting to dismiss the question.

"That is a nonanswer," Q9 said. "It offers no information."

"Perhaps because I have none," Ebrihim replied,
quite testily. "Honestly, Q9, you can be most aggravating. When we land, I hope to contact members of my
family who will help us stay hidden while we gather
more information. Our prime duty is, of course, to the
children. We must ensure their safety. How we are to do
that, I do not know."

"No one knows how to do the impossible," Q9 said,
rather tartly.

"They do seem to have a talent for trouble," Ebrihim
conceded.

"That," said Q9, "is one of the great understatements
of all time."

*   *   *

Jaina, Jacen, and Anakin lay flat on their backs in their
beds, cooped up in one of the *Falcon*'s tiny cabins. They
were all properly belted in, doing their best to lie still
and behave. At least the twins were doing their best.
Anakin was having a bit more trouble repressing the
impulse to squirm and fidget.

"Gotta get *up*," he announced.

"No, you don't," Jacen said, more than a little tired of
being in charge of his little brother. He and Jaina were
taking turns being responsible for him. In another ten
minutes Anakin would be her problem, and for that,
Jacen was thankful.

"I need to get up," Anakin said again.

"Why?" Jacen asked, calling his kid brother's bluff.

"What is it you *need*?" He knew perfectly well that what Anakin really had in mind was rushing to the *Falcon*'s cabin to help push the buttons. Of course, the scary thing was that he'd probably push all the *right* buttons. Anakin's skill with electronics and machinery was more than a little disconcerting, even to Jacen. It was like Anakin's Force skills had taken some sort of weird hard left turn. But, all that being said, "probably" wasn't good enough on a spaceship—especially one as wonked out as the *Falcon* usually was.

"Well, um, I gotta—"

"And don't tell me it's the bathroom," Jacen said, guessing what was going to come next. "You just went."

"Oh, yeah," said Anakin. "Well, um, I gotta get up and—and—find my bookchip. I need it to read."

"Oh, brother," Jaina said. "How dumb does he think we are? Jacen, did *we* used to do this?"

"We must have," Jacen said. "I just hope we were better at it."

"Better at what?" Anakin demanded. "What?"

"Being sneaky," Jaina said. "If you're going to tell a fib, at least think up the whole thing before you start. No one believes you when you stop halfway through like that. And besides, the bookchip is a really bad excuse. You can barely read yet."

"I know my letters and numbers."

"But you can't read a whole book to yourself yet, can you?"

"Almost," said Anakin, but even he seemed to realize he wasn't very convincing. "But I *still* need to get up."

Jacen let out a sigh. "Anakin, you *can't* go to the cockpit. Period. That's it. If we let you go, Chewbacca would just throw you right back out, and you'd be in trouble and we'd be in trouble, and it all would be for nothing."

"Well, okay," Anakin said. "But would it be okay if I just got up and looked for my bookchip?"

"*No.* You can't get up. None of us can. The grown-ups are all busy, and we can't interrupt them, and we can't be wandering around, in case the *Falcon* hits a bump. I can't get up, you can't get up, no one can get up until Ebrihim says we can. All right?"

"All right." Anakin said, his voice turning sulky. "But can I just—"

"No!" Jacen said. "Just lie still and be quiet." He waited a minute to see what his little brother would do next. It would either be a tantrum or a sullen silence with occasional mutterings about the injustice of the universe. Jacen devoutly hoped for the latter. It was a lot quieter.

After a minute's silence he heard mumbling from the bunk below his, and breathed a sigh of relief. Now the trick was to be quiet until Anakin forgot he was mad, or else Anakin would get mad all over again that *he* had to be quiet while the other kids could talk.

Not for the first time in the last few days, Jacen found himself beginning to appreciate just how much his parents had to put up with.

He and Jaina had been forced to do a lot of growing up in the last few days. The escape from Corona House had been chaotic and terrifying, and the flight to Drall had seemed to have consisted of terror, tension, tedium, and low comedy. The terror had come early, when the Corellian PPBs had attacked them and done some damage before Chewbacca could shoot them down. The tension had come in waiting to see if Chewbacca's improvised repairs would hold together long enough to get them to Drall—or anyplace at all, even at the minimum power levels that were all the Wookiee was willing to risk. Tedium barely described the long dull days it took to get to Drall. As for the low comedy—well, it came along more or less automatically whenever Chewbacca, Q9, and Anakin were in the same compartment.

It didn't help matters that no one had had a chance to pack anything in the frantic rush to escape the havoc on Corellia. Each of them had exactly two sets of clothes—whatever they had happened to be wearing at the moment the attack started, and one set of cut-down ship's coveralls each, scrounged from whatever their parents had happened to leave on board. Q9 had proved surprisingly skillful in cutting children's clothes out of adult ones, but the coveralls didn't fit properly, and it was a perfect nuisance the way Ebrihim insisted that they wash everything out between wearings. Seeing how he didn't wear any clothes at all, it hardly seemed fair. In any event, considering that they had almost no clothes, there certainly a lot of laundry to do.

And then there was Anakin.

It had fallen to Jaina and Jacen not only to take care of themselves, but to keep Anakin in line as well—and the twins had learned very quickly that keeping their kid brother out of trouble was a lot less entertaining—and a lot more difficult—than helping him get into it.

But learning how to do laundry and baby-sitting were far from the only growing up they had done. There were more serious problems as well.

There was the question of secrets, for example. Back on Corellia, before the trouble started, Anakin, somehow, had sensed the presence of a huge, ancient, underground facility of unknown purpose, and led Jacen, Jaina, and Q9 straight to it. The children had told their parents, Ebrihim, and Chewbacca about it, but no one had the slightest idea what the installation was. All anyone knew for sure was that the Human League was looking for it, though no one knew why. It seemed obvious to Jacen that *something* had to be done about the place Anakin had found, but he could not think of what. It was starting to dawn on him that grown-ups had to deal with that kind of ambiguity a lot.

And that was not all that had happened on Corellia.

The night before the attack on Corona House, all three children had eavesdropped on a meeting between their parents, Governor-General Micamberlecto, and Mara Jade, and overheard a lot of top-secret things about the starbuster plot, stuff that had not gotten out to the general public. The children hadn't *meant* to hear such vital information, but they had. Jacen was virtually certain that Ebrihim, Q9, and Chewbacca knew nothing about that meeting.

And *that* made the three children the only people off the surface of Corellia who knew about the plot—except the bad guys, of course.

And what they were supposed to do about *that,* Jacen had not the faintest idea.

*   *   *

Ebrihim looked through the viewport at the surface of Drall, compared it against the map display, and then nodded. "This is approximately the right position," he said. "You may begin your descent from orbit."

Chewbacca grunted unhappily, but worked the controls and started bringing the *Falcon* in.

"I still don't see how we are reduced to navigation by dead reckoning," Q9 said. "How could this ship have such primitive location equipment?"

Chewbacca looked back over his shoulder at Q9 and bared his fangs.

"If you wish to place blame, Q9, place it with me and with my Aunt Marcha. I did not memorize the precise coordinates of her estate last time I visited, and it would seem she has never gotten around to installing a landing beacon in her back garden."

For once, Q9 had no reply.

The *Millennium Falcon* moved down from orbit as she had moved into it—stealthily and slowly as she could, doing as much of her maneuvering as possible over unpopulated parts of the planet, where detection would be more unlikely.

The ship drifted into atmosphere and the night sky over Drall, cruising silently along. Ebrihim did not much like the idea of coming in during local night. It would be difficult to find his aunt's home even in broad daylight. But no one had any idea what sort of reception the *Falcon* might receive if it were detected.

There had been reports of disturbances on Drall, but there was no way to know the current state of affairs. All interplanetary communications had been shut down by the hugely powerful jamming that had started up after the attack on Corona House. Still, Ebrihim couldn't quite believe that things could be *too* bad on Drall. Drall were too sensible to be swept up in the sort of hysteria that seemed to be gripping Corellia. Even so, there was no point in taking chances.

Chewbacca moved the *Falcon* lower and lower, down into the night. At last he pulled her nose up and brought her into a gentle banking turn. They had reached the point on the map Ebrihim had noted as being more or less near his aunt's country estate.

"Good, good," Ebrihim said as he looked out over the low rolling hills. "I must admit I wasn't sure how close we were going to be, but we are quite near indeed. I have often flown this way in an aircar. There," he said, pointing out the window. "Follow that river to the north. Aunt Marcha lives on the western bank."

Chewie turned the *Falcon* northward and brought her in to treetop level—then below treetop level, swooping down to fly only ten or fifteen meters over the surface of the river itself.

"Goodness!" Ebrihim cried out, in a voice that was embarrassingly close to a squeak. "I appreciate that we need to avoid detection, but do we need to fly *quite* so low?"

But it seemed Wookiees had little patience for the

faint of heart. Chewbacca merely laughed, and brought the *Falcon* down just a trifle lower.

Ebrihim was more than a little unnerved, but even so, it was a breathtaking experience, swooping so low over the blue-black waters of the wide river, the trees to either side little more than indistinct shapes that rushed past in the darkness, coveys of startled white-winged aviars springing into the air as the *Falcon* soared past their roosts. It took an act of will to break away from the scenery and look forward, upriver, watching for his aunt's house.

He had not been this way in many a year, but the night flight over the water brought back any number of memories. When he was a cub, he had played on the banks of this river, swum in it, frolicked on the great lawns of his aunt's mansion. Peaceful, splendid days. But now—now the world, the Galaxy, had changed, and not for the better.

Wait a moment. That small island in the river. Yes. Yes. "Gain some altitude, friend Chewbacca. That island is a bit larger than it looks. And slow the ship as well. We are getting close. Very close."

Chewbacca brought the *Falcon* to about a hundred meters' altitude and slowed it almost to a hover, so the ship was barely crawling forward.

"There!" Ebrihim pointed toward the tree-lined riverbank. "That small pier there, with the white boat tied up. That is my aunt's. Fly in away from the river, past the tree line."

Chewbacca swung the ship around and moved over the trees. A large white house came into view, and he brought the *Falcon* to a halt, so it hovered in place, a silent shape in the sky.

The house was a central hemispherical structure about twenty meters high, with two long wings on either side. The unbroken white of the dome made a striking contrast with the dark slate roofs of the wings. The wings were three stories high, and the whole house was easily a hundred meters from one end to the other. Though there was little decoration on the exterior of Aunt Marcha's home, it was not a severe-looking building, and even in the darkness, it seemed a welcoming place. The gardens and the trees were lovely, and decorative vine plants crept up the side of the dome and the walls of the two wings. It was the sort of place Ebrihim's vast family could visit all at once—and often did.

"Yes, that is my aunt's home," Ebrihim said eagerly. "But . . ."

"But what?" Q9 asked.

"But something is wrong. It is only an hour after dark. The house should be brightly lit and full of people—but all the windows are dark."

Q9 extended his dataport and plugged into the *Falcon*'s sensor system. "I read nothing unusual," he said. "No significant weapons or shielding. No communications activity. An infrared sweep reveals two Drall-sized life-forms. Four vehicles in the outbuilding to the rear of the house. Power charge near depletion on three of them, if that tells us anything."

"You have just read a great number of things that are unusual," Ebrihim said. "There should be, at the very least, four or five Drall in the house. Even if Aunt Marcha herself were not in residence, the staff would still be there. And the house staff would never let the power charge on the vehicles get that low."

Chewbacca let out a low rumbling hoot.

"I don't know what we should do," Ebrihim said. "Let me think for a moment." He and the others were practically fugitives. They needed help. They needed someone who would hide them. But who was that down below in the house? Was one of the Drall Q9 detected indeed Aunt Marcha? Or was she not there for some reason? Were those interlopers down below? Or suppose it *was* Aunt Marcha? What was she doing in the house with just one attendant and the lights off? Could she be in trouble? And would they bring more trouble on her by coming here? But where else could they go? On the other hand, if she were in trouble, perhaps Ebrihim and his party could help her. A highly maneuverable modified Corellian stock light freighter with turbolasers, shields, and all the rest of it did have its uses, and those aboard the *Falcon* did have a fair number of skills.

That decided him. "Put her down," he said. "Try and get her in down under the trees as much as possible so she won't be so easy to spot from the air."

Even if Ebrihim had not understood Wookiee, the dirty look he got from Chewbacca would have told him what the hoot and the blat meant. *Don't tell me my business.*

The *Millennium Falcon* eased her way down toward the ground and sidled over to one side of the house, moving over the spacious lawns toward the woods. Chewbacca brought her to a halt in midair well under the forest canopy, and then brought her in for a gentle, perfect landing.

Ebrihim breathed a sigh of relief. They were safe. "Q9, for heaven's sake unstrap me from this blasted pilot's chair."

Q9 unclamped himself from his position in the rear of the cockpit and rolled forward. He extruded a pair of worker arms and rapidly undid the straps. Ebrihim hopped down from the chair and stretched, grateful to be free.

Q9 hit the cockpit door control and they all stepped out into the ship's corridor. Ebrihim went to the door of the children's cabin and knocked. "Jaina, Jacen, Anakin. We've landed safely. You can unstrap now and come out."

Ebrihim tried to step out of the way quickly, but he was nearly trampled all the same as the three children tumbled out of the cabin.

By the time he got himself untangled from them, Chewbacca and Q9 were ready to open the airlock bulkhead door and lower the access ramp. "Wait just a moment!" Ebrihim called out, and hurried over. "I'd best go first, alone."

There was a brief chorus of protests from all hands, but Ebrihim shook his head firmly. "No," he said. "I go alone. I am known here, and you are not. They might well have spotted our landing from the house, and could be a trifle nervous about it. Things could go badly if they saw a stranger coming out of the ship."

"Well," said Jaina, "I guess you're probably right. But hurry back! We've been cooped up in this ship *way* too long."

"I'll be back as fast as I can. However, friend Chewbacca, it might be just as well if we were ready for a quick takeoff. It's possible that my aunt isn't here, and that we'll encounter a somewhat, ah, less *hospitable* welcome than we might like."

Chewbacca nodded his agreement.

"Anakin, if you would be so kind as to open the hatch and let the ramp down," Ebrihim said.

"Sure thing!" Anakin cried, delighted at the chance to do real work with real machinery. He punched in the proper codes and watched with obvious pride as the inner hatch opened and the ramp dropped smoothly down into the dark night. The night air of Drall wafted into the ship, cool and inviting, redolent with the soft, flat tang of a river breeze.

"I'll be back as soon I am able," Ebrihim said, trying not to sound nervous. And, indeed, why should he feel nervous? This was his family seat, his home. If there were any place in the universe that he ought to feel safe, and comfortable, it was here.

He walked down the ramp, out into the dark night of home. As he stepped onto the soil of Drall for the first time in years, he was surprised by how soft it felt underfoot.

Stepping clear of the ship, he walked a little ways toward the house, but then stopped. There is a bit of folklore common to the spaceways, a little piece of knowledge that all believe to be true. In its crudest terms, it is that there is no place like home. You can never be as comfortable as on your own home planet, with the air pressure, the atmosphere, the gravity, and all the other things exactly as you knew them as a child. It felt *good* to Ebrihim to be back under Drall's lighter gravity, breathing its sweet air. Even the hooting and cawing of the night creatures, the hums and buzzes of the local insects, seemed to reach out to him, soothe him, remind him of days gone by. The very air seemed perfumed, laden with all sorts of—

BLAM!

A high-powered blaster bolt blew up the ground right in front of him.

Ebrihim dove for the ground and landed face-first in a thicket of big, blue, foolish-looking flowers that gave out a cloyingly sweet scent. His aunt's prized garden.

"Who's there?" a familiar voice cried out. "Did I hit anybody?"

His *aunt.* What was she doing out here packing heavy weapons? "Don't shoot!" Ebrihim cried out. "Don't shoot. It's me, your nephew Ebrihim!"

"Ebrihim?" his aunt's voice asked. "What the devil are you doing out there? Did you come on that raider ship that's lurking back there?"

"It's no raider!" he called out. "Those aboard are friends! We are here seeking help!"

"Then why land like thieves in the night?" she asked, coming close enough for Ebrihim to see her by starlight. She looked a bit older and stouter than he remembered, but seemed as vigorous as ever. Of course, the oversized blaster rifle she was carrying added to the impression of vigor. "It *is* you, Ebrihim," she said, in a slightly irritated tone of voice, as if she were expecting him to have changed into someone else. "Get yourself up. You look ridiculous down there."

"Yes, ma'am," Ebrihim said, scrambling to his feet and brushing the dirt out of his fur.

"Now then, tell me quick and no foolish answers. Why did that pilot sneak up on the house? Why did he land in the trees, if you have nothing to hide?"

"We weren't hiding from *you*," Ebrihim said. "We were afraid someone from the outside might spot us. The pilot put down there to try and keep out of sight from above."

"Hppphm. I see," said Aunt Marcha. She slung the blaster rifle over her shoulder and bent down to examine one of the bright blue flowers Ebrihim had crushed when he dove for cover. Straightening up, she surveyed the ground under the *Millennium Falcon*'s landing pads. "Next time," she said, her voice more peeved than ever, "tell your pilot friend to land somewhere besides my nannarium beds."

CHAPTER FIVE

Seems Like Old Times

The bucketful of water hit Han square in the face. "Wake up," an unpleasantly familiar voice told him as he sat upright, spluttering and coughing. "Show's over."

Han opened his eyes cautiously, and instantly knew that caution was called for. He was back in his cell, and the light was none too bright. Even so, it hurt his eyes. For that matter, pretty much every part of him hurt. That Selonian, Dracmus, packed one heck of a wallop.

Thrackan tossed the empty metal bucket into the far corner of the cell, and its clattering was enough to set off a pounder of a headache at the base of Han's skull.

"Come on," Thrackan said, his voice impatient. "Snap out of it. My medics checked you over, and they told me you'd live. Said you were too mean to kill easy."

"Being mean was always your department, Thrackan," Han said, his voice barely more than a croak. He opened his eyes a bit more fully, and watched as his cousin laughed, pulled up a stool, and sat down facing Han on the cot.

"There's the Han I always knew," Thrackan said. "Good to hear you show some spirit."

Thrackan was close to Han. Oddly close. Han suddenly realized he could smell alcohol on his cousin's breath. He noticed that Thrackan was carrying a bottle of what looked very much like Vasarian brandy. His cousin was at least a little drunk. "What do you want now, Thrackan?" Han asked, not sure of what was going on. "You've had your entertainment."

"Don't push it, Han. Don't have much patience left for *you,* believe me."

"So why are you here?" Han asked, unable to control his temper completely. "Is it a slow day, and you want to kill an hour or two pulling my fingernails out?"

"Don't give me ideas," Thrackan said. "I don't need any. I already have an idea. A surprise for you. But I'll show you that in a little while. First I want to talk with you."

Han tried to laugh, but the sound came out as a strangled cough. "Yeah, we have a lot of catching up to do. What is it that brings you down here? *Besides that bottle you have in your hand.* At a guess, his cousin had started feeling just a trifle guilty about what he had done, and had come down here to force Han to say it was all right. Not the most logical train of thought, but it was the sort of thing Thrackan would do.

"Wanted to see you," Thrackan said, a trifle indistinctly. "Besides, there's something I wanted to tell you before the surprise. And something I need you to do."

"All right," Han said. "What did you want to tell me?"

Thrackan let out a sigh. "I'm here because I need your help. Otherwise, I'd have executed you by now f'r the attack on the spaceport."

"Did you think that having a Selonian beat me to a pulp would inspire me to help you?"

"That was necess'ry," Thrackan said dismissively.

"Real-life theater for the officers. You're the most important prisoner we have taken—and you know as well as I do about family loyalty on this damn planet. All those stories about a man who sacrifices principles and duty to take care of his family. My men needed to see I wasn't influenced by that sort of thing."

"Glad I could help demonstrate your integrity," Han said. He remembered those stories a bit differently, of course. The moral of those stories was that it was *good* to put family first. Apparently, there would be none of that nonsense in the Human League. "But why do you need me?"

Thrackan looked his cousin straight in the face. "For two reasons. First, I'm gonna let everyone know *you* are where *I* am. You'll be a sort of insurance policy. This place is hidden pretty good, but they've found better-hidden places than this. Pretty strong place, too, but get a big enough bomb and aim it carefully enough, and no structure will stand."

Han smiled. "If anyone gets a chance to take a crack at you, I doubt they'll be much worried about taking me out at the same time."

"Brave words, but not true. If—and it is a *very* big if—Governor-General Micamberlecto manages to stage a counterattack, or if the New Republic manages to join the party, they won't wanna make any attack that would endanger you. Do you *really* b'lieve the Governor-General and your wife would order a bombing run 'gainst the structure *you* were in? Or that a fleet of New Republic ships, captained by all your old buddies, would wanna try it? Never," Thrackan said, with a flat finality. "Maybe they'd take a crack at some sort of crazy commando raid to rescue you, but lemme tell ya, we are all *set* to deal with that eventa'lity." Thrackan seemed to realize that he had a little trouble with that last word and frowned.

There was enough truth in what Thrackan was saying

that Han didn't wish to pursue it further. "What was the second reason you need me?" he asked, hoping to change the subject.

Thrackan took another pull off the bottle, and then made a vague sort of gesture with his free hand. "Right now I'm telling *lies* to the world. All part of the plan. When the time comes for me to tell the truth—or at least to let the truth get out—*you* will be a very useful messenger. People—the people who matter—will believe *you.*"

"Telling lies and truth about what?" Han asked.

Thrackan smiled. "Oh, no. No, no. No. I'm not taking chances. Might've said too much already." Thrackan paused for a moment, and looked Han straight in the face. He put his hand on his cousin's knee, and gave it an affectionate little squeeze that sent fresh spasms of pain through Han's bruised body. Thrackan clearly did not notice. "You know, much as I hate to admit it, it's *good* to see you. Maybe we're enemies at the moment, and you're my prisoner, but I suppose that old family feeling is still there. Takes me back to the old days."

"Same here," Han said. Not that the old days with his cousin were anything he wanted to remember, but his dancing lesson with Dracmus had certainly reminded him of them. Still, if Thrackan was in a talking mood, he wanted to encourage him. "But it seems to me that we have a lot to worry about here in the present."

"That we do. At least *I* do. *You're* not going to be going anywhere or doing much of anything for a while."

"I sort of figured that."

Thrackan made an attempt to put a crafty expression on his face, and shook his finger at Han. "But can I *count* on your cooperation while you're here? When the time's right, you'll be released, and we'll give you a message to carry—unless, of course, you've caused so much trouble in the meantime that it's not worthwhile keeping you around."

"Thrackan, I don't now how to say this, but I *am* something close to a prisoner of war in all this. It's my job to cause trouble."

"I was afraid you'd see it that way. I don't suppose I could get you to give me your parole, the way Dracmus did?"

"Sorry. No can do."

"And even if you did, I don't think I'd trust *you* as far as I'd trust her," Thrackan said. Amazing, really, the casual arrogance of the man. One moment he was waxing nostalgic over the old days spent beating smaller children to a pulp, and the next he was tossing off a contemptuous insult of Han's honor that was made worse by being completely unconsidered. "We almost got your kids, you know. Our spotters saw that Wookiee pal of yours hustle them into your ship, and we scrambled a flight of PPBs to go after them. If we had caught *them*, we'd *really* have some leverage on your wife."

Han stared at his cousin, astonished in spite of himself. It took a very special kind of mind to come up which such schemes, to see so much and yet be so blind. "How can you do it, Thrackan? How can you go against the best traditions of our people? *Never involve the innocent. Always protect your family.* Don't those words sound familiar at all?"

"I don't run *my* life according to the morals from old nursery stories," Thrackan said.

"So how *do* you run your life?" Han asked, his temper starting to get the better of him. "What *are* the moral lessons you live by?"

Thrackan chortled and took another pull at his bottle. "Fine questions coming from a pirate and a smuggler and a traitor."

"I've been called worse," Han said evenly. "But we're talking about you. I really want to know. How did you get to where you are?" There was no such thing as enough information about the enemy. Han knew the size of his cousin's ego. If Han could twit his vanity, get him talking about himself, Thrackan might well reveal something valuable. "When I left Corellia," Han went on, "you weren't much more than an Imperial bureaucrat. How did you get to be the Grand Exalted Hidden Leader, or whatever it is they call you now?"

Thrackan sneered. "They call me by my *proper* title. They call me the Diktat. And it's a title I have ev'ry right to claim."

"How so? How did you earn it?"

Thrackan smiled coldly. "The old-fashioned way," he replied. "With old-fashioned determination. Determination and ambition."

"With maybe a little backstabbing and skulduggery thrown in for good luck," Han said.

"Watch what you say to me, Han, or I'll—"

"You'll what?" Han said, tired of playing nice. "Beat me to a pulp? Try and kidnap my children? Order a rocket attack on the building my family is in? Don't tell me a man capable of all that didn't play a trick or two here and there on his way to the top."

"And suppose I did play the game? There'd be nothing new in that. Lots of other leaders have to do it on their way up."

"Now there's a fine moral lesson for you. *Everyone else does it.*"

"I should have let the Selonian kill you," Thrackan muttered.

"Yeah. What a pity you seem to need me. But you were telling me about your heroic climb to the top."

"Maybe I *will* let her kill you," he said, in a sulky tone. "But about me, there's not that much to tell. Let's just say that I maneuvered my way into progressively more important posts. By the time your stinking Rebellion won its first battles against the Empire, I was the heir presumptive to the Diktat. Dupas Thomree was the

Diktat, Daclif Gallamby was heir apparent, and *I* was third in the line of succession."

"*That* would be news to a lot of people," Han said. "I remember Thomree, of course, but I've never heard of Gallamby—and I never knew you were up there, too."

"Th' fact was not widely known," Thrackan said, once again trying to speak in formal tones—and not quite pulling it off. "But the Imperial government of Corellia had a *tradition* of secrecy. We din't answer to *anyone.*"

"You're forgetting your close personal friend the Emperor. You must have answered to *him.*"

"Not really. The Emperor believed in order, and *we* kept order here. I can assure you of *that.* In exchange for keeping order, which we would've done anyway, and for swearing absolute loyalty to the Emperor's external policies, the Emperor granted Diktat Thomree permission to run the sector any way he pleased. There was no reason for the public to know the arrangements for the succession. Even the most *powerful* members of the leadership were unknown to the public. People jus' knew who the Diktat was. Secrecy was a real handy thing for those in power."

"So what happened?"

"When the war against the Rebellion started, Thomree kept *his* side of the bargain. He provided troops and ships for the Emperor. But not long after, Thomree, ah, well, he—he died unexpectedly."

"I bet it's a real interesting story how *that* happened," Han said, noticing his cousin's hesitation. "There might even be more than one version."

"I had nothin' to do with it," Thrackan said. "But I won't kid you. Lots of Diktats died under suspicious circumstances. *I* think Thomree figured he had protected himself from assassination by makin' a nobody his successor. Wouldn't be the first time someone tried that—or the first time it failed."

"So who *did* succeed?"

"Gallamby took over. He was the last Diktat. If you can call him that. Jus' a figurehead, a puppet on a string—"

"Were you one of the ones pulling the string?" Han asked.

"Nope. I tried, but others got to 'im first. They managed to control policy. *They* called for economy. They cut back on Thomree's support of the war against the Rebellion." Thrackan paused a moment and shook his head. "How close were some of those fights, cousin?" he asked. "Do you think maybe a few more Corellian ships, a few thousand more Corellian troops, might've tipped the balance? Do you think maybe Gallamby and his gang might've won the war for you?"

Han did not answer. It was no secret that the Rebel Alliance had won more than once by the skin of its teeth.

"Yeah, don't talk," Thrackan said. "*I* say a few fools eager to save a credit or two lost us the war."

"There was more to it than who had the most ships, Thrackan. We had other things going for us."

"Skywalker, you mean."

"Well, yes. Luke Skywalker. And maybe the forces of history."

"I've never believed in fate," Thrackan said. "I've always made my *own* fate."

"Except the Rebel Alliance defeated the Empire," Han said. "You weren't able to do much about that."

"Why do you take such *pleasure* in baiting me, when I could have you killed or tortured any time I want?"

"Mostly because I don't like you," Han said. "But I want to hear this story and you want to tell it. What happened in the Corellian Sector when we defeated the Empire?"

"Even up to the end, I was struggling, behind the scenes, to return Corellia to her former policy."

"You were trying to seize power."

"Of *course* I was, y' fool. Gallamby was letting everything fall apart. Act of patriotism to try and kick 'im out. And by the time of the battle of the second Death Star, I was almost ready to get rid of him. We were all set." Thrackan paused for another swig on his bottle, and his face darkened. "But then we heard about the Emperor's death, and about the defeat at Endor. *That* was enough for the alien scum here, and for their sympathizers."

"Aliens? What aliens?"

"You know damn well. The nonhuman scum here on Corellia."

"The Selonians and the Drall."

"Right."

"How could they be aliens? They've lived here for thousands of years."

"They aren't human. So they're aliens." Obviously, as far as Thrackan was concerned, there could be no argument. "And they all figured that without an Emperor, there wasn't any Empire. There were *celebrations* here when the Emperor died, if you can believe that."

"Do tell," Han said. "Amazing." He was starting to understand something. Somewhere, in the back of his mind, Thrackan couldn't quite believe that Han, his own flesh and blood, could not see the true way. It must be that Han had never heard the real story, in all its self-evident logic. But once it was all explained, once Han understood what had *really* happened, the scales would fall from his eyes. He would be converted to Thrackan's way of thinking. Han could play along with that, if need be. "Even his enemies mourned the death of a worthy adversary." That, of course, was a bald-faced lie. News of Emperor Palpatine's death had been met with dancing in the streets. But telling Thrackan that wouldn't accomplish much of anything.

"Thanks, Han, for telling me that. Here, they celebrated. Nearly all of 'em. Even the troopers and the navy crew. Deserted in droves. No one *defeated* the Empire in Corellia. It jus' *collapsed*." Thrackan stood up a little straighter and made an effort to focus himself. "A regime without authority cannot rule," he said, very grandly. "And the regime here lost all authority."

"The people stopped being afraid of you, is that it?"

"Fear," Thrackan said, "is a great organizing principle. But the end of fear wasn't the only thing that made it crack. It was us startin' to fear *them*. Gallamby made a run for it. Him and his handlers. Took half the credits in the treasury with them. And that was just the start of it. Scavenger hawks. They came in like scavenger hawks and grabbed everything that wasn't nailed down. And then people started to get hold of *files* and started arresting gov'ment officials, trying them for crimes committed in office. Crazy stuff. How could anythin' done in service of the Empire be a *crime*?"

"Beats me," Han said. "So the Empire collapsed. What did *you* do? How did *you* get here?"

"I started planning. Plotting. Thinking of the long term. Finding friends one place, favors someplace else. Started searching out people who'd done all right under the Empire, and wanted the old days back."

"So that's your goal. Bring back the Empire? Give up now, Thrackan. It's dead, dead and gone."

"I know *that*," Thrackan said. "I don't like it, but I can see it. Could see it the day Palpatine and Darth Vader died. All over. But Palpatine's New Order, the Imperial *system*—that we can bring back, at least here. Just no Emperor over the Diktat. No one telling the Corellian Sector what to do. In-de-pen-dent. Just us here, putting the aliens back in their place."

"I thought you were going to kick them off the planet Corellia," Han said. "I heard the announcement. If the New Republic didn't move all the nonhumans off the planet, you'd blow up another star?"

Thrackan laughed. "Yeah. I bet you heard it. Everybody on this planet did. That's one of the lies I've been telling. No way to do that. No way. Impossible. But it makes them *sweat.*"

"What's impossible?" Han asked, a bit too eagerly. "Moving the nonhumans off, or blowing up another star? Did you *really* blow up that first star?"

But Thrackan just laughed. "Oh, no," he said. "I can't tell you that. That would spoil the surprise." He frowned for a moment. "That reminds me," he said as an extremely nasty smile spread across his face. "I almost forgot. *Another* surprise. Reason I came down here. Got a big treat ready for an alien lover like you."

"What—what do you mean?" Han said. Something in his gut tightened up. Thrackan's surprises were rarely pleasant.

"You wait right there. I'll bring it in."

Thrackan stood up, a bit unsteadily, and walked toward the cell door. He pounded on it three times, and the door swung inward. Thrackan turned back to Han. "Be back in just a secon'," he said.

Han stood up, and discovered just how painful standing could be. As best he could tell, there was no permanent damage from his fight with Dracmus, but it would be a while before he healed altogether.

Dracmus . . .

All of a sudden Han had a very good idea what his cousin's surprise was going to be.

Thrackan came back into the cell, a trooper at his back. The trooper took up a position watching the door and drew his blaster, aiming it through the doorway.

The Selonian, Dracmus, stepped into the cell, followed by another trooper with his weapon drawn.

Thrackan looked from Han to Dracmus and back again, a wild grin on his face. "Han," he said. "My dear old cousin. My dear old alien-loving traitor cousin. Traitor to the Empire, traitor to the Emperor, traitor to your *race.* I think it's time you said hello to your new cell mate."

*   *   *

The weary travelers came out of the *Millennium Falcon*. Being careful not to step on any more nannarians, they walked toward the house, Ebrihim's Aunt Marcha in the lead, her blaster rifle slung over her shoulder. She led them to the central dome and up the low stairs to the large doors that led inside. Once at the top of the stairs, she turned toward her nephew and looked at him expectantly.

Ebrihim understood, and turned toward the others. "Our tradition requires a brief and simple ceremony of presentation when a guest first enters the home of the host," he explained. "If there are none who know both parties, the visitors are expected to present themselves. However, if there are people who know both groups, the most junior person knowing both parties is expected to do the honors. In this case, that is myself."

"You're the only one," Jacen objected.

"But I am also the most junior. That is what decides. In this way, we honor those who are our seniors."

"You getting this, Anakin?" Jacen asked in a loud whisper.

"Quiet, Jacen," Jaina hissed.

"It is also expected," Ebrihim went on in a more severe tone of voice, "that the elders will behave in a way *worthy* of honor."

"Sorry," Jacen said.

"Then, if we may begin. Chewbacca. Jaina Solo. Jacen Solo. Anakin Solo," said Ebrihim. "Permit me to present the Duchess Marcha of Mastigophorous. If she will so deign to honor us, she will be your hostess. Pray do her honor."

"You never told us your aunt was a Duchess," Jacen said accusingly.

"You never asked," Ebrihim replied evenly.

Jaina curtsied prettily, and managed somehow to look quite ladylike, considering that she was in rumpled, oversized ship's coveralls. "Pleased to meet you, Your Grace."

Chewbacca bowed, and did so with a surprising grace. Ebrihim turned toward Jacen and Anakin and waited in silence until Jaina gave her twin a poke in the ribs.

"Huh? Oh." Jacen bowed awkwardly, popping up and down rather clumsily. Anakin got the idea, but imitated his sister's curtsy instead of his brother's bow.

"Close enough," Ebrihim muttered to himself. Then he turned to his aunt. "Your Grace, may I present the Wookiee Chewbacca, and the humans Jaina Solo, Jacen Solo, and Anakin Solo, all of the planet Coruscant."

"Ignored again, I see," Q9 muttered.

As good manners required, the Duchess paid the droid no attention whatsoever. "I am most pleased to meet you all," she said, nodding gravely. "I am honored to have such guests. Please make my home your home—"

"Within reason." Ebrihim said with a warning look at the children.

"—and accept all that my hospitality may offer," the Duchess concluded, not missing a beat.

"Thank you," the three children said in chorus.

"Come, then, and enter," said the Duchess, and gestured toward the door, which opened on its own.

She stood aside and let her guests go. The children went first, followed by Chewbacca and Q9. Ebrihim and Marcha entered side by side, and waited while Chewbacca and the children admired the interior of the dome.

Ebrihim remembered his own first visit to the dome. No one could set foot in it without stopping just to *look*. It was a special and magic place. The plain white walls of the hemispheric dome rose up to the ceiling, peaceful and perfect, its warm white featurelessness drawing the eye upward. The columned entryways to the two wings of the house faced each other, each as elaborate as the exterior of the building was plain. One entry was carved in purest white marble, the other in jet-back ebony. Monsters and fabulous creatures out of legend and history clambered and slithered and flew up and down the doorframes and around the columns.

The elaborate entryways faced each other across a formal courtyard filled with planters and flowers of all kinds. A jet of water danced in the center of the dome, tempting those who dared to thread their way through the hedgerow maze that surrounded the fountain itself. A dozen species of Drallish aviars and Corellian birds and other flying creatures flittered and fluttered about the dome.

After a moment or two of wide-eyed admiration, the children rushed into the dome, eager to explore. Ebrihim saw Anakin rush straight into the maze, and wondered whether the lad would break all records in solving it, or whether he would vanish into it for all time.

"We have to conserve power everywhere else to do it," Marcha said to Ebrihim and Chewbacca, watching the children race about, "but by the stars, I am going to keep this dome green and alive." She began to walk about the garden, Ebrihim by her side, and Chewbacca and Q9 walking behind.

"I am glad of that, Aunt Marcha," said Ebrihim. "But we have just now arrived from Corellia, where there has been a complete news block. What has caused the power shortage?"

"Bandits. Terrorists. Drallists. Call them by the names they have earned, or by the name they give themselves. It doesn't much matter. They cut the power lines and sabotaged the local backup generator. All we have is the auxiliary house generator, and *that's* been balky. I had to send all the help home, not just to conserve power, but for their own safety. Driggs is the only one here with me. He's been caretaker here since before you were born. This *is* his home."

"Aunt, please, tell me. What is a Drallist?"

His aunt turned and looked at him solemnly. "If you do not know the answer to that question, you did well to come here," she said. "The Drallists are Drall who say Drall for the Drall! Foreigners out! No Selonians. No humans. Everyone with a tail off the planet! Everyone without fur off the planet!"

"Not here, too," Ebrihim said. "The madness has not reached our people as well."

"Oh, yes it has, dearest nephew. Yes it has." She paused to regard Chewbacca and Ebrihim. "But it is late, and you have had a long journey—and it will take some doing to get those human cubs to bed, if I am any judge. We shall talk more in the morning."

Chewbacca bowed low and let out a low moan and a quiet little whoop as he pointed back toward the ship outside.

"What is it your friend is saying, Ebrihim? I never did learn Wookiee."

"He is offering to run power from his ship to the house and to take a look at your generators. And, I might add, our ship is in need of repairs. Nothing major, I take it, but the hyperdrive needs a bit of work, along with some other adjustments."

"I thank you for your offer of help, and will gladly accept what assistance you can provide," Marcha said to Chewbacca. "And you are, of course, welcome to repair your ship here, but not much joy will you have of a hyperdrive. Don't you know about the interdiction field? The broadcast comlinks are down, but we still get news over the fiber cable links, and *we* heard about it."

Ebrihim looked at her blankly. "What interdiction field? As I said, we have just come from Corellia. The last news we got was of Thrackan Sal-Solo using the starbuster to demand all nonhumans be thrown off Corellia—"

"*What?* What in the heavens are you talking about?"

"The threat to blow up more stars if the Human League's threats aren't met."

"There has not been the slightest mention of that on Drall," Aunt Marcha said. "If there had, it would have been all over the planet in an hour. How did you get this remarkable news?"

"It was on an all-channel broadcast that *Millennium Falcon*'s com system recorded automatically while were making our escape. Chewbacca and I played it back later, and we agreed not to tell the children about it. No need to frighten them. I take it you did not hear any of this on Drall."

"Nothing. Not at all."

"But what would be the point of making the threat on only one world?"

"How could anyone seriously threaten to blow up stars to begin with?" Marcha asked.

"A very good question," Ebrihim said. "But they have. And they claim to have done more than merely threaten. They claim to have actually blown up a star. And for heaven's sake, don't tell the children. But you still haven't told me about the interdiction field."

"But how could you not—ah. Of course," Aunt Marcha said. "With your ship's hyperdrive out, the instruments that would tell what had happened would also be inoperative."

"*What* interdiction field?" Ebrihim asked again.

"Plainly," said the Duchess Marcha, "we have a lot to talk about."

CHAPTER SIX

Meetings and Lies

Gaeriel Captison adjusted her cloak and threw back its hood to reveal a cascade of brown-blonde hair that was her crowning glory. Perhaps the red cloak was too formal for the meeting with the Coruscant group. Whatever it was they wanted, it was supposed to be a private working group, not an official delegation. Nonetheless, she wanted to make a good impression.

Gaeriel sighed and began pacing again. Foolishness. Absolute foolishness. Why pretend? She did not care one little bit what sort of impression she made on the delegation. She was through with politics, for the most part, and glad of it. While it had always pleased her to be able to do good, she finally had lost all patience with the posturing, the positioning, the worry over appearances that went with it.

But Luke Skywalker. He was part of the delegation— and she wanted to look good for *him*. Why hide it? It was vain and foolish and pointless, but that did not make it any less true.

Suddenly the door annunciator chimed, and there was no longer time to worry. They were here.

Gaeriel could have sent a servant, but after all, this was supposed to be a secret meeting, so she had sent the servants away. She went to the door of her private apartment, paused for a moment to compose herself, and then pressed the door control button.

The door slid silently into its recess.

And Luke Skywalker stood there, all alone. He was dressed in a fighter pilot's flight suit, cleaned and neatly pressed, but unadorned by any insignia. He wore his lightsaber clipped to his belt in place of the standard-issue sidearm. He was bareheaded, his hair was cut a bit shorter than she recalled, as if the adult Luke was stricter with himself than the youth had been. He looked, if not exactly older, then more mature. The rigidly controlled passion, the determination held in check by that same inner discipline—that was all still there. She could read that in his eyes, at a glance.

"Master Skywalker," she said. "I bid you welcome. You were expected, of course. But you come alone."

Luke flushed and bowed slightly. "The others of my party will be along in a few minutes, Lady Captison. But I thought it best if I saw you alone, at first, so that we might—we might—"

"That we might have the awkward scene we are having without an audience. Of course. That was most thoughtful of you, Master Skywalker."

Her visitor stood stiffly in the doorway. "It would—it would please me if you would call me Luke," he said.

"Good. I'm glad to hear it. You and I should not be formal with each other."

"Thank you—Gaeriel." Luke craned his neck slightly forward. "Is it all right if I—"

"Oh, yes, of course. Where are my manners? Please, please come in."

Gaeriel stepped back and ushered her guest in. "Come this way, into the garden. We can talk there."

She led him through the light and airy house to the central courtyard, open to the sky. She had planted her garden there—bright flowers, straining toward the sun, sharing their beauty with the world. There was a little marker-stone in the shadiest corner of the courtyard, still looking a little new, a little out of place, like a plant that had not quite set its roots down yet. Her husband's ashes slept under the simple cube of stone. Sitting down on the bench facing the marker, she looked from Luke to the stone, and then from the stone to Luke. What was she thinking of, bringing Luke here for their first talk? So her dead husband could serve as chaperon? She felt a twinge of what?—guilt? embarrassment? shame? Whatever the precise emotion, it made no real sense.

It was all so ridiculous. Gaeriel pushed the feeling out of her mind and gestured for Luke to sit down beside her. She considered pointing the marker-stone out to him, and explaining what it was, but what would be the point of that, beyond making the man feel more awkward than he already did?

Once Luke was seated, at a more-than-respectful distance, she couldn't help but note, she began to speak with a certain forced cheerfulness. "So, Luke," she said, "what brings you to Bakura?"

Luke looked down at his feet for a moment, and then straight in her eye. "The present," he said. "Not the past."

"Ah," Gaeriel said. "I see."

"You meant a great deal to me, Gaeriel," he continued. "You still *do* mean a great deal. There have been many, many times over the years when I have wanted to contact you, send you a message, come for a visit—"

"And why didn't you?" Gaeriel asked. *And why did I never go to see you?* she asked herself. There was an odd thought. In all the long years she had thought of seeing Luke again, it had never once entered her head that she might go to him.

"Because I could never be a part of your life, not really. Not when I might be called away to who knows where at any moment. Not when your political career, and your duty to your people, would have made it impossible. I could only have disrupted your life, and then disappeared from it again. Would that have been fair to either of us?"

"No," Gaeriel said. "It was hard enough that first time, looking at you and saying good-bye. To have had you return, and then leave again, over and over, to have seen what I wanted, and to have the seeing remind me that I could not keep it—no, Luke, you were quite right."

"But—but the thing of it is that time passes," said Luke. "I remember what I felt for you, but that's not the same as *still* feeling it. You have a piece of my heart, but it's a different, calmer, quieter piece than it used to be."

Gaeriel looked toward her husband's tombstone and smiled again, more sadly this time. "I certainly got over you, Luke, if that helps."

"Yes," Luke agreed, "you did. You married, and had a child, and—"

"And my husband died," she finished for him. "And here we are. But you are here for the present, you said, not the past."

"Yes." Luke agreed, and let out a deep breath. "We need your help," he said. "When the others in my party arrive, we can explain it in more detail. Some of it I have learned very recently, from an NRI agent traveling with me by the name of Kalenda. She got out with the latest information we have. The basic facts are these. There is a crisis. There seems to be a revolt in the Corellian system. Those who started the revolt claim to be able to blow up stars at will, and they might be telling the truth. Worse, they are prepared to blow up stars in inhabited systems. It's at least possible that they will do just that if we interfere, though they have not explicitly said so. Our Chief of State—my sister—was caught in the revolt, along with her husband and children."

"What help do you need of us?" Gaeriel asked.

"The leaders of the revolt seem to have chosen their moment carefully. They commenced their rebellion at a moment when the New Republic Navy was heavily committed, and those ships not committed were undergoing repair. We don't have any ships to spare. We need yours."

Gaeriel looked at Luke in astonishment. "I hardly know what to say, Luke. I must admit that I'd imagined seeing you again more than once over the years. But somehow I never imagined you calling on me to ask if you could borrow our navy."

"It's not the most gracious way to renew an old acquaintance, is it?" Luke asked, smiling ruefully.

"No, it isn't. But at least it has the benefit of being original." Gaeriel thought for a moment. If they wanted help from the Bakuran Navy, they would have to talk to Ossilege. And he'd want to bring in his tactical people. *And* she'd need to talk to the new Prime Minister as well. He'd certainly want a representative sitting in. . . .

Gaeriel was lost in thought when the door annunciator chimed again. She blinked and came back to herself, surprised at how quickly her mind had turned toward the practicalities, the ins and outs of making things happen on Bakura. The chimes sounded again.

"Ah, that will be my friends," Luke said.

"You go let them in," she said, standing up. "Now that I know what this is about, I know who to call. Give me a half hour and I can get together the people you need."

*   *   *

Han Solo sat on his cot and stared at Dracmus the Selonian, and Dracmus the Selonian sat on her cot and stared back at him. The two of them had sat there, silent, for half the night. Han had no idea what to do. Was this creature his ally or his enemy? Was she wondering whether to befriend him, or was she just waiting for him to doze off, and amusing herself in the meantime by considering which part of his anatomy would make the tastiest appetizer?

"Apologize my asking in the Basic," Dracmus said at last, speaking so suddenly that Han jumped in startlement. "My Basic I have not used much for long, and it is not good. As I use, will come back. But *must* use. *Must* ask. Cannot ask in my tongue, as Selonian has not the word. So, in Basic. That man Thrackan Sal-Solo is your *cousin*? Yes? That is how you say the thing?"

An anticlimactic way to start the confrontation, but the way things had been going, Han would take all the anticlimaxes he could get. "Yeah, that's right. My cousin."

"Which is a kind of relative? A relation of the blood? Of what sort, please, does it mean?"

"There are various kinds of cousin," Han said slowly. "But the sort he is to me is of the closest sort, a first cousin. That means a child of your parents' siblings. Thrackan is my father's sister's son."

"Ah," said Dracmus, still staring fixedly at Han. "I make confession that I do having the trouble getting human family concepts straight," she said.

"Yeah," Han said, a bit slowly. "I can see how that might be." He had not known what to expect of Dracmus. He had been worried that she might bear a grudge about the fight, but it seemed she wasn't going to mention it. Well, if she wasn't, *he* certainly wasn't going to. Still and all, he hadn't expected her to start off asking about cousins. Why cousins? Han didn't know a great deal about Selonian family life, but he knew something.

Selonians were hive animals, living somewhat like certain social insects, in groups they called dens. Normally the whole den lived together, but members might travel far and wide, and some might live apart from others. It was the bloodline of the den, and not the physical proximity of den members, that mattered.

Each den normally contained a few fertile males and exactly one actively fertile female, the queen. That one queen, the single breeder female, gave birth to all the rest of the den's offspring. She would have four or five birthings of five or more every year, a pace she might keep up for thirty or forty standard years. Only one birth in a hundred was a male, but all males were fertile. One birth in five hundred was a fertile female. The vast majority of a given den was made up of sterile females. Strangely enough, the fertile males and females, the breeders, were an oppressed, albeit pampered, minority. The steriles treated the fertiles as breeding stock. Power was vested not in the fertile queen, but in one of her sterile daughters or aunts or sisters, who, in effect, owned her.

A very odd setup, and Han could see how human family relations would seem just as odd to Dracmus. "You Selonians do things a bit differently," he said.

"Yes, yes," Dracmus said, a bit absently. "Very differently." She curled her tail on her lap. "But this your cousin. He is not like you."

Han felt his head reeling just a bit. It had been a hard enough day already without some Selonian trying to play anthropologist. Still, there was something in her tone of voice that told him she was the persistent sort. He wouldn't get any peace until he satisfied her curiosity. "He is and he isn't," he said. "We *look* a lot alike and *sound* a lot a like. But we don't *think* alike. Which is why he's out with his drinking buddies and I'm in a cell."

"Is that the rule with human cousins? Look alike, not think alike?"

"There's no rule," Han said. "It varies. It varies an awful lot. Thrackan and I look a lot more like each other than most cousins. Cousins don't usually *act* much alike."

"Very much of interest," Dracmus said. "Very much. And he is your enemy? Deeply and truly so? Of your blood, your close blood, and yet you work against each other?"

"Oh, yes," Han said. "Very much so."

The tip of Dracmus's tail whipped back and forth moodily. "Amazement. We Selonians, we *know* other species are so, but having know is not understand. Against blood."

"Yeah. Against it," Han said. He was exhausted, and not quite sure how much longer he could keep up the small talk without passing out on the spot. Still, he really didn't want to insult Dracmus. Especially considering how sharp those teeth were. He hesitated a moment, then decided to take the chance. "Look, no offense, and I really am glad it seems you're not going to tear me limb from limb, but I'm not in such great shape just now. Why does this matter? Can't it wait?"

"It matters much," Dracmus said. "I believe now you *are* not like him, though I wonder *why* you are not. I am glad you are not the same. So you should be glad."

"And why is that?" Han asked.

"Because one is enough bad. If I decided you *were* him like, I would have torn your throat out by now."

Han nodded and smiled to himself. "In that case, I *am* glad you don't think we're the same. But I'm beat."

"Beat? Yes, I beat you hard. Apologies."

"No. I mean yes, but that's not what I meant. It's a slang expression meaning 'I am exhausted.' "

"Ah. You need to rest. Understandable."

"Right. So if you promise not to tear my throat out overnight, can we continue this in the morning?"

Dracmus hissed low, the Selonian equivalent of a laugh, as she lay back on her own cot. "I promise, honored Han Solo. Your throat is yours till the morning. I not harm you this night. But we have much to discuss."

"I bet we do," he said as he eased himself back down on his cot. He felt safe now, at least for the moment. Most Selonians were ferociously, relentlessly, honest. If Dracmus said she would not harm him tonight, then he was safe from harm.

Until the morning, at least. Han could not help but notice she had left herself an out.

He shut his eyes and was instantly asleep.

*   *   *

Lady Tendra Risant of the planet Sacorria looked through her macrobinoculars at the night sky and knew something was happening. Something that was not good.

The macrobinoculars were high-powered and set up on a tripod with a sophisticated autotracking system that allowed her to track an object in orbit quite easily. Not that she needed any such power and capacity, since the larger ships in the fleet of orbiting spacecraft were visible to the naked eye, if you knew where to look. And after a little bit of extremely quiet research, she knew *exactly* where to look.

Tendra Risant had never had much to do with anything outside her own life until a few weeks before. Then she had met Lando Calrissian, and somehow, everything had changed. She was not in love with him, nor he with her. Perhaps they never would be in love. And yet, there had been a sense of connection between them, a sense of *possibility* that she had never felt before.

And then, mere hours after he and his friend Luke Skywalker arrived on Sacorria, they had been thrown off the planet by the local authorities. They had lifted off, en route to Corellia—and vanished altogether, even as all traffic in and out of the Corellian system was stopped dead by the huge and mysterious interdiction field, and all communications with the Corellia system were jammed.

Sacorria was one of the so-called Outlier Worlds of the Corellian Sector, somewhat isolated from the rest of the sector. The planet had always assured itself that it could get along just fine without Corellia's help, and even dreamed of being free of Corellian control—but the people of Sacorria had received a pointed lesson in the dangers of getting what you wished for. And now they were scared. Without Corellian trade, the economy had not so much stopped as it had slammed face-first into a brick wall.

Something had happened, something big—and Lando was in the middle of it.

Lando. Perhaps she was reading too much into the—the possibilities with him. Perhaps Lando had been nothing more than smooth talk. Perhaps, even if nothing had happened on Corellia, he never would have come back, all his pretty words to the contrary. But none of that mattered now. He had gotten her started wondering and worrying. And it did not take her long to find a lot more to worry about—starting with the Triad, the government of her own planet. The population was restive and fearful, yet the government was blandly reassuring. According to the Triad's proclamations, they knew nothing more than the average human or Drall or Selonian in the street. Of course, if there was one word to describe the Triad, it was "paranoid." Most dictators who got to the top via plots and coups were justifiably concerned about falling victim to more of the same. A trio of dictators, each of a different species, each forced to watch both of the others, could not help but be even more concerned about plots and schemes.

And yet there were no hysterical pronouncements, no mass arrests of enemies and subverters of the status quo. The only clue that something was not right was that the military had vanished. In normal times, it seemed as if every third person walking down the street was in uniform. Now, suddenly, they were all gone, all leaves canceled, all units on alert, if you believed the scuttlebutt. *That* made sense if there was a crisis, if the Triad was mobilizing against whatever mysterious threat had struck at Corellia. Except, as Tendra had learned with just a little digging, the mobilization had been ordered two days *before* the Corellian interdiction field went up—in point of fact, just an hour or two after Lando and Luke arrived on planet.

That would explain why they were allowed to land, but immediately required to leave, at any event. But it also suggested, very strongly, that the Triad knew about the Corellian interdiction field in advance. Whether that meant they were part of the plot that had caused it, or whether they had pulled off some sort of intelligence coup and gotten the word from their spies, Tendra had not the faintest idea.

But the thing that had her worried most was the fleet assembling in orbit. There were too many ships, far too many—at least ten times the number the Triad admitted to publicly. Even allowing for secrecy and paranoia, it was quite a feat to hide ninety percent of your striking force. Besides, Sacorria was not a particularly populous world. A little quick arithmetic demonstrated that it would take something like half the adult population of the planet to provide crews for a fleet that size. Therefore, many, if not most, of the ships and crew were from off-planet. But where were they getting them? And what did they plan to use them for?

The answer to the latter question seemed obvious, though she could not see the details clearly. It had to be that this fleet was heading for Corellia. For what purpose, and under whose command, she had no idea. But it had to be Corellia. Nothing else made sense.

But suppose they were part of the organization that had thrown up the interdiction field? And suppose they could turn the field on and off at will, allowing their ships, but no one else's, to move? It didn't take much imagination to see what a powerful weapon that could be.

But what was she supposed to do about it? She had no great love for the Triad. She felt only the slightest twinge of patriotic guilt over the idea of warning someone about what she had found out. After all, Sacorria was her home world. But whatever she might owe the planet, she certainly owed nothing to the Triad. They were thugs and tyrants, nothing more or less.

Then what to do? Get to Coruscant, give them a warning? A moment's thought convinced her there would be no point to such an action. Even if she were able to find someone who would listen to her, she would not be telling them anything they didn't know. New Republic Intelligence had no doubt been crawling all over Sacorria before the Corellian crisis blew, and no doubt had redoubled their effort since then. No, if NRI hadn't been able to find out everything a private citizen could discover by keeping her eyes open, then they didn't deserve to know.

But Corellia. The people in the Corellia system would not, could not know. And they were the ones who *needed* to know. And if it just so happened that was where Lando was supposed to be, then so much the better.

Good. That much was decided. She would go to the

Corellian system and warn Lando—warn everyone—of the fleet gathering here.

Which only left the trifling question of how, exactly, to go about doing that.

* * *

"Are you awake, honored Solo?"

Han opened his eyes to see a mouthful of very sharp teeth very close to his throat. "I am now," he said, with the utmost sincerity. It might not be the most pleasant way to be awakened, but the sight of that mouthful of cutlery first thing in the morning certainly was an effective means of making a person fully alert. "Why? What's happening?"

"I wished to speak with you."

"And it can't wait?"

"I think not. There is one reason of which I cannot speak. But also when they find we have not done battling during the night, they might become disappointed, and separate us again."

"You could have a point," Han said, "but I'm all for disappointing them." He sat up, moving cautiously, and was pleased to find he hardly winced. He might be getting older, but it would seem that he was still a quick healer. "So what do you want to know?"

"I must know about certain lies. But it is like cousins, this lying thing," Dracmus said as she returned to her own cot and sat back down on it.

"What?" Han said. "What are you talking about?"

"Forgive. A strange way to say it. I am meaning, I suppose, we Selonians have cousins, yes, and uncles and nieces and all such, if you look at chart of descent. At least I think we do. I am not sure of precise meaning of all those words. But though we have these relationships, we never *think* of them. We do not understand the ideas well."

"I guess not," Han said. "You don't have families that way."

"No, we do not. And this idea of cousins being different and same—all Selonians in a den near identical. Closer genes than in your brother and sister. We are more alike than that. Closer to being hundreds of identical twinses."

"That much I knew," Han said. Selonian genes did not randomize as much as human genes did. Each breeder male would father a certain portion of the sterile population, and all those with the same father were said to be in the same "sept." All the sterile females in a given sept were, for all intents and purposes, clones, with each individual's genetic structure all but identical to that of every other member.

"By way humans use word," Dracmus said, "Selonian not even *have* of families. We have dens. In *your* terms, I have three hundred sisters and half sisters. I may have brothers, but I know not of them. They would have been sent elsewhere to breed. So I have not *idea* of sister and brother as you do. When we see human parents, see human woman pregnant out in public, we find it odd and some unpleasant. Breeders should be in den. We think, how strange you treat your breeders—and then we remember, *all* you are breeders. 'Wife, husband, mother, father.' We do not *think* in such ways."

Han looked at Dracmus. He had never really stopped to think about it. The Selonians might have breeding pairs, but they did not have husbands, or wives, or marriages. How could they? As with every intelligent species, Selonian culture was driven by Selonian biology, and marriage was not compatible with a species where one breeder queen might have a thousand sterile, asexual daughters. The human way must seem equally strange to Dracmus.

Human marriage was, of course, associated with breeding, and to Selonians, that was an extremely distasteful subject. Han knew perfectly well that many Selonians looked down on races where everyone was a breeder. "You might not *think* in such ways most of the time, but you're going to have to learn if you're going to deal with humans."

"A true thing," Dracmus said. "Before now, I have not gotten out much. The tasks of dealing with humans fell to my—you would say—elder sister, but she died eight days ago in accident. Now I have job."

"I'm sorry your sister died," Han said.

"As am I. My training in human dealing was not yet complete."

Han looked at Dracmus in surprise. How could she say such a callous thing? But then he stopped himself. Thinking about it, how upset could she afford to *get* over one sister's death if she had three hundred? It must have been more like the death of a distant aunt to a human. And if the steriles in a given sept were all near clones anyway, how much sense of loss could there be at the death of one sister when she had twenty or fifty more, all virtually identical? "Well, it seems to me that you're doing fine, even with only partial training."

"That is most kind, honored Solo, but we are drifting away from point. We must speak of lying. Lying to us is as strange as families. We Selonians *can* do lying, but we have no practice at it. We see it is a bad thing. Not a little bad thing, as with you, but a *big* bad thing, like murder."

"Lies *can* be a big bad thing," Han said, but then thought for a moment about some of the exceedingly tall tales he had told over the years. "But, ah, mostly they're not."

"You see? You have *skill* at lies. You understand them, know big from little. Selonians terrible sabacc players, bad at all games that require concealment of truth. I think lie for human can be small because you are so alone. Lie can touch only one, hurt only one. It can be kept secret. For Selonian, together in den, lie touches all. All know of it. No secrets, all hurt. Do you follow?"

"Just about," Han said, trying to parse the slightly scrambled sentences. "I take it that there are some lies someone told you that you want to ask me about."

"Yes! Yes! Glad I did not kill you in the fight."

"The pleasure is all mine," Han said. "But what are the lies in question?"

"First, please, can you tell when Thrackan your cousin is lying?" Dracmus asked.

"Sometimes," Han answered. "Last night he thought I knew less than I did. He told me things that were in direct contradiction to what I already knew. He even told me that he was telling lies—but he didn't say what they were."

"But when you *aren't* sure. Can you tell when all you have is the words of his speaking?"

Han thought for a minute. "At times. A little. And I can make some guesses about things that might be true inside his lies."

"Like for what? Tell me some, that I get feel of it."

"Why is this so important to you?" Han asked. He wondered just how far he could trust Dracmus. So far she had behaved very well indeed—but he had not the slightest idea what she was up to, or why she had been thrown in a Human League prison. About all he had to go on was the idea that the enemy of his enemy might well be his friend.

"I will give explain later, if time. But it is important. Please."

Han considered, and decided the stakes were too high. He needed more than that. "No. Tell me first. Why did you need to know about human lying?"

Dracmus hesitated. She stood up, walked toward the door of the cell, and then back to her cot, her tail lashing. "Is a terrible problem. I need to know much more of human doings than I do. It is a great trouble that my sept sister died."

"What's the problem?" Han asked.

"I ask you to explain human lying, but if can explain then is because you are skilled at it. I think you a good liar, I am sure, honored Solo."

"Thanks," Han said. "So I've been told."

"Was a deadly insult, not a compliment," Dracmus said. "But you make my point stronger by taking it so. If I tell you more, I tell you things others must not know. But how can I trust human proud of his good lying?" She waved her arm about to indicate the whole underground complex. "This could all be trick to make me say what I am about to say."

Han smiled. "I see Selonians are good at paranoia, even if they are not so good at lies."

"Oh yes. Paranoia, that we are very good at."

"Then you should be careful of what you say to me in any event. There could be all kinds of spy eyes and hidden microphones in this cell. They could be recording everything we are saying. Maybe we should switch to Selonian."

"Pointlessness," said Dracmus. "I am sure they are *not* snooping us, but if they were, they would record all and play back to Selonian speaker."

"True enough. But how do you know they are not recording?"

"I must say no more about that."

Interesting. Whatever else you could say about Selonians, they were clearly not much good at concealing the presence of a secret. How could a race of inept liars be otherwise? It was plain that Dracmus knew more about this place than she was supposed to, but at the moment Han figured it was best to play along. "What *can* you say more about?" Dracmus stared at him, her eyes piercing and intense, but she said nothing. Han sighed. "Would it help if I gave an oath on—on the lives of my children—that I will not reveal what you tell me to Thrackan or his people?"

"A strong oath, if you mean it. In the Selonian way of oath taking, mine is the right and duty to hunt your children down and kill them if you transgress."

Han hesitated a moment. Suppose they used torture or mind probes or drugs on him? Would that matter to Dracmus? He doubted it. But Thrackan and his goons had shown no signs of wanting to interrogate him—and even if he was tortured, and he cracked, and Dracmus decided to hunt down his children, she'd have to find them first—and get past Chewbacca in the process. It was Chewbacca that decided Han. No one got past *him.* "I take the oath," Han said. "I will not betray you. But what of you?"

"The lives of all my sept sisters be forfeit if I betray you," said Dracmus.

"I can't ask fairer than that," Han said. "Talk to me."

Dracmus let out a sigh and sat down on her cot. "Very well," she said. "Let me tell you a tale."

Han settled in to listen.

"Was a riot in Selonian enclave of Bela Vistal city that started crisis, and was Selonians who riot after intolerable and forever provocation from the Human League—but I not think was we who started it. Must admit that even I not sure if the street scuffle that sparked it all was real, or staged by Human League. I believe it was League."

"It had to be," Han said. "Things spread too far too fast for it to all be chance. The timing was very convenient from the League's point of view. They probably don't even much care if everyone really believes they touched things off, as long as no one can prove it. They wanted an excuse, a justification, not a reason."

"Yes! For many reasons, most well-timed. But I think you do not know the all of it, the biggest of it."

"How do you mean?" Han asked.

Dracmus paused again, then plunged in. "I believe this—am all but certain that Thrackan is bluffing. His Human League could *not* have blown star that went supernova. *That,* I think, is his lie."

"What?" Han asked.

"Think of it," said Dracmus. "Their group is too small, too stupid. Yes, now they win a fight, they will grow fast, but just a little ago, League was little more than Thrackan and a few hangers-on. Had not resources, ability—or brains—to do such a thing. Nor the money to buy those who could do it. Making starbuster system is massive breakthrough, huge endeavor. *You* think could these drunken fools who watched us fight make it happen?"

"So you're saying that Thrackan is bluffing," Han suggested. "You think the star when nova by itself."

"Yes and no," said Dracmus. "I believe *Thrackan* didn't do it, League didn't do it, but star could *not* have gone nova on its own. Wrong star type. *Someone* set it off. Somehow. For some reason. I believe was meant to be secret test shot."

"Secret? But everyone knows about it."

"Think, honored Solo! A messenger drone had to bring proof of the explosion to Corellia. Otherwise none would notice that it had gone nova for years yet. The star was in uninhabited system. Speed-of-light delay means light of the nova not reaching inhabited system for decades. Only came to notice *because* of the anonymous message sent by Thrackan's people. And was Thrackan Sal-Solo's people who sent message. No doubt of that."

"How do you know all this?" Han asked. "Some of this information no one is supposed to have."

"I must say nothing at all about that."

Dracmus was definitely not good at hiding secrets. "I'll say one thing for you. You're consistent. All right, you can't say how you know. But go on."

"It is all logic. The star could not blow on its own. Human League no science lab. They could not blow star. Thus must be some others blew that star—and likely must be could blow others."

"Your logic is plain enough, if you grant the idea that our hosts aren't up to the job. So who blew the star, and how did the League find out about it, and how do they relate to the League—and how kindly are they going to take the League taking the credit?"

"No ideas on that. But whoever organization is, has not shown itself yet, for whatever reason. Perhaps they never show selves at all. Might be suits their purposes to have Human League taking the credit, and blame. Who shall search for real conspirators while believing League is to blame?"

"So that's what you want my opinion on? You want to know if your logic is right, and that Thrackan is lying about the starbuster?"

"Yes," Dracmus said. "Opinion, please."

Han thought it all through, as carefully as he could. "You're right. The League isn't the sort of outfit to be much on technology or science, and if anyone had the starbuster for sale, it's got to be that they could have found a higher bidder. *If* you are right on that point, then I think the rest of it must be right. Someone else is allowing the Human League to take credit for the starbuster."

"If all so, then the questions become *who* controls this interesting device, why they do it, and what is their relation to Human League?"

Han shook his head. "I have no idea. Whoever they are, the starbusters haven't shown their hand yet. But somehow, thinking about it all, I am starting to wonder if the Human League is just a front."

"A front? A front to what?"

"Sorry," Han said. "Another idiom. A false front. Something put up just to hide what's behind."

"Ah. The starbuster people hide behind the Human League who are in front, and the League's actions provide an explanation for various activities."

"Right," Han said.

"But this brings us no closer to finding the starbusters themselves."

"Wait a second," Han said. "Maybe we are close. Much closer than we thought, or than we would want to be. Maybe the person who delivered the message was much more than just the messenger."

"I don't understand."

"Before the revolt started. *After* the nova went off, but *before* anyone knew about it, we got a message. Governor-General Micamberlecto, my wife, and I. It told all about the supernova and warned us to obey further instructions, or else stars of inhabited planets would be exploded."

"Yes. But what of it?"

"Mara Jade."

"Mara Jade? The trader? She has had many dealing with the Selonians. We know her well, and trust her."

"Yeah, well, Mara Jade is a lot more than just a trader. Did you know that she used to be the Emperor's Hand? The Emperor's personal, private, secret agent and assassin?"

"No," Dracmus said, clearly startled. "Do you speak truly?"

"Very much so," Han replied, a trifle excitedly. "It also would explain how the bad guys managed to get hold of the Chief of State's private diplomatic cipher. She used to be a spy. She knows how to get that kind of stuff." He thought for a moment and then spoke again. "It all fits. Mara Jade brought us the message, and she gave us some long complicated story about how it got to her. From what was on the message container, it looked as if it had been meant for Luke Skywalker, but that they had used Mara as a backup when that failed. But what if that was all an elaborate charade—one that we bought into all the way?"

"You are suggesting Mara Jade brought a message she had written herself? That she is part of the starbuster plot?"

"Yes!" Han said. "*And* she was nowhere to be found the day Corona House was attacked."

"Ah! Of this I can speak, and glad to do so, to defend the honor of Mara Jade, which I wish to do. She has been sighted in Corona House since day after rocket attack."

"How do you know that—okay, okay, I should have known. You must say no more about it. You're just full of secrets you can't tell, aren't you? But I don't know that her being there *before* the attack and *after* it, but not being around *during* it is much of a defense."

"But why would she do it? What would be motive?"

Han hooked a thumb at the cell door. "Our kindly hosts are very obviously all either ex-Imperial or people who just want the good old Imperial days back. Thrackan said as much to me. Now, I grant, she has done a lot of good for the Republic over the years, and she hasn't gone around chanting the Emperor's name out loud or anything, but Mara has never been one to show her hand. She always was good at keeping secrets. I doubt anyone is ever quite sure of what she intends. Suppose, just suppose, that Mara has changed her mind again. What if she's decided she wants the Empire back after all? Maybe she looks at Corellian and figures you have to start somewhere. I grant it's a little hard to believe, but it seems to me we're in the position of having to choose between improbable explanations."

"The idea has logic, but does not convince," said Dracmus. "I do agree Jade is hard-edged, ruthless. But she has *honor,* and we speak of wiping out whole planets. Could she truly be capable of such brutal savagery?"

Han nodded. "I grant you have a point. She's always

been tough, and hard, but never barbaric. I can't see her as the sort to murder millions. But maybe we don't have the whole story. We might be missing something. Remember the first nova didn't hurt anyone. Maybe the threat to inhabited systems is a bluff."

"Mine is another theory," said Dracmus. "I believe the folk behind this are indeed ex-Imperial, but not Imperial spies. The Imperial Navy. Some remnant formation of Imperial ships has finally made an old Imperial superweapon work. Starbuster is like Death Stars or world devastators. A huge weapon, meant for terror, not true military use."

"No way," Han said. "A lot of time has passed since the last of the Imperials were beaten back, and we've had a good look through the Imperial archives. Virtually all Imperial forces have been accounted for. You might be able to spin out a story where someone managed to scrape together a task force from ships mistakenly listed as destroyed. Some people say there are whole fleets out there that no one knows about. But even if that were true, where are the thousands of trained crew supposed to come from? Every time anything goes wrong anywhere in the Republic, some conspiracy buff or another trots out a theory of a cabal intent on reviving the Empire. If someone runs out of place mats in the palace commissary, it's an Imperial plot. I for one no longer believe in that particular bogeyman. The Empire is as dead as Darth Vader. I still say it's Mara Jade. She's a master trader, and an ex-Imperial intell operative. She's got ships, resources, technical centers, and spies everywhere, and she's real. She's no imaginary fleet of ships drifting in the Sand Crab Nebula. She had means, motive, and opportunity."

"Unless, of course, we are both right," said Dracmus. "To make conspiracy is to draw many together. Perhaps one plot pulls in Jade, Imperial Navy fragment, Human

League, and others, too. But I hope you are all wrong, honored Solo. I truly do."

"Why, Dracmus?"

"It is not obvious? If she is behind this plot, she has quite deliberately arranged things so she is where she is right now, to be where she can do the plot the most good."

"What's your point?" Han asked.

"Right now," she said, "Mara Jade is in same place with your wife."

CHAPTER SEVEN

Trust

I *must* be granted access to working communications equipment!" Leia Organa Solo told the guard, not for the first time. She stood there, her fists balled up, seething with rage, as the guard ignored her and set the tray down on the table. She had been locked up in Corona House, for days now. Until a few days ago, it had been the Governor's residence, and now it was a Human League prison. It was not a place she wanted to be any more. "Didn't you hear me? You must grant me access—"

The Human League guard was puffing a bit, as he always did when he brought in the food. Once he had set the tray down and caught his breath, he seemed to feel he could pay attention to his captive, and proceeded to laugh in her face, not for the first time. "Guess what?" he asked. "I'm not gonna do it. I'm not going to grant you access to nothing. But tell you what. You go on *telling* me to do it every time I bring your food up from downstairs." The guard leered unpleasantly. "I don't mind, and maybe it makes you feel better." He plopped down the lunch tray and took away the breakfast tray. "You can tell me to do it again at dinnertime, if you like." He seemed to think that was all very funny, and laughed louder than ever as he headed out of the guest room, now made over into an improvised cell, where Leia was being held.

Just before he reached the door, he turned back and spoke again. "Oh," he said, "I almost forgot. We're rearranging the cells. Seems one female prisoner had a fight with another. Gotta divide 'em up. Right after lunch, you get a new cell mate." The guard laughed one more time as he stepped out into the hallway.

Leia heard the lock snick shut behind him. She always heard the lock. Why was it the one thing this bunch of incompetents always remembered to do was lock the door?

Leia forced herself to calm down. She opened up her fists, and took three deep breaths. There were Jedi exercises she could have done to calm herself more completely, but she didn't *want* to be completely calm. She wanted the luxury of a little anger.

Though she was not in the least bit hungry, and the food appeared to be poorly prepared field rations again, Leia forced herself to sit down at the table and eat it. She needed to keep her strength up. Sooner or later the Leaguers were going to decide what to do with her, and she needed to be rested, ready, alert. She took a sip of water to wash down whatever the unappetizing glop on her plate was, and tried to think.

If the secret message they had sent her was to be believed, the League was going to blow up its second star, Thanta Zilbra, in three and a half weeks, unless the New Republic agreed to their demands—and yet the demands were impossible.

Why make demands so outrageously unrealistic in the first place? Leia wondered. And why had the League gone to all the trouble of sending a secret message when the League publicly announced a slightly less detailed version of the same information only a day later?

Something did not fit. Either something had gone seriously wrong with the League's plan of action, and they were now merely improvising, as best they could, bluffing it out. Or else the secret message had been a piece of misdirection, intended to serve some other, as yet unknown purpose.

Leia realized that she had finished her meal, though she still wasn't all that clear on *what* she had been eating. She shoved the tray aside and tried to think. None of it made sense.

The problems, the contradictions, the illogic went around and around in her head. Leia could find nothing she could get a handle on. It might have been two minutes or two hours later that she suddenly realized someone was unlocking the door.

Yes, of course. The guard had said something about a new cell mate. Good, she thought. It will be nice to have someone to talk to. Maybe the Human League thought she would interpret forcing her to have a roommate as some sort of elaborate insult, an invasion of the sanctity of the Chief of State's quarters, or whatever. If so, they were going to be disappointed. Leia Organa Solo was a diplomat, first and foremost. She would give the newcomer a proper welcome. Leia stood up, came around the table, and put a smile on her face.

The door swung to, and a grinning Human League trooper shoved Leia's new companion into the room. Leia's smile faded away.

It was Mara Jade.

The door slammed shut, and the two women stood staring at each other. Mara Jade. *Why her?* Leia wondered. There were too many unanswered questions about Mara's role in this whole crisis. She had brought the message, but there was no evidence, beyond Mara's own word, that she had received the message cube in the way she described. She had vanished completely during the attack on Corona House, and only reappeared the next day, picking her way out of the rubble of one of the ruined upper stories, claiming to have been trapped there during the first assault. Again, there was no evidence of that but her word. And now here she was, in Leia's cell. Was it chance? Did the guards do it with some vague idea that Mara and Leia would not hit it off, and put them together for their own amusement? Or was she a plant?

How many attempts had she made on Luke's life? That was all supposed to be in the past—but suppose it wasn't? Leia wasn't sure what to think.

The tableau held for a moment longer, but then Mara made the first move. "Hello, Leia," she said, stepping forward and nodding her head very slightly, her tone and behavior formal, even if she called Leia by her first name. "It is good to see you." She made no effort to offer her hand, or come closer. She looked cool, calm, well-fed, well rested. The troubles of the last few days— if they had indeed been troublesome days for her—had left no mark on her. Mara was tall and slender, with a dancer's body and grace. Her red-gold hair flowed over her shoulders, set off by the plain black tailored jumpsuit she wore.

"And it's good to see you," Leia said, not quite sure if she was lying or not. She turned and went back around the table, and retook her seat there, if for no other reason than to break up the awkward scene. "However I must admit I am surprised."

"I think it would be a bit more accurate to say you're not quite sure what to think," Mara said evenly, taking a seat opposite Leia at the table. "If *I* were in your shoes, I'd be wondering about me. You're no fool, and neither am I. I can see all the reasons you might suspect me. Nothing I can say will convince you that I had no role in all this. I don't know how strong your Jedi powers are, but I doubt they are strong enough for a complete probe of my mind."

"Not one that I'd have any faith in," Leia admitted.

"So there we are," Mara concluded.

"Are you saying I'll just have to trust you?"

Mara shrugged. "Trust me to do what? We're not allies in this, so far as I know. The one thing we can both be sure we have in common is that we'd both like to escape."

"Can I even be sure of *that*?" Leia asked.

Mara smiled. "Yes," she said. "You can. I want *out* of here. The longer I am cooped up here, the worse it will be for my trading business. You've never known me to be shy about admitting my personal interests. I'm losing time and money sitting here."

"And that's supposed to satisfy me."

"No," said Mara, "but it's all I've got. I'm not involved in this madness, but how can I prove a negative?"

Leia looked long and hard at Mara. She had the very strong impression that Mara could say more if she wished, but it was clear she was not going to say another word on the subject. "What can you tell me about what's going on out there?"

"Not much," Mara said. "I've been locked up three doors down. My ex-roommate accused me of being a League sympathizer, it got a little sticky, and so here I am. I haven't heard anything more than you."

"How about a theory, then?" Leia asked. "I've had nothing to do but think about the situation, and I can't make sense of it at all. The pieces don't fit together. What do *you* think is going on?" The question was broad enough for Mara to answer however she liked, and that was the point. Leia wanted to know Mara's opinion—or, perhaps likelier, Mara's pretended opinion.

"I don't have a theory, exactly," Mara replied, "but it seems very clear to me that Diktat Thrackan Sal-Solo knows what he is doing. He's controlling the situation, and he knows it. He's smart enough, has enough political savvy, that he'd be able to predict the results of his actions. I don't think he has to do anything. I think he just has to say he's going to do things."

"And the results of what he has said about kicking nonhumans off the planet has been riot and upheaval," Leia said. "His words have caused further hardening of bad feelings between the three races. People have been radicalized, pushed into extreme positions by extreme circumstances."

"And my guess is that is exactly what Sal-Solo hoped would happen," Mara said. "Maybe he just wants to make the New Republic look bad. He's certainly put *you* in a bad position."

"That's for sure," Leia said. "He's set it up so I have to make one of two politically, and physically, impossible choices. Let thousands, maybe millions, die as their planet is wiped out, or else forcibly deport millions of people from their ancestral home. Whatever I do, the New Republic's reputation is going to be badly damaged, if not wrecked beyond all repair."

"That might be his ultimate goal," Mara said. "The destruction of the New Republic. He wants to set up the Corellian Sector as an independent state. Seems to me that the weaker the New Republic is, the more luck he's going to have making his independent state last."

"So he doesn't much care what happens or what we do, so long as we end up looking bad. Is that it?"

"It's one theory."

"But we can't do anything at all as long as we're prisoners," Leia said. "What good does it do him to hold us?"

"None that I can see," Mara said. "So I don't think he will, much longer. I think he is going keep his troops in Corona House until he is satisfied that the situation is under control. Then he'll withdraw the troops and shut off the jamming. You and Micamberlecto will be able to give whatever orders you like—to whatever forces you can reach. Except you won't have much in the way of forces to order around by then. You'll be very ineffectual. And you won't be able to leave the system. There's still the interdiction field. He's not going to drop that. That keeps you from getting out, and keeps your friends from getting in."

"But the interdiction field won't stop the New Republic from intervening," Leia said. "It will just slow it down. If they have to spend a month or two or three flying at sublight speed to get here, they will."

"Leia—Madame Chief of State. With all due respect, I am a master trader. Information is the lifeblood of my work. If I know the Republic Navy is in no shape to fight right now, and if the enemy can read your private cipher, I don't think they know less than I do. They probably know as much as you do on the subject."

"If not more," Leia conceded. "And even if Thrackan sets us free, he'll keep very close tabs on us. He'd try and bully me into talks, and I'd be negotiating with a gun to my head." She paused. "No thank you. No way. I have to get out of here before that happens."

Mara looked hard at Leia. "I was sort of coming around to that," she said.

"What do you mean?" Leia asked, immediately suspicious. "You have something in mind."

Mara hesitated a moment, and then shrugged. "I give up. There's no way I can tell you this without it sounding like a setup. So I'm just going to tell you and let it sound like whatever it will. I have a slave-circuit controller for my ship, the *Jade's Fire*."

Leia stared at Mara, but her mind was anywhere but on Mara's appearance. Suddenly there were a dozen new variables in the equation. A slave-circuit control was basically a remote control for a spacecraft. The simplest of them were no more than homing devices. Push a button and the ship would come to you. The more sophisticated slave systems could operate virtually every major system on a starship. Leia didn't quite know how to react to the news. It was easy to imagine all the ways this might be a trap. It shouldn't have been a surprise that Mara had such a device, but on the other hand, if she had it, why hadn't she used it by now? "Where is the control unit?" Leia asked.

"It's hidden—well hidden—in my quarters on the twelfth floor. I never had a chance to get to it. For that matter, I still don't see any chance."

"Nor do I," Leia agreed. "Unless you can come up with a way to get through locked doors and breeze through their guard stations on the stairs. I know from the door numbers that we're on the eighteenth floor— but I also know the League probably has its own barracks set up on the sixteenth or seventeenth."

"And how do you know that?"

"My quarters were on the fifteenth floor," Leia said, "and I saw what shape the building was in before we got locked up. Fifteen was a mess after the attack, and everything between eight and fifteen is even worse, so they can't be lower than sixteen. And my guard mentioned bringing food from downstairs, and he's always out of breath when he shows up."

"That's it?" Mara asked. "That's all you've got?"

"It seemed pretty convincing to me," Leia said. "But this slave controller of yours. Wouldn't the guards have found it yet?"

"I doubt this bunch of thugs would be able to find their own heads in the dark," Mara said. "I got the distinct impression that they were more interested in browsing through whatever valuables they could slip into their pockets."

Leia thought fast. She was starting to get an idea. "It's possible—just possible—that I could help you get the slave controller. If I can, and if the controller is still there, can you make it work?"

"How are you going to get the controller?" Mara asked.

"Let's just say that maybe I could," Leia said. There was a flaw, an obvious one. "The jamming," Leia said. "How is your slave controller going to get past that?"

"The Human League isn't the first to jam com frequencies. The slave unit has a backup mode, a comlaser mode that works on line of sight." Mara stood up, went to the window, and drew open the curtains. She pointed out the window. "There's the spaceport. She's just a dot on the horizon from here, but I can see her. The *Jade's Fire* is out there, sealed up tight and locked down. As long as the slave controller can see her, I can bring her in. It might take a little extra doing through the jamming, and at this range, but I can do it."

"So you think that if you got the controller, you could get the ship here."

"Something can always go wrong, but I'd say the odds were about ninety-five percent."

"But could you bring her close enough alongside the building so that we could get aboard?"

Mara frowned. "It would take some piloting. I'd put that at about seventy-five percent."

"That's better odds than we have at the moment," Leia said.

"But how are you going to get to the slave control?" Mara asked again.

Leia looked hard at Mara. There was no more proof than before that the trader was not involved with the Human League, but somehow, now Leia believed her. But suppose Mara *wasn't* on the level. Then what? How bad could things get? The worst-case scenario that Leia could see was that she might get killed. Not an appealing prospect, needless to say, but from the standpoint of what was best for the New Republic, a martyred Chief of State was probably preferable to one forced to choose between letting millions die or helping to deport a whole planetful of innocent people. Death she would risk for a reasonable chance of escape. "It's going to take some luck," Leia said at last. "And more than a little bit of planning. Let's sit down and get to it."

CHAPTER EIGHT

The Hard Way

I have the start of wondering if I should have said one thing to you about your wife's circumstance," said Dracmus.

"I thought you said you'd speak Basic better once you had a little practice," Han said as he paced back and forth in the cell.

"Oh, I would been having to get better," Dracmus said, "but honored Solo is driving me bolts by acting so nervous. I cannot concentrate."

" 'Nuts,' " Han said. "The expression is 'driving me nuts.' "

"Bolts or nuts, you are going around the corner."

"The bend," Han said as he paused to examine the door of the cell for at least the hundredth time. "I'm going around the bend."

"Truly so," said Dracmus.

"Listen. I think I have this figured out. Two guards bring our meals. One carries the food, and the other covers him with the blaster. I take my food tray from the first guard, and throw it in the face of the second guard. He dodges the tray, and I grab his blaster while you knock out the first guard and take his weapon. Then we get out into the corridor—"

"And while bravely you are hurling your dinner buns

131

at the first two guards the third guard and the fourth guard and the fifth and sixth and seven guard shoot many holes in all of us both," Dracmus said, calmly sitting on her cot. "And just in case they *all* miss, all the exits will be getting locked up hard, and all in complex go on lovely red alert until they hunting us nicely down."

Han glared at the Selonian. "You're an awful big help. You know that?"

"More so than you think. Patience, honored Solo. All that is required is just a little patience."

"Patience! You're the one who reminded me that my wife is right under Jade's thumb. I've got to get out of here and warn her, rescue her!"

"Dead you cannot do this," Dracmus said. "Dead I can also do nothing, and I wish to do more than nothing, and your mad plans will get us killed both. Remain calm. Remain calm."

"Calm? What is there to remain calm about?"

But suddenly Dracmus was on her feet, her head cocked to one side, her hand signaling for quiet. "Please, silence!" she said.

Han stared at his cell mate. "What are you—"

"Zzzzsss!" Dracmus said. "Silence!"

Han stood stock-still, listening. Finally he heard it. A low, far-off humming, with an occasional clittering, clattering noise.

Dracmus turned toward Han and bared her teeth in a disconcerting Selonian equivalent of a smile. "Do you hearing that?" she asked. "I wonder what that could be."

*   *   *

"Are you ready?" Mara asked.

Leia smiled. "Not really, but I'm not going to get any readier. Let's just hope it all works." The plan seemed more logical than practical, somehow. In theory, it ought to work. In practice, lots of things were bound to go wrong.

"Let's get started," Mara said.

Corona House had been designed as the Governor-General's residence, not as a prison. As such, it had no holding cells, but a good number of guest suites and state apartments of various sizes and degrees of luxury, depending on the rank of the guest. The smaller rooms more or less resembled conventional hotel rooms, and it was these that the Human League had pressed into service to confine its New Republic prisoners. As such, they lacked such amenities as bars on the windows, although the beds were provided with linens. Now that night had fallen, Leia and Mara planned to take advantage of both these features of the room.

Step one had already been accomplished. They had stripped the sheets and blankets off both beds, sliced them into strips using a dull knife quietly swiped from Leia's dinner tray, and tied the strips together to form a crude rope—which Leia hoped was stronger than it looked. Step two was a bit trickier. There are ways to smash out a window quietly, but they are not foolproof. It would be far better if they could get the window open, but that was not going to be easy. The guards had spot-welded all the windows on the floor shut. At least they had more or less done so. They had done a proper job on one of Leia's windows, a solid weld that nothing was going to shake, but the weld on the other was downright sloppy, a weak little splotch of melted metal that didn't look strong enough to hold anything.

Except that it proved to be stronger than it looked. They spent twenty minutes taking turns trying to lever a crack into the weld. First Mara and then Leia and then Mara tried to wedge the knife into the seam between window frame and sill. The effort left them no farther forward than before, aside from a badly bent knife and a well-gouged windowsill. Leia was well into her second turn with the knife, and just about ready to give up and risk smashing the window, when something went *snap* and the weld cracked clean in half. Leia looked at Mara with a grin, and slid the window up. It was the work of a moment to gouge a hole in the screen and tear it open.

Then came the hard part.

They tied one end of the improvised rope around the bed frame. Leia tied an improvised climbing harness onto herself, snaked the bedsheet rope through it, then climbed up onto the windowsill and threw the end of the rope out the window.

"Wish me luck," she said to Mara.

"Oh, I do," Mara said. "After all, I get to go next."

Leia swallowed hard and stepped out onto the ledge just outside the window. She gave the rope a good hard tug. It seemed to be holding. She paused, just a moment, and looked around. The night was cool and clear, the wind blowing steadily, just enough to catch at her hair and blow it into her face. The city of Coronet was spread out below her—directly below her, if she looked straight down, which she chose not to do. But looking out toward the horizon was all right. She could do that without any problem. Without window glass between her and the view, everything seemed closer, sharper, nearer to hand.

The city was quieter than it should have been. There should have been the sounds of traffic, the occasional far-off voice carried by the wind, perhaps a snatch of music floating up now and then. But all Leia could hear was the muffled boom and roar of the surf, far off on the horizon. She looked out to the water and could just barely make out the line between sand and sea. She could see the lines of whitecaps moving into the shore. She turned her gaze toward the city of Coronet itself.

Large stretches of the city were blacked out. Even in the places where there were lights, there were not enough of them. The city in the cold, clear night seemed lonely, half-empty, half-abandoned. And maybe it was. Surely any nonhuman with a modicum of sense would have gotten out of town or gone into hiding by now.

But looking at the city was not what she was out here for. She made sure the rope was running through the crude climbing harness properly, took another deep breath, tested the strength of her climbing rope one more time, and put her weight on it as she eased her way over the window ledge. She started down the side of the building, hoping against hope that she and Mara had worked out the distances properly and the improvised rope was going to reach to the fifteenth floor.

The going was a lot easier than she had expected, at least at first. The rope was taking her weight without any trouble, and the knots holding the lengths of torn bedding together were likewise behaving, sliding around her body, and through the climbing harness without undo fuss. So far, so good. Leia moved slowly, carefully, down the wall. She paused when her feet were just about at the top of the seventeenth-floor window. Pushing off against the wall, she walked herself over to one side of it, both trying to get herself out of view of the window, and trying to avoid walking on the glass. Probably the glass was strong enough to support her weight, but on the other hand someone had been shooting at this building not so long along, and the window might well have taken some damage.

She managed to get over to one side of the window, though with considerable difficulty. Gravity wanted her to hang straight down from the tie-off point of the rope, and it was hard to get enough purchase to hold herself off to one side as she eased down the sheer side of the building.

A gust of wind blew in from the opposite direction of the steady breeze. It lasted only a few seconds, but it seemed to blow right through her clothing, chilling her to the bone and, worse, blowing her hair back into her face, blinding her. Making *very* sure she had a good solid grip on the rope with her left hand, and even surer that the rope wasn't going anywhere, she let go of it with her right hand long enough to push her hair away and force it back behind her ears as best she could. She realized as she let go of the rope how stiff and cold her hands were already.

Leia looked down at the window ledge coming up below her. Almost there. Almost there. She glanced at the window itself, and saw to her relief that the shades were drawn. But she knew she still had to be careful. Noises outside windows tended to be very noticeable seventeen stories up.

She reached the window ledge and was very much relieved to put her feet down on something solid, if only for a moment. But even standing here, she was by no means safe. She could slip and fall. The wind could blow her off. She still had the climbing harness on, and she needed to keep some tension on the rope, with the result that part of her weight was still on it. If it broke, over she would go. Nevertheless, being on the ledge was an improvement on dangling on the end of the rope.

She rubbed her hands together and blew on them, trying to get at least some circulation back. There was no excuse for further delay. She flexed her fingers, took hold of the knotted sheets she was trusting her life to, and stepped backwards off the edge of the window ledge.

Almost immediately, she realized something was wrong. The rope was showing more and more stretch, sagging down a bit more under her weight with every step she took. That was not good. Not good at all. If it stretched enough, if one crucial bit of thread snapped under the strain and unraveled, and that opened a wider tear, then—

Leia looked down, straight down, and instantly

wished that she hadn't. If the rope broke, she would fall, and that was all there was to it. "Come on," she whispered to the rope. "You don't have to kill me. Lots of other things can go wrong and do that for you."

For example, walking down the wall of the sixteenth floor might do the trick. If her suspicions were correct, this was where the Human League guards had their barracks. She looked down and saw the top of the sixteenth-floor window—with her climbing rope dangling right in front of it. She swore under her breath and wondered how she could have been so negligent.

Never mind. Never mind. She walked herself sideways, away from the window, and asked the wind to blow the right way and keep the rope from being visible from the window. Of course, the rope would then be visible from the next window over, but never mind. Leia moved down the wall, struggling to keep well away from the window. She looked at the window, and was alarmed to see the shades were open. Worse, she could count at least four Human League troopers in the room, asleep on their Imperial-Army-Standard-Issue–Surplus cots.

Leia took a deep breath and moved on. Quiet. Careful, slow movements. There. Below her. The next window ledge. Set down on it, but just for a moment. Resist the strong temptation to do more than catch your breath and flex your fingers one more time. Move.

Leia went over the next ledge, down to the fifteenth floor, the VIP level, a double-high floor built to give the residents therein very high, grand ceilings. This was the level her apartments had been on. Leia didn't expect to be lucky enough to come in on top of her own window, and she wasn't. But one piece of luck she was hoping for was to find a smashed-out window at least nearby. The fifteenth floor had taken a lot of damage in the attack, and unless the Leaguers had been spending all their waking hours replacing broken windows, she ought to be able to find a way in.

She paused after she got over the last ledge and breathed a sigh of relief when she saw that virtually all the windows were blown out, curtains billowing out into the wind. That was the good news. It would be easy to get in. The bad news was that she had forgotten that the double-high ceilings meant it was twice as far down to the window ledge. They had made their rope as long as they possibly could, but she had no idea if it would reach down a whole extra story. It was impossible to make any sort of useful eyeball estimate of how much rope she had. It was dark, it was hard to judge a straight vertical drop, and the rope was blowing in the wind.

Suddenly Leia's foot slipped, and she was swinging through the air, bouncing off the side of the building as the rope slid and twisted. She dropped a half meter or so as the rope cleared some snag or another on one of the two ledges above.

Leia scrambled as best she could and finally managed to steady herself against the building, resisting the temptation to stop and catch her breath. That might do nothing more than give her a chance to get the shakes, and that she could not afford.

But she had received a very clear reminder that the rope had two ledges to rub against, tear against. She had best get off it as soon as possible. There, directly below her, was some sort of smashed-open window. It would have to do. She rappelled down the wall until the wall wasn't there anymore, and she was face-to-face with the missing window. She slid down the rope, praying that chance would not pick this moment to send another gust to send her swinging back and forth.

The drapes of the blown-out window billowed below her, and there was very little she could do to avoid getting tangled up in them. She kicked them out of the way as best she could, but they simply blew back into her. She kicked them back again, and then again—and then she was past them, just in time to be blinded again as the wind knocked her hair back into her face.

And then her foot hit the ledge, hard enough that she turned her ankle. Never had Leia so welcomed a jolt of pain. She was down. She set both feet firmly on the ledge—and discovered that the rope ended just a meter below the surface of the ledge. That was cutting things awfully close. The drapes slapped her in the face again, but she ignored them, and just stood there for a moment, eyes closed, trying to settle herself down.

But there was no time for more than that. She shoved the drapes out of the way and stepped through the broken window onto the windowsill. She slid the rope out from her climbing harness and pulled on it three times, paused, pulled three times more, paused again, and pulled three times more. The signal told Mara she had arrived safely.

The rope immediately twitched and jerked as Mara signaled back.

Being careful of the broken glass that was scattered everywhere, Leia stepped down off the low windowsill and into the darkened room. She would have to go back out in a moment to help Mara in, but she could take just a minute to collect herself.

It was all going well so far, and, in a sense, that was the frightening part. She was chilled to the bone, her hands were aching and raw, she had twisted her ankle and nearly fallen at least twice—and everything was going well.

If only she had developed her Jedi skills the way Luke had. If she had, she probably could have simply walked down the side of the building, carrying Mara in one hand and swinging her lightsaber in the other—a gross exaggeration, of course, but never mind. As things were, she knew that her skills were too undeveloped and unreliable to put much faith in them at a time like this.

Once her eyes had adapted to the gloomy room,

she spotted a knocked-over chair. She set it upright, brushed the broken glass off it, and sat down. So far so good. There were dozens of things that could still go wrong, but they had made a start . . . assuming that Mara wasn't involving her in some incredibly elaborate setup, and the guards weren't about to bust in the door so she could be "shot trying to escape," or whatever.

That was a happy thought, and one that inspired her to get up and check on Mara's progress. Going to the window, she climbed back up on the sill. The rope was flailing around most vigorously in the wind. Leia's first impulse was to grab at it and try to steady it, but it was hard to know if that would make matters better or worse. She decided to leave well enough alone. One thing she *could* do was to pull the heavy curtains into the room and shove them out of the way. She got that done and went back out on the window ledge and looked up, watching for Mara.

The rope was bouncing and gyrating more and more vigorously as Mara came closer. In a surprisingly short time Mara herself appeared, coming over the last of the ledges, moving well. Down she came. She paused just over the top of the smashed window and looked down. "Leia," she shouted above the rising wind. "I've got to get down fast. Spot me coming down."

Had something gone wrong? Leia positioned herself as best she could on the narrow ledge and watched Mara come in. The rope was clearly stretching more and more. Leia would not want to trust it again.

Down Mara came, her expression grim and intense, her hair flying wildly about in the wind. Leia reached up and steadied the rope as Mara slid the last two meters or so of the climb down. She guided Mara through the broken window and hurried in after her.

"The rope," Mara said, massaging her hands and stamping her feet. "It was getting more and more stretched out. The wind caught it and it banged against the sixteenth-floor window where the guards were sleeping. It'd take a bloody miracle for them *all* to have slept through it."

"Maybe I can keep them from spotting where the noise came from," Leia said. "I'll be right back." She stepped onto the windowsill and grabbed at the rope. She could not help but notice it had stretched itself out by at least another half meter. Well, that might be all to the good at this point. She pulled the rope along to the next smashed-out window. Still holding the rope, she stepped inside and examined the situation. The window frame was still in one piece, even if the glass was gone. Good. She pulled the frame open, snaked the rope through it, and pulled it as taut as she could. She slammed the empty frame shut on the rope and then went back out the way she had come.

She paused on the ledge, just before she rejoined Mara. Was it her imagination, or was there a different feel to the air, in just the few minutes that had passed since she had been inside? Coronet was a seaside town, and the weather had a way of coming up suddenly. At least it had waited until they were in off the rope. But would the comlaser mode of Mara's slave controller work with a rainstorm sweeping through the area? No way to know.

Mara was in the same chair Leia had been in. "That climb takes it out of you," she said.

"That's for sure," Leia agreed. "I pulled the rope along to the next window and snubbed it off. With a little luck, the angle will keep them from seeing it from the window. I think I pulled it tight enough that it won't bang against any more windows, either. But they might have spotted it already. And I think we might have some weather on the way. We'd better keep moving."

"Weather? That's not good," Mara said, getting up. "We have to hurry. So where to?"

They were on the fifteenth floor, past the main barracks of the Human League, and on the same floor where Leia's quarters had been.

"Follow me." Leia started searching for the way out of the suite of rooms that led into the central foyer for the floor. She fumbled through the near-total darkness and was forced to backtrack twice before she got her bearings. The going was not easy. There seemed to be a great deal of debris strewn about, and most of it might as well have been invisible. Leia longed for some sort of handlight or glowlamp, but the Human League guards had not been so considerate as to provide such amenities to their prisoners. She considered trying to get the lights on, but that would be sure to attract unwanted attention.

At last she found the way out of the apartment, into the central foyer. She had been worried about locked doors or other obstacles. If the way into her apartment were sealed, they would be forced to backtrack and walk around the exterior of the building, on the window ledges—and *that* did not strike Leia as an attractive option. But the moment they were in the central foyer, she breathed a sigh of relief. The Human League troopers had done a fairly efficient job of looting on this floor, that much was clear. Even in the darkness of the foyer, she could see all sorts of odds and ends flung about— and the doors to all the apartments left wide-open, the faint, ghostly radiance of starlight glowing through them. She moved toward her own door, Mara right behind her.

Leia stopped just short of the door, and Mara nearly walked up her back.

"What's wrong?" Mara asked. "What is it?"

Leia knelt down and picked up the small object she had spotted. How she had seen it in the virtual darkness, she could not say. It was a little model hover car, one of Anakin's toys. Suddenly it all hit her hard. Her child's toy. Had he dropped it there himself in the midst of the frantic escape during the attack? Or had the Human League's thugs seen fit to root through the children's toy chest in their search for loot? What had happened to her children? Where were they? Were they safe? Could Chewbacca protect them?

Stop. Stop. She had a job to do. For them, as much as anyone. She had to get free, and set about organizing some sort of resistance to the monsters who had scattered her family. Nor did it escape her that it was a member of her family who was responsible for all this. Thrackan Sal-Solo would pay.

Leia wrapped her hand around Anakin's toy, around the bit of plastic and metal that was suddenly all she had of her son. She slipped it into her pocket and then moved on without explaining to Mara what had made her stop. How could she expect Mara to understand?

She stepped into the apartment that had been her home not so long ago. The furniture had been thrown about, and the windows smashed to bits. She smelled the damp, cold smell of a long-dead fire mixed with rain, but forced herself not to think of home and family. In all probability the League thugs were already searching for them. There was no time.

She went straight to the kitchen and knelt down by the main cooking unit. There was a storage cabinet under its heating compartment. She opened it up and pulled the pots and pans out as quietly as she could, though every unavoidable clatter and rattle seemed deafeningly loud. She reached into the rear of the compartment and found what she was looking for. Two cloth-wrapped packages. She pulled them out.

One package was covered with the finest black velvet and tied with a silver ribbon. That one she opened first. Her lightsaber, a gift from her brother Luke. He had given it to her just before she had set off on this trip. She rolled the velvet up and shoved it in a pocket, suddenly unwilling to leave anything more behind. She clipped the lightsaber to her belt. The other object was wrapped in much plainer cloth, a scrap from one of Han's old shirts.

She hesitated before opening it. But there was no point in not going the whole way at this point. If Mara had wanted to kill her, all she would have needed to do was cut the rope when Leia was dangling out over nothing at all. She unwrapped the scrap of cloth. Han's spare blaster was inside.

"Take it," Leia whispered.

Mara looked at Leia, her expression unreadable in the dim light from the shattered windows, she made no move to take the weapon. "Are you sure you want me at your back with this thing?" she whispered back.

"No more than you want me at *your* back with my lightsaber. But we can get back to not trusting each other later. Right now isn't the time. Take it."

Mara took the weapon—but Leia hung on to the scrap of cloth and stuffed it in the same pocket with the velvet and Anakin's toy. Her husband was gone, too. That little bit of torn shirt might be the last she would have of him. But there was no time.

"All right," Mara whispered. "Anything else from here?"

Leia thought for a moment. They needed light, and there should be some sort of portable lamp somewhere in the apartment. But how could she find it in the dark —and suppose the League thugs had grabbed all the lamps when they had looted the place? No. No time to waste searching for what might not be there anymore. "No," she whispered. "Nothing I'd be sure of finding. We have to move."

"Anybody there?" Mara and Leia froze. It was a man's voice, a bit sleepy, and coming from inside the apartment. Suddenly Leia's heart was pounding in her chest.

"Magminds, is that you? Magminds?"

The sound seemed to be coming from the upper level of the apartment, from the bedrooms. Obviously, at least a few of the Human League troops had found themselves better billets than surplus Imperial Army cots.

If they ran, they'd make noise and give their friend time to raise the alarm. If they tried to get to their friend upstairs, they'd have to blunder through the darkness of the living room, get up the stairs to the upper level, and search the upstairs bedroom—and it seemed highly unlikely they'd be able to manage all that unimpeded.

Sometimes inaction was the best policy. Leia looked toward Mara and put a finger to her lips. Then she pointed to herself and to Mara, and then at the floor. *Stay quiet and stay still. Wait.*

Mara nodded, but held her hand out flat at shoulder level and then brought it down slowly. *Duck down. Hide.*

They were trapped.

* * *

Han Solo watched as the vibroblade came up through the stone floor and, with a high-pitched squeal, began slicing out a perfectly circular slab. The vibroblade withdrew, and the slab of stone lifted itself up, until it was hanging in midair a half meter over the open hole, a portable antigrav unit attached to its underside.

A Selonian hand-paw reached up out of the hole and shoved the slab to one side. It slid along on its antigrav unit and floated into the corner, where it bounced gently off the wall and came to rest.

A Selonian head popped up out of the hole and nodded cheerfully at Dracmus. "We are glad to have located the proper cell," she said in Selonian. "It caused some awkwardness when we detected that you had been moved."

"It is of no consequence," Dracmus said. "But let us be on our way." She turned toward Han and spoke, still in Selonian. "Come, honored Solo, we must go. Or would you still prefer distracting the guard by throwing buns at him?"

Han hesitated a moment. He had no idea what the sides in this fight were, let alone whose side Dracmus was on. Was he being rescued, or just becoming someone else's hostage? But on the other hand, the idea of facing Thrackan after Dracmus had escaped was not very appealing either. "I am coming," Han said.

"For a moment there, I thought you were about to refuse," Dracmus said.

"I almost did," Han said as he sat down on the edge of the hole and got ready to drop through.

Dracmus sighed. "Humans. Always determined to do things the hard way. Come on. We must begin to move."

Han went down the hole.

CHAPTER NINE

Getting Involved

Leia crouched down in place, deeper into shadow, putting out her left hand to balance herself a bit. Now if only whoever that was would decide he had been hearing things, or that the wind had blown in through the window and made noise, all would be well. He would go back to sleep, and Leia and Mara could get on about their business.

"Magminds?" The voice was closer, more distinct this time, and sounded a bit more worried. Leia saw a sudden little bloom of light sweep over them and heard a stair creak. He was coming down stairs.

She turned to Mara—and realized that Mara was not there anymore. There was a bump, a thud, from the main room, and the shifting shadows in the kitchen told Leia that the beam of the man's handlight was sweeping across the room. "Hold it," the voice said. "I've got a blaster trained right on you and—"

The light of a blaster shot flared, briefly illuminating the kitchen like a bolt of lightning that was there and then gone. A crash, a thud, and the glow from the handlight died. Leia's lightsaber was in her hand and on in an instant. She rushed out of the kitchen—and stopped dead in her tracks as she saw the scene lit by the blood-red glow of her lightsaber blade.

147

There was a heavyset man—or at least the remains of one—sitting up on the stairs in his nightshirt, a neat hole through his chest. The look on his face was one of pure astonishment.

"He dropped the handlight and broke it," Mara said, clearly irritated with the dead man, as if he had broken the light on purpose. "We could have used that. The fool didn't even have a blaster."

"That's all you've got to say?"

"That's all there's time for, if we want to live through this," Mara said. "If it helps, I was going to try and knock him out, not shoot him, until he claimed to have a gun."

"It doesn't help much," Leia said, staring at the dead man. He was their enemy. If he had managed to raise the alarm, or caught them himself, or if he *had* had a blaster, things would look very bad. But telling herself those things didn't make him any less dead. And there *was* no time. "We have to move," she said, coming out of it. "If there was one of them sleeping here, there might be more. And someone might have heard—or this one might have called it in before he came out for a look."

"Right," said Mara. "Back to the foyer and down. Unless you want to try another three floors on a home-made rope."

"No, thank you," Leia said. There were risks in heading down the inside of the building, but nothing like those involved in another run down the outside. "Let's go."

It was time to move fast. Leia led the way back to the foyer, stumbling in the darkness once or twice. She had been in the emergency stairs once before, just after the attack on Corona House, but even knowing her way, it was almost impossible to navigate in virtually complete darkness through the heaps of junk that seemed to be strewn about everywhere.

"Step back from me," she said to Mara, "and shield your eyes for a second. I'm going to switch on my lightsaber."

Leia shut her own eyes as she unclipped the lightsaber from her belt and activated it. The weapon came alive with the familiar low thrum of power. Even through her closed eyelids, the light from the blade seemed remarkably bright after the gloom and darkness. She gave her eyes a moment to adjust, and then opened them cautiously, being careful not to look at the lightblade itself. She held the blade vertically and looked around the foyer, now lit by the ruby-red glow of the lightsaber.

"First time I've ever seen one of those used for a handlamp," Mara said.

"You work with what you've got," Leia said. "There's the door to the stairs. Let's go."

They picked their way through the broken furniture and heaps of discarded loot and made their way to the stairs. The door to the stairs was slightly ajar, and Leia prodded it with her toe. It swung open a bit but stopped before the opening was wide enough to go through. Leia shoved a little harder with her foot, then with her hip, forcing the opening wider.

Lightsaber at guard, she stepped onto the landing and forced herself to repress the impulse to jump back when she saw what had blocked the doorway.

It was a body, the dead body of a young man, wearing the uniform of the Governor-General's tech staff. The corpse was lying on its back, and had a neat hole between its open eyes. The shifting red shadows cast by the lightblade made the dead man seem a strange and alien thing. Leia recognized him, though she did not know his name. He had been the one who told her about the interdiction field, just after Han had vanished. How long ago was that? Just a few days? Half a lifetime? He had seemed a nice young man. Now here he was, shot dead and left to rot in a stairwell for some trivial and unknown offense. The Human League made itself awfully easy to hate.

She gestured for Mara to follow her and stepped over the body, down the stairs. Mara came after. Leia made her way down the darkened stairs in a moving pool of dim red light cast by the lightsaber. The emergency staircase was a cold, harsh place, its plain unfinished stresscrete walls looming up hard and gray, every flaw in their surfaces wildly exaggerated by the elongated shadows. Even here, the looting troopers had discarded whatever they could not use. A broken desk lamp, a flurry of papers scattered about, a vase, a hat, a comlink rendered useless by the jamming the Human League had imposed.

She could imagine the League troopers tromping down these stairs a day or so ago, arms full of whatever they had grabbed, not much caring if a woman's shoe fell out of the heap, deciding that the heavy iron Frozian statue wasn't worth carrying. Somehow the crime of theft, the act of looting, was made worse when it was this wasteful, this pointless, this mindless.

"Psst."

Leia turned and saw Mara holding a finger to her lips, signaling for silence. She pointed to her ear. *Listen.*

Leia could hear a distant, low booming, and the wind moaning through the building. *Rain,* she mouthed, and pantomimed rain falling.

Mara shook her head, pointed at the lightsaber, and put a finger to her lips again.

Leia shut off the lightsaber for a moment to silence its hum. They stood in the darkness and listened. The sounds of the rain came through far more clearly with the lightsaber off, but clearly that was not the sound Mara was worried about.

Then Leia heard it, very faint, coming from up above. Voices, rough male voices, speaking in harsh, urgent tones, and the clatter and shuffle of men hurrying about in the background. It was impossible to make out the words, but equally impossible to mistake the cadences of the voice. It was clearly one man giving orders to others.

Their escape had been discovered. Maybe someone had spotted the rope. Maybe the dead trooper in Leia's apartment had managed to call in before his death. How didn't matter. Leia switched the lightsaber back on, and the two of them hurried faster down the stairs, past the fourteenth, past the thirteenth floor.

When they reached the twelfth, Mara's floor back before the world turned upside down, Leia grabbed the door handle and pulled hard. It didn't budge. She pulled again. Nothing. Had it been welded shut by the League? Had the explosions jammed the doors shut? No way to tell, and no time to examine the door for clues. Not when the League troops were going to start searching for them any second now.

Leia swung the lightsaber down hard, in a carefully-aimed vertical cut down the latch side of the door. She gave the door a good solid kick and it bounced back against the doorframe and swung out toward them. Leia and Mara stepped through it, and Mara pulled the door shut behind them. The lightsaber cuts on the door would provide a clue that even a Human Leaguer could read, but maybe, just maybe, no one would think to look.

Leia turned to Mara. "All right," she said in a loud whisper, "twelfth floor. Where to now?"

Mara shook her head. "It's a little hard to say." Leia looked around, and saw Mara's point. They were in the twelfth-floor foyer, and if the equivalent space on the fifteenth had been a mess, this foyer was barely there anymore. There had been a major explosion here that had cracked open the floor and left boulder-sized chunks of stresscrete wall and floor lying everywhere.

The handsome wood paneling had been splintered into ruin and half the doors leading to the private rooms were blown clear open. One wall of the foyer had been completely flattened, doors and all, so that the rooms beyond the wall were exposed to view. Most of the remaining doors had been wrenched partly or completely off their hinges. Virtually every window was shattered, and the wind was blowing in everywhere. Leia could hear the splattering rush of rain pouring down. The smell of cold rain seemed to grab at her, speak to her of wet, miserable nights and the trouble yet to come. But there was another, and a worse, smell: the sickly-sweet odor of rotting flesh. People had died here when that rocket hit, died and been smashed as flat as the walls. The dead were buried here, somewhere in the dark, under the debris that had killed them.

But if the ghastly scene was affecting Mara, she did not show it. "My room is this way," she said.

"If it's still anywhere at all," Leia said, following close behind. Mara led her almost to the end of the hallway, far enough away from the blast that the doors were still on their hinges, and one or two were still closed and latched.

Not so the door Mara stopped in front of. It was bent backward at a crazy angle, held in place by just the upper hinge, blocking the entrance rather effectively.

"Allow me," Leia said, and slashed the lightsaber down on the offending hinge. The door dropped to the floor with a resounding crash, and the women walked over it to the interior of Mara's quarters.

It was a smaller apartment than Leia's, but then, Leia was the Chief of State and Mara was just a Master Trader. The apartment was really no more than a bedroom, a refresher, and an autokitchen set into one wall, but the furnishings were opulent and handsome. At least they had been.

Here the wreckage was caused not by looting, but by

the violence of the rocket attack. A big chunk of the stresscrete ceiling had fallen in onto the bed, crushing the frame. Leia looked up and saw the hole it had left. The rest of the room was in no better shape. The paintings and other decorations had come off the wall, the chairs and table were overturned, and broken glass was everywhere. She looked toward the window and saw that the rain was coming down in earnest now, a real storm. The rain flared and pulsed in a dull throb of light as a bolt of lightning flashed somewhere nearby. The rumble of thunder rolled in the window as the sodden drapery flapped in the wind.

Mara wasted no time looking around, but went immediately to the closet and wrenched the door open. The contents spilled out onto the floor, and she knelt down and dug through them until she found a small satchel with a long strap. She stood up, put the strap over her shoulder, and opened the satchel, digging through it until she came up with a handlight. She switched it on, and instantly the weird shadows cast by the lightsaber vanished. After the bloodred glow of the saber, it was an amazing relief to see by the warm yellow light of the handlamp. Suddenly even the room full of wreckage seemed like a normal, understandable place, instead of a den of looming shadows.

Leia shut off the lightsaber, but did not clip it to her belt. The League troopers could still show up any moment. "So where's the slave controller?" Leia asked.

Mara set a side table upright, put the handlamp on it and pointed it at the bed. "Under there. The good news is it's obvious no one else could have gotten to it. The bad news is that I'm not sure it'll much matter if we can."

"You think it might have been crushed?" The largest hunk of stresscrete was about half a meter long and twice as wide, and about eight centimeters thick.

"One way to find out," Mara said. "Give me a hand clearing the bed off."

"Stand back and let me get the problem down to size first," Leia said. She swung the lightsaber down and it slashed through the hunk of stresscrete again and again, chopping it up into smaller pieces. Leia was careful to keep the lightsaber under tight control so as not to slice into the bed beneath it. Needing both hands free, she shut off the lightsaber and clipped it to her belt. "Here," she said, "grab the other end. And stay away from the cut edges—they're going to be plenty hot."

The two women heaved the chunks of stresscrete off the bed, working together on the biggest ones. "That ought to be good enough," Mara said. "Help me flip the bed over."

They stood next to each other, got their hands under the broken frame, and heaved up on it. The broken bed came up, and a minor avalanche of debris clattered down onto the floor. The bed wobbled back and forth a bit, but stayed balanced on its side. "Well, we've made enough noise to bring in every Leaguer in the building," Mara said, "but I don't know how we could have done this quietly."

"Let's just hope the rainstorm shields the noise," said Leia.

"Except that rain isn't doing us any favors. There's no way we can get line of sight on the *Jade's Fire* through that. We'll just have to wait until it clears up."

"No chance of using the comlink frequencies and getting through the jamming?" Leia asked.

Mara shrugged. "No harm in trying, but I can't see how it could possibly work. Assuming the controller hasn't been smashed flat. Bring that handlight around here and let's see what we've got."

Leia retrieved the light and held it for Mara. There it was, a neat, flat little metal package taped to the center of the bed frame's underside. No one could ever have found it without upending the bed. Even then, they might have missed it. Either by chance or design, it was exactly the same dark brown color as the underside of the frame.

Mara peeled the package off the frame and turned it up on its end. The package was a bit crumpled in one corner, but it looked to be more or less in one piece. Mara opened it up and pulled out a small, jet-black device, liberally festooned with buttons and switches. She pushed in the power button and all the other buttons lit up. "That's something, anyway," she said. "At least it *thinks* it's working."

Leia was about to make some sort of encouraging reply when they heard a bang and a thud, and muffled voices. Leia immediately shut off the handlight, and both women ducked behind the upturned bed.

They knelt there, staring at each other in the dim light cast by the slave controller, listening. They heard the clatter and rattle of bits of debris falling down, and the sound of heavy boots tromping on the rubble. The voices and footsteps came nearer, became more distinct. Leia unclipped her lightsaber once again, her thumb on the power button. Mara shut off the slave controller to extinguish the lights on its control panel, shoved it in the satchel that still hung over her shoulder, pulled Han's blaster out, and held it at the ready. Then she slipped her hand into the satchel again, and pulled out a smaller blaster from there.

Suddenly one set of footsteps sounded so loud Leia thought the walker was going to step on her. A handlight beam flared into the darkened room and swooped around, casting huge, distorted shadows everywhere. "You check the next one over," the trooper shouted out into the hall. "I got this one."

They could hear the mangled door creaking a bit as the trooper stepped on it, the crunch of his boots on the broken glass, his breathing as he stepped fully into the room, the sounds mixing with the steady low roar of the storm outside. Leia could hardly believe the trooper could not hear her heart pounding against her ribs.

He stepped around the bed and looked into the corners of the room, his back to Leia and Mara.

Mara had her pocket blaster aimed straight at the man's heart as he finished his cursory check. He turned back the way he had come, little realizing that he was staying alive by keeping his back to the upended bed.

The trooper headed back out into the hallway, and the two women relaxed, if only a trifle. Neither needed to tell the other that the trooper or his friends could be back at any moment. Leia tapped Mara on the shoulder and pointed to the smashed-out window. Mara frowned and nodded reluctantly. Neither of them could work up much enthusiasm for standing on the narrow ledge in the middle of a rainstorm, but they were running out of hiding places.

Leia clipped her lightsaber back on her belt and climbed up onto the windowsill one-handed, carrying the handlight with her. She immediately found she had to be careful of her footing. The glass in this window had not come out anywhere near as cleanly as it had on the floors above. Jagged shards still hung in all the window frames, and broken bits of it were all about. But with a little care, she managed to get clear of it all.

The trouble started the moment she stepped out onto the rain-swept ledge and moved toward the right side of the window, trying to get out of sight. The rain instantly soaked her to the bone, and the wind was deafeningly strong. Moving on the rain-slicked stone was like walking on wet ice. Leia put her back to the wall, grabbed onto one of the sodden drapes flapping the window, and hung on for dear life. Knowing it was a bad idea, she glanced downward, down toward the ground twelve flights below, made invisible in the driving rain. So easy to put a foot wrong and—

But then Mara was coming out onto the ledge, and Leia had other things to worry about. Mara was moving a bit faster than she should have. She slipped, and Leia caught her just barely in time. Mara twisted awkwardly and managed to recover, catching her left calf on a jagged piece of glass in the process. Mara grabbed at Leia and hung on for dear life. It took her a moment to compose herself, and then she clambered over Leia to get past her on the ledge. Leia let her pass, and then, still holding on to the drape, edged out of view of the window. She put her back to the building's outer wall and braced herself there, with her eyes shut, able to do nothing more than concentrate on the need to keep breathing.

They were here, they were alive, and that was about the best that could be said. Sooner or later the Leaguers would search again, and someone with more brains than yesterday's rancid gumbah pudding would notice the telltale marks of a lightsaber on the door of Mara's room, or on the neatly sliced strips of stresscrete, and then, perhaps, even think of looking out the window. Or else the wind would shift, and simply blow them clean off this ledge. Or they would drown like hive rats in the rain.

Or else Mara could get that blasted slave controller working, and her ship would come and rescue them.

Leia opened her eyes and looked over to Mara. She already had the controller out, trying to work it in the driving rain. Leia glanced toward the open window and decided that the odds were very low they could see a light through all the rain, so long as she was careful. She adjusted the handlight so it put out a tight beam and pointed it down at the controller.

Mara glanced up at her and nodded her thanks, and tried the unit again. Then she shook her head. "No good," she shouted into Leia's ear, struggling to be heard over the pouring rain. "Comlink mode is jammed for sure, and there's not a chance in the Galaxy of a laser punching through all this. We'll just have to wait out the rain."

Leia nodded. Mara turned off the slave controller and shoved it into her satchel. Leia turned off the hand-light and tucked it inside her blouse.

"Wait," she said to herself, in a voice so low that Mara could not possibly hear. She knew as well as Mara that they could not wait for long. She told herself that she should look on the bright side. If this rain had come out while they were on the rope, they would never have made it. At least they had gotten this far. Besides, these rainstorms never lasted long. The faster they came up, the faster they blew themselves out. "Just wait," she said, "and hope to the stars that slave controller is really working—"

Suddenly the wall of rain in front of her bloomed with light, light coming from inside the building, from the room they had come from. Someone was back in there, looking around. Leia gave Mara a very gentle nudge to get her attention and nodded toward the light. Mara's eyes widened, and she nodded back. But what could she do?

They were trapped, but Leia was not interested in going down without a fight. She mouthed the words "pocket blaster" to Mara. The trader nodded, pulled the blaster out of her satchel, and handed it over. Leia took it in her right hand. Her left hand was still holding onto the drapery, and she let go of it and moved the blaster to that hand. She unclipped her lightsaber and held it at the ready in her right hand. Anyone who came out that window was going to pay dearly for doing so.

But then the light from the inside went away. Another reprieve. Leia realized she had been holding her breath, and forced herself to exhale. Maybe it was going to be all right.

At that moment the wind shifted, and suddenly the

rain was fading away, the line of squalls passing over Coronet and moving on to other business elsewhere on the coast.

Leia looked to Mara, but she already had the slave controller back out and powered up. She aimed it in the general direction of the spaceport and switched it on. Almost immediately a new light flashed on the control panel. "Positive lock!" Mara said, looking back toward Leia—and then, in the same instant, behind Leia.

Leia had the lightsaber on before she could turn back around. A Human League trooper had his head out the window, was bringing his blaster to bear. She had the lightsaber up over her head for a downward strike before she was finished turning. The trooper fired, and she deflected the shot with her lightsaber. She swung the blade around for an upper cut that chopped through the blaster before it sliced the trooper's head off at the neck.

The man's head tumbled down into the darkness, and his body fell back into the room. Now it was too late. Another man stuck his head out, out of range of the lightsaber, and Leia fired with the pocket blaster. He pulled his head back in. Either she just clipped the man or else he had the sense to retreat.

A hand appeared, threw a mini-detonator toward Leia, and then vanished. Leia caught the detonator on her lightsaber blade and flipped it back into the building. It went off a split second later, with enough force to have thrown her off the ledge if she hadn't dropped the blaster and grabbed at the drapes again. A gout of flame spewed out the window, close and hot enough to singe her hair. She could feel Mara grab onto her right arm, and it took all the presence of mind Leia had to shut off the lightsaber before the backswing on the blade sliced a few parts off both of them.

Flames were blossoming inside what had once been Mara's room. They were running out of time and chances and choices with alarming speed. Leia looked toward the spaceport, off toward the horizon. There it was! She could see it. A spot of light headed straight for them at high speed. It had to be the *Jade's Fire,* riding to the rescue. She pointed it out to Mara, who nodded and let go of Leia. She worked the controls on her slave controller, looking back and forth between the incoming ship and the controller. They still weren't out of the woods. Mara had to fly that thing right to them.

Leia looked to the burning room, watching for more unwelcome visitors. Nothing from that quarter, and not likely to be unless they had some troopers who didn't mind being roasted alive. She looked over her right shoulder and checked the window on the other side, behind Mara—and saw lights and movement inside. "Mara!" she cried—but either Mara had been deafened by the blast, or else flying the ship by remote was too delicate for anything else to interfere. Leia let go of the drapes, scooped up the pocket blaster, and spun around. She fired behind Mara's head, straight at the hand coming out of the window. She hit the blaster the hand was holding and blew it up, clearing the threat from that corner for the moment, but starting another fire—and leaving her completely flash-blinded.

Leia closed her eyes and shook her head. She reopened her eyes and looked out into the sky. There. Coming close enough to be a recognizable shape. The *Jade's Fire,* rushing closer.

But there, behind it, were other dots of light rising from the spaceport. PPBs—Pocket Patrol Boats—sent to chase down the ship that had suddenly launched itself.

The flames were growing brighter on either side of Leia and Mara, but Leia could hear the *chuff, chuff* of fire extinguishers being brought into play. The troopers would have the fires under control soon.

"Leia!" Mara shouted over the roar of the flames.

"Get ready. I'm not sure how close I'll be able to fly her in, but the second she's close enough, jump! You might not get a second chance. If you get aboard, go to the pilot's station and be ready to take control once I'm aboard!"

"Will do!" Leia shouted, and watched as the *Jade's Fire* rushed closer. She was a bigger ship than Leia had expected, significantly larger than the *Millennium Falcon*. She was a craft of graceful lines. She had a snubbed-off nose and a wide fuselage that blended into the two thick elliptical wings. She was painted in a flame-pattern of oranges and red. Leia certainly wouldn't want to try flying anything that size up to the side of a building by remote. And it looked like the job was giving Mara just a bit of trouble at that. The *Fire* slowed as it came nearer, and wobbled a bit in flight. Turbulence.

Mara swore under her breath and made the slightest of adjustments to the controls. The *Fire* slowed down even more, and eased down just a trifle, bringing the top of the craft more or less even with the window ledge. Mara brought her in to a complete halt in midair, about fifty meters from the ledge. At that moment a blaster fired from one of the upper windows of Corona House. The shot pinged off the *Fire*'s hull. A door opened in the top of the fuselage and a gun turret popped out. It immediately swiveled about and returned fire. "Shoot-back system," Mara shouted before Leia could ask. "Automatically returns fire at anything that shoots at it. Which reminds me. Don't do any more shooting yourself, or that thing will paste you for sure."

"Thanks for the tip," Leia replied. Better late than never. She shoved the pocket blaster into her pocket and clipped the lightsaber to her belt.

Mara began sidling the *Fire* in closer, slowly closer, in toward Corona House. Another blaster fired, and the topside turret responded with a torrent of fire. Closer,

closer. A topside hatch was opening, yellow light streaming out of the ship's interior. Leia looked down at the portside wing of the big ship, and judged the distance as about two meters. A meter and a half.

Close enough. Don't give yourself time to think, she told herself. She jumped.

She landed hard on the upper hull of the ship and for a long, heart-stopping moment felt herself sliding down and off the rain-slicked hull. But then her hand found a purchase, and she pulled herself up and was on her feet, scuttling toward that open hatch, trying not to think of all the troopers in the building who might decide she would be worth taking a potshot at.

She heard a bump on the hull behind her and hoped to hell it was Mara, but there was no time to look back. She jumped down the hatch, not worrying about how she was going to land or what her ankle felt like, interested only in getting hull metal between herself and the line of fire.

Leia managed to land full on her twisted ankle, and collapsed in a heap on the deck at the intersection of two corridors. She pulled herself up just as Mara came swarming down the hatch ladder. Mara hit the hatch-close button the moment her head was clear of the hatch and came down the ladder.

Leia caught Mara as her leg collapsed under her, and saw the blood soaking through the left leg of her coverall. That cut on Mara's calf must have been worse than it looked. But no time for that. "This way," Mara shouted, pointing down one of the corridors.

Heavier blaster fire sounded from the rear of the craft, nearly knocking them over. The overhead shootback system returned fire. "That'll be the PPBs," Leia said. "Can the hull take that fire without shields?"

"For a while," Mara said. "But let's not try and find out how long." Leia half-carrying Mara, the two women hurried for the control room. They stopped in front of a hatch, and Mara punched codes into a keypad. The hatch slid open. Mara half lunged, half fell into the pilot's station and instantly powered up the shields. "That'll hold the PPBs," she said, and then hit the throttle. The *Jade's Fire* leaped forward, grabbing for speed and altitude.

Leia got herself to the navigator's station and collapsed. Soaked through to the bone, her teeth chattering, her ankle throbbing, her body no doubt a mass of bruises and sores she couldn't feel yet, onetime Princess, onetime Senator Leia Organa Solo, Chief of State of the New Republic, breathed a sigh of relief. They were going to make it. She watched through the forward viewport as the *Jade's Fire* left Corellia behind.

She was not sorry to say good-bye.

CHAPTER TEN

Getting There

Gaeriel Captison sat down at one end of the long table and nodded to the man standing at the far end. "Admiral," she said, "I think we are ready to begin."

"Thank you, Madame Captison." Admiral Hortel Ossilege of the Bakuran Navy looked around the table. "I wish to review the situation," he said, "and make sure that I understand it completely. Mr. Skywalker, once more, please, how long until your New Republic can refit and redeploy its ships in order to assemble a fleet of its own?"

"Our best estimate is that massing a force and preparing for action will take another forty-five standard days," Luke said.

"Indeed?" Ossilege asked, eyebrows raised. "I begin to wonder how you won against the Empire." He was a small man, of slight build, well-scrubbed and pink-skinned, completely bald on top of his head, but sporting a quite dramatic pair of bushy black eyebrows and a sharply pointed goatee. He wore a Bakuran dress naval uniform of creamy white, with a perfect fruit salad of ribbons and decorations on his chest. On the face of it, he should have looked ridiculous, a comic-opera caricature of the sort of officer who only fought—and won—

the sort of battles that took place in buffet lines, and in front of promotion boards.

Luke had learned very early on that appearances were deceiving. In a day and a half of talks, Ossilege had demonstrated that his was a first-class mind, and that he had little time for nonsense of any sort. "Readiness is very low. There's no doubt about that," he said. "But we have good evidence that the plotters on Corellia have penetrated our security system and timed their operation carefully."

"In short, they caught you with your pants down," said Ossilege. He turned toward Kalenda. "Lieutenant, once more, please, your best estimate of the enemy's naval strength. Have you any reason to revise your opinion?"

"No sir, but I wish I did. I am forced to report that, from all I could see, the naval strength of the Human League and their allies is almost negligible. They seem to have a large number of fighter craft and corvette-class craft, but nothing at all larger. That's the evidence, but I just can't believe it. I think it would be suicidal to take that information at face value. They *must* have more ships somewhere. We have to assume that they are hiding their strength. We just don't know where they are hiding the ships, or why they are hiding them."

"Doesn't your outfit keep track of that sort of thing?" Lando asked.

Kalenda shrugged. "The NRI does its best to track ship inventories, but it's almost impossible. And it's hard to get the information you have to the people who need it. We've got agents all over the Outlier Worlds, but their intelligence reports would go through Coruscant before they were sent on here. The reports haven't caught up with me yet. Maybe a courier ship will bring all sorts of news tomorrow. On the other hand, maybe it won't. And even if does, I wouldn't put much stock in the information. The Galaxy is pretty big. You can hide whole fleets full of ships, or whole shipyards, without much trouble. And there's an awful lot of surplus hardware from the Republic–Empire war floating around."

"You have no way of counting ships?" Ossilege asked in astonishment. "You, the much-vaunted NRI?"

"With respect, Admiral, you only have your own star system to contend with. But we have to watch everything. Suppose someone patches up a derelict cruiser and sells it on the black market in a system our people have never been to? Or what if a shipyard takes on a military-to-civilian conversion job and tears all the weaponry out of a frigate, and turns the frigate into a cargo for a nice, peaceful, well-established shipping company—except it turns out that the weapons were never actually removed, and the shipping company never existed except in whatever database the slicers got into? How are we supposed to deal with that? Or suppose someone just builds whatever ships they want for themselves, and never tells anyone about it? How would *you* count all the ships fitting that description within a thousand light-years of Corellia?"

Ossilege raised one bushy eyebrow. "You have just described a large fraction of the Bakuran procurement process," he said, "a subject I would prefer not to discuss further. I take your point." He turned toward Lando. "Captain Calrissian. You were to attempt a more detailed analysis of the so-called starbuster plot. Your findings?"

Lando turned his palms upward in a gesture of helplessness. "The droids and I went over every bit of data we could squeeze out of the datachip Kalenda brought out. Nothing. We crunched the numbers as hard as we could, and it still came up ambiguous. There is no way to prove, absolutely, that the message to Leia was sent before the star blew up—and likewise no way to disprove the idea that the message was sent *after* the explosion, in such a way as to make it look as if it were delayed. But one thing we do know for sure—*someone* blew that star. There is simply no natural explanation for its having detonated on its own.

"There is also the imagery sent to Governor-General Micamberlecto, showing the star blowing up at close range. That *could* have been faked, but it would be extremely difficult. If we assume it's genuine, either whoever shot the imagery just happened to have the probe in exactly the right position at exactly the right time, or else they had a probe waiting and ready to collect the imagery that would prove their claims."

"There's another related issue," Luke said. "The New Republic has to at least try to evacuate the next planetary system on the starbuster list. Plans weren't finalized before we left, but more than likely the *Naritus* and two or three other ships currently on patrol duty in the Coruscant system will be diverted to that job. That means that many fewer ships for operations in Corellian space."

"Very well," Ossilege said unhappily. "It would appear I already know all I am going to know. I would call upon Madame Captison to discuss the political side of the situation before we discuss the military side."

Luke looked toward Gaeriel, along with everyone else at the table. "It is fairly straightforward," she said. "The Prime Minister and the government have ordered the Navy to assist the New Republic in this crisis, and authorized the Admiral to lead a task force for the relief of Corellia."

"Wonderful!" Luke said. "Please convey our thanks to the Prime Minister."

"Thank you, Madame Captison," said Lando.

"Thank you, ma'am," Kalenda said.

"You are all most welcome, and it goes without saying that all Bakura will be proud to repay some part of the great debt we owe the New Republic. There is one other matter, a minor one perhaps, but it might be worth noting. While Admiral Ossilege will be in full military command of the operation, the Prime Minister has appointed me as her plenipotentiary, with full powers to speak for Bakura in matters of policy. She felt this was necessary because the communications jamming would render normal consultations with Bakura impossible."

"But, Gaer—uh, Madame Captison," Luke objected. "What of your child?"

"Malinza will stay with family here, of course. I am not the first parent called to hazardous duty."

"Yes, of course," Luke said. He wanted to protest, to object to the idea of Gaeriel going along, but he knew there was no chance of his winning the argument.

"Thank you for your concern, Jedi Master," Gaeriel said, "but that decision has been made. Admiral, I think it best that we turn to you and discuss the practicalities of the mission."

"Yes, ma'am," said Ossilege. "First and most important, I must tell you that Bakura, by herself, cannot fight this war for you. Grateful as we are for the New Republic's aid in the past, we cannot strip all the defenses from our own world for months on end—and months on end it would be if we had to fly our ships in and out of the Corellian system in normal space. We cannot perform that task. But, I believe there is at least a fighting chance that we can do something at least as valuable. I believe we can get in, locate the interdiction-field generator, and knock it out, opening the door to whatever New Republic forces can be mustered in the meantime. And I believe we can do this without being unduly inconvenienced ourselves by the Corellian Field."

"How so?" Lando asked.

"We believe we have developed a partial countermeasure to the interdiction field." Ossilege held up his hand to the eager questions from all three of their visitors. "We do not know for sure if it will work in these circumstances or, if it does work, how well it will. There have been only limited tests to date. But the principle is quite simple. As you know, an interdiction field simulates the mass lines produced by a naturally occurring gravity well. A ship cannot travel in hyperspace inside a steep gravity well, and thus is decanted out into normal space, or realspace.

"We have spent some time developing a device called a hyperwave inertial momentum sustainer or, as the technical staff insist on calling it, HIMS. I prefer the term hyperwave sustainer. It uses a gravitic sensor that provides a fast cutoff for a ship's normal hyperdrive, causing it to shut off instantly before it can risk being damaged by the interdiction field. It simultaneously activates a static hyperspace bubble, produced by a hyperspace coil *designed* to burn up and blow out in the presence of an interdiction field.

"The static hyperwave bubble cannot provide any thrust, of course, but it can hold the ship in hyperspace while the ship's forward momentum carries it along. The first blowout coil activates the second, the second activates the third, and so on. In effect, the ship flickers in and out of hyperspace, jumping into it and being thrown back out of it, over and over again, until its forward momentum carries it clear of the interdiction field, and the normal hyperdrive system comes back on-line."

"Very elegant." Luke said, impressed.

"Yes, I suppose, in a crude sort of way. It's brute-force engineering, and our tests show just how rough a ride it is, but it does get the job done."

"At least it allows the ship to escape any interdiction field of *reasonable* size," Gaeriel said dryly. "Not the monstrosity you two found out there. There are limits."

"What sort of limits?" Luke asked.

"Installing a hyperwave sustainer is no simple or inexpensive task," Ossilege said. "It is costly and time-consuming. We have, at present, only four ships—three destroyers and one light cruiser—equipped with the sys-

tem. Installing every static hyperwave bubble generator
we can on the ships, we estimate that we can hold the
ships in hyperspace for roughly three quarters of the
distance from the edge of the interdiction field to its
center. The ships will not be able to hold formation, and
might well become somewhat scattered. But they will be
able to drop into the Corellian planetary system well
inside the defense perimeter—and within close striking
distance of Selonia."

"Selonia? But what good does that do?" Lando
asked. "I thought we had figured out the interdiction-
field generator had to be somewhere in the double-
planet system, somewhere on Talus or Tralus. Why go to
Selonia?"

"Because Selonia provides us with a target of opportunity, and a diversion from our attack on the Double
Worlds," Ossilege said. "Let me show you." He pushed
a series of buttons on the control panel by his hand. The
room's light dimmed, and a standard wire-frame schematic of the Corellian planetary system appeared, floating over the center of the table. "These are the present
relative positions of the five inhabited planets of the
Corellian system. As you can see, Corellia is on the opposite side of the star Corell from Tralus and Talus.
Drall is about ninety degrees ahead of Corellia, but
Selonia is nearly at its closest approach to the double
planets, Tralus and Talus. As you can also see, Selonia's
orbit is exterior to that of the double planets. If we
make a direct coplanar radial approach to Tralus and
Talus from the system's exterior, we more or less have to
pass by Selonia. And Selonia is a major target. The
rebels there will be forced to defend it."

"If there are rebels there," Luke said. "We know almost nothing about what's going on there."

"I am not sure there are any rebels anywhere," Ossilege said. "Simultaneous uprisings by independent
groups on five worlds? That's stretching the bounds of

credulity. I believe there is a more—intimate—relationship between the various rebellions. I do not wish to speculate further on that issue just at the moment. But in regard to your point, Mr. Skywalker, one reason I wish to mount an assault at Selonia is to find out what happens there, find out who reacts and how. We can learn from their reaction to us. If they welcome us as liberators, all to the good. If they attack, as I suspect they will, I expect we will learn a great deal as well—as well as forcing them to commit their short-range forces. I hope that by drawing them out at Selonia, we can weaken the forces they can mass at Tralus and Talus."

Lando looked over the tactical display. "It makes a certain amount of sense," he said, "but it's risky. Extremely risky. You have a small force operating without support deep inside enemy territory, with no way to withdraw if things go badly."

Ossilege faded out the tactical display and brought the room lights back up. "Your point is well taken," he said. "But audacity is a weapon, as sure as that blaster at your side is one. But both are useless left where they are. Audacity is a weapon that must be drawn from its scabbard from time to time."

"That's very poetic," Lando said, "but with all due respect, I have some experience in these matters. I must say that you might be asking too much of four ships."

Ossilege smiled thinly. "It is *my* experience," he said, "that you achieve more by asking too much rather than by asking too little."

Luke Skywalker said nothing. But he was coming to realize just how dangerous a man Ossilege was.

The question was, of course—dangerous to whom?

*   *   *

Han Solo crawled along behind Dracmus down the tunnel, bone weary of the journey, and wearier still of not

knowing what was going on. It had been two days since
the Selonians had rescued the two of them from the
Human League's hidden fortress, and just about that
long since Han had been clear on the situation. The
rescue party had escorted Han and Dracmus out of the
escape tunnel to a main passageway, and then said their
good-byes. Han and Dracmus had been traveling by
themselves ever since, occasionally encountering other
Selonians, but for the most part on their own.

He still was not sure if he was a prisoner, or if he was
being taken to a place of safety, or both. Dracmus had
revealed an impressive ability to avoid answering unwanted questions.

All Han knew for sure was that she was taking him
someplace, and that he had to do a lot of crawling to get
there, through a seemingly endless series of low-ceil-
inged tunnels lit in the gloomiest, dimmest red imagin-
able.

"Is it much further to some place I can stand up?"
Han asked, raising his voice a bit so Dracmus could hear
him. Dracmus was ahead of him in the tunnel, as she
had been for most of the journey. Han had spent an
awful lot of the last few days watching her hindquarters
and tail as she moved ahead of him.

Dracmus laughed, making that hissing noise of hers.
Han would not miss that sound if he never heard it
again. "Always you want to stand. Is it not a nice rest to
be off your hind feet? Stretch yourself, let forelegs do
some of the job."

The Selonian hadn't answered his question *that* time,
either, though Han could see no point to avoiding a
reply. He had the distinct impression that Dracmus had
received instructions from the rescue party to keep
quiet and answer no questions. Han had asked her
point-blank if that were the case, but if it was, then the
prohibition extended even to questions about the prohibition. If she had received orders to keep quiet, she was

obeying them in a rather slavish and literal-minded way. What harm in letting Han know how high the ceiling was a bit farther along? But he and Dracmus had had some variant of this same conversation at least a dozen times since her friends had sprung them from the Human League prison. Han had yet to receive a straight answer, and he was still on his hands and knees three-quarters of the time.

Han understood the reasons for the low tunnels, of course. Selonians were as nimble on four feet as on two —perhaps more so. They were in large part creatures of the underworld—tunnelers, diggers, burrowers. Tunnels dug for Selonians going on four feet had to be only a meter across and a meter high, while tunnels dug for Selonians walking on two feet had to be at least two meters high—and Selonians didn't see the point of digging out twice as much rock, just for the sake of a vertical posture. Unfortunately, understanding the logic didn't make the crick in Han's neck go away, or relieve the throbbing ache in his knees.

At least he wasn't the first human to come up against the problem. The Selonians had provided him with a helmet, knee pads, and padded gloves, but there were times when he wondered if the solutions weren't worse than the problem. The helmet was heavy and unventilated, and was not quite the right shape for a human head. The gloves were too big and clumsy, and the knee pads threatened to slide off with every step he took—if you could call moving on your knees stepping. It took hours of awkward trial and error before he learned the peculiar little extra lift and twist required of each knee to keep the pads in place.

Once or twice he had considered the idea of not going forward, of not doing what Dracmus said, of striking out on his own through the tunnel system. But he knew the idea was hopelessly impractical. Dracmus could move through the tunnels a lot faster than he could, for one thing. And Dracmus knew her way around the tunnel system, for another. Besides, Dracmus could call for an awful lot of help, if need be. Han and she were far from alone down there.

Han heard a sort of chuffling sound behind him, and then a double hoot from the same quarter, followed by a squeak and a warble from Dracmus. The sounds were not any part of the Selonian language Han had learned. They were tunnel-talk, signals meant to be clearly understood even in the echoing confines of the underground ways. It had not taken Han long to find out what they meant. Space knew he had heard them often enough. *Here I come from behind you,* called the Selonian in the rear. *Please feel free to overtake us,* Dracmus replied. Han let out a sigh and lay down flat on his stomach. "Here we go again," he muttered to himself.

He heard the skittering and clicking of claws on stone behind him, then the pause as the Selonian behind him, surprised to find a human, stopped to snuffle at his feet and his clothes before scrambling over his body, managing to put all her weight on Han's chest and then step on his head. Han sighed again. Another set of aches and pains he would have to get over. The ones who overtook from the rear always seemed to find new places to set their claws. The ones who came from the front all seemed to walk on the same spots on his back and the backs of his legs.

The overtaking Selonian scuttled over Dracmus in turn, and that was some comfort, if not much. Selonians were used to it. But Han could not help but hope that Dracmus got at least a *little* bit of a jab in the ribs. However, if she did take a bit of damage, she didn't show any sign of it.

Han got back up off his hands and knees and followed after his guide.

Unless, of course, she was his jailer. He still wasn't quite sure.

* * *

The Duchess Marcha of Mastigophorous liked to reassure herself that all of her nephew Ebrihim's eccentricities could not possibly come from her side of the family. And yet there was no question that he had inherited one or two traits from her side of the bloodline. Ebrihim had endurance, even if he did not always take advantage of it. But when the circumstances called for it, he could keep going long after everyone else had collapsed from sheer exhaustion.

And he had the skills of a good scholar, even if he did not put those skills to good use. He could report on the facts, discuss them objectively, and then analyze a situation dispassionately, speculate about it responsibly, and never get facts muddled up with opinions or ideas. And, of course, endurance was a great help in scholarship as well. One needed to keep going, to keep chasing. No doubt, Ebrihim could have made something of himself if he had not also had the temperament of a dilettante. Everything interested him, with the result that he had never pursued any single subject far enough.

But tonight, for once, he was putting all his scholar's skills to use. The children were long ago asleep, that Wookiee fellow Chewbacca had likewise turned in, and even Q9-X2, Ebrihim's absurd droid, had returned to the ship in order to recharge.

But Ebrihim was wide-awake, and alert, fresh as a dressel flower on a dewy morning. She and he had been sitting up in the kitchen for hours, talking over endless pots of strong tea and a stack of good, solid, hardbiscuits, the sort that really exercised the jaw and the gnawing muscles, the sort that chipped human teeth.

The family news had come first, of course. It had

often been said of the Dralls that if the universe were
swallowed by a mammoth black hole, and it happened
on the same day a favorite cousin broke off an ill-
advised love affair, no member of the cousin's family
would even be able to work in a mention of the end of
the universe for days.

But even though Ebrihim had been gone for a long
time, sooner or later even family gossip had to give way
to the wave of crises that seemed to be drowning the
Corellian planetary system. "Things have never been
this bad," Aunt Marcha said. "It seems that a half-
dozen separatist groups popped up over night, all of
them squawking how they hate the Corellian Sector
government and chittering on about how the New Republic is no better than the Empire, and urging everyone to band together to oppose the Human League
oppressors, and they all seem to hate each other most of
all. All sorts of nonsense. Most un-Drallish."

"Which were the ones that gave you trouble?"
Ebrihim asked. "You mentioned something about a
group called the Drallists?

"Those are the ones. Of all the foolish groups, the
Drallists are the worst. They're the ones who have been
cutting power links and terrorizing travelers. It seems
they denounce someone else for being a collaborator
every day. Declared *me* a collaborator, if you can believe that. They didn't bother to say who I was collabo-
rating with, or who my imaginary collaborators were for
or against. They seem to be in favor of chaos, and
against everything else. But I knew what being a collab-
orationist could mean. Houses have been bombed, you
know."

"What!" Ebrihim said. "Dralls blowing up the houses
of Dralls! I can't believe it."

"I could not believe it myself, nephew, but I could not
endanger others on my behalf. I sent away everyone I
could—relatives, servants, friends, everyone. The house

seems so empty without them all. I hope they can all come back when the trouble is over. If it ever *is* over."

Marcha shook her head and refilled her nephew's tea mug. "I don't know what is to come next. Truly I don't."

"Nor do I, Aunt Marcha. Neither do I."

"Do you want anything else?" she asked, her reflexes as a hostess taking over. "Another hard-biscuit, perhaps?" she said, offering the bowl.

"I'd be delighted," Ebrihim said. "Your biscuits are splendid, as usual. Hard as wood, and most flavorful. I had forgotten how much I enjoy them. Human food gives no benefit to the incisors."

"I am glad to hear that you enjoy them, nephew. But what of you? How in the stars did you end up here with three human children and a Wookiee?"

"Those are not just any human children, Aunt Marcha. Didn't their names mean anything to you? Their parents are people of note."

"Well, perhaps they are," she said with a sniff. "I have never made much effort to see what airs humans are putting on at the moment. I take it you have been tutoring the children of some minor member of the Corellian aristocracy. All very well, I suppose, but you can't expect me to recognize their names."

"I expect even *you* have heard of their people. Their father was a hero of the war against the Empire—and, it appears, the cousin of the Human League's leader, though he was less than pleased to hear that, I can tell you! Their mother is Leia Organa Solo, Chief of State of the New Republic. Their uncle is Luke Skywalker himself."

"Heavens!" Aunt Marcha said, impressed in spite of herself. Marcha, as head of a very grand family, had always known that there were times when long family lineages merely meant that a pack of idiots had been reproducing for too long. She had always been more interested in accomplishment than in hereditary status.

But some families *were* impressive. "You *are* traveling in interesting circles, nephew. Tell me all."

"Very well, Aunt Marcha. But I warn you, it is a long story."

"I have never known you to tell a short one, nephew."

Ebrihim took another cup of tea and proceeded to tell her a remarkable tale, of all that had happened since he had been hired by Leia Organa Solo. Clearly, intrigues had been swirling around Corellia for some time. It was typical of Ebrihim that he would manage to get himself right in the middle of it all.

Marcha had always worried about her nephew. To humans, perhaps, he seemed levelheaded, sensible, even dour. By Drallish standards, he was flighty, irresponsible, a flibbertigibbet. She had long ago given up on him settling down and starting his own family. It did not take much knowledge of psychology to tell her that his affection for the human children might be some sort of substitute for the children of his own he would never have. On the other paw, it took even less knowledge of psychology to suspect herself of reading too much into it. The Duchess of Mastigophorous had little time for nonsense, especially her own.

But, nonetheless, every family had its eccentric nephews and cousins, and there were unquestioned benefits to that arrangement. The Duchess Marcha learned this anew as she listened to Ebrihim's account of his adventures with the Organa Solo family. The spying, the secret attacks, Han Solo's kidnapping and release, the attack on Corona House; all of it was quite remarkable.

But the one thing that shocked her most was, of course, his using the family's high status as a means of getting into an archaeological dig, for no other reason than so he could see the dig himself. If the dig proved interesting to his employers, and educational to the children, so much the better. The sheer effrontery of it was breathtaking. Even most humans would have trouble taking advantage of their position in that way. No sensible Drall would have gotten mixed up in such goings-on. At least good had come of it. For if they had never gone to the dig, little Anakin would never have found that strange, huge chamber.

But the story reminded her of something. Something strange she had seen in the news some time before. "Nephew," she said. "Have you ever heard of such a thing as an archaeological dig on Drall?"

Ebrihim looked at her and frowned. "Of course not," he said. "That was part of why I was so interested in seeing one. There's no such thing as Drallish archaeology, any more than there's such a thing as human tail grooming."

"That," said Marcha, "was my impression. We have no need of archaeology. There is nothing worth digging for." The Drall were a tidy people, and an ancient one, much given to keeping good records and keeping things organized. For thousands of years, everything of importance had either been neatly filed away in storage or else recycled. There was no such thing as Drallish prehistory, or preliterate history. At least, if there were, they were so long forgotten that they might as well not exist. "That is why it surprised me some time ago to see a brief mention in the press recently of a large archaeological project near the equator."

"That's absurd!" Ebrihim protested.

"I quite agree," she said. "I found it peculiar enough that I tried to learn more. I was able to establish the exact location of the dig, but that was all. There were no further news stories, and I could not get anywhere at all making private inquiries. It was nothing more than idle curiosity that made me pursue the question, and perhaps I gave it up too quickly. What intrigues me is that the account of the dig made it sound a great deal like the one you described."

Ebrihim looked at his aunt in openmouthed astonishment. "Aunt Marcha! The implications of what you are saying—"

"I know, I know. They are enormous. But I don't see that we have any choice but to pursue the question. I think we have to know more—a great deal more—about what the children discovered."

*   *   *

Tendra Risant guided her newly acquired ship through hyperspace toward the Corellian planetary system—and whatever awaited her there. The ship was a slow and elderly Corellian runabout she had named *Gentleman Caller,* and the *Gent* wasn't much to look at. But looks didn't count for a great deal. The ship would get her there—eventually. That was all that mattered.

She was only half a day out from Sacorria, but had already learned a lot of interesting things about interstellar travel, and she was eager to sit down and talk about them with Lando, if and when she ever found him. She had a feeling they were the sorts of lessons he often found useful in his work.

The first and greatest lesson was that money made nearly all things possible, and most things dead easy, especially when you were ready to throw cold hard cash around in the form of bribes and other encouragements. Embargoes? Orders grounding all spacecraft and forbidding the sale of used spacecraft? Registration filing? None of those impediments could stand up to a good strong dose of money properly applied.

The second was that people were awfully spoiled about space travel. Everyone seemed to assume that the interdiction field around Corellia might as well have been a solid, impenetrable wall, impossible to get through. Nonsense, all of it. The interdiction field simply prevented a spacecraft from entering the Corellian system while moving faster than the speed of light; nothing more.

Getting to Corellia was no problem, provided you didn't mind taking your time on the way. The navicomputer told her the trip from the edge of the interdiction field to the planet Corellia would take her three long months at the *Gentleman*'s best sublight speed, but Tendra half-expected she would not have anywhere near that long to wait. The Corellians could not keep the interdiction field in place forever. They would have to take it down some time—if someone else didn't take it down for them. Or perhaps the jamming would end, even if the interdiction field stayed up.

Besides, Tendra knew she might well be able to do a great deal of good without ever getting close to Corellia. All the normal comlink frequencies might be jammed, but that meant nothing to the special communications gear Lando had given her before he left for Corellia. He had intended it as a romantic gift, a way for them to send secret lovers' messages back and forth to Sacorria, but the system could be put to other uses.

It was a strange old system he had given her. It transmitted and received modulated electromagnetic radiation in the radio band of the spectrum. Because the signal sent by the system used electromagnetic radiation, the broadcast was limited by the speed of light. Lando had said it was called a radionics communications system. While Tendra could see no particular reason the system could not be adapted to send visual images, the unit she had was sound only. Very crude. You spoke into a microphone, and your voice went out as modulations on a radio-band carrier signal, ambling out into the universe at the speed of light.

But even the speed of light was faster than a spacecraft limited to sublight speeds. The Corellian planetary system was only a few light-hours across. If Lando were in-system, and if he—or anyone else—happened to switch on a radionics receiver tuned to the proper frequency, then Tendra's warning about the fleet massing at Sacorria would reach them in only a few hours, once she was in-system. It was a long shot proposition. Tendra knew that. But even long shots paid off every once in a while.

And besides, it got her off Sacorria.

CHAPTER ELEVEN

The Tale of Ratiocination

On the morning after their arrival at the villa of the Duchess Marcha, the children had nothing more in mind than getting breakfast eaten as soon as possible so they could get started exploring the huge house and its grounds.

But Q9 was waiting for them in the kitchen, and even though he served them breakfast in a most helpful and efficient manner, the news that Ebrihim and Aunt Marcha wanted to have a little chat about the huge underground chamber that Anakin had found put a most effective damper on their enthusiasm. Breakfast suddenly took on the feel of the condemned prisoner's last meal.

There has never been a child living who did not feel that special twinge of fear when summoned in by the adults to explain something. Even the most innocent childhood problems seem to have a way of ballooning out of control when exposed to grown-up viewpoints.

When the offense was the accidental breaking of a window, things were bad enough. Even given that accidents happen to everyone, a sensible child must approach the interview armed with the knowledge that adults often have a very different idea of what an "accident" is.

When the offense was the semiaccidental discovery of a huge, ancient, alien, much-sought-after, and mysterious underground facility, the problem was, of course, far worse. Jaina instantly conjured up two or three ways that finding the chamber could get them in big trouble. Maybe, despite their precautions, they had left a clue that had let those Human League creeps find it. Maybe it was some strange, huge, burial chamber and they had violated someone's taboo. Maybe, worst of all, finding it had been what had set off the whole war. She could not see *how* that could be, but that didn't mean it couldn't have happened.

Anakin tried to sneak off with an excuse that he had to go help Chewbacca fix the *Falcon,* but that one didn't even fool Q9. None of them were getting out of it.

"So did they say what they wanted to know?" Jaina asked as she poked her spoon around her bowl of diced fruit.

"Only that they wished to hear from you, in your words, all about the chamber Anakin found. I have told you that three times now. I should think the first two times should have been clear enough."

"Well, maybe I want more of an answer than that."

"Then I suggest that you ask more of a question."

"Look, Q9," Jacen said. "The one *big* question is—are we in trouble?"

"In trouble for what?" the droid asked.

"I don't know," Jacen asked. "If I knew, I wouldn't have to ask."

"How can I tell you what you want to know when I don't know what it is?" Q9 asked.

"But I want to know if you know what I don't," Jacen said.

"But I can't know what that is if you don't tell me," Q9 replied.

"Yes, but—"

"Quiet!" Anakin shouted. "Too loud."

"I'm with Anakin," Jaina said. "Let's eat our breakfast and then we'll find out."

* * *

The children finished eating in a nervous sort of silence, and then followed Q9 from the kitchen to Aunt Marcha's study, an odd little room with a door so low that Jacen had to duck just a bit to get through it. The room was windowless, and the walls and floors were rounded, and merged one into the other, and there was a dry, loamy smell to the room. The walls were painted a swirly sort of dark brown, and the furniture consisted solely of what appeared to be big, flat rounded rocks scattered about. The rocks, however, turned out to be soft and comfortable cushions, and the children settled into them very happily.

"Why does this room look so funny?" Anakin asked.

"Anakin!" Jaina cried. "Don't be rude."

"It's quite all right," said Aunt Marcha. "There's never any harm in an honest question respectfully asked. And though you *might* learn how to ask things like that a *bit* more politely, I'll tell you. Long, long ago, all Drall would hibernate in underground burrows during the cold, cold winter. Some Drall still believe that Drall were *meant* to hibernate, and do so to this day. I don't go quite that far, but many Drall like the idea of a place that is like a snug underground burrow, warm and safe against the cold. It relaxes us. I think this is a very good place to think and talk. What do you think?"

Anakin looked around and nodded. "I kind of like it," he announced.

"Good," said Aunt Marcha. "Now then, let's get

started. Children, Q9-X2 has shown us the images he recorded when you visited that cavern. But let's pretend we didn't see them. Tell me everything you can about it. Don't leave out a single thing."

"Well," Jaina said, "okay." Aunt Marcha didn't sound mad. Maybe things were not as bad as she thought. Maybe they weren't in trouble after all. Unless Ebrihim's Aunt Marcha was one sneaky old character. "We didn't find it, first off. Anakin did. And I don't know how, either. It was like he saw some sort of line or arrow or something we couldn't see, something under the tunnel floor, and the invisible arrow led him to it."

"Anakin does weird stuff like that," Jacen said blandly.

"I see," said Aunt Marcha, in a tone of voice that made it clear she did not.

"All three children are very strong in the Force," said Ebrihim. "Anakin's abilities are—ah—most unusual."

"Yeah," Jacen said. "He's spooky-good with machines. Stuff like that. Mom and Dad say he might grow out of it."

"Or I might not," Anakin put in. Jaina had the feeling her little brother thought they were blaming him for whatever-it-was. "I don't think anyone's *mad* at you for finding the chamber," she said reassuringly.

"Quite the contrary," said Aunt Marcha. "It might be very, very important that you found it. But go on, please. Anakin, ah, followed this invisible guide. Then what happened?"

Jaina and Jacen told the rest of it, finishing each other's sentences and adding details to whatever the other said, in the way twins often did. Anakin chimed in now and again, but as often as not, no one quite knew what to make of his contributions. Nevertheless they managed to give Aunt Marcha a good idea of the place, in however disjointed a fashion.

They described the way Anakin had led them to one

stretch of blank wall, seemingly just like all the others, and the way he had found the hidden keypad control and opened the massive door. They described the strange silver walkway behind the door, and the platform it led to. And they described the huge conical chamber spread out below the platform, with six silver cones in a circle at its base, and a seventh cone in the center.

Ebrihim's Aunt Marcha stopped them now and again to ask questions. She had Q9 project all the imagery he had recorded, and went over it with the children in detail, asking how old things looked, how hot the place had been, if they had noticed anything about the top of the conical chamber. The children answered as best they could, and Aunt Marcha generally seemed to get the answers she was expecting.

At last she seemed to decide she had all the information she was going to get from the three of them. "Thank you, children," she said. "What you have told me is very important. More important than you could imagine. I think that Ebrihim and I need to sit down and talk about it all for a while. You may go."

Jacen and Anakin scrambled to their feet and headed for the door of the odd little den. But Jaina stayed where she was. Ebrihim's aunt might think she knew all she needed to know, but she was wrong. Jaina felt sure of that. There was something more, something besides the strange hidden chamber. It had been preying on her mind for a long time, and she was determined to say something, even if it left her in a world of trouble. "Um, ah, Your Grace?"

"Yes, child? What is it?"

"There's something else you should know about. Something that we all heard, that we weren't supposed to hear."

"Jaina!" Jacen protested. "Don't!"

"We *have* to, Jacen. It might be real important. And we can trust her. We *can*. We *have* to."

Jacen turned away from the door and sat back down. "I think it's a mistake," he said.

"Well, if it is, it's my mistake," Jaina said. She turned back toward the Duchess. "The night before the attack on Corona House, our parents had a meeting with Governor-General Micamberlecto and a lady named Mara Jade. She's a—"

"I know all about Master Trader Mara Jade," said Aunt Marcha, in studiously neutral tones. "Go on."

"Well, she brought them a message from someone who sounded a lot like Dad. . . ." Jaina told the Duchess all about the meeting the children had overheard, and about the written message they had seen projected on the wall and the spoken message they had heard, about the threat to blow up a whole series of stars, culminating in Corell itself. Aunt Marcha listened carefully, asking occasional questions. Jaina went through the whole story, but she hesitated a moment at the end. No. She had to go the whole way. "There's another thing. I can't quite say how, or why, but there's some sort of connection between what we heard in the message and the place Anakin found. I can't explain it, exactly, but somehow they *felt* the same."

"I don't see how that could be," said Aunt Marcha. "Not if my suspicions about the place Anakin found are right—and I am almost certain they are."

"If it is any comfort, Jaina, I don't think you gave away any secrets," said Ebrihim. "Chewbacca and I heard a similar message that was broadcast to all of the planet Corellia the very next day. We didn't want to tell you about it, because we didn't want to frighten you. Little did we know."

"But the message we heard said to keep everything a big secret!" Jaina protested. "Why tell it to the whole world the next day?"

"That," said Ebrihim, "is an excellent question."

"I have my own questions," said Aunt Marcha. "Most of them about that list of times and coordinates. Where were they? What were the times? If we knew the schedule, that might tell us something very important."

"I *know* what they are!" Anakin announced. "I could write 'em down for you."

Marcha smiled at him. "I'm sure you could, Anakin. But we need the real numbers, not pretend ones that—"

"Oh, he could write down the real ones," Jacen said in a very casual tone of voice. "Do you have some paper and something to write with?"

"What?" Marcha asked. "How could he—"

"If you'll allow me," Ebrihim said. He stood up and opened the front of a cupboard built into the wall. He extracted a large sheet of paper and a pen and handed them to Anakin. Anakin put the paper on the floor, lay down on his stomach, and began writing neat, precise rows of numbers. "The boy's memory is—ah—somewhat remarkable."

"If he sees it, he remembers it," Jaina agreed. "Of course he doesn't know what it all means, but he remembers it."

"What do you mean he doesn't know what it means?" Marcha asked.

"Well, he can't really read so well yet," Jacen said, "but he knows his letters and numbers really well."

*   *   *

A very long hour and a half later, Ebrihim and Marcha sent the children away, once it seemed they had gotten all they were going to get out of them—and they had certainly managed to get a great deal. Anakin, with some prompting, had been able to recite virtually the whole conversation of that night, word for word, with Marcha's office system recording and transcribing it all.

They had gone over Sal-Solo's public message as re-corded by the *Millennium Falcon*. They had plotted out the perfectly accurate star positions that Anakin had written down.

And they had not gotten much of anywhere.

"Nephew," said Aunt Marcha, "we have a mystery on our hands. One we *must* solve. And yet I do not know how to begin. One message, the one the children heard, offers proof—or at least compelling evidence—that the authors were able to blow up a star. The message de-mands secrecy, does not reveal the identity of its au-thors, and yet offers many details concerning when and where the next attacks will come. It demands the recipi-ents comply with instructions, and yet gives no instruc-tions.

"The second message, the one you heard, came scarcely a day later, and told everyone on the planet the authors could destroy stars, made absolutely impossible demands, and the system-wide jamming and the in-terdiction field were activated immediately afterward, making it absolutely impossible for anyone to even *try* to carry out the demands. Furthermore, the second mes-sage was *not* transmitted to the other planets. However, given the prohuman, anti-Drall, anti-Selonian nature of the second message, I can understand why they would not want it transmitted anyplace where those races might take out their revenge on the human populace. It makes no sense. No sense at all."

"Quite true," said Ebrihim. "If you assume that both messages were sent by the same people."

"But of course they were. How could they not be?"

"I see clues in the first message that strongly suggest otherwise."

"Explain yourself."

Ebrihim picked up the printout from the transcriber. "To do so requires a certain amount of ratiocination, of deductive reasoning. We can deduce certain things from

the fact that some information is not there. 'This will be
your only notification prior to events,' " Ebrihim read.
" 'Inform no one of this message and await instructions
so as to avoid the need for further action. We will be
monitoring all communications. Do not attempt to call
for help. Any violation of instructions will result in an
acceleration of the schedule.' That was all the speaker
said. Consider that the first message was in two parts—a
written list of times and coordinates that did not refer to
the anonymous recorded voice, and a recorded voice
that makes no reference to the written list.

"From what the children said about the voice resem-
bling their father's, I think it is highly likely that the
speaker was indeed Thrackan Sal-Solo. Let us suppose
it was. Suppose he was handed a script and told to read
it, without being told what it was about. Perhaps the
authors of that message wanted someone with a Corellian accent. Perhaps they wanted Thrackan's voice so
that when Thrackan did reveal himself, they would be
linked with him. Perhaps he just happened to be handy
when they wanted the words read.

"In any event, the message was recorded. If Mara
Jade was not part of the plot, then it could have been
recorded no more recently than about three weeks ago,
when it came into Jade's possession. Of course, if she *is*
part of the plot, it could have been recorded at any time
up to the moment Leia Organa Solo opened the message cube. But let us assume Jade is not involved. In
that case, the message could have been taped months,
even years, before."

"What of it?" Marcha asked.

"Then all is explained. Let me tell you a tale, if you
will. I think something like this happened: Sal-Solo is
approached by the senders of the first message, for
whatever reason. My guess is that he was involved in
some aspect of the plot, and they wanted a Corellian
voice.

"However the details work, he reads the spoken message, and then, somehow, learns the content of the written message—or, at least, learned of the starbuster plot. And he decides to invent his own piggyback conspiracy. He knows when the message is going to be delivered, or at least can learn when it has been. All he has to do is watch for Mara Jade to arrive and contact Leia Organa Solo. He immediately puts his own plan for an uprising into effect. He makes his broadcast claiming he controls the starbuster, and then activates the jamming and interdiction field."

Aunt Marcha shook her head. "I can go with you part of the way, but not the whole distance. What of the simultaneous revolts on the other worlds? Your theory requires either Sal-Solo to mastermind antihuman revolts, or else an astonishing degree of coincidence. From what we know of it, the Human League does not sound like the sort of operation that can operate a massively powerful jamming system, let alone develop superweapons like the system-size interdiction-field generator or the starbuster. Besides, if you give the jamming and the interdiction system to Thrackan, you have *two* shadowy organizations capable of developing technology. Make him nothing but a messenger boy and a powerless malcontent, and the plot only needs one."

Ebrihim thought for a moment. "Will you let him control the jamming system? It is a brute-force sort of technology and does not require any new invention. I think I can make a case that Thrackan did that much."

Aunt Marcha nodded cautiously. "I suppose," she said. "See if you can convince me."

"Thank you. Let's see if I can present a revised scenario." Ebrihim paused for a moment and thought it through before he spoke. "Thrackan Sal-Solo's group is assigned to deliver the message before the nova explosion, thereby proving the authors of the message could blow up stars at will. Either by chance or by choice, Sal-

Solo's people bungle that assignment, so that it arrives *after* the star has detonated. Sal-Solo's people are also instructed to report to their masters when the message reaches Leia Organa Solo, as that will be the cue for all the revolts to take place. Leia Organa Solo gets the message, and the orders to start the revolutions go out.

"What the masterminds of the plot intended was for the interdiction field to be activated, trapping the New Republic's Chief of State in-system, and preventing the New Republic from interfering. However, communications were to be left open so that negotiations could take place—after the entire system erupted in chaos, with the masterminds' lackeys, recruited from among local hotheads and malcontents, overthrowing the various planetary governments. The masterminds would then negotiate with the New Republic government, destroying one star after another until they got what they wanted. The masterminds would then control the Corellian planetary system, and thus the Corellian Sector, with their lackeys in control of the planets.

"Except Thrackan Sal-Solo double-crosses his masters. He starts his revolt, but then broadcasts his message, falsely taking credit for the starbuster—and then jams all communications so that the masterminds of the plot cannot respond. He either seizes control of the interdiction generator, or else simply prevents the masterminds from getting to it and shutting it off.

"Having created chaos, he then exploits it. Perhaps he plans to grab the Corellian system for himself, before the masterminds of the plot can respond. He cannot keep up the jamming forever, and sooner or later the interdiction field must come down. But by the time they are shut down, by the time the smoke clears, he will be in command of the entire Corellian planetary system."

The Duchess looked at her nephew unhappily. "I must concede that you have offered a convincing theory," she said. "But it is, unfortunately, a most disturbing one. If you are correct, then the conspirators have already fallen out with each other and are fighting among themselves."

"Unfortunately, even if my hypothesis is correct—and I believe it is at least close to the truth—we do not have the whole story," said Ebrihim. "None of it explains what it was that the children found in that chamber—or why the Human League seemed to be searching desperately for it, or what if any connection any of this has to the archaeological dig here on Drall."

"I think there is the closest of connections," Marcha replied. "Based on Q9's imagery, and what I have heard about the dig here, I would say the two sites are all but identical, the only difference being that perhaps more of the installation has been excavated on Corellia. I have a pretty fair idea what the children found, and I suspect an identical chamber can be found in the archaeological site here on Drall. But we have to find it first, and for that I am afraid we are going to need help from the children—or at least from Anakin."

Ebrihim looked at his aunt. "I assure you, if you need Anakin, you need all three of them. The two older ones seem to be taking their responsibilities toward him very seriously indeed in the past few days. Beyond which, they seem to be the only ones who can get him to do anything."

"I see. I must say that doesn't surprise me. Be that as it may, I intend to take the children to the dig here, and let Anakin see if he can find a similar chamber. There will be some slight risk involved. Do you think the children will be willing to cooperate?"

"I would expect so. Human children tend not to worry as much as they should. But that is not the issue. You are on shaky ethical ground in asking children to assist in a risky enterprise, and they are far too young to judge the balance of risks and benefits. They are well below the age of informed consent for humans."

The Duchess Marcha looked over the list of star coordinates Anakin had written. A list of stars in an oddly precise child's hand, a list of stars with planets full of people. A list of stars that someone had marked down for destruction. "I do not relish the thought of using children," she said, "but I do not see that we have a choice."

*   *   *

Tendra Risant sat in the pilot's chair of the *Gentleman Caller*, rigidly alert, trying to watch every instrument at once. She was near, very near, to the edge of the Corellian interdiction field, and did not quite know what to do. "Near" was a relative term. She knew she was *approximately* at the edge of the field, but the information she had been able to buy concerning the Corellian Field was vague in the extreme. She might be right on top of it, or she might have another billion kilometers to go. In theory, there was nothing preventing her from dropping out of hyperspace deliberately, here and now, and sailing toward Corellia in normal space. But suppose she was a billion kilometers off? That would add another week or ten days to her transit time, and after only a few days aboard the *Gent,* she was quite certain she did not want to extend the trip if she could help it.

No, she would stay in hyperspace as long as she could, and let the interdiction field knock her back into normal—

WHAM!

The *Gentleman Caller* shuddered from stem to stern as the ship was thrown out of hyperspace into the universe proper. The viewports flared with a tangled crazy-quilt of jumbled star lines, and every alarm in the ship went off at once. Tendra, very much a greenhorn pilot, panicked for a moment and froze up as the lights cut out and the ship started pinwheeling across the darkness. Then she snapped herself out of it, and reached out for the manual hyperdrive cutoff switch.

Half the alarms cut out as soon as the hyperdrive went off-line, and was no longer trying to hold the ship in hyperspace. With any luck, she had cut the drive off before it could burn out. Not that it would matter anytime soon, of course. She hit the resets on the other alarms and set to work regaining attitude control of the tumbling ship. No rush on that, in practical terms, of course, but it was more than a little disconcerting to see the entire universe tumbling past the viewports in all directions.

Besides, she wanted the view steadied down enough so she could see where she was going.

There. There it was. Still distant enough that it did not show a disk. There, the close, bright star. That was Corell, the star that shone on Corellia.

It might take her a while to get there, but she was on her way. Well on her way.

CHAPTER TWELVE

Under the Iceberg

Han had lost all track of time. On and on through the scarlet-lit tunnels they went, moving at a snail's pace. There was something indefinably old about the tunnels, something that, in spite of the fact that all were dry, well-made, well-kept, told Han they had been here a long time. Well, why not? There had been Selonians on—and more to the point, *in*—Corellia for untold thousands of years, and a tunnel, once dug, had a tendency to remain where it was. There must have been thousands of kilometers of tunnel under the surface in the capital region alone.

Han, however, would have been just as pleased if they had built fewer tunnels but made them bigger. Now and again his wish came true, and they would come to a larger passage, sometimes merely wide enough for two Selonians to walk side by side, sometimes a vast artificial cavern hundreds of meters across, all of it lit in that same dark, lurid red. Han was glad to see any such place, so long as the ceiling was high enough for him to stand upright—even if he was no longer capable of standing. The endless hours of crawling in the cramped

197

tunnels had left him hunched over, his back aching, his knees so bashed and battered and sore he could barely straighten them. But even tottering along stiff-legged, with stabbing pains shooting through his back, was preferable to crawling through the low tunnels.

Nor was there anything private about his ordeal. There were plenty of folks in the audience. Any chamber large enough to hold large numbers of Selonians was doing exactly that. There were dozens of them, hundreds of them, everywhere, busily working on bits of machinery Han could not quite identify, carrying things back and forth, talking and arguing and shouting and laughing in both the standard Selonian Han had learned and the whistles-and-hoots language he had first heard in the tunnel. It was plainly time to start wondering just how standard "standard" Selonian was.

Everywhere he went, they all watched him, all eyes locked on the strange apparition from the upper world. In the more crowded chambers, they did their best to steer clear of him—whether out of fear or disgust or respect, or simply because they were ordered to do so, he had no idea. Once or twice he was jostled as some Selonian on an urgent errand failed to look where he was going.

Han didn't mind that so much. It made him feel as if he were really there. He even almost didn't mind the staring from all corners. He could sympathize with it. After all, Han was, if anyone ever had been, a born tourist. Even in the midst of his misery, he was determinedly struggling to see all he could see, knowing full well what a rare privilege it was.

He even caught a glimpse of the other castes, the breeder males and females—or at least he thought he did. In one large chamber he passed through, he saw four or five larger, plumper-looking Selonians off to one side, and they seemed to have a great number of attendants fussing over them. And yet there was nothing the least bit servile about the attention being paid to the plump Selonians. Instead, there was something impersonal and cold-bloodedly efficient about it all. Han saw one attendant bring a plate of food to the breeders—but there was no ceremony about it, nothing at all fancy about the meal. Somehow it looked more like a farmer bringing feed to the cattle, rather than a servant catering to royalty.

He gradually became aware of a faint, spicy scent in the tunnels, not unpleasant, but sharp and tangy. It was the fragrance of many Selonians together in one place. Han found it soothing, comforting somehow.

Han had never had the slightest idea that the Selonian tunnels were so extensive. Growing up, he had had some vague notion that the Selonians liked to live underground, but somehow that had always been presented as some part of the primitive past, something that had happened long ago. Modern, urban, civilized Selonians didn't live in tunnels under the ground. They lived in nice, normal houses and apartments, the way humans did, the *normal* way.

It was beginning to sink in with Han that the Selonians humans saw in the cities were but the tip of the iceberg, especially trained for the task of dealing with outsiders. And it was getting more and more obvious that they were mere window dressing, carefully trained to make humans comfortable, to make Selonians seem less alien, less strange to them. There had always been some sort of half-awareness on his part that the old ways of dens and septs and underground passages still lived on, but he had always thought that such things were vestiges of the past, unimportant in the modern day of Selonian life. He was beginning to understand that it was the modern ways that were unimportant.

He was seeing things that he never knew existed, and yet, clearly, they had been part of the world he had grown up on, part of the world he called home. Just how blind had he been, had all humans on Corellia been, to the true nature of Selonian culture? And what of the Drall? Could it be that they had secrets just as deep?

Han had gotten that far in his thinking when they came out of a particularly tight crawlway tunnel and into a huge chamber, easily twice the size of anything Han had seen so far. It was something close to the size of an underground town, and a crowded one at that. There was something frantic in the air of the place—quite literally so. That spicy aroma of many Selonians was there again, stronger than ever. There was a strange bite to the scent, a tang of what could only be fear-sweat.

Han followed Dracmus out of the tiny side tunnel and climbed painfully to his feet. It seemed as if every square centimeter of his body had its own special ache or sore or twinge. He still hadn't gotten completely over the pasting Dracmus had given him for Thrackan's amusement. That had only been a few days ago, and yet somehow it seemed a half a lifetime at least. Those injuries would have been hard enough to get over without the further punishment of the trip through the Selonian tunnels. It was something of a wonder he could even move at all. But in spite of all, it was, undeniably, a pleasure to stand up straight again. He pulled himself fully erect—and suddenly changed his mind as shooting pains stabbed down his back. It was not so much of a pleasure after all.

But there was more going on here than an aching back. He looked around himself. He noticed that there seemed to be a number of badly injured Selonians in the throng, several of them laid out on stretchers. Some wore bloody bandages, and under the general hubbub of crowd noises, Han could hear a high-pitched keening, a sound of pain and fear, someone unseen crying out, a cry that was past all hope of help or relief, a mourning

call of loss and sorrow. Even those who seemed unin-
jured looked lost, afraid, gaunt, shell-shocked.

"Who are they?" Han asked.

"Refugees," Dracmus said, her voice hard-edged and
angry. No matter what orders she had about answering
questions, she could not restrain herself. "Refugees of
the making of your cousin Sal-Solo and his Human
League. Their surface homes burned, gas bombs in their
tunnels. Chased and hunted and shot at. The main transit ways clogged with more of them, and all other transit
must take the backways, the small tunnels.

"We fought back when we could, but the Human
League had numbers and weapons and surprise. So we
flee, we retreat, we hide. Supplies ruined or far away,
and there is nothing we can use to help them. No bandages, no medicine, not even any food. We can get none
of these, because the Human League blocks our access.
My people suffer because Thrackan Sal-Solo, a human
of your blood, says they must, and for no reason other."

Han wanted to protest, to say again that it was not his
fault, that Thrackan was Han's enemy as much as
Dracmus's. But then he realized that it was not true.
Thrackan Sal-Solo was never going to hunt down all the
members of Han's family for the crime of being human,
or demand they all be ejected from the planet of their
birth to make room for another race.

Han tried to look at the situation the way Dracmus
did. Selonian family relationships were irrevocable in
ways human relationships were not. You were born into
your sept, your clan, and there was no way out—or even
any thought that there could be any way out. You were
part of the whole in ways that humans never were. The
clan, the sept, the den moved as one. A sept-sister
would no more act against the sept than a person's hand
would try to wrap itself around its owner's neck and
strangle her. In Selonian eyes, Han was a part of the
whole of his cousin's family. If the misery before him

was the treatment a member of his family offered to Selonians, Han was starting to understand why the Selonians distrusted him so much.

Actually, the only surprising thing was that they had not killed him yet. He just hoped the operative word wasn't "yet."

"Come, honored Solo," said Dracmus. "We must keep moving. The end is near, but time is short."

The end is near? There was a phrase with unpleasant connotations. Han didn't even dare ask what it meant. The other statements, though— "Moving to where?" Han asked as he struggled forward. Even standing still for that short a time had left him stiff and tired. "Time is short until what?"

The expression on her face was unreadable, even for a Selonian. "I have said too much already," she replied. "Come now."

Han stumbled forward, following Dracmus through the tumult of the huge chamber.

*   *   *

Luke Skywalker stepped into the courtyard gardens of Gaeriel Captison's home, and sat quietly on the bench that faced the marker-stone. Beneath it, as he had learned, were the ashes of Pter Thanas, Gaeriel's dead husband. It was hard for him not to look at that stone, hard to avoid thinking about that man it remembered. A good man, and by all accounts, a good husband for Gaeriel.

But that husband had not been Luke Skywalker. There. There it was. That was the one thing he had found hardest to face. Another man had been to her what he might have been, perhaps would have been if fate had molded events differently.

But events had been as they were. There was nothing to be done about it. Now, on the morning of leave-taking, it was time to accept things as they were, and move on. The Corellian Sector, his sister, his family, were in trouble. He had to worry about them, not about might-have-beens.

Leaving the past behind, however, would not be quite so easy. Not this morning. He heard a sound behind him, stood up, and turned around. There they were, coming down the rear stairs. Gaeriel. Gaeriel and her daughter, Malinza.

The little girl had luxuriant black hair, and wore it in long tresses that hung down her back. She was pale-skinned with serious-looking brown eyes. Mother and child were both wearing long white robes, quite plain and undecorated. Gaeriel was coming down the stairs at a slow, dignified pace, but Malinza was making a game of it, hopping down the stairs one step at a time, and singing a little song to herself.

Luke walked toward them and met them at the bottom of the stairs. "Good morning, Luke," said Gaeriel. "It's good of you to come. I wanted the two of you to meet."

"I wouldn't have missed it for anything," Luke said.

Gaeriel smiled. "I'm glad," she said, and turned toward her daughter. "Malinza," she said. "I want you to meet a very special friend of mine. He's going with me on my trip."

Malinza stopped singing to herself and looked up at Luke, her face very serious indeed. "Hello," she said. "Are you going along to take care of my mommy?"

Luke knelt down in front of the child. The time he had spent with Leia's children had taught him a few things. He knew that some questions needed to be turned on their side if you wanted to understand what the child was really thinking. Malinza was a little worried about who would take care of *her* while her mommy was gone. Best to try and direct the conversation to that point and reassure her as best he could. "I'm not going along to take care of her," Luke said, "but I will watch out for her. And even if your mother has to go away for a while, she'd never do it if she didn't make sure someone was here to take care of *you*."

"That's right, Malinza," Gaeriel said, kneeling down next to her daughter and giving her a pat on the shoulder. "Madame Boble will stay with you, and Lady Corwell will come by every single day to make sure everything is all right. And all your family will be here, too. *They'll* all watch out for you."

"But I want *you*, Mommy," said Malinza.

"I know you do, sweetheart. It would break my heart if you didn't. But sometimes grown-ups have to do things they don't want to do. I don't want to leave, but I have to. Luke's friends helped us an awful lot, a long time ago. Now *they* need help, and we have to pay them back."

Malinza looked at Luke, her face solemn. "Do you really need my mommy to help you?" she asked.

Luke thought of his own niece and nephews, cut off behind the Corellian interdiction field, missing in action aboard the *Millennium Falcon*. Without Gaeriel, they would have no Bakuran fleet. And without the Bakuran fleet, there would be no rescue of Corellia. "Yes," he said. "We really do need her help."

Malinza thought for a moment, and then nodded. "All right," she said, her voice very serious. "But you watch out for her, like you promised."

"I will," said Luke. "I will."

*   *   *

The *Gentleman Caller* moved in toward Corellia at a leisurely pace, crawling along at sublight speeds on a course that would get the ship to the planet—eventually.

Tendra Risant checked the radionic transmitter for

the hundredth time. It *seemed* to be working. All the indicator lights were showing green, and it was drawing as much power as it was supposed to, and the message repeater was definitely sending out her hailing call over and over again. She had checked that enough times. "Tendra to Lando," her voice said from the speaker. "Please respond on pre-assigned frequency." Pause. "Tendra to Lando. Please respond on pre-assigned frequency." Pause. "Tendra to Lando. Please respond on pre-assigned frequency. . . ." Then a ten-second pause, and then the same message over again, ad infinitum.

But it had been days now, and there had been no response. Lando had told her that the radionic unit aboard the *Lady Luck* was always on, always scanning for messages. So why hadn't he answered yet? Was he even in-system? Was he away from the *Lady Luck*? Was he dead? Or was it that some component that cost a tenth of a credit had failed, some gizmo inside her transmitter or his receiver? Maybe Lando was sending a reply back, over and over again, and wondering why *she* did not respond. But the receiver seemed to be working just fine as well. At least, when she turned the volume gain up all the way, she got a low hissing sound, which had to be static from natural sources. If the unit could pick up static, surely it could pick up a signal. Or did that necessarily follow? Tendra realized she did not know anywhere near enough about radionics.

But she was getting to be a Galaxy-class expert on waiting. And worrying.

She turned up the gain on the transmitter-monitor again, just to be sure that it was still working. "Tendra to Lando. Please respond on pre-assigned frequency. Tendra to Lando. Please respond on pre-assigned frequency. Tendra to Lando. Please respond on pre-assigned frequency. . . ."

CHAPTER THIRTEEN

Yggyn's Choice

"Time's up," Mara said to Leia. "It's time to decide."

Mara sat at the pilot's station of the *Jade's Fire,* looking calmly at Leia. Leia, seated at the navigator's station, returned her gaze with an expression steadier than her emotional state. "So it is," she agreed. "Time to decide."

Once she had shaken their initial pursuit, Mara had simply left the *Jade's Fire* into a random orbit of the star Corell, letting the craft drift where she might, running under minimum power on all systems. The idea was that a random, unpowered flight pattern would give them the best chance of escaping detection from whoever might try and come after them. Their course was an unstable one; the ship would spiral into Corell in a few months' time if left to her own devices.

Not that any such thing would happen. They could change course at any time. The problem was, they had to decide which course to follow. They had helped each other escape, but neither had had any clear plan of action beyond that. They had attempted to come up with a plan just after their escape, but neither of them was in any shape to do so. The discussion had degenerated into pointless bickering. It had become clear in very short order that they were too tired to decide anything. Both women had needed at least a little time to recover from their injuries and rest up, and it seemed as if there was no burning need for an immediate choice in any event. They had agreed on thirty hours' rest and recuperation before coming to a final decision.

The time to choose a destination and a plan had come, but Leia had a very strong hunch doing so was not going to be easy. "I take it," said Leia, "that you still want to head back to Corellia."

"Yes, I do," said Mara. "That's where it's all going on. Whatever happens in this system is going to be decided there."

"Why should that be of any importance to you?" Leia asked. "Why should you care who's up and who's down in this planetary system? You're not a Corellian, and if you have no love for the Human League, you certainly have no more for the New Republic. Why do you want to be where things are going on? Why don't you just get out?"

"I do care what happens," Mara said. "I run a trading business, and we've made a large investment in Corellia. We've put in time and money and energy here, and it was just starting to pay off. We were just beginning to do some very promising routing through this sector. My costs went through the roof when the revolts started. I want stability so I can make a reliable profit. Stability doesn't have much to do with tinpot dictators. And even if I don't much care for your New Republic, maybe the idea of someone wiping out whole star systems full of people bothers me." Mara paused for a moment, and looked straight at Leia. "But that's not the real point of your question, is it?"

Leia rejected the impulse to deny what Mara was implying. No sense pretending when both sides could see the truth. "No," she said. "It wasn't."

"You wanted to know if I could offer up a plausible

explanation for my still being here, a motive for my behavior that wasn't suspicious. After all, the message about the starbuster came through me. You have to wonder if I'm part of the plot. Might I remind you of the reasons I have for suspecting *you* in the plot? The message itself was keyed to your personal characteristics, and the senders went out of their way to demonstrate that they could read your private cipher. Plus, that message contained data that could only have come from classified New Republic sources."

"What possible motive would I have for overthrowing the New Republic's government in the Corellian Sector?" Leia demanded.

"I have no idea," Mara replied. "On the other hand, what motive would *I* have for disrupting this system? You seem to have no trouble at all suspecting me of things without quibbling over motive. Why shouldn't I have the same luxury? Besides, I could spin a perfectly feasible scenario, where you set up some sort of plan to flush out the Human League and the other rebels, and trick them into showing themselves, with the intent of smashing them once you knew where they were. That would be a dangerous game, to say the least, and if it's what you're playing at, it has clearly gone wrong. But it's possible."

Leia smiled thinly. "Why stop there? Why not let the imagination run wild? Maybe *both* of us are involved in the plot, but the plot's so compartmented neither of us knows the other's in it. Maybe one of us, or both of us, are dupes, unknowing pawns in someone else's game. You know as well as I do that once you start playing the game of wheels within wheels and hidden plots, it's very hard to stop."

"True enough," said Mara. "Nonetheless, the point is, I can't entirely trust you or your motives any more than you can trust me or mine."

"Well, that much at least we can agree on," Leia said.

"But let's pretend we can trust each other. What do you want to do?"

Mara leaned back in her pilot's chair and stared out at the stars. "The absolutely logical thing would be to say this is not my fight and I don't wish to get killed in someone else's cross-fire. The sensible move would be to point this ship's nose straight out of the Corellian system and power up the sublight engines. It might take us a good long *while* to get out of here, but we *would* get out. And I doubt it would take as long as one might think."

"Agreed," said Leia. "They can't keep that interdiction field on forever. It's *got* to draw huge amounts of power, and it can't be easy to maintain. Even if maintaining it is no technical problem, sooner or later being isolated is going to do them more harm than good. Politically, economically, and so on."

"Right," said Mara. "That's the way I see it. Even so, I don't want to leave, no matter how sensible it might be. Someone has caused me a lot of trouble, and I want to return the favor. Besides, we also have to bear in mind that the moment we relight the sublight engines, and the longer we have them on, the higher the odds we will be detected and shot down."

"You know this ship and how detectable she is," Leia said. "Can that help us decide? Is there one destination that we can get to with the lowest odds of being spotted?"

"Nice thought," Mara said, "but it doesn't get anywhere. We're still close enough to Corellia that we'd barely have to light our engines to get there. If we did a night-side approach over the oceans, and treetop flying to get to where we wanted to be, the odds on spotting us would be very low. Selonia and the Double Worlds, Talus and Tralus, are just about at their point of closest approach to each other. They're furthest from here, on the opposite side of the sun. On the other hand, we

would have the sun behind us, making it harder for anyone watching from Corellia or Selonia or the Doubles to
detect us. Drall is closer, making for a shorter flight, but
we wouldn't have the sun's glare to hide in. However,
my best information is that Drall has the least advanced
spacecraft detection net of any of the planets. It all
comes out about even."

"All right, then," Leia said. "You don't want to leave
the system, and the odds of reaching any one of the
plausible destinations are about the same as any of the
others, but you want to go to Corellia, on the grounds of
it being the center of the crisis. I think returning would
be suicidal. They'll be hunting for us, and they'll be mad
at us. It's the one place where we're certain to get a
hostile reception by the folks in charge."

"And you want to go to Drall, because that is most
likely where your children are, right?" Mara asked.

"Yes I do. The only native Corellian onboard the *Millennium Falcon* was a Drall. He'd direct the ship to the
place he knew best, where he could keep the children
safest."

"And I say that's pointless," Mara said. "We don't
know anything about what's happening on the other
planets, but we have to assume things are pretty bad. If
Ebrihim does have your children there, he has them in
hiding, for their own safety as well as his own. And *we'd*
have to go into hiding as well—not easy when there are
only a few hundred humans on the planet. How are we
supposed to stay hidden, find another group who is hidden, and meet up with them?"

"Through the Force," Leia said. "Get me anywhere
near that planet, and I'd be able to sense their location.
I know it."

"Which would do us a lot of good if they are under
lock and key. Even if we do manage to find them, what
do you do *then*? Pat your children on the head and hide
with them? Would a human ship coming in make them

safer or put them in more danger? I'd guess danger, if things are as unsettled there as on Corellia. And what do *I* do? Drall is a sleepy backwater. For that matter, what would *you* do there? We're not going to be able to accomplish anything on Drall."

Leia said nothing at first. Mara's arguments made a little too much sense. Finding her children would make her feel better, but it would not improve the situation. She could only truly make them safe by putting an end to this crisis. "I can't abandon my children," she said to Mara.

"No one's asking you to. Look, think it through. If they are alive and well and on Drall, they have Chewbacca and the *Millennium Falcon* and their Drallish tutor and all of his contacts. All that's working to protect them. Would getting to them make them safer— or just make you feel better?"

Leia frowned. "All right," she admitted. "Maybe I shouldn't go to them—yet. But I am not going to stay away from them one minute longer than I have to." She paused for a moment. "It's obvious," she said, "that we have reached a stalemate. It seems to me that we could come up with good arguments against every single possible course of action."

"And how can one of us persuade the other when neither trusts the other's arguments?" Mara asked. "I could be trying to talk you into a trap, or vice versa." Mara was silent for a moment. Then her eyes seemed to light up, and she turned toward Leia. "I just thought of something," she said. "Are you familiar with the concept of a Yggyn compromise? It's broken the logjam in more than one trade negotiation."

Leia smiled. "I know it well. If neither party can accept the other's proposal, both agree to a third alternative. I want Drall. You want Corellia. Under Yggyn rules, we'd head to Selonia."

Mara shrugged. "I was thinking of Talus and Tralus,

but Selonia will do. We need someplace to go, and at least on Selonia there's some chance of a friendly reception. Anything beats sitting here arguing until we crash into the sun."

"Very well, then," Leia said, taking a deep breath and looking out into the starry darkness. "Very well. We go to Selonia."

*   *   *

"I still wish we had brought the *Millennium Falcon*," Q9 said. "This hovercar cannot defend itself."

"*And* it's awfully crowded in here," Anakin complained from the rear seat. "When are we going to get there?"

"Uh-oh," said Jaina, sitting in the front. "Jacen, get his mind on something else quick, or you're going to hear that question about a zillion more times."

The Duchess Marcha was sitting in the hovercar's front seat, wedged in between Jaina and Chewbacca, who was doing the flying. She had never been quite so close to a Wookiee before, and she was not finding it to be the most relaxing of experiences. But she couldn't understand why Jaina was so agitated by her little brother's question. "Can't you just tell him the answer and then ask him to be quiet?" she asked Jaina in a low voice. She was quite baffled by the skills required to manage a small human child. Besides which, she wouldn't mind knowing how long it would be herself. It was not easy getting information out of Chewbacca.

"Doesn't work that way," Jaina whispered back. "Answering would just get him focused on the question, and he'd ask, 'When are we going to get there *now*?' two minutes from now. And two minutes after that, and after that."

"I see," said Aunt Marcha, though that was a bald-faced lie. Such strange creatures, these humans, the children far more so than the adults. How they had ever risen to a position of prominence in Galactic affairs was quite beyond her.

But at least the older ones knew how to manage the younger one. "Anakin!" Jacen said, having found a suitable distraction. "Look down there! See? That's the Boiling Sea."

Anakin, sitting in the seat behind Jacen, next to Q9, looked down at the dark water below. "I don't see it boiling," he objected.

"It doesn't always boil," Jacen said. "Only sometimes. In the summer. But Q9 will tell you all about it."

"I will?" the droid asked.

"Yes, Q9," Ebrihim said, from his seat next to Jacen. "You will. Quietly. That is an order."

"Very well," Q9 said, clearly unenthusiastic. The droid started telling Anakin all about how, in the summer months, the temperatures below could become high enough for part of the small, landlocked sea to boil, and how the winter snows and rains cooled and replenished it. For a wonder, Anakin listened, even when Q9 got to the part about the sea being a temporary feature that would no doubt vanish in a few thousand years due to upstream erosion.

Marcha shook her head once again. Why in the stars that sort of thing should be of interest to a small boy child she had no idea, but she was grateful just the same. The trip was getting a little long, but that was to be expected, flying an evasive route at night over land and sea at something close to treetop and wave-top level. Say what one might about his social skills, she was glad they had a pilot of Chewbacca's skill on the job.

Then, at long last, Chewbacca let out a low hoot and slowed the car to a halt, bringing it to a full stationary hover about ten meters off the ground. Marcha switched on the infrared view system and peered at the screen. She zoomed in on a low hill about three kilometers away. There, glowing a ghostly green in the infrared view, was a low, boxy-looking building, sitting near the top of the hill. "That's it," she said. "Has to be. Move in, very slowly. Circle around the base of the hill until you are due south of the building. Bring us in as close to three and two tenths kilometers due south of the building as you can, but be sure you land out of sight. And I trust your running lights are off."

Chewbacca glared at her, but made no other reply.

Marcha paid no mind. She had other problems. Finding the archaeological dig had not proven to be much of a problem. Getting into it—and back out—was going to be the tricky bit. If her theories were correct, Anakin would be able to help . . .

If they could now get his mind off the Boiling Sea. Q9 was running out of information on the subject.

CHAPTER FOURTEEN

Underground Activity

For whatever reason, the passages and tunnels were getting larger as they went along. At least Han thought they were. Perhaps they had simply by-passed the larger tunnels in the previous sector, or they had been shut down by the refugee flow. Or maybe Selonians in this part of the world preferred walking erect. The tunnels here were cool, dry, and slightly musty like all the others, lit with the same dark, lurid red. The tunnel floors and walls were as squared off and smoothed out as the ones they had left behind—but these tunnels were bigger, and much less crowded.

Whatever the reasons for the change, Han was grateful for it. A few minutes of walking fully upright did wonders for him, stretching out the worst of the knots in his back and his legs. It also had the added benefit that they could make better time. Han's slow progress through the crawlway tunnels had driven Dracmus to the edge of distraction. The mere fact that he now was able, more or less, to keep up with her seemed to set her much more at ease.

It did not, however, make her any more forthcoming,

so Han decided to try another tack, ask different questions. "Honored Dracmus, I know you cannot tell me where we are going or why, but can you at least tell me something—anything—about the source of your orders?"

Dracmus did not answer, did not even say she could not answer. Han took that as a sort of tacit admission he was on the right track. "Is this strictly inside your sept?" he asked, pressing the point just a trifle. "Or is it something bigger? An alliance, a group of some kind?"

"Honored Solo—please! I have the—the strongest of orders from the highest of places. You have the right to know more, to know all, but you must not, you cannot, learn it from me."

That was more than he had gotten so far, even if it wasn't much. Han thought about it as they walked along. Even if he didn't have any solid information, maybe he had enough to do some guessing. *All right,* he told himself. *They don't trust you, but they haven't killed you or left you behind. What does that say?* The answer was obvious, if hopelessly vague. The same old story. They wanted him for something. There was something he could do, something he could say, that they needed. It could be anything. Technical help, political connections, military expertise, access to some bit of knowledge he possessed without being aware of its importance. His recipe for double-strength Mutant Zombie coolers. It could be anything.

Except that couldn't be *exactly* right. If they *needed* him, they wouldn't be stringing him along in this information-free limbo. More likely they knew they *might* need him. They *might* want him. Until such time as they were sure it was worth the risk of trusting him, they would keep him on ice. That had to be it, Han told himself. They wanted him for something, but they were not sure they could trust him. Or perhaps they were not sure he would cooperate.

For that matter, Han was not sure himself. He had no idea what side they were on, or what the sides were in this fight. He wasn't even strictly certain which fight this was. Even before he was captured by the Human League, the situation in the Corellian system could have been described as the fight of each against all. There was no way of knowing how the situation had evolved— or degenerated—since then. By this time of day, Dracmus's den could be for or against practically anybody.

Han had reached that happy conclusion when it suddenly dawned on him that he could hear something off in the distance. A series of low, methodical, mechanical sounds, clicks and whirs and hums. And they were moving closer to the sounds. He started to hear voices, Selonian voices, calling to each other, and there was something in the rhythm and tone of the shouts and calls that sounded irresistibly like a construction gang at work.

Dracmus heard the sounds as well, and her step grew more lively, more eager.

Suddenly Han realized they were very near the end of their journey, or at least this part of it. He hurried along behind Dracmus, down a long ramp. Yellow-white light shone up from the lower level, and Han was astonished at how cheered he was by the mere sight of something besides the bloodred illumination of the Selonian tunnels. He stumbled eagerly toward the light and the sound.

The ramp opened out on a chamber, not of bare stone, but of metal and gleaming plastic, echoing with hurry and rush and bustle. It was a transportation hub, that much was obvious. A pocket-sized landing field stood at its center, with three small spacecraft sitting on it, maintenance crews working on them. Han looked up and saw that the ceiling of the place was a retractable dome. On the far side of the dome's base a bullet train sat on its track, waiting to depart, ready to hurtle down the rail tunnel that came through one wall of the chamber and back out another. Runcarts zipped in and out of the tunnel mouths on this errand or that. "Quite a place," was all he could think to say.

"There are many like it," Dracmus said. "It is like all the others."

That surprised Han. "But I thought that you just walked in the tunnels," he said.

"Why think that? Do you not think Selonians can build their own machines and vehicles, should we choose so to do? We are just ignorant primitives who live underground without help from our fine human friends?"

"All right, all right," Han said. "I wasn't thinking. My apologies." He looked about, and realized just how deep in he was. This place was secret, known only to the Selonians. He had no proof of that, but even so, he knew. Drall and humans did not come here, were not told of it. "Who knows about this place?" he asked. "Besides the Selonians?"

"You do," said Dracmus. "No one else."

"Exactly the answer I was hoping not to get," Han said. That *would* be the one question Dracmus would be willing to answer clearly and unequivocally. Han did not like learning secrets involuntarily. What if they decided, later on, that it was not such a good idea that he knew it? There really was only one way to make a person unlearn something. . . .

"Come now," said Dracmus. We must move on." She led him down a path from the tunnel mouth down toward the center of the transportation complex.

Han had half-expected to be put aboard one of the runcarts and brought to some local official's office in a nearby tunnel. Failing that, they were most likely putting him on the train to some place or another.

Instead, Dracmus led Han straight to the closest and

largest of the three waiting spacecraft. A spacecraft? Where the devil could they be taking him? Someplace else on Corellia, presumably, someplace far enough away that it would take too long to get to by tunnel. But where? And why?

Han took a closer look at the vehicle. He knew at a glance that it had not come out of any of the human-operated Corellian shipyards. It had to be that the Selonians had built it themselves. It was a small short-haul craft, definitely not capable of interstellar flight. It was a flattened cone shape about twenty meters high and twenty across. It was unusual in being a forward-flight-vertical craft. Most modern spacecraft were built like the *Millennium Falcon*, with the direction of forward flight horizontal to the landing jacks, with the pilot looking out the side of craft at liftoff. This bird had her forward viewports in the apex of the cone, so the pilot would be looking straight up during launch. The design was crude in many ways, but simple and effective. For one thing, the structural loading design was a lot simpler when thrust only came from one direction. The *Falcon* had to handle thrust-loads not only through the aft propulsion system, but through the landing-pad repulsors. That put a lot of stress on a vehicle—and the *Falcon* had not always been up to that stress. In any event, it was clear that the Selonians built more than their own run-carts and bullet trains.

While Han was looking over the ship, a hatch popped open about a meter and a half off the base, and a boarding ladder unfolded itself from inside the hatch and extended itself down to the ground. A peppery, energetic-looking Selonian climbed down the ladder and came over to Dracmus and Han. She grinned at Han, and gave a hissing laugh. "So this is the baldskin I've heard about," she said in Selonian that was almost too fast for Han to follow. "Not much to look at, is she?"

"A he," Dracmus said mildly. "This one is a male,

young Salculd. And he has been through many a priva-
tion, many injuries, and much difficulty. That he is here
to look at all says much about him."

Han was more than a little surprised to hear Dracmus
offer any praise of him. "Is most kind of you to saying
so, honored Dracmus," he said, in his somewhat labored
Selonian.

Salculd looked at Han with her jaw half-opened, the
Selonian equivalent of raised eyebrows. "She—he—can
speak Home Talk! Or near enough, anyway. Very well,
honored Dracmus. I will remember there is more here
than is seen." She turned toward Han. "Come along,
you."

Han looked toward Dracmus. "Salculd takes me?" he
asked in Selonian. "You come not?"

"I must consult with—certain others—before I board
the craft and we all depart. I shall join you soon. Pilot
Salculd will—watch over you—while I am away."
Dracmus hesitated a moment, then spoke in rapid Basic, clearly intending that Han would understand and
Salculd would not. "Our pilot is of an odd sept, and
Selonian pilots are often strange," she said. "She might
act odd from time to time. Pay no attention, and don't
be alarmed."

"Why don't I find that comforting?" Han said.

"I really do not know, honored Solo. I shall rejoin you
on the ship soon." Dracmus gave a shallow bow to Han,
and a deeper one to Salculd, then went on her way.

"What was that about?" Salculd asked in Selonian.

For some reason Han had already formed the impression that this Salculd was someone he could talk to.
"She warned that you are little strange," Han replied in
the same language.

"Oh, that," Salculd said. "They all think that. They
like being underground, or where they can get inside if
they need to. They don't like the idea of space, that's all.
Come on aboard, ah—what did she call you?"

"She call me Solo. Han Solo. Friend call me Han."

Salculd smiled and took the hint. "Then I'll call you Han, and you can decide how odd I am. Come on aboard."

Han followed Salculd up the boarding ladder and into the ship, looking at everything very closely. Even from the outside, there had been something home-built in the looks of the conical spacecraft, something rough-and-ready. The sight of the interior fittings only strengthened that impression. "Good ship," Han said in Selonian and stretching the truth for the sake of diplomacy. He pointed to himself. "Am pilot, have own ship. Can you show me yours?"

Salculd cocked her head to one side and looked at Han quizzically. "You're a pilot, huh? They never told me that. Sure, I'll show you around."

It was plain that Salculd didn't quite believe Han's claim to be a pilot. She wanted to test him, see if he knew what he was talking about. Han was more than glad to take up the challenge. He was willing to do anything that might give him more information. It only took a few minutes of asking the right questions, recognizing pieces of equipment, and making sympathetic noises concerning the problems of pilots everywhere—unreasonable passengers, bulky cargo, clumsy ground crew, and the like—for Han to convince Salculd of his bona fides. Once that point was established, there was no slowing Salculd down. She wanted to show Han everything, and Han did his best to be an appreciative audience.

As they ranged about the ship, it did not take Han long to realize that practically everything aboard fit into one of two categories. First, general-purpose hardware bought off the shelf, the sort of thing that was widely available as new, used, surplus, or even scrap. Things like the boarding ladder, or the pilot's chair, or the power couplings.

Second, there was the specialized gear, either modified from its original use, or purpose-built and custom-made. Everything in the second category replaced something that would be easy to trace if purchased on the open market—or the black market. The navicomputer and the boost-land repulsor units, for example, were clearly hand-built, and no one hand-built those if they did not have to.

That piece of information told him a great deal. The human-run Corellian shipyards were among the most famous in the Galaxy, and rightly so. The *Millennium Falcon*—or at least the stock freighter that had become the *Falcon* after a few thousand modifications—had been built there. The Corellian yards had churned out any number of ships of every type, from the smallest runabout to the most powerful star destroyer, for any number of clients. With the trading economy in the shape it was in, Han knew that ships—and secondhand ships more capable than this one—were cheap and easy to come by.

But why go to all the trouble and expense to build one's own vehicles, inferior to what you could get cheaper? Even chop-job Uglies would be safer and more reliable than this thing. There was really only one explanation, and Han did not like it. You built your own ships when you didn't want anyone to know what you were doing, when you wanted to stay hidden, and secret.

And that, in its turn, told Han even more about the Selonians who had him, something he had suspected for some time now.

He was in among the rebels.

Or at least, a collection of Selonians that viewed themselves as rebels. But rebelling against whom? The Human League? The New Republic Government? Or perhaps it was even some group that had opposed the Empire, and had remained in hiding, not trusting to outsiders, ever since the Empire's fall. Anything was possible. All Han had ever really learned about Selonian politics was that it was quite impenetrable to outsiders.

Well, maybe that was true, but on the other hand, it never hurt to ask—and he had learned more from Salculd in the last two hours than he had from Dracmus in the last few days.

"Honored Salculd," he asked, struggling to speak his best Selonian, "who are you all? What group is it that has me? What is going on?"

Salculd looked surprised at the question. "No one has told you this?" she asked.

"No one," Han replied.

"We are the Hunchuzuc Den. We and our den wish Selonians on Corellia to be free."

"Free of what? The New Republic? The Human League?"

"What? No! What concerns of ours are those? We wish to be free of the Overden, the central power on Selonia. All else is secondary to that fight. We use this fight as something to hide behind, a chance to act while the Overden has its own worries. And you are part of the plan."

"But what *is* my part?" Han asked. "What are you going to do with me?"

Salculd looked surprised again, and cocked her head to one side. "We take you to Selonia, of course. What did you expect?"

* * *

The hovercar drifted down out of the Drallan sky and settled in behind a convenient crag of rocks. Everyone piled out as quietly as possible. It was a cold and windy night, particularly cruel to furless humans—and the children certainly looked cold. Ebrihim sent them back into the hovercar while the two Drall adults reconnoitered, and Chewbacca got the sounder and borer ready, assisted—or perhaps harassed—by Q9. Ebrihim took the chance to get his aunt by herself and ask her a few questions. "Do you still think Anakin can find it for us?"

"I believe he can."

"Aren't you expecting rather a lot of a little boy?" Ebrihim asked.

"I am not expecting," Marcha said. "I am hoping that a being—a young being—with extraordinary abilities will be able to help us. I believe we are in the right spot, in any event. I took all of the tracking information from Q9's movements through the tunnel system on Corellia. That showed that the chamber we want was exactly three and two tenths kilometers due south of the main entrance, with the top of the chamber one hundred ninety meters below the level of the main entrance. According to our instruments, we are just that distance from the entrance on the hill—and ground level here is one hundred seventy meters below the entrance point. Unless I am very, very much mistaken, we should be able to dig twenty meters straight down into the tunnel system from here."

"Perhaps so, dearest aunt. Assuming all your guesses are right. Assuming our Drallist friends up on top of the hill are not already looking for us, and aren't about to descend upon us. Assume all goes well. Assume what you want. But after tonight, don't ever call me the reckless one in the family."

Marcha smiled. "Agreed," she said.

Just then the ground shook with an odd, low, *thud* that lasted a trifle too long to be anything natural. Chewbacca already had the sounder up and running. They went over to see how he was doing, and felt another of the deep long thuds rattle through them just as they got to where he was working.

Chewbacca was examining a datapad readout. He

nodded in satisfaction, and then moved the sounder over another few meters to take another reading.

The sounder and the borer were compact mining tools that Chewbacca had dug out of the *Millennium Falcon*'s cargo bays. The *Falcon* carried many such tools, the sort of things that came in handy to a ship that was out on its own.

The sounder consisted of a beating device which struck the earth with a series of very rapid sledge-hammer blows, and a sonic detector that used the resultant vibration patterns to develop a three-dimensional map of whatever lay beneath the surface. After getting readings from four or five different points on the surface, Chewbacca had enough data to put together a reasonably clear three-dimensional map of the subsurface. He set the sonic detector down on a convenient rock and activated its holographic display.

A complicated image appeared, showing a density map, running from blue for most dense to red for average density to yellow for least dense. Chewbacca worked the controls and made all the blue imagery go away, and then all the red. A bright bar of yellow light glowed in the display, about thirty meters away to the north.

"Excellent," said Marcha. She pointed at the display. "We dig there."

Ebrihim reached for the display controls. He brought the red and blue back in and pulled the image out to show the maximum volume of space. "I don't see anything in this imagery like the sort of chamber we're looking for," he said.

"Of course not," said Aunt Marcha. "Remember how carefully hidden the one on Corellia was. So too with this one. It's shielded from any form of detection."

"I only wish I was as sure of myself as you are, dearest aunt. Very well, friend Chewbacca. Let's see about getting that drilling machine set up."

The borer was a simple device as well—a bank of

what were in effect high-power short-range blasters set into a spinning drill head about seventy centimeters wide. The drill head spun, and the blasters fired, disintegrating the rock or soil in front of them. The drill head rode in a sleeve that it pulled along behind itself. A long flexible tube was attached to the end of the sleeve.

Chewbacca set up the drill head and the sleeve over the selected drilling point, hanging the head from a tripod-mounted winch. The tripod holding the winch unfolded to stand about three meters high. The winch helped control the descent of the drill head, and would extract it once the hole was made. Chewbacca walked the end of the exhaust tube as far downwind as possible from the drill hole and the car. He staked the end of the tube down carefully and checked his work. The vaporized, superheated rock and dirt and dust were blown out the end of the tube at high pressure, effectively sandblasting anything in its way, and Chewbacca did not want that exhaust tube giving him any surprises.

Chewbacca checked the hookup one last time, then spoke for what was, for him, a long time, a very complicated series of whoops and roars and growls. Ebrihim listened carefully and nodded. "I understand. If anyone is watching in infrared, or listening, they will be able to spot us very easily. I have seen no sign of surveillance or monitoring, but it is senseless to take needless risks. I will have the aircar at the ready, and be in the pilot's chair, prepared to take off at a moment's notice." Chewbacca nodded.

Ebrihim turned toward Marcha. "Will you come with me, my dear aunt?" he asked. "The noise is likely to be quite ferocious."

Aunt Marcha shook her head. "No," she said. "I am too eager to see what happens next."

"Very well," he said.

Ebrihim went back to the car and opened the door as quietly as possible. Sure enough, the car was full of sleeping children. Even Q9 seemed to have powered himself down. Ebrihim got into the pilot's seat, where Chewbacca had been, and readjusted it so that he was looking out the viewports rather than at the bottom of the control stick.

He waved at Chewbacca, and the Wookiee waved back—and then hit the start button.

The sound was remarkably loud, even inside the car. It was a huge roaring boom that went on and on, and then dropped an octave or two in tone and quite a few decibels in loudness as the drill head bit into the ground. Then came a sort of rattling, whirring sound as the exhaust tube bucked and swayed a time or two, and then, suddenly, with a low rumbling whoosh, a solid plume of rock dust jetted out the tube, still hot enough that it was glowing faintly red as it spewed out into the darkness.

"That thing is really kicking out some power," said Jacen as he woke up, climbing up into the front seat to get a better look.

"Sure hope no one's close enough to hear it," Jaina said, yawning.

Anakin climbed into his brother's lap and frowned thoughtfully. "Chewie's got the blaster matrix focus too tight," he announced.

"How do you know that?" Ebrihim asked, vaguely thankful that the child was sleepy enough that he wasn't tempted to go retune the thing.

"I dunno," Anakin said with a yawn. "But I guess it's working okay anyway." He looked out the window and seemed to be working something out in his head. "It ought to take about twenty minutes," he said.

CHAPTER FIFTEEN

Posture and Repulsion

A dmiral Hortel Ossilege stood on the flag deck, overlooking the bridge of the *Intruder,* the Bakuran light cruiser that would serve as his flagship on this mission. The other three ships of his command, the destroyers *Watchkeeper, Sentinel,* and *Defender,* were keeping good formation and reporting themselves at full battle readiness. All was well. He drew himself up to his full height and puffed out his chest to stand there, resplendent in his gleaming white full-dress uniform.

"You seem pleased with the situation," Luke said to the Admiral. "Glad to be back in action again?"

Ossilege was a full head shorter than Luke, and yet when the Admiral looked up at Luke, there was so much confidence, so much authority in his expression, that Luke felt very much like a schoolboy about to be firmly corrected. "No sane person who has been in 'action,' as you put it, could ever wish to experience it anew. The thrills, the excitement, do nothing at all to compensate for the terror and the bloodshed. The task of an officer in battle is, too often, to choose which of those you command should die. That sort of action I would be pleased to avoid for the rest of my life."

Ossilege hesitated a moment, and then spoke again. "And yet, honesty requires me to say more. There *is* a special excitement to it all. I cannot deny it. I am not proud of it, but I do feel it. Do you think it strange for me to feel such contradictory emotions?"

"I would never presume to question your judgment, Admiral, especially on the eve of battle. But it is a wise commander who is aware that he both loves and hates battle. The trouble is in finding the balance between the two."

"You put that well, Master Skywalker. But a commander must also remember the price of excessive caution. That, I think, is something symbolized by the names of our ships. The three destroyers were originally built to guard against the possible return of the Ssi-ruuk, and were modified to get through an interdiction field. *Watchkeeper, Sentinel, Defender.* Those are, no doubt, fine names, and they speak to the primary mission of our navy: defense against a possible return of the Ssi-ruuk. But a wholly defensive force cannot win a war. It is never enough merely to resist. One must be able to strike back."

"But here we are aboard the *Intruder,*" Luke said.

"Precisely! Exactly the right name for the first ship specifically designed to escape an interdiction field, don't you think? Bakuran strategic thinking has for too long been focused on defense. I am pleased to see our government finally taking advantage of a chance to display a more aggressive posture."

"I am less concerned about our posture, Admiral," Luke said, trying to pick his words carefully—"than I am about accomplishing our mission."

Ossilege looked at him again, smiling faintly. "That sounds something like a rebuke to me, sir. Perhaps a deserved one. But let us see how the situation develops.

You will learn, soon enough, whether I know my business or not."

Somehow, it was not an entirely comforting notion.

*   *   *

The thundering roar of the blasters gradually faded away as the drill head bit deeper, dying away into a low, muted rumble that was all but drowned out by the whooshing roar of the exhaust tube. At just about the twenty-minute mark, the drilling noise cut out abruptly and the sound from the exhaust tube growled down into silence.

"Cutoffs came on!" Anakin announced. "Must be through to the top of the tunnel. Come on!"

Ebrihim, the three children, and Q9 got out of the hovercar and went over to the top of the drill head. Chewbacca was just winching it out of the hole, moving very carefully around the still red-hot components. The winch lifted the drill head high enough that Chewbacca could peer into the hole. The children clustered around him and peeked down as well. Ebrihim joined them, and was rewarded with a blast of heat to the face, and not much else. Not too surprisingly, there was nothing much to see but a black hole. Jacen shone a light into it, and if Ebrihim tried very hard, he could almost imagine that he saw a splotch of dark brown at its bottom.

Chewbacca spent the time waiting for the hole to cool by erecting a second tripod winch next to the first one and using a complicated set of pulleys to transfer the drill head to it, getting it out of the way. That left the first tripod, with its winch, still directly over the hole.

"I suppose we'd better start down," Ebrihim said, none too enthusiastically. A nice snug burrow was one thing, but pits sunk into ancient alien tunnel systems were quite another. "Down you go, Q9."

"What? Why me? Why should I go first?"

"Because I ordered you to do so, and because you have all those built-in sensors you're so proud of. You might actually be able to detect something with them. We'll listen in over the hardwire line and you can tell us all about it."

"You just think I'm expendable, that's all."

"Don't encourage the notion," Ebrihim growled.

"What if—if I see something?"

"If you report danger, we'll pull you back out and we'll all get out of here. Now get moving."

Q9 floated over to the drill hole with obvious reluctance. The droid's low-power repulsors were nowhere near strong enough to allow him to float down into the pit. He would have to be winched down, just like everyone else. Chewbacca hooked him up to the winch and checked all the hookups one last time. The system-wide jamming had even affected extremely short-range com systems, requiring a direct physical link before two ends of a com system would work.

Ebrihim plugged a comlink into the appropriate jack on Q9 and put on a headset attached to the same line. "Off you go, then," he said to his droid, and signaled to Chewbacca. He watched as Q9-X2 was lowered into the hole.

"My infrared sensors show that the walls of the hole are still quite warm," Q9 said. "However, they are cooling rapidly, and should be cold enough not to harm your precious hides, if you should happen to work up the nerve to come down here."

"That's quite enough, Q9. One more word along those lines and I'll shut you down and let Anakin rewire you."

"I believe it would be prudent to treat that as a legitimate threat," said Q9. "Just coming out of the bottom of the drill hole. I am indeed in a tunnel very similar to what we saw on Corellia, though it is in much poorer

repair. Stop lowering me, please. I am far down enough
to use my repulsors."

Ebrihim signaled Chewbacca to quit paying out cable.
The Wookiee pulled a lever, and the winch stopped
abruptly.

"Fleep! Dowzer!" Q9's voice cried out, followed by a
series of electronic tones that cut out after a moment.

"Q9! Are you there! Q9!"

"I'mm ball richt," Q9 said. "I'm all right. That hard
stop just scrambled my voice matrix for a moment. But
tell the Wookiee not to hit the brakes so hard next time.
I am going to detach myself from the winch line and the
communication cable and have a look around. Please
stand by."

There was silence on the line for a minute or two, and
then a click as Q9 plugged himself back into the communication cable. "All is quiet down here," he said. "I
can detect no sound or movement or energy use. You
might as well all come down."

*   *   *

Chewie was the last of them to descend, and the drill
hole was something of a tight fit for him. He brought
himself down using a hardwired remote control for the
winch, and left the control hanging on its wire next to
the winch cable.

By the time he had reached bottom, the others had
made at least a little progress in exploring the tunnels.
These were identical in design to the Corellian ones—
big and cut out of the living rock. But the walls and
floors of these tunnels were cracked and broken, and
there were signs that the tunnel had flooded repeatedly
over the years. The thin layer of dust over everything in
the Corellian tunnels was a thick, grimy layer of mud
here. Nor were there any lights functional here. The
group had to rely on their handlights in the otherwise

absolute darkness. Q9 extruded a pair of floodlights from his topside dome. One he directed at the ceiling to provide some sort of general lighting. The other he aimed through the direction of his forward travel.

The tunnel was full of looming shadows and weirdly lit figures that appeared in and vanished from the beams of the handlights. The tunnel was cold and dank, with a clammy feel to the air.

Ebrihim had worried that the children might be afraid in the dark forbidding tunnels, but he soon realized that he had underestimated them once again. They were clearly used to dealing with odd circumstances.

There was another bit of good news that quickly became apparent—the Drallists were unlikely to find this particular piece of tunnel anytime soon. An underground subsidence, many years before, had collapsed the main tunnel back toward the main entrance. In all probability, it wasn't the only such cave-in. Maybe their backs would be safe.

On the other hand, Ebrihim reflected, the Drallists could drill a vertical hole just as well as anyone else. It would be best not to let their guard down.

Ebrihim tried to stay out of the way while people got organized. There seemed to be enough going on without his adding to the party. Chewbacca was checking the winch gear to make sure they could get back out, Aunt Marcha had wandered ahead down the tunnel, and Q9 was hovering about, generally getting in the way. Meantime, the two older children were doing what they could to get Anakin on the job, encouraging him to reach out with his ability in the Force and see if he could find anything like the whatever-it-was he had detected in the Corellian tunnels.

"I can *sort* of feel it," Anakin said, a bit doubtfully. He reached out his hand and seemed to be trying to catch something floating in the air. "Not as strong as it was the other place. Not sharp. Just sort of floating there. Like it got broke. Maybe when the roof fell in back there, something gone torn up."

"Try, Anakin," said Jacen. "Try."

Anakin shrugged helplessly. "I *am* trying," he said. "But it's just not *strong* enough."

"Excuse me," said Q9. "Perhaps I can be of help. Your Grace, you believe that the entrance to this chamber will be in exactly the same position relative to the entrance as the one on Corellia?"

"That is correct."

"Then I can use my inertial tracking data to lead us to the proper coordinates. My best estimate is that we still have some way to go, and are probably not in the right cross-corridor. However, I should be able to get us within thirty meters of the correct point."

Anakin nodded eagerly. "Get me that close, and I can find it!"

"Then allow me to lead the way," Q9 said, the pride in his voice plainly apparent.

The droid set the rest of the group a fairly brisk pace, especially considering that none of the others had the benefit of repulsor skirts and had to contend with the increasingly uneven floors and the mud slides. *How long had these tunnels been here, anyway?* Ebrihim wondered.

The two Drall had the hardest time keeping up with the others. The children could climb over anything, and Chewbacca could walk faster than anyone else in the group could run. But the Drall had evolved from exclusively ground-dwelling animals, not brachiators like the humans and the Wookiee. Their short legs and arms, and their limited climbing ability, made negotiating the various obstacles far more difficult for them.

Q9 was getting farther ahead with every moment, the beams of his floodlights zipping along down the tunnel. Three times he stopped abruptly at cross-corridors and dove down the left side passages. Twice he came back. The third time, it would seem, he found the path he was looking for. Ebrihim and Marcha puffed along as best they could, trying to keep up. They made the left turn and came around the corner just in time to see the Wookiee and the children making a right down the next corridor. The two Drall redoubled their efforts, but they were just barely able to keep Q9 from getting still farther ahead.

The children, however, were actually closing the distance between them and Q9 as Anakin grew more eager in the chase and the other two children urged him on.

"Keep trying, Anakin!" Jaina shouted as her brother paused for a moment, looking a little lost. Anakin nodded, then pointed at something invisible under the floor.

"Can you feel it now?" Jacen called to his brother as he climbed over a pile of collapsed rock. "Can you?"

"Yeah!" Anakin said. "Starting to! It's there in the floor, just like in the other place. Q9! Stop! You're going too far."

The droid stopped and turned—and managed to blind everyone for a moment as his forward-view floodlight swept across their eyes. "Q9! Shut that thing off!" Ebrihim shouted, feeling irritable. He didn't like being left behind.

"I beg your pardon, Master Ebrihim," said the droid, and doused his forward-view flood. "Have you found it, Master Anakin?"

"Yeah! There!" the boy said, pointing at a blank spot on the muddy wall. "Someone lift me up and—*ooof!*" Anakin got the wind knocked out of him as Chewbacca scooped him up in his arms, but he scarcely even noticed as he squirmed with excitement. "There! There!" he called out, pointing to where he wanted to go. He pushed on a section of wall, but nothing happened. "All this *junk* on it," he muttered to himself, and clawed away a patch of the caked-on mud until he had cleared an area about fifteen centimeters square. The wall underneath still seemed pretty blank to Ebrihim, but

Anakin pressed on it again, harder this time, and a section of wall popped away, as if it were trying to open, but it got stuck with less than a finger's breadth of space clear. Anakin put his fingers around the open edge, but couldn't get it to go any farther. Finally Chewbacca simply tucked Anakin under one arm and pulled the little door open himself. Even he had to strain a bit to get it to move, but then it popped clear and came open smoothly as clots of mud and dirt rattled to the floor.

A thin layer of mud hid the interior, and Anakin eagerly scraped it off. He revealed a five-by-five grid of green buttons that flickered to life, with a purple light backlighting the buttons. Anakin frowned at the buttons and muttered to himself, "Might not be working too well. Just have to try." He punched a combination into the buttons and waited a few seconds for something to happen. Nothing did. He balled up his fist and punched the top of the keypad. The green light buttons came on more brightly, and stayed on. Anakin tried the combination again—and this time something very definitely happened.

There was a clunk and a thud and a deep, unnerving sort of rattle, and then suddenly the muddy overlayer of the wall in front of them shuddered and fell off in a heap, spattering everyone with mud and dirt. The stone wall under the mud dropped down onto the floor.

In the Corellian tunnels, the panel behind the false wall had been a gleaming silver. The panel here was tarnished and splotched. But the panel worked properly, even if it did show signs of age. A line appeared in the panel, then began to form into a seam. Suddenly there was an enormous door in the wall, and it swung open, forcing everyone to scuttle out of its way. The big door bulldozed the heaps of mud out of the way as if they weren't even there.

Behind the door was a long corridor of silverstuff, all

of it perfect and untarnished, exactly like the one on
Corellia.

Light from the corridor flooded the muddy corridor,
and everyone shut off their handlamps. Q9 powered
down his overhead light and retracted both of his lights
back into his body.

Chewbacca set Anakin down and stepped up into the
silver corridor, moving slowly and cautiously, the twins
and the other adults and the droid behind him. The
Wookiee had to lower his head in order to fit in the
corridor, which meant he had to move even more
slowly. But Anakin was in motion as soon as the
Wookiee put him down. He raced down the corridor
ahead of everyone else.

"Oh, boy," Jaina said to her brother. "If he falls off
the edge, Mom and Dad will kill us." The twins hurried
after their brother, even though there was no hope of
catching him before he got to the end.

The corridor ended in open space, with the platform
they were standing on jutting out into nothingness,
forming a rounded view ledge roughly five meters on a
side. There were no guardrails. Chewbacca was uncon-
cerned by the sheer drop. He went right over to the
edge and looked down. The others stayed bunched up,
close to the center of the platform.

The cavern was an exact duplicate of the one hidden
away on Corellia. It was a sharply angled cone about a
half-kilometer tall, all the surfaces made of the same
silvery metal—if it *was* a metal.

The children and Q9 had been forced to leave the
huge chamber on Corellia almost the moment they
found it, for fear of leading the Human League to it.
There had been no chance to examine it closely or explore it. This time, there was the chance—but no one
quite knew how to proceed. The obvious thing to do was
to get to the base of the chamber, but short of jumping
over the edge, there seemed to be no way to accomplish

it. Ebrihim was on the verge of asking if they could do something with the winch when events overtook him. The viewing platform started *moving,* sidling up the side of the cone toward its apex. It was enough to startle even Chewbacca, who leapt back toward the center of the platform as he spun about to see what had happened.

Ebrihim turned around at the same moment as the others, and everyone was rooted to the spot by a terrifying sight. Anakin had found another concealed keypad, this one set into the surface of the platform. He was kneeling over it, punching in commands. As they watched, the platform surface under the keypad extruded itself upward to form a control station about a meter off the ground. The keypad canted itself down a bit to be easier to reach. Anakin got to his feet and punched in a rapid series of commands. The platform stopped, then moved sideways. It seemed as if it were still attached to the wall of the chamber, but how he could not tell. The two simply flowed into each other.

Just below their present position, and off to one side, they could see the opening of the corridor they had come down. They heard a low solid boom coming from the corridor, and Ebrihim realized that the outer door to the tunnel system had just closed itself.

Then the silver walls of the cone puckered in around the corridor opening, irising in to seal it off, until it shrank away and vanished altogether. Almost immediately, the platform started moving again, sliding smoothly and perfectly and impossibly up the side of the conical chamber.

"Anakin!" Aunt Marcha shouted. "What on Drall are you doing! Stop this platform at once!"

But Anakin did not reply, or even seem to be aware of her existence. He was completely focused on the keypad in front of him. Ebrihim made a move toward him, to try to stop him, but Jacen held up a warning hand.

"Don't!" he cried. "Whatever he's doing, he's doing it, and doing it right. If you try and interrupt him, and he gets confused and pushes the wrong button . . ."

Ebrihim saw Jacen's point. What if he accidentally pushed a button that made the platform vanish altogether? Up and up they went, the far sides of the cone coming closer and closer, more and more of the view downward getting cut off—though not even Chewbacca was too eager to look down any more.

They were approaching the apex of the cone. "We are going to be mashed flat in a moment," Q9 announced in a calm, conversational tone. The platform moved closer, and closer, and closer to the apex—and then, perhaps twenty meters short of the top, it stopped.

And something happened to the top of the cone. It shimmered, and its surface rippled and wiggled, until it settled down to a regular series of upward pulses. They could hear the sound of something big and hard smashing into rock, over and over again.

"It's like it was *pushing*," Jaina said. "As if it was trying to get—"

And with a sudden, final, thunderous roar, the pulsating point of the cone rammed upward, and broke free, slamming tons of rock and soil out of the way. Suddenly they could see the night sky.

Loose rock and debris fell down into the chamber, but a strange flicker of—of *power;* there was no clearer way to describe it—swept past the platform they stood on, and grabbed at the debris, and threw it back upwards, out of the hole, up into the night.

All was quite abruptly quiet and still. Where the apex of the cone had been, there was now a perfect cylinder, about thirty meters across.

Anakin pushed another button, and the platform moved upward again, growing wider as it rose until the sides of the platform merged with the sides of the cylinder, and the platform moved straight up, toward the night.

When it reached the surface, it stopped. They were standing in the dark on a silver disk thirty meters across on the surface of Drall, looking up at a cold night sky pocked with stars, Talus and Tralus visible near the horizon. Ebrihim could see the hovercar, about a kilometer or so away, visible by an interior light.

"Anakin," the Duchess asked, in a sort of half-strangled attempt at a casual tone of voice, "can you make it go back down? Can you make it go up and down whenever you like?"

"Sure!" said Anakin. "All I have to do is—"

"No!" Marcha cried, before Anakin could reach for the controls. "Not now. Not just yet. But I think we need to stay here, inside the chamber, set up camp. We need to study this place, but we need to remain concealed as well. If we go in and out of it, we are sure to be spotted, and we can't risk that. We need to study this place, master it, and keep the wrong sort of people from getting near it."

"What *is* this place?" Ebrihim asked. "What does it do? Who built it, and when, and why?"

"I can answer *some* of those questions, nephew, and I expect you could do the same, if you gave it a bit of thought. You saw how it shoved those rocks back up as they fell. That confirmed what I suspected. This place is a repulsor, a planet-sized repulsor, powerful enough to move the whole world of Drall. It *did* move the world of Drall, once, long ago."

"What?" Ebrihim said. "It shoved some rocks out of the way. How could it move a planet?"

"Easily," she said. "You saw a giant swat at a gnat. Does that mean the giant is not able to do more? I knew from the first moment that I saw the images from the Corellian chamber that it had to be a repulsor. The configuration of forms is identical to the earlier Drallish repulsors, albeit scaled up tremendously."

"But I don't get it," Jacen objected. "What do you mean, the repulsors moved the planet? Move it from where?"

"Another star system. Scientists have argued for generations about the theory that the Corellia planetary system could not have formed naturally, that someone must have moved all these planets here from elsewhere. Well, here, at last, is the proof. We are standing on the roof of the device that propelled this world from—from wherever it came from, who knows how long ago? We know there is an identical device on Corellia. There must also be identical installations on Selonia and Talus and Tralus. All the worlds were brought here, so long ago it was forgotten when we began our civilization, at the dawn of the New Republic. As to who, and why, I have no idea." She shook her head thoughtfully. "And we Drall thought we knew our past."

"But why has everyone been searching like crazy for these things?" Jacen said. "It's interesting and important, but why would guys like the Drallists and the Human League be looking for ancient machines? They don't care about that kind of stuff."

"No," agreed the Duchess, "but they do care about weapons. A repulsor this size could do any amount of damage. A repulsor that can move a planet can also move a spacecraft—or smash it to pieces. It is a massively powerful defensive weapon. With a planetary repulsor operational, a planet could hold off any conceivable attack."

"That's all very well, Aunt Marcha," Ebrihim said tartly, "but there is no threat of such attack—or wasn't before the current troubles. Besides, all the planets had perfectly good defenses beforehand. I can't believe there's all this fuss over a defensive weapon. The planetary repulsors would be nice to have as weapons, but not so vital or urgent that they would be worth all the trouble that's been taken to dig them up."

"You may well be right, nephew, but we must argue that point at a later time. Right now I suggest that we leave Q9 here to watch this entrance while the rest of us go to the hovercar and warm up before we get back to work on the repulsor."

"But what do you plan to do with it, besides keeping the bad guys from getting it?" Anakin asked.

The Duchess of Mastigophorous shook her head, a worried look on her face. "If I knew, my dear, I would tell you."

CHAPTER SIXTEEN

Arriving Signals

" Thirty seconds to projected edge of interdiction field," the tactics officer reported, her voice echoing through every compartment of the *Intruder.* The moment had come, and they were exactly as ready as they were ever going to be. The crews of all four ships were strapped in and ready for what was bound to be a rough ride. "Twenty-five seconds."

Luke looked down on the bridge from the glassed-in confines of the flag deck that looked down on the bridge proper. Luke and all his companions were there, strapped into their seats and ready for action. Belindi Kalenda, Lando, Gaeriel, Artoo, and Threepio. And Ossilege, of course, along with his staff officers.

The bridge down below was a fairly standard arrangement, borrowing as much from Imperial ship design as anything else. There was a central raised walkway, with the various control stations in sunken trenchlike operations centers that lined the perimeter of the bridge.

Luke glanced over at Lando and grinned. "Let's see if we can make it all the way in this time," he said.

Lando smiled back. "Absolutely," he said. "I don't like getting doors slammed in my face."

"Twenty seconds."

"I don't know why they bothered with the countdown

clock," Lando said. "That's just a best-guess estimate of the edge of the field. It's bound to be off."

"It never hurts to give the crew something to focus on," said Admiral Ossilege. "And it makes it a great deal easier to coordinate between the four ships."

"Fifteen seconds."

"I quite agree with Captain Calrissian," Threepio volunteered. "I've always found this sort of thing terrifically disturbing."

"Threepio, pipe down," Lando said. "And I don't ever want to hear you agreeing with me again. Is that understood?"

"But, Captain Calrissian—"

Artoo cut Threepio off with a rude noise.

"Well, I never!" Threepio said. "Such language! Artoo, you ought to be ashamed of yourself."

"Ten seconds."

Luke looked over to the tactical display, showing the colored dots of the four ships moving toward the dotted blue line of the field's estimated limit. Then he turned back to the forward viewport, determined to see the actual moment of the *Intruder*'s impact on the interdiction field.

"Five seconds."

"Four."

"Three."

"Two."

"One."

"Zero."

Nothing happened, but then, Luke hadn't really expected it to. He looked over to Lando, and Lando shrugged. The two of them had done the best they could to measure the field using the *Lady Luck*'s instruments, but they knew better than anyone how rough and ready those measurements had been. It was no surprise at all that they were off by a substantial margin.

"Plus two seconds."

"Plus three."

Lando looked toward Luke. "Hey, who knows?" he asked. "Maybe they dropped the field. Maybe we can do this the easy—"

KA-RAM! Luke was slammed forward into his restraint harness, and thrown to one side at the same time. The forward viewport was suddenly a blaze of surging light, reds and oranges slashing down as star lines flared into view and then vanished again.

"WE ARE IN THE INTERDICTION FIELD!" the tactics officer shouted over the sudden din of hooting alarms and emergency systems. *"MAINTAINING STATIC HYPERSPACE BUBBLE. FIRST STATIC BUBBLE GENERATOR DECAYING AT EXPECTED RATE. COLLAPSE IMMINENT—"*

BLAM! The whole ship bucked and shuddered as the first bubble generator blew out and the second cut in. The main lighting died for a moment, but kicked back in before the emergency systems had a chance to come on. The shaking and shuddering got worse, moment by moment, and Luke heard the far-off crash of something slamming into a bulkhead on a lower deck.

BLAMM! The second generator blew, and the third snapped on, more abruptly than the first two. An overhead lighting fixture overloaded and blew out, throwing a shower of sparks across the flag deck. One spark managed to start a fire on the deck carpet, but Artoo had his built-in extinguisher out and on before Luke could even call out a warning.

BA-LAAMM! The third generator blew, and the fourth cut in. "Maintaining hyperspace bubble!" the tactics officer called out, the noise level down enough that she did not have to shout quite so loud. "Losing hyperspace momentum at rate inside projections. Projecting virtual full stop relative to interdiction field in thirty seconds."

"If we hold together that long!" Lando shouted.

There was another crash somewhere belowdecks, as if to emphasize his point.

BAA-LAAMMM! There was no doubt about it. Each bounce in and out of hyperspace was a bit slower—but a bit less violent—than the one before it. They were through the worst of it. Now if only the ship could hold together for whatever punishment was yet to come—

WHAMMM! The shock was the hardest yet, and suddenly the ship's artificial gravity failed, just as the lights died again. The ship began to tumble, end over end, as new alarms began to blare and honk. The red emergency lights came on, revealing a scene of chaos. Two or three bridge officers had been thrown clear of their stations, and were flailing about in midair, struggling to grab hold of something, anything, and hang on.

Dozens of small objects had been thrown loose by the impact, and they were caroming about the interior of the bridge. A similar cloud of debris filled the flag deck. A command station down below on the bridge sparked and flared, throwing lurid shadows in the red-lit gloom.

"Main power coupling off-line!" the tactics officer announced. "We have lost positive ship control, but hyperspace bubble is holding."

Ossilege punched the com key that linked him to the ship's master. "Captain Nisewarner! Cut the hyperspace sustainer! Drop us into normal space at once."

"At once, sir," Semmac's voice replied. A moment later, a long, rumbling *thud,* almost below the threshold of hearing, a sound more felt than heard, rolled across the ship. The star lines flared almost halfheartedly to life before dying out, leaving the stars of Corellia gently pinwheeling as the *Intruder* tumbled her stately way across the sky.

"Fleet status," Ossilege ordered, his eyes staring out into the sky.

One of the flag-deck technicians checked his displays, listened on his headphones for a moment, and then reported, "*Defender* and *Sentinel* have just dropped out of hyperspace in approximate formation with us, within projected parameters. *Sentinel* reporting only minor damage, *Defender* reports all boards green. As of yet, we have no track on *Watchkeeper.*"

"What is the *Intruder*'s location?" Ossilege asked, still watching the viewports.

"No navigational fix as yet, sir. Stand by, data coming in."

The main lights suddenly cut back in, and an automated voice boomed out, "*Warning. Warning.* Artificial gravity resumes in thirty seconds. We will ramp up from zero to one hundred percent of full standard gravity over a twenty-second period. Stand by for resumption of artificial gravity."

The bridge officers who had been thrown into midair had all managed to find handholds by this time and were scrambling across the overhead bulkheads to whatever ladders or guide wires they could find. The gravitics came on again with a low hum that vanished into the subsonic almost at once. The debris caught in midair started floating downward, thudding and clattering to the deck as weight returned.

The stars stopped pinwheeling past the viewports as the navigation crew regained attitude control. Luke could see one of the destroyers—the *Defender,* it looked like—come into view as it took up station keeping.

"We now have a solid navigational fix," the flag-deck technician announced. "We are off projected course line by approximately ten million kilometers, and we are seventy-two hours from Selonia at flank speed."

"Are we capable of flank speed at this time?" Ossilege asked.

"Damage assessment still coming in, sir. Engineer reports maximum advisable acceleration is one third flank. It was a pretty rough ride. Stand by. Sir, the *Watchkeeper* has just dropped out of hyperspace. Attempting to plot a navigational fix on the *Watchkeeper*. We are not receiving any com- or data-link from *Watchkeeper*. Power emissions from *Watchkeeper* below normal minimums. She is tumbling badly, sir."

"Tried to ride the hyperdrive sustainer a little too long, it would appear. Very well," said Ossilege. "My compliments to the masters of *Intruder, Defender,* and *Sentinel.* Use laser visual signaling to order ships to get under way and rendezvous at *Watchkeeper.* She's the furthest toward the inner system, and we may need to render aid. Inform me of any change in status of any ship."

"Very well, sir."

Ossilege turned to Luke and Lando. "Well," he said, "it would seem we came through that in reasonably good shape. And I expect our friends on Corellia will be more than a bit surprised to see us pop out of hyperspace a mere three days out from the inner system. I wonder if they will be in any position to respond in time?"

*   *   *

R2-D2 was running at capacity. There was so much to do, so many demands on his attention. There was only so much one droid could do. He was responsible not only for the flight-readiness of Master Luke's X-wing, but for Lando Calrissian's *Lady Luck* as well. Handling the standard diagnostics and maintenance and navigational updates on two ships at once was not, in itself, enough to present him with any great problem. His master, Luke Skywalker, also required his attendance a fair amount of the time, and negotiating for supplies, equipment, and datalinks with the Bakuran droids was extremely time consuming. It took a great deal of background effort to make everything go smoothly.

Artoo was aboard the *Lady Luck* at the moment.

Lando Calrissian's ship was safely in its lockdown point on the *Intruder*'s flight deck, right next to Luke's X-wing, in the midst of the Bakuran fighter craft. Techs and droids were swarming over all the Bakuran vehicles, making sure they had ridden out the *Intruder*'s violent arrival. The Bakurans were using at least one human tech and two droids on each fighter check-out. Artoo was left to do the same check-job on the X-wing and the *Lady Luck* by himself, and both of them were far more complex spacecraft that the Bakuran fighters. He was on his own, save for the extremely marginal assistance of Threepio.

Artoo began his checks of the navigation systems. He plugged his dataport into the main navigation sensor arrays, and noted the dorsal infrared unit was slightly out of alignment. That he could fix from here by sending commands through the dataport link. He switched over and tested the navicomputer itself. The unit passed easily, solving all of the simulated problems with high precision.

Satisfied that the navigation systems were operational, Artoo moved on to test the communications equipment. As all normal com frequencies were being jammed, rendering all the com gear useless, communication testing was at lower priority than normal, but sooner or later the jamming would be lifted. It would be prudent to at least do a cursory check.

The standard hyperwave channels all tested out normally, with no aberrations. It was impossible to do detailed checks under jamming conditions, of course, and the laser line-of-sight communications could likewise not receive a full check until the ship was out in clear space. But all the circuits seemed functional, and the com control system was operational.

"Artoo! Where are you?" Artoo could hear Threepio calling from somewhere near the *Lady*'s main hatch. Artoo elected to complete his present task before responding. He continued the com check, moving on to tests on the ship's lowest priority communications device, the radionics system.

All the radionics systems seemed functional. But there was one odd thing. In spite of the jamming, it seemed to be receiving a signal. But of course. The archaic electromagnetic-radiation signaling system could not be affected by jamming of hyperwave subspace frequencies anymore than poisoned human food could hurt a droid. There was no way for the radionics system to detect subspace signals, let alone be jammed by them.

Artoo began to examine the signal. It was repeating, over and over again. A beacon, perhaps, or a distress call.

"Artoo! Artoo! Where are you!" Threepio's voice again, closer and more insistent this time. Artoo tried to concentrate on interpreting the signal. It was quite a simple pattern in many ways, but he was not used to dealing with nondigital signaling, or with radionics. It appeared to be an analog transmission, though he could not be sure of that without—

BLANG! Threepio's hand slapped down on the top of Artoo's sensor dome. "Artoo! Look alive, will you? Master Luke wants you on the flag deck at once to record the tactics report. Stop running those redundant checks, unplug yourself, and come with me at once!"

Artoo ceased his analysis at once, disengaged from the *Lady Luck*'s data port, and hurried after Threepio. The tactical report could well provide vital data. Analysis of low-priority signals would just have to wait.

*   *   *

Han sat back in his flight chair, immensely restless. Watching Salculd do a semicompetent job of flying her ship was not doing his mood much good. Han was aboard the Selonian's nameless cone-shaped ship as it lumbered across space, taking its own sweet time about the passage to Selonia. Han was starting to lose whatever slight patience he had for the situation. They were a day and a half out from Corellia with perhaps another day's travel to go. Unfortunately, the key word in all that was "perhaps." Han was starting to believe they were never going to get anywhere.

The coneship had already suffered two propulsion failures, and Han had been drafted to perform repairs both times. What he saw of the propulsion systems in the process had not put him at his ease. It seemed the whole sublight propulsion system was held together with spit and string.

Nor had Dracmus, serving as the ship's commander, shown the best judgment. Dracmus had ordered three evasive course changes in response to what seemed to be wholly imaginary threats from the handful of craft that were braving the spaceways. Given the extremely limited capacity of the coneship's sensors, there seemed very little point to any attempt at evasive maneuver. The only ships they could detect were the ones moving very slowly and not very far away. Nor could the coneship run fast if she were attacked, and she could not shoot at all. Unless they were attacked by an overburdened spacetug, they were fair game for anyone. There was, therefore, very little point in trying to stay out of sight. Dracmus, however, was not convinced by these arguments. It was starting to sink in with Han that the Selonians might be the masters of the underworld, but they needed a little practice to get good at ship handling, to put it charitably.

Of course, there were benefits to being a passenger on a slow-moving ship. Being onboard any ship, even one this crude, meant getting off his hands and knees, meant a chance to take at least a sponge bath and rinse out his clothes—opportunities he had not had since being captured by the Human League forces. It meant a chance to rest, to recuperate, to let a full day pass without sustaining a new injury, to use the medkit to patch himself up at least a little.

Yes indeed, looked at it that way, there were benefits. Maybe he should take a little nap. He was just on the verge of closing his eyes when the alarms blew. He was halfway out of his restraint harness, about to rush to battle stations, when it dawned on him that he had no battle station on this boat.

Dracmus materialized from her stateroom. "What is it?" she called to Salculd.

Salculd was at her pilot's station, frantically twisting dials and setting switches, and did not answer at once. It took a full fifteen seconds for her to get the alarms cut off and the flight system back under some sort of control. *Good thing it wasn't a real emergency,* Han thought. *Otherwise we'd all have been killed before she had the alarms reset.*

"Detector alert," Salculd said at last. "Another ship. No, *three*—no, *four* others. They just popped out of nowhere, out of hyperspace."

"But what about the interdiction field?" Han protested.

"It's still there," Salculd said. "But the ships got through it, somehow. They're coming from starboard, moving straight for us, and for Selonia."

"Full evasive!" Dracmus ordered at once, not waiting for details.

"Wait! Hold it!" Han shouted, trying to get them to stop in time. A glance at the display boards made it clear the newcomers were at least two and a half days away at any sort of reasonable acceleration. Besides which, who would send four big ships in pursuit of this glorified go-cart?

But it was too late. For all of Salculd's irreverent posturing, she had never been anything but quick off the mark in obeying Dracmus's orders. She slammed the sublight engines up to maximum and heeled the nose of the ship hard over.

"Don't throttle up so hard!" Han shouted. "Your power relay inverters can't handle too many hard power-ups!"

And the sickening thud they heard a moment later told Han he had understated the case. The inverters could not handle *any* more hard power-ups.

"You've blown the primary power regulator!" Han shouted. "Throttle down before you lose the backup, too!"

Salculd looked over at Han, a wild look in her eye. "But Dracmus ordered me to—"

"But nothing! You can't perform evasive maneuvers if the engines blow out! Throttle down!"

Salculd needed no more convincing. She lunged for the controls and pulled the throttle back.

Nothing happened. The ship continued to accelerate wildly.

"Backup regulator's blown!" Han said. Without the regulators in place to mediate—and end—the power reactions, the ship's sublight engines would do nothing more than run flat out at maximum power, until they melted down or exploded, taking the ship with them.

Han scrambled out of his flight chair and dove for the access ladder to the lower deck. He swarmed down the ladder and rushed to the power relay inverter array. He popped the access panel open and spent a frantic moment or two searching through the mishmash of nonstandard components for the manual emergency cut-off switch. He spotted it and yanked it down hard. The sublight engines died with a sickening lurch. The switch was already hot enough to burn his fingers. A moment's examination confirmed his worst fears. The power coupling runaway had blown out the sublight engine initiator link. No point in even checking to see if the engines had held together. Without the initiator link, there was no way to start the engines in the first place.

They were stranded but good.

Han made sure that the array had dropped into cooldown mode properly and then went back forward to the control cabin at the apex of the cone, stopping off at the head just long enough to wet down a towel and wrap it around his burnt hand.

"We're all right for the moment," he announced. "I found the cut-off in time to keep the ship from blowing out. But we're derelict."

"Derelict?"

"We can't maneuver the ship," Han said. "Whatever course we had at the time I threw the cut-off is the course we're going to have, unless someone comes along and rescues us."

"Is there no way to fix it?" Dracmus asked.

"*Maybe,*" Han said, "if we're very lucky and we don't crash into a planet or into Corell or starve to death before we can do the job. If the engines themselves haven't melted down, all we have to do is make ourselves a new initiator link—but that could take months." The coneship made the *Millennium Falcon* look maintenance-free. "Who maintains this ship for you—your worst enemy?"

"In a sense, yes," said Dracmus. "It is because our enemies have denied us access to regular spaceports and seized all our ships that we are forced to use these craft. They've been in storage for twenty standard years."

"And you just wheeled them out, pushed the 'on' switch, and hoped for the best?" Han asked.

"We didn't have much choice in the matter," Dracmus said. "We are in a fight for our lives, and the question of what is an acceptable risk suddenly has different answers."

"But why is it worth risking both of your lives and a nonreplaceable ship just to get me to Selonia?"

"Perhaps we do not put such an excessive value on our own lives, as you humans do. We are more willing to sacrifice ourselves for the good of all."

"Speak for yourself," Salculd muttered.

"Your question is still a good one," Dracmus went on, ignoring the interruption. "However, I must say no more about it."

"I had a premonition you were going to give that answer," Han growled. "Still, it doesn't exactly fill in all the blanks, if you know what I mean."

"If you ask me," said Salculd, "it's time that we—"

Suddenly another alarm squawked. Salculd turned back toward her controls. "What have we got left that's not shut down—" She checked the displays. "Uh-oh," she said. "More bad news. The navicomputer just crashed."

"That's not bad news anymore. With the engines down, who cares about the navicomputer?" Han said. "Look on the bright side. If we can't navigate, it doesn't matter if the propulsion system is melted down to slag."

*   *   *

The *Jade's Fire* was farther sunward from Selonia, but she had far better detectors—and a far better stealth ability than the coneship. The *Jade's Fire* could see the coneship—though they had no reason to pay her any mind. However, the coneship could not see the *Fire*. Beyond that, the *Jade's Fire* also had a far superior ship-type database. The coneship had spotted the sudden arrival of four large incoming blips. The *Jade's Fire* had them nailed as Bakuran warships—three destroyers and a cruiser—the moment they came into range.

And there was one other difference. Those aboard

the *Jade's Fire* reacted somewhat more calmly to the Bakurans' arrival.

"What the hell are they doing here?" Mara asked. "And how did they beat the interdiction field? And who's aboard?"

"I don't know how they got here," Leia replied. "But I'm glad to see them. And as for who is aboard, I think I have a very good idea." She reached out with her Force sense and closed her eyes. But no, the range was too great. Maybe Luke could reach out that far, but she could not. She hadn't really expected to sense from here. She would try again later. But even so, she *knew*.

"Who?" Mara asked. "Who is it you think is aboard those ships?"

"Luke," she said. "Luke is there. He came to the rescue. He brought the ships in. I knew that when I saw they were Bakuran. The Bakurans owed a debt to Luke, and he got them to pay it. Don't ask me how, but he did. And don't ask me how the Bakurans beat the interdiction field, but they did."

Mara looked at Leia and frowned as she thought it through. "It's exactly the sort of thing he *would* do," she conceded. "And the Bakuran connection clinches it. I think you're right. Luke just arrived. But that's a battle formation out there, and communications are still down. Luke or no Luke, I don't think it would be the smartest idea to head over that way for a little visit. We keep our heads down and stay on course for Selonia."

The infuriating thing was that Leia knew perfectly well that she was right.

*   *   *

Belindi Kalenda was delighted to be where she was—or, more accurately, she was glad to be anywhere where she could do something useful. She felt as if she had been lost in the shuffle since her arrival in the Coruscant system, bringing her messages from Corellia. Others might have been swept up in the drama of great events, but once her task as messenger was complete, she had been promptly relegated to the background while the grown-ups took over.

But here they were, back on Corellia, and it would have been a gross understatement to say the Bakuran intelligence staff did not know its way around. They had a fair amount of book knowledge and database information about the planet, but nearly all of it was badly dated. Several of their references referred to its role as an Imperial base, which was bad enough, but she had actually stumbled across several "update" reports in the Bakuran files that were clearly written during the Old Republic. They needed all the help they could get.

But she had bigger jobs than updating the historical record. There was any amount of real-time analysis to do. Her primary job at the moment was to get the best figures possible on the size, dimensions, and intensity of the interdiction field. The Bakurans had brought along special instruments for the purpose of tracking the field —and with every reading those instruments got, it became clearer and clearer that both the jamming signals and the interdiction field were centered on the Double World system. They had suspected that right along, of course, but it was nice to get it confirmed. But Kalenda had just gone one better than that. The data she had just pulled in and processed made her all but certain that she had detected the precise position of the field generator. And while she didn't know about the others, the news certainly was enough to give her a surprise.

Kalenda checked the time and swore under her breath. She was supposed to give the tactical report in five minutes. She wouldn't have time to freshen up or change. Well, it wasn't her fault the confirming data had chosen this moment to come in. It wasn't as if the data would be any better if it came from an officer in a fresh uniform.

* * *

"Now then, the first order of business is fleet status," Kalenda said to the staff assembled on the flag deck. "The news is not good, but it could certainly be worse. The good news is that *Intruder, Defender,* and *Sentinel* have all effected repairs and are under weigh and in formation, making for Selonia at three-quarters flank. The bad news is that although *Watchkeeper* has managed to restore her life-support systems and her attitude control, she has not been able to restore her propulsion system, and is not expected to be able to do so for some time. She is drifting in toward the inner system, but it will take her several years to get there on her current course. Her crew will be safe onboard in the meantime. The other three ships will perform a flyby of her, but will not stop to render aid. However, we plan to launch an uncrewed shuttle vehicle loaded with spare parts toward her as we come in on closest approach."

"I've ordered all but five of her fighter craft to transfer over to the operational ships," Ossilege said. "Five fighters should provide sufficient cover against attack, and the fleet is going to need all the firepower it can get."

"Anything further on what we'll be up against?" Lando asked.

"Yes, there is," said Kalenda, "and it's most interesting. We are seeing small fighter craft launching from the Doubles, Corellia, and Drall, all headed for a very clear intercept point directly in our path for Selonia. There are three or four larger craft—none of them even the size of the *Lady Luck,* but nearly all the craft we have seen so far are light fighters. The ones boosting from Corellia are all PPBs, and the craft from Drall and the

Doubles are roughly equivalent. We can assume the Selonians will launch their own craft when we are closer. They save on fuel and consumables by holding their ships on-planet as long as possible. However, it seems clear that craft from all the planets are joining in a coordinated attack. At least they are trying to join in."

"What's the problem?" Lando asked.

"One of timing," Kalenda said. "We are now just over two days out from Selonia, and the intercept ships just started launching a few hours ago. Our analysis of their sublight-engine emissions strongly suggests that most of the craft are boosting for the intercept point at maximum thrust, but course projections show they aren't going to get there in time. Nor have the intercepts been timed for simultaneous time-on-target, which would provide the maximum firepower to them. Rather, the fighters are straggling in over a prolonged period of time, giving us the chance to fight a few of them at a time. That strikes me as very poor coordination."

"Not very surprising with virtually all communications jammed," said Gaeriel Captison. "My guess is that the coordination was agreed to before the jamming started. 'If a ship comes into the system, this is what you do.' That sort of thing."

"But the fact that there is any coordination at all seems quite remarkable," said Kalenda. "Five independent sets of rebels on five planets, many of them the self-declared bitter enemies of each other, all banding together to attack us. You were right, Admiral Ossilege. We are learning things from this assault.

"On another subject, I can now report that moments before this meeting, we pinpointed the exact source of the jamming and the interdiction field. Not surprisingly, they are both coming from the same place. More surprisingly, that place is Centerpoint Station."

"Where?" Gaeriel asked.

"Centerpoint Station. I'm not surprised the name

isn't familiar to you. It's not very well known outside the system. It is a very large space station that sits in the barycenter, or balance point, between the Double Worlds of Talus and Tralus. Put another way, it occupies the point in space about which both of those worlds revolve."

"I must say that news surprises me a great deal," said Ossilege. "I assumed that the interdiction field was so powerful that it had to be coming from a ground-based source. How could a space station be large enough to generate that much subspace energy?"

"Centerpoint is a very large installation," Kalenda said. "That being said, I would agree that we can't see how it could be generating or controlling the field. But it is comparable in size to a Death Star, and, I believe, much more massive. And it seems to be putting out one hell of a lot of power. Far more than is indicated in any of the historical records we have, for what that is worth. It's like it's come alive after being dormant."

"If it controls the jamming and the interdiction field, then Centerpoint Station is the key to this whole system," Ossilege said. "May we see some imagery of it?"

Kalenda punched in the proper commands, and a holographic image of the station appeared over the table. The main body of the station was a massive gray-white sphere. Long fat cylinders, covered with all sorts of piping and hardware and antennae, extended from either side of the sphere, with the whole system spinning on its long axis. "The main sphere is a shade over a hundred kilometers in diameter. From end to end, the whole station is about three hundred fifty kilometers in length. It's so old that it has to spin to provide artificial gravity. It predates the invention of our form of artificial grav, and no one knows who invented *that*, or how long ago."

"Interesting. Very interesting indeed. But why put the interdiction generators and the jamming equipment on a space station? No matter how large it is, wouldn't you agree that a space station would be intrinsically more difficult to defend than a planet-based installation?"

"In many ways, yes, sir."

"And yet. And yet. Our opponents can read a positional display as well as we can. They must know that we have instruments capable of charting the interdiction field and locating its origin point. And they must know as well as we do that the control of the interdiction field is vital to their plans. *And yet* there is no indication of any effort that I am aware of to protect this Centerpoint Station. Fighters from the Double Worlds are moving toward the intercept point."

"Sir, if I might interrupt for a moment. Our tracking isn't absolutely solid at this range, but we are fairly sure that we've also spotted fighters launching from Centerpoint and heading toward us."

"Indeed?" Ossilege raised his eyebrows. "That makes it even more remarkable. They chose to send fighters away from what they must defend most strongly? But their failure to defend is only part of the problem. They must also know that even a somewhat coordinated attack demonstrates that the seemingly independent rebel groups are working with each other. The Human League's propaganda goes on and on about how much they hate all the other groups. I would assume the others sing a similar tune. In those circumstances, this coordination amounts to consorting with the enemy. Should it get out, it will be politically damaging to all of them. These are fairly closed societies, of course. Yet stopping us is seen as a vital enough task that they are ready to risk that damage, though they are deploying a force of light fighters that is too weak to stop us.

"Why light fighters? Either they do not control any larger ships, or else they do not feel the need to risk them in combat. But they would appear to have no reason to be so confident. It is all most puzzling. Had these points occurred to you, Lieutenant Kalenda?"

"Yes, sir, they had."

"And what do they tell you?"

"Only that we are missing something. Something very big. Something that makes them confident that they can stop us at Selonia."

"I quite agree," said Ossilege. He thought for a moment. "How long until closest approach with *Watchkeeper*?"

Kalenda checked the time. "Ah, we will do the flyby in about eight hours, sir."

"I see. I see. Very well." Ossilege stood up abruptly and turned toward his flag communications officer. "Set up a direct laser line-of-sight link with the captain of the *Watchkeeper*. Patch it through to my cabin, full privacy scramble." The com officer saluted and set to work at his console. "As for the rest of you, suffice to say that Lieutenant Kalenda's report has inspired me to make a change in plans. I will inform you of those changes as soon as I have completed my consultations with the *Watchkeeper*. That is all. Good day to you."

And with that, Ossilege swept out of the room.

Everyone stood up and made their way toward the door. "What was all that business about consulting with *Watchkeeper*, Lieutenant Kalenda?" asked Captain Calrissian.

"I don't know, sir," she replied. "But I've got a hunch that I wouldn't want to be the captain of the *Watchkeeper* just at the moment."

"Oh, yeah," Calrissian agreed. "When admirals take a sudden interest in disabled ships, it's almost always time to start worrying." *That* much was beyond debate.

CHAPTER SEVENTEEN

All Together Now

Tendra Risant was close to despair. It seemed as if she had been stuck aboard this ship for years instead of days. The *Gentleman Caller* had appeared a roomy enough ship when she had first boarded and explored her, but now the craft felt no larger than a coffin—an image she did not much care for.

She was not sure how much longer she could hold on. Tendra had never solo-piloted a ship before, never been this *alone* before. The silence, the solitude of space seemed to close in around her, and the vast open emptiness seemed to confine her. The ship had enough food to sustain her, and the recycling system would keep her air and water pure for at least a year without any trouble at all. But was there enough *sanity* left aboard the craft to keep her going? The ship could keep her body functioning as long as need be—but it could do nothing to keep her mind working.

Why didn't Lando *answer*? What had happened? What had gone wrong? Had she gambled everything in her life on a foolish whim, and lost?

She reached over and listened again to the radionics monitor speaker as it echoed what the transmitter was sending. She knew that hearing the message could do her no good at all, and might simply reduce her to tears once again. But she had to hear it, had to know it was still going out.

"Tendra to Lando," said the voice, her voice, from the speaker, sounding far more sensible than she had felt for a long time. "Please respond on preassigned frequency." Pause. "Tendra to Lando. Please respond on preassigned frequency." Pause. "Tendra to Lando. Please respond on preassigned frequency. . . ."

*　　*　　*

Admiral Hortel Ossilege stood on the flag deck of the *Intruder,* resplendent, as usual, in his dress white uniform. "The time has come," he said, "to explain the situation. As you know, we have taken the *Watchkeeper* in tow and transferred virtually all of her crew to the other vessels. You no doubt are wondering why we are taking a near-derelict craft in tow as we enter into battle. I will tell you flat out now. I intend to sacrifice her."

If that statement was intended to elicit a general murmur of astonishment, it succeeded. Ossilege waited for the room to quiet down. "We have been baffled by the badly timed arrival and inadequate coordination of the opposing fleet," he said. "We are now only a few hours away from contact with the first elements of that fleet, and yet the tail end of it has barely begun to form up. We have just now started to track launches from Selonia itself.

"I have analyzed the ship placements of the enemy, and I can tell you this—they *are* very bad, if the enemy does in fact try to do what we think he will try to do. If he offers a straight fight, he will lose, and lose badly.

"*But.* If they intend instead to draw us, to herd us, to move us around by offering themselves as a target and then retreating—*then* they have deployed themselves very well indeed.

"The obvious question is, of course, draw us toward

what? I intend to find out, and without risking all of my command.

"We have managed to restore a very small percentage of the *Watchkeeper*'s propulsion power, and will shortly rig a slave system capable of flying the ship by remote control, at least well enough for our purposes. I will operate the main remotes myself. I recognize that it is the traditional prerogative of the ship's captain to fly the craft at such times, and I do wish to make public acknowledgment of the fact that Captain Mantrony asked, very strenuously, for that privilege. I have refused her. If the *Watchkeeper* is indeed attacked in some novel way, we need to fly her so as to find out as much as possible about that weapon. Captain Mantrony would be less than human if the laudable instinct to protect her own ship did not interfere with that need. Her protests of my actions have been recorded.

"I want my fleet to be led toward whatever trap they have set—with the *Watchkeeper* well in the lead. I do not want our fighters to be overly aggressive. They should take battle if it is offered, but not seek it out. I want a defensive, not an offensive, posture. I think there is no doubt that we can deal with any number of these PPBs and other light fighters at the proper time. For now, I simply want to preserve our force and probe the enemy's capabilities.

"So," Ossilege said in solemn voice as he looked out over the faces of his officers. "Let it begin." He nodded to the *Intruder*'s tactical officer.

"All crew to battle stations," she ordered. "All fighter pilots to their spacecraft. Stand by for fighter-craft launch."

The briefing was over, and the officers and pilots stood up and began to file out.

"Defensive posture," Lando muttered to Luke as they followed the others out. "If he really wanted a defensive posture, we could all just stay aboard ship."

"Hey, come on," Luke said. "You're my wingman out there. I don't want you *too* defensive."

"Look, you'll be lucky if I even remember how to fly my ship," Lando replied. "What with all the planning meetings, I haven't even been aboard her since we entered the Corellian system."

Luke grinned and slapped his friend on the back. "Well, they say once you learn, you never forget. Here's your big chance to find out if that's true. Come on. Let's get to our ships."

*   *   *

Now, Leia thought. *Now* they were close enough. At this distance she could reach across and sense her brother's mind, if he were indeed there. She shut her eyes, and used her power in the Force to *reach,* to spread her senses outward.

And she felt him, at once, immediately, felt him strong and clear across the darkness and the distance. Leia smiled, reveled in the warmth of the contact, of the pleasure of knowing her brother was near, and coming closer. But that was only half of it. She knew that Luke would sense her in the Force in the same moment, would instantly know where she was.

Even if her ability was not strong enough to allow any meaningful communication, just the simple knowledge that he was there, that he would know she was here, was a tremendous comfort.

*   *   *

Luke was halfway up the access ladder of his X-wing when he felt his sister's touch through the Force. He froze and looked up, with his mind's eye, through the bulkheads and decks and durasteel of the *Intruder,* up and out into the clean darkness of space. He could *see* her spirit there, shining in the dark, as clearly as he could see Artoo being lowered into his socket on the X-wing. She was here. She was alive. She was all right. What else could matter as much as that?

Luke got an answer almost before he could form the question.

For now that he was reaching out with his Force sense, he realized there was someone else out there as well.

*   *   *

Leia felt the same contact, almost by accident, as her Force sense swept across space. In some ways, a much fainter presence, a being not endowed himself with the slightest ability in the Force. But all living things were present in the Force, and this life shone bright with vigor and determination—and it shone especially bright for Leia.

"Han," she said, the joy and amazement plain in her voice, turning to Mara. She worked the detector controls and brought the sensors to bear on the right piece of sky. "There!" she said, pointing to a small blip in the detector display. "Han is on that blown-out coneship. Luke is aboard the largest Bakuran ship, but Han is here, too." She shut her eyes and concentrated again. "Two other beings as well; Selonians, I think. I'm not sure about them, but it is Han. I *know* it's Han."

*   *   *

Leia is here, Luke thought. Leia is here, and Han is here, and there isn't a thing I can do about it. Things were moving too fast. He buttoned up the canopy of his X-wing and ran his cross-checks with Artoo. He checked the deployment roster.

His X-wing and the *Lady Luck* were scheduled to

launch from the belly of the *Intruder* in thirty seconds. Barely time to feel thankful that she and Han were all right. In between nav checks, system tests, and bringing the X-wing to hover, there was no time for anything else.

Not even time to use the laser link system to tell Lando the news.

That was perhaps fortunate, as Lando had his own startling news to contend with.

*   *   *

Strictly speaking, there wasn't really any point to running the automatic com check. Not when all the standard com systems were shut down by the jamming, and there was no way to test the laser link system onboard ship. But Lando tried to be a careful pilot, when he had the chance. And that meant full systems checks if he hadn't flown the ship in a while. He didn't expect any surprises, though. Artoo had run systems checks recently, and he was always careful to take care of the *Lady*.

But what one expected rarely had much to do with what one got. He learned that much when the radionic scanner picked something up—and put it on the cabin speaker.

"Tendra to Lando," said the voice—Tendra's voice—from the speaker. "Please respond on preassigned frequency." A pause, and then it repeated, "Tendra to Lando. Please respond on preassigned frequency." And repeated, "Tendra to Lando. Please respond on preassigned frequency. . . ."

Lando was stunned. Absolutely stunned. How had she gotten to Corellia? What in the name of stars and skies was Tendra doing here? *Why* had she come here? How far away was she?

Lando checked the launch clock. Just under half a

minute to go. Barely time to do anything. But he had to do *something*. He punched up the com system, switched it to the rarely used radionics mode, and set it for repeater transmission. He thought for a minute before he replied. There was so much to say, and so little time. "Lando replying to Tendra. It's a long story why, but I only arrived in-system very recently, and have just now received your transmission." He paused for a moment, and then went on, feeling more than a bit awkward. "It, ah, might sound melodramatic, but I'm about to go into battle, and there is no time for anything. There's a lot I want to say—but all of it will have to wait. The main question is, where *are* you? I will do my best to monitor your original frequency from here on in. Good luck to you, and to all of us. Lando out. Message repeats."

Lando just sat there for a moment, thinking of all the ways he should change that message. It said too much, and it said not enough—but there was no time. It would have to do. Ten seconds until launch. Lando hit the continuous transmit-repeat button, brought his sublight engines to standby, and began concentrating on staying alive.

* * *

Han Solo was not a happy man. There are few things that make a pilot feel as helpless as being aboard a derelict ship. It was bad enough for a pilot to be a passenger aboard a craft with someone else, anyone else, at the controls. But when no one is at the controls, when the ship is *out* of control, the sensation was far worse. The nameless coneship might as well have been an asteroid, a lump of spacerock, for all that could be done to maneuver it. All they could do was wait. Sooner or later someone would shoot them down, or they would crash into something, or the food would give out, or the air and water would go bad. With the luck this ship had, it wouldn't be more than a day or two before two or three of those things happened.

Unless. Unless Han could jury-rig *some* sort of propulsion system and bring the navicomputer back on-line. The odds for success weren't good, of course. But Han had never been one to give up easily. And the first stage of the job was clearly to make a detailed survey of the damage. It was lucky that they had nothing but time on their hands, because that was what this job would take. A lot of time.

Han stared at the ruined initiator link, trying to fix every part of it in his mind, doing his best to memorize it before he touched it. He was going to have exactly one chance to repair this thing, and he had to get it right. He noticed a slender crack in the base of the impeller bracket. If that crack went all the way through, the bracket would be useless. Well, he'd just have to build a new one. Maybe he could find something on the ship that would—

"Honored Solo!"

The voice boomed down from the upper deck, loud enough and suddenly enough that Han nearly jumped out of his skin. "Dracmus, don't *do* that!" he shouted back. "Scared me half to death. I could have snapped the impeller bracket clean off, if I had been touching it."

"My apologies, Honored Solo," Dracmus called back. "But there is another matter, an urgent one. A ship is about to dock with us."

"What!" Han forgot all about the impeller and scrambled up the ladder to the upper deck. "What are you talking about?" he demanded. He looked up at the detector screen and saw from the visual-mode display that there was indeed another ship out there, only a half kilometer away and closing fast. He looked up through the cone-apex viewports and spotted the ship easily. "Salculd, why didn't you spot it until now?"

"She came up from our stern," Salculd said apologetically. "Our stern detectors were never very good, and the overload must have damaged them in some way the diagnostics couldn't spot."

"Great," Han said. "We've been flying blind and we didn't even know it."

"But what do we *do*, Honored Solo?" Dracmus asked.

"Do? What *can* we do? We have no com system with the jamming, so we can't talk with them. We have no propulsion system, so we can't move—unless we all get out and push." He pointed to the fast-approaching ship and shrugged hopelessly. "All we can do is put out the welcome mat and hope they're friendly. I'd say I hoped they were on our side if I knew what side that was—" Han stopped talking and looked harder at the incoming ship. "Wait a second," he said. "I know that ship. I know that ship—"

"What ship is it?" Dracmus demanded. "Are they friend or foe?"

"I'm not sure. Dracmus, Salculd, both of you. Grab sidearms and get to the air lock. Hurry!"

Salculd and Dracmus both froze for a second, not sure whether to obey Han. "Go!" he shouted again. "Now!"

That got them moving. "I have two blasters in my cabin," Dracmus announced, and rushed to get them, Salculd hard on her heels.

Han scrambled back down the ladder and rushed over to the air lock, wishing for a wrench, a hammer, anything big and heavy. But there wasn't time. He heard the thud of hull clamps linking to the coneship, heard a high-pitched hum as a force field coming on vibrated through the hull. Standard operating procedure when two ships with nonmatched hatches docked up. One would activate a tubular force field between the two air locks, allowing free transit from one ship to the other.

Assuming all parties cooperated. Han briefly considered disabling the air lock, preventing the boarders from coming over. But there would be very little point to that. Any cutting laser worth its salt would be able to slice through the coneship's hull metal in a matter of minutes. Better to let them aboard and take it from there. And besides, she might be friendly. She *might* be . . . But then he heard the coneship's outer doors slide open. It was too late to worry about it.

"Solo!" Dracmus shouted as she rushed down the corridor, blaster at the ready. "Solo! What is going on? What ship is that?" She stopped short, and Salculd almost knocked her over. "What is going on?"

"That's the *Jade's Fire* that just latched herself to our hull," Han said. "Mara Jade's ship. Your swell friend has just tracked me—or you, or us—halfway across the Corellian system. And I can tell you right now, I am *not* giving her any more benefit of the doubt. She had better do a damned good job of convincing me she's on our side or—"

The inner airlock door slid open, and Han stopped talking. He just stood there, openmouthed and in shock, for a full five seconds. And then, somehow, suddenly, they were in each other's arms, seemingly without either of them crossing the distance between them. "Leia," he said. "Leia, how did you—"

Leia Organa Solo wrapped her arms around Han and hugged her husband. "Hello, Han," she said. "I missed you."

*   *   *

Luke Skywalker kept his X-wing in formation with the *Lady Luck*, both craft flying escort on the *Intruder*. The four ships of the Bakuran task force were set in a modified flying-wedge formation, a three-sided pyramid with the *Watchkeeper* at the leading point and the other three ships forming up in an equilateral triangle directly behind her. The hope was that the opposition would not be able to detect the tractor beams the three other ships were using to hold *Watchkeeper* in formation. At any rate, the formation *looked* impressive, and that was most of the point.

"—uke, come in, Lu—"

It was Lando on the line-of-sight laser com system. The best that could be said about the system was that it worked, which was a great deal more than could be said about any other com system available to the fleet. However, it did not work *well*. It just about sufficed for conversation between a fighter and his wingman. Anything else, and it was hopeless. "Still breaking up a bit, Lando," Luke said. "What's up?"

"—emme re-ibrate this -ing again. There we go. I just wanted to know if you had any better idea what we're looking for out there."

In other words, Lando wanted to know if Luke had sensed anything through the Force. "Not really," he said. "I don't feel anything much from the other side, besides the emotions you might expect before a battle. My guess is that they don't have any more idea than we do. The brass knows, but the troops don't."

"Great," Lando said. "How about Leia and Han?"

"They're still out there. I can sense the two of them together now—and someone else, too, now that I know where to focus my awareness. Mara Jade. I think they're on her ship now, and if I'm matching up my Force sense with the tracking data properly, they are on the shortest, fastest course that will get them clear of the battle zone."

"Can't blame them for —at," Lando said, still breaking up just a trifle. "But I sure wish Mara had decided to join in the fun. Her ship packs some serious firepower. We could use the help."

"Not really," said Luke. "Ossilege was right. The en-

emy formations are all wrong for fighter-to-fighter battle. If that was what this was about, we'd wipe them out
in a minute. They have to know that. They aren't going
to offer battle. Not unless they're suicidal."

"—o what *are* they going to offer?" Lando demanded.
"Musical entertainment?"

Luke shook his head. "I don't know," he said. "But
we're about to find out. Here they come."

A wave of Corellian PPBs came in from sunward, trying to stay hidden in Corell's glare. They went straight
for the *Watchkeeper,* but broke off their attack almost
before it had started, only getting off a few token turbolaser shots before shifting course and diving away. A
flight of Selonian light attack fighters came in right behind the PPBs and performed almost the identical maneuver, coming in just a trifle closer—and being
rewarded by a series of rapid bursts from the
Watchkeeper's main battery. The *Watchkeeper* scored two
direct hits on the LAFs. Luke had to hand it to Ossilege,
who was flying the *Watchkeeper* by remote. That was
some pretty fair shooting.

The surviving LAFs moved off on the same heading
as the PPBs, on a bearing that would take them just
over the limb of Selonia. Luke reminded himself that
they were coming up on the planet. It would be downright embarrassing to get preoccupied with the dogfight
and crash into it. More PPBs came in from directly
above the Bakuran ships, diving straight into the center
of the wedge formation to come up behind the
Watchkeeper and give her a dose of firepower from
the rear. The other big Bakuran ships opened fire on
the interlopers, but they were restrained by the fear of
firing on their own ship. Shooing them away was a job
for the fighters, and several flights of Bakuran fighters
took up the task.

Luke decided to join them. "Lando, let's encourage

those PPBs to go on about their business," he said. "Form on my port wing and follow me in."

"I'm with you, -uke," Lando replied.

Luke brought his fighter's wings to attack position and lit the engines. The X-wing dove into the center of the flying wedge, the *Lady Luck* off her port wing. Luke spotted a pair of PPBs below and off to starboard. He swooped in on them, locking his guns—but both PPBs blew up before he could even fire.

"Score two," Lando announced. "At least I think it was me. Lot of shooting going on. Luke! Coming up from the rear and below!"

Luke had his X-wing in a diving barrel roll before he could see the threat. You had to trust your wingman. And sure enough, there was a PPB and an LAF coming straight for him. Both of the light fighters opened up on him, and the X-wing took a glancing hit to the portside lower wing. Artoo bleeped protestingly but recalibrated the shielding to compensate.

Luke fired two short bursts. The first hit the LAF and blew it sky-high. The second burst only caught a piece of the PPB, sent it tumbling out of control and out of the fight. Luke forgot about it and pulled the X-wing's nose up, heading back toward the *Watchkeeper,* coming up under her keel.

"That's it," Lando said. "They've broken off."

"Yeah," Luke said. "And they're heading for that same piece of sky as all the other flights bugged out toward. That's where they want us to go."

"And that's where we are going," Lando replied. "*Watchkeeper*'s changing course to pursue. Just what Ossilege said they'd want him to do."

"Great," Luke said. "But I'm not sure who's outsmarting who in all this. I'm going to fly formation on the *Watchkeeper,* high and to the rear. Stay with me."

"Received and understood," Lando said. "Don't get

too close to her, though. If Ossilege is flying into a trap on purpose, I don't want to go along for the ride."

"Agreed. Double standard formation distance."

The *Watchkeeper* broke formation with the other big ships and lumbered toward the massed formations of PPBs and LAFs. The *Watchkeeper* was very definitely not moving fast. Whatever propulsion they had managed to patch together for her wasn't anything much, that was for sure. But she was moving, for all of that. Luke slowed his X-wing to match her velocity and took up station keeping five kilometers behind and three above her stern.

"Luke, another —ight of LAFs coming in fr— —low the *Watchkeeper,*" Lando warned.

"Let 'em come," Luke said. "Shields at maximum, but don't respond or return fire."

"But—"

"Just do it," Luke said. "I want to see how they respond. But be ready to drop shields and fight if they come back for a second pass."

The LAFs came up from behind, six of them. Four turned to take a firing pass right over the topside of the *Watchkeeper,* doing a strafing run across her upper deck. Explosions flickered and flared over the decks of the *Watchkeeper,* but her shields held. The main batteries swung about and poured fire at the LAFs. Two of them flew right into the battery fire before the others peeled off and headed for that same slice of sky.

But Luke had very little time to worry about that. The other two LAFs were on them, sweeping past in a blaze of turbolaser fire, catching both ships with repeated hits; but with shields at maximum, the small lasers on the LAFs weren't able to do any appreciable damage. Of course, with the shields maxed up, neither ship could fight back, either, but that scarcely mattered just at the moment. The two LAFs swooped past, unmolested— and followed their fellows down the same vector, toward

the limb of the planet, which every other enemy fighter
had taken. All of them were rendezvousing there now,
coming together in a mass formation.

"Now I get it," Lando said. "That clinches it for me.
They are trying to draw us toward that one point at all
costs, and they are under very strict orders to do so.
There isn't a fighter pilot living who wouldn't want to
take another crack at two nice big fat slow-moving
targets who didn't shoot back. Luke, you sure five kilometers up and three back is distance enough?"

"Not really," Luke admitted. "Make it ten and six and
re-form at that station-keeping point. But what are they
trying to pull us toward?" he asked as he flipped the
X-wing around and flew toward the new escort point.

"Got me," Lando said. "A big cloaked ship, or some
kind of minefield, maybe."

"Except a ship or mines would have to be between us
and the fighters for that to make sense," Luke said,
watching the *Watchkeeper* move forward in leisurely pursuit of its tormentors. "Their fighters just flew straight
through that patch of space." The *Watchkeeper* sailed
on, bringing her main battery to bear on the enemy
fighter fleet. She fired again and again, making a lot of
hits. "Whatever it is, they're willing to pay a big price to
get a ship to it. But what is it?"

"You've got me, Luke. Maybe they've got some sort
of—"

Suddenly, out of nowhere, a giant, invisible fist
slammed into the *Watchkeeper*. The lower hull slammed
upward, pancaking it against the upper hull, as huge
sections of ship broke free and flew off into space. Massive explosions ripped through the ship, and merged
into a single fireball that completely engulfed it.

"Evasive!" Luke called out, and flipped his X-wing
around to boost away from the expanding fireball at
maximum thrust. The *Lady Luck* was beside him,
matching the X-wing's acceleration, but the shock wave

of the explosion was moving faster. Luke cut the X-wing's engines and went to maximum shields a half heartbeat after the *Lady Luck* did so. The shock wave rushed past the two ships, slamming into them, sending them tumbling off wildly into space before it passed by them. Debris of all sizes clattered into the shield, bouncing the ship around even more.

At last the explosion shock wave was past them, and Luke was able to bring the X-wing back under control. But he could not see the *Lady Luck*. "Lando!" he called. "Lando!"

"I'm here," he said. "Behind and below you. Took some hull damage and lost the port sublight engine, but I'm here. You okay?"

"I'm okay," Luke said. He brought the nose of the X-wing about and looked back toward the point in space where a destroyer had been swatted like a fly. Where the *Watchkeeper* had been was nothing, absolutely nothing at all. "But what happened?"

"I was about to ask you. Luke—what *was* that?"

"I don't know," Lando. "But I've got a very nasty hunch we haven't seen the last of it."

*   *   *

"It is as we feared," said Dracmus as she watched the main display aboard the *Jade's Fire*. "The fools have used it. They have gone ahead and used it."

"Used what?" Han asked. "What *was* that?"

"A planetary repulsor," said Dracmus. "Similar in principle to the repulsors used in spacecraft to make them hover, but immeasurably more powerful. The device itself is buried under the surface of Dracmus. There is such a device hidden on each of the planets on this system. It was by use of the planetary repulsors that the long-lost architects of the Corellian system transported the various planets here."

"What?" Leia said.

"The Corellian system is an artifact, a built thing, Honored Chief of State. Built when, and by whom, and for what reason, I could not say. But it was built."

"A huge buried repulsor," said Han. "That was what the Human League was looking for!"

"Yes," said Dracmus, "though they may well have found it by now. The Dralls and the folk of the Double Worlds are searching for their repulsors as well. We Selonians found ours first, and quickly made it operational. Not surprising, given our skill at underground work. I am told that aiming the device is still quite difficult, which was why that ship needed to be lured to a certain point. But our engineers will soon solve that, I have no doubt. Then we will be able to strike any point in the sky, at will, whenever we choose."

"We? We?" Han said. "Your people, your den, control that thing?"

"I don't believe so. But, in truth, I am not sure. My information is old, and the struggle to gain control of it has been tremendous, as you might imagine. The fight over the repulsor got swept up in other issues, and got out of control, until we had something close to civil war, in fact.

"There were two factions. One—mine—calls itself the Republicanists. We sought to use the repulsors as a bargaining chip. We wished to turn our repulsor over to the New Republic in return for a guarantee of Selonia's sovereignty inside the New Republic and the Corellian Sector government. That was why we wanted to bring you to Selonia, honored Solo. It was hoped that we might use you to open the negotiations."

"And the other faction?" Han asked.

"Calls itself the Absolutists. Sought to use the repulsor as a weapon to establish absolute Selonian independence. But the issues became so complex, and the fight so desperate, that either side could have used it as the weapon."

"But there were fighters from all the Corellian worlds here," Mara objected.

"Yes. Precisely. A huge irony. We have long suspected that all the revolutionary groups—the Absolutists, the Human League, the Drallist Front, all of them—were being *coordinated* by someone outside themselves. We have proof of that now—but we are no closer to knowing who that outside force was, or what they did it for."

"It's incredible," Han said. "I can't believe it."

"But how does it all fit together?" Leia demanded. "What does it have to do with the starbuster plot? Who blew up that first star? And why the race to find the repulsors on the other planets?"

"I don't know," said Dracmus. "I don't know what to think." She paused a minute and looked toward the screen, where they had just seen the Bakuran ship destroyed. "All I know for certain is that my planet has just declared war on the New Republic."

CHAPTER EIGHTEEN

On the Clock

"*L*ando replying to Tendra. It's a long story why, but I only arrived in-system very recently, and have just now received your transmission. . . ."

Tendra listened to the words, over and over again, her eyes filled with tears. He was here. He was alive. And he was *fighting*. Relief swept over her, even as she felt renewed fear for his safety. She thought of the long speed-of-light delays that was one of the most clumsy features of radionics. It took hours for a radionic message to get from the inner system to Tendra aboard the *Gentleman Caller*. What if something had happened in those hours? What if Lando had lived long enough to send her a message, but died in battle before she could hear it? No. No. She would not believe it. She would not ever consider it. She had work to do. She had come here with a purpose, and at long last she could act on that purpose. With the radionic link to Lando established, she could send warning of the fleet massing in the Sacorrian system. She had long since composed a detailed message, telling all she knew, but now that the moment had come, she could not resist reading it over one last time. After all, with all the effort she had made, she might as well be sure she got it right.

*   *   *

Marcha, Duchess of Mastigophorous, rode up the strange silver disk elevator to the surface, Anakin at the controls, as usual. Down below her, the *Millennium Falcon* was concealed, and Chewbacca was working Ebrihim and Q9 and the twins hard, setting up a snug little underground camp in the huge, hidden repulsor chamber. They would be able to hide out there for quite some time, and be able to study the repulsor in detail. With a little luck, they would find a way to keep anyone else from using it.

But all that was for later. Right now Marcha simply wanted to get up out from underground and stand under the bold night sky of Drall. The disk elevator rushed smoothly upward and inward, to the apex of the huge chamber. The point of the cone opened itself as the edges of the disk merged with the edges of the chamber, and they were moving up a smooth, perfect cylinder, rising out of the ground into a brilliant night, the sky awash with stars.

And more than stars. There, off to the east, Corellia and Selonia were two fat points of light near the horizon. And to the west, floating a bit higher in the sky, the Double Worlds of Talus and Tralus, with Centerpoint Station so tiny a fleck of light Marcha was not sure if she saw it, or simply imagined that she did.

"They're out there somewhere, aren't they?" Anakin asked, taking Marcha by the paw and leaning into her a bit.

"Yes, dear, they are," she said, wrapping her free arm around him. "Your parents are out there, I am sure of it, working and fighting and struggling to set things right."

Anakin nodded thoughtfully. "They always do," he said. "Is that why we have to stay here? So we can help them by figuring out this repulsor thing?"

"Yes, dear," said Aunt Marcha. "That's it exactly."

"Gee," said Anakin. "I sure hope we don't let them down.

* * *

Somewhere out on the edges of the Thanta Zilbra system, Wedge Antilles brought his Enhanced X-wing in for a landing on the flight deck of the *Naritus,* and wished to the devil he had an enemy he could shoot at. Instead, they were evacuating people from a whole star system, just because the paranoids at NRI had heard some crazy rumor. The story was that someone had blown up one star, and was threatening to blow up Thanta Zilbra next, and then some other star—and it seemed to Wedge that the rumor mill had named practically every star in the Galaxy as being the next on the list.

It all sounded absurd on the face of it. How the devil would anyone go about blowing up a *star*? Zero hour was less than twelve hours away now, and there had been no sign of anything happening. And what about the rumors that the Chief of State was caught up in the middle of it, in serious danger? Wedge hope that part of it was wrong. He knew how much the New Republic needed Chief of State Organa Solo—and he knew how much Leia meant to Wedge's friends Han and Luke.

But the scuttlebutt about Leia was a rumor, nothing more. Some of the fliers in his squadron had heard that the whole exploding-star story was a fake, though none of them could name any source beyond the usual friend of a friend of a buddy who knew someone who heard something in the staff canteen. Wedge ignored it all. Rumors were not his department. His job was to follow orders, and at the moment that meant flying evacuation support missions—a few in his X-wing, and but most passenger runs in a small runabout. He also had to ride herd on Rogue Squadron, and keeping that bunch of loose cannons under control was no easy task.

They were keeping him busy on this one, but that was to be expected when the fleet mission was to evacuate every single sentient being from the entire Thanta Zilbra system—including those who did not want to go.

Those were headaches enough without wasting time worrying if orders made sense. At least he was flying fighters again. For a while there, it had seemed as if he had been drawing every duty but the one he was best at.

Not that running courier jobs and running emergency spares to transports was the most exciting kind of flying. But at least it was nearly over. The fleet was supposed to jump into hyperspace no later than one hour before zero hour. Another shift and a half, and it would all be over—and more than likely they'd have to move everyone off the transports back to their homes, with apologies all around for the inconvenience. Of course, a fair number of the people of Thanta Zilbra had saved them the trouble. Unable to believe there was any danger, they had simply refused to go. A fair number of the New Republic representatives trying to convince them were not all that convinced themselves, and that didn't help matters.

But enough of all that, just for the moment. He needed to unwind, at least a little bit, before he went back out. He popped his canopy and pulled himself out of the fighter. He waited for the ground crew to bring in the egress ladder, then climbed down out of his ship.

He went to the pilot's ready room, stripped out of his flight suit, treated himself to a very brief but very needed shower, and got into a fresh set of coveralls. Thus refreshed, and feeling a bit restless, he decided to wander over toward the operations center to see what had gone wrong while he was out on patrol sorting out the last foul-up.

The *Naritus* was the flagship for the three warships

and eight large transports involved in this mission, and the ops center was the nerve center for the whole operation. It was from ops that ships were dispatched and recalled, from ops that the word came to try this solution instead of that, or just to give up and go on to the next problem. It was from here that the fleet officers placed their comlink calls to the leaders of this mining outpost or the captain of that in-system freighter, urging them, cajoling them, pleading with them to get out now, before it was too late, before disaster struck. It was from here that the mission commanders tried to smooth things over aboard the overcrowded transports. There had already been fights and one or two near riots. Tempers were running hot.

Wedge arrived at the ops-center hatch, punched his access code into the keypad, and the hatch slid open. He stepped inside—and instantly noticed something was wrong. Ops was calm. Quiet. Usually it was a madhouse, people tearing around, trying to manage the flow of ships and refugees and information.

But something had happened. And he realized it was not calm that had brought the room to silence, but horror. Everyone in the room, without exception, was staring at one or another of the monitor displays.

No one was bellowing orders into headsets, or punching commands into control panels, or flipping back and forth through a dozen com frequencies to hear from all the participants in a given crisis. None of them were doing anything but *staring*. Wedge looked from one face to another and saw the same expression. Dumb shock, disbelief, astonishment, terror.

Wedge hurried over to the fighter communications station. "Parry, what is it?" he asked the duty officer.

Parry shook his head and pointed at the main display screen. "The star," he said. "None of us believed it. Not us, not the people on the stations we were supposed to evacuate. But it just started to happen. Look at it. *Look at it.*"

Wedge turned and looked at the infrared image of the star's disk. Only an hour before, it had been a placid, featureless blob, with nothing more threatening than a sunspot or two to blemish its appearance.

Now it was a roiling, tortured inferno, bubbling over with flares and spicules and prominences, its surface churning away so violently that Wedge could *see* the movement as he watched. "It's going to blow," he said. "It's really going to blow. I didn't believe it could happen. I *don't* believe it."

"And now what do we do about all the people who believed as little as we did?" Parry asked.

Wedge stared at the monitor screen and frowned. "We have to go back and get them," he said.

*   *   *

Wedge lost count of the number of missions he flew that day, all of them in the runabout, most of them with the ship way over its authorized carrying capacity. One look at the change in their sun, and suddenly everyone was convinced it was time to go. Back and forth he went to the settlement on Thanta Zilbra, jamming as many warm bodies as he could into the craft before lumbering back into the sky. The landing fields were chaos, so bad it was hard to find a place to land, and his runabout was repeatedly mobbed before he could even get the hatches open.

The *Naritus* was not in much better shape. They did not have the time or the available ships to transfer civilians to the transports, and they were overcrowded anyway. Somewhere in the nightmare fog of that day, he heard a voice over his headphones, a voice at ops confirming what Wedge already knew: the information given to the mission planners badly undercounted the population of Thanta Zilbra.

All he could remember later were faces, images, moments. There was no way to assemble anything like a complete, orderly chronology. A crying child in her mother's arms, another baby thrust aboard his craft by a father who could not get aboard himself, the stale smell of too many bodies jammed into too small a space, the stink of fear in the air. Doing an overflight of a fire burning out of control in the middle of the Thanta Zilbra settlement, nosing his runabout through a throng of hysterical refugees piled onto the flight deck of the *Naritus,* making it impossible to continue operations. The voice of a stranger, some other pilot somewhere else in the operation, coming into his headphones, softly singing a lullaby. Was she aware she was singing? Was she trying to soothe herself, or some terrified child jammed into her spacecraft?

An old man, sitting on a box in the middle of the landing field, flatly refusing to leave, despite the pleading of his family. Was he determined to give up his spot to someone who had longer to live, or was he just stubborn, or crazy, refusing to believe in any danger that required him to leave his home? Smashed-open luggage, the most precious belongings of a lifetime abandoned on the landing pad, some of them forcibly discarded when the owner refused to believe it was a choice between his suitcase and someone else's life.

The chaos of small spacecraft of all kinds, civilian and military, bobbing and weaving and flying in and out among the larger ships of the rescue fleet. A collision in space, as a civilian pleasure boat slammed into an X-wing, and both craft exploded. No one lived through that.

And then, at last, sitting at the controls of his runabout, asking for launch clearance to go back for the next load, and hearing the request denied. There was no time to go back. It was over. The fleet had to leave. Screaming into the mike, demanding clearance, insisting there was time plenty of time, for at least one more run, knowing there were still people back there. He knew they were there. He had seen them, spoken with them, promised them he would return.

And hearing the order to secure for the jump to light-speed. *That* order, that moment, he remembered clearly. The *Naritus* activated its hyperdrive, if only for a few moments, and suddenly she was gone from Thanta Zilbra, escaped, away. Wedge could feel the change in her engines as she dropped back into normal space, a light-week or so away from the doomed sun.

Suddenly the urge to shout, to scream, to protest, was gone as well. He sat there, empty, wooden, spent. After a time he released his seat restraints, disembarked from the runabout, and shouldered his way through the crowds of refugees on the flight deck, pushed his way toward a viewport. From here, seen by light that had left the star seven days before, Thanta Zilbra still seemed healthy and well, a warm, inviting dot of light in the sky, not far off at all.

But that was not the way it really was. Not anymore. Wedge shoved his way back through the crowds of sobbing, terrified, stunned people, back toward the operations center.

They were all watching it there, of course. There was nothing else left to do. The cameras from the stay-behind drones were sending their signals via hyperwave link, and so Wedge could see it, see it happen. The star seemed to grow darker, shrink in on itself. Its surface seethed with energy as it backed down in on itself, collapsing down until—

Until it flared, blasting outward in a blinding gout of white starfire that bloomed past the incinerating planets, past the vaporized space stations, until it reached the stay-behind camera and—

The screen went black.

"Right on schedule," Parry said, half to himself. Wedge had not even noticed he was there. "Bovo Yagen is next. That's confirmed, too. No rumor. Estimated system population twelve million—if you want to believe estimates after today. And they're spread out over two inhabited planets and dozens of stations, asteroids, and habitats. If we couldn't pull ten or fifteen thousand people out of this system, what the hell are we going to do there?"

"I don't know," said Wedge. "I don't know."

All he knew for sure was that unless some way could be found to stop the next nova, millions of people were going to die.

TO BE CONCLUDED

ABOUT THE AUTHOR

ROGER MACBRIDE ALLEN was born in 1957 in Bridgeport, Connecticut. He graduated from Boston University in 1979. The author of a dozen science-fiction novels, he lived in Washington, D.C., for many years. In July 1994, he married Eleanore Fox, a member of the U.S. Foreign Service. Her current assignment takes them to Brasilia, Brazil, where they will live for the next two years.

The World of
STAR WARS Novels

In May 1991, *Star Wars* caused a sensation in the publishing industry with the Bantam Spectra release of Timothy Zahn's novel *Heir to the Empire*. For the first time, Lucasfilm Ltd. had authorized new novels that *continued* the famous story told in George Lucas's three blockbuster motion pictures: *Star Wars, The Empire Strikes Back,* and *Return of the Jedi.* Reader reaction was immediate and tumultuous: *Heir* reached #1 on the *New York Times* bestseller list and demonstrated that *Star Wars* lovers were eager for exciting new stories set in this universe, written by leading science fiction authors who shared their passion. Since then, each Bantam *Star Wars* novel has been an instant national bestseller.

Lucasfilm and Bantam decided that future novels in the series would be interconnected: that is, events in one novel would have consequences in the others. You might say that each Bantam *Star Wars* novel, enjoyable on its own, is also part of a much larger tale beginning immediately after the last *Star Wars* film, *Return of the Jedi.*

Here is a special look at Bantam's *Star Wars* books, along with excerpts from these thrilling novels. Each one is available now wherever Bantam Books are sold.

THE TRUCE AT BAKURA by Kathy Tyers
Setting: Immediately after *Return of the Jedi*

*The day after his climactic battle with Emperor Palpatine and
the sacrifice of his father, Darth Vader, who died saving his
life, Luke Skywalker helps recover an Imperial drone ship
bearing a startling message intended for the Emperor. It is a
distress signal from the far-off Imperial outpost of Bakura,
which is under attack by an alien invasion force, the Ssi-ruuk.
Leia sees a rescue mission as an opportunity to achieve a
diplomatic victory for the Rebel Alliance, even if it means
fighting alongside former Imperials. But Luke receives a vision from Obi-Wan Kenobi revealing that the stakes are even
higher: the invasion at Bakura threatens everything the Rebels
have won at such great cost.*

Here is a scene showing the extent of the alien menace:

On an outer deck of a vast battle cruiser called the
Shriwirr, Dev Sibwarra rested his slim brown hand on a prisoner's left shoulder. "It'll be all right," he said softly. The
other human's fear beat at his mind like a three-tailed lash.
"There's no pain. You have a wonderful surprise ahead of
you." Wonderful indeed, a life without hunger, cold, or selfish
desire.

The prisoner, an Imperial of much lighter complexion
than Dev, slumped in the entchment chair. He'd given up
protesting, and his breath came in gasps. Pliable bands se-
cured his forelimbs, neck, and knees—but only for balance.
With his nervous system deionized at the shoulders, he
couldn't struggle. A slender intravenous tube dripped pale
blue magnetizing solution into each of his carotid arteries
while tiny servopumps hummed. It only took a few mils of
magsol to attune the tiny, fluctuating electromagnetic fields of
human brain waves to the Ssi-ruuvi entchment apparatus.

Behind Dev, Master Firwirrung trilled a question in Ssi-
ruuvi. "Is it calmed yet?"

Dev sketched a bow to his master and switched from human speech to Ssi-ruuvi. "Calm enough," he sang back. "He's
almost ready."

Sleek, russet scales protected Firwirrung's two-meter
length from beaked muzzle to muscular tail tip, and a promi-
nent black **V** crest marked his forehead. Not large for a Ssi-
ruu, he was still growing, with only a few age-scores where

scales had begun to separate on his handsome chest. Firwirrung swung a broad, glowing white metal catchment arc down to cover the prisoner from midchest to nose. Dev could just peer over it and watch the man's pupils dilate. At any moment . . .

"Now," Dev announced.

Firwirrung touched a control. His muscular tail twitched with pleasure. The fleet's capture had been good today. Alongside his master, Dev would work far into the night. Before entenchment, prisoners were noisy and dangerous. Afterward, their life energies powered droids of Ssi-ruuvi choosing.

The catchment arc hummed up to pitch. Dev backed away. Inside that round human skull, a magsol-drugged brain was losing control. Though Master Firwirrung assured him that the transfer of incorporeal energy was painless, every prisoner screamed.

As did this one, when Firwirrung threw the catchment arc switch. The arc boomed out a sympathetic vibration, as brain energy leaped to an electromagnet perfectly attuned to magsol. Through the Force rippled an ululation of indescribable anguish.

Dev staggered and clung to the knowledge his masters had given him: The prisoners only thought they felt pain. *He* only thought he sensed their pain. By the time the body screamed, all of a subject's energies had jumped to the catchment arc. The screaming body already was dead.

THE COURTSHIP OF PRINCESS LEIA
by Dave Wolverton
Setting: Four years after *Return of the Jedi*

One of the most interesting developments in Bantam's Star Wars *novels is that in their storyline, Han Solo and Princess Leia start a family. This tale reveals how the couple originally got together. Wishing to strengthen the fledgling New Republic by bringing in powerful allies, Leia opens talks with the Hapes consortium of more than sixty worlds. But the consortium is ruled by the Queen Mother, who, to Han's dismay, wants Leia to marry her son, Prince Isolder. Before this action-packed story is over, Luke will join forces with Isolder against a group of Force-trained "witches" and face a deadly foe.*

In this scene, Luke is searching for Jedi lore and finds more than he bargained for:

Luke popped the cylinder into Artoo, and almost immediately Artoo caught a signal. Images flashed in the air before the droid: an ancient throne room where, one by one, Jedi came before their high master to give reports. Yet the holo was fragmented, so thoroughly erased that Luke got only bits and pieces—a blue-skinned man describing details of a grueling space battle against pirateers; a yellow-eyed Twi'lek with lashing headtails who told of discovering a plot to kill an ambassador. A date and time flashed on the holo vid before each report. The report was nearly four hundred standard years old.

Then Yoda appeared on the video, gazing up at the throne. His color was more vibrantly green than Luke remembered, and he did not use his walking stick. At middle age, Yoda had looked almost perky, carefree—not the bent, troubled old Jedi Luke had known. Most of the audio was erased, but through the background hiss Yoda clearly said, "We tried to free the Chu'unthor from Dathomir, but were repulsed by the witches . . . skirmish, with Masters Gra'aton and Vulatan. . . . Fourteen acolytes killed . . . go back to retrieve . . ." The audio hissed away, and soon the holo image dissolved to blue static with popping lights.

They went up topside, found that night had fallen while they worked underground. Their Whiphid guide soon returned, dragging the body of a gutted snow demon. The demon's white talons curled in the air, and its long purple tongue snaked out from between its massive fangs. Luke was amazed that the Whiphid could haul such a monster, yet the Whiphid held the demon's long hairy tail in one hand and managed to pull it back to camp.

There, Luke stayed the night with the Whiphids in a huge shelter made from the rib cage of a motmot, covered over with hides to keep out the wind. The Whiphids built a bonfire and roasted the snow demon, and the young danced while the elders played their claw harps. As Luke sat, watching the writhing flames and listening to the twang of harps, he meditated. "The future you will see, and the past. Old friends long forgotten . . ." Those were the words Yoda had said long ago while training Luke to peer beyond the mists of time.

Luke looked up at the rib bones of the motmot. The Whiphids had carved stick letters into the bone, ten and twelve meters in the air, giving the lineage of their ancestors. Luke could not read the letters, but they seemed to dance in the firelight, as if they were sticks and stones falling from the sky. The rib bones curved toward him, and Luke followed the curve of bones with his eyes. The tumbling sticks and boulders seemed to gyrate, all of them falling toward him as if they would crush him. He could see boulders hurtling through the air, too, smashing toward him. Luke's nostrils flared, and even Toola's chill could not keep a thin film of perspiration from dotting his forehead. A vision came to Luke then.

Luke stood in a mountain fortress of stone, looking over a plain with a sea of dark forested hills beyond, and a storm rose—a magnificent wind that brought with it towering walls of black clouds and dust, trees hurtling toward him and twisting through the sky. The clouds thundered overhead, filled with purple flames, obliterating all sunlight, and Luke could feel a malevolence hidden in those clouds and knew that they had been raised through the power of the dark side of the Force.

Dust and stones whistled through the air like autumn leaves. Luke tried to hold on to the stone parapet overlooking the plain to keep from being swept from the fortress walls. Winds pounded in his ears like the roar of an ocean, howling.

It was as if a storm of pure dark Force raged over the countryside, and suddenly, amid the towering clouds of darkness that thundered toward him, Luke could hear laughing, the sweet sound of women laughing. He looked above into the dark clouds, and saw the women borne through the air along with the rocks and debris, like motes of dust, laughing. A voice seemed to whisper, "the witches of Dathomir."

HEIR TO THE EMPIRE
DARK FORCE RISING
THE LAST COMMAND
by Timothy Zahn
Setting: Five years after *Return of the Jedi*

This #1 bestselling trilogy introduces two legendary forces of evil into the Star Wars *literary pantheon. Grand Admiral Thrawn has taken control of the Imperial fleet in the years since the destruction of the Death Star, and the mysterious Joruus C'baoth is a fearsome Jedi Master who has been seduced by the dark side. Han and Leia have now been married for about a year, and as the story begins, she is pregnant with twins. Thrawn's plan is to crush the Rebellion and resurrect the Empire's New Order with C'baoth's help—and in return, the Dark Master will get Han and Leia's Jedi children to mold as he wishes. For as readers of this magnificent trilogy will see, Luke Skywalker is not the last of the old Jedi. He is the first of the new.*

In this scene from Heir to the Empire, *Thrawn and C'baoth meet for the first time:*

For a long moment the old man continued to stare at Thrawn, a dozen strange expressions flicking in quick succession across his face. "Come. We will talk."

"Thank you," Thrawn said, inclining his head slightly. "May I ask who we have the honor of addressing?"

"Of course." The old man's face was abruptly regal again, and when he spoke his foice rang out in the silence of the crypt. "I am the Jedi Master Joruus C'baoth."

Pellaeon inhaled sharply, a cold shiver running up his back. "Joruus C'baoth?" he breathed. "But—"

He broke off. C'baoth looked at him, much as Pellaeon himself might look at a junior officer who has spoken out of turn. "Come," he repeated, turning back to Thrawn. "We will talk."

He led the way out of the crypt and back into the sunshine. Several small knots of people had gathered in the square in their absence, huddling well back from both the crypt and the shuttle as they whispered nervously together.

With one exception. Standing directly in their path a few meters away was one of the two guards C'baoth had ordered out of the crypt. On his face was an expression of barely controlled fury; in his hands, cocked and ready, was his crossbow. "You destroyed his home," C'baoth said, almost conversationally. "Doubtless he would like to exact vengeance."

The words were barely out of his mouth when the guard suddenly snapped the crossbow up and fired. Instinctively, Pellaeon ducked, raising his blaster—

And three meters from the Imperials the bolt came to an abrupt halt in midair.

Pellaeon stared at the hovering piece of wood and metal, his brain only slowly catching up with what had just happened. "They are our guests," C'baoth told the guard in a voice clearly intended to reach everyone in the square. "They will be treated accordingly."

With a crackle of splintering wood, the crossbow bolt shattered, the pieces dropping to the ground. Slowly, reluctantly, the guard lowered his crossbow, his eyes still burning with a now impotent rage. Thrawn let him stand there another second like that, then gestured to Rukh. The Noghri raised his blaster and fired—

And in a blur of motion almost too fast to see, a flat stone detached itself from the ground and hurled itself directly into the path of the shot, shattering spectacularly as the blast hit it.

Thrawn spun to face C'baoth, his face a mirror of surprise and anger. "C'baoth—!"

"These are *my* people, Grand Admiral Thrawn," the other cut him off, his voice forged from quiet steel. "Not yours; mine. If there is punishment to be dealt out, *I* will do it."

For a long moment the two men again locked eyes. Then, with an obvious effort, Thrawn regained his composure. "Of course, Master C'baoth," he said. "Forgive me."

C'baoth nodded. "Better. Much better." He looked past Thrawn, dismissed the guard with a nod. "Come," he said, looking back at the Grand Admiral. "We will talk."

The Jedi Academy Trilogy:
JEDI SEARCH
DARK APPRENTICE
CHAMPIONS OF THE FORCE
by Kevin J. Anderson
Setting: Seven years after *Return of the Jedi*

In order to assure the continuation of the Jedi Knights, Luke Skywalker has decided to start a training facility: a Jedi Academy. He will gather Force-sensitive students who show potential as prospective Jedi and serve as their mentor, as Jedi Masters Obi-Wan Kenobi and Yoda did for him. Han and Leia's twins are now toddlers, and there is a third Jedi child: the infant Anakin, named after Luke and Leia's father. In this trilogy, we discover the existence of a powerful Imperial doomsday weapon, the horrifying Sun Crusher—which will soon become the centerpiece of a titanic struggle between Luke Skywalker and his most brilliant Jedi Academy student, who is delving dangerously into the dark side.

In this scene from the first novel, Jedi Search, Luke vocalizes his concept of a new Jedi order to a distinguished assembly of New Republic leaders:

As he descended the long ramp, Luke felt all eyes turn toward him. A hush fell over the assembly. Luke Skywalker, the lone remaining Jedi Master, almost never took part in governmental proceedings.

"I have an important matter to address," he said. For a moment he was reminded of when he had walked alone into the dank corridors of Jabba the Hutt's palace—but this time there were no piglike Gamorrean guards that he could manipulate with a twist of his fingers and a touch of the Force.

Mon Mothma gave him a soft, mysterious smile and gestured for him to take a central position. "The words of a Jedi Knight are always welcome to the New Republic," she said.

Luke tried not to look pleased. She had provided the perfect opening for him. "In the Old Republic," he said, "Jedi Knights were the protectors and guardians of all. For a thousand generations the Jedi used the powers of the Force to guide, defend, and provide support for the rightful government of worlds—before the dark days of the Empire came, and the Jedi Knights were killed."

He let his words hang, then took another breath. "Now we have a New Republic. The Empire appears to be defeated. We have founded a new government based upon the old, but let us hope we learn from our mistakes. Before, an entire order of Jedi watched over the Republic, offering strength. Now I am the only Jedi Master who remains.

"Without that order of protectors to provide a backbone of strength for the New Republic, can we survive? Will we be able to weather the storms and the difficulties of forging a new union? Until now we have suffered severe struggles—but in the future they will be seen as nothing more than birth pangs."

Before the other senators could disagree with that, Luke continued. "Our people had a common foe in the Empire, and we must not let our defenses lapse just because we have internal problems. More to the point, what will happen when we begin squabbling among ourselves over petty matters? The old Jedi helped to mediate many types of disputes. What if there are no Jedi Knights to protect us in the difficult times ahead?"

Luke moved under the diffracting rainbow colors from the crystal light overhead. He took his time to fix his gaze on all the senators present; he turned his attention to Leia last. Her eyes were wide but supportive. He had not discussed his idea with her beforehand.

"My sister is undergoing Jedi training. She has a great

deal of skill in the Force. Her three children are also likely candidates to be trained as young Jedi. In recent years I have come to know a woman named Mara Jade, who is now unifying the smugglers—the former smugglers," he amended, "into an organization that can support the needs of the New Republic. She also has a talent for the Force. I have encountered others in my travels."

Another pause. The audience was listening so far. "But are these the only ones? We already know that the ability to use the Force is passed from generation to generation. Most of the Jedi were killed in the Emperor's purge—but could he possibly have eradicated all of the descendants of those Knights? I myself was unaware of the potential power within me until Obi-Wan Kenobi taught me how to use it. My sister Leia was similarly unaware.

"How many people are abroad in this galaxy who have a comparable strength in the Force, who are potential members of a new order of Jedi Knights, but are unaware of who they are?"

Luke looked at them again. "In my brief search I have already discovered that there are indeed some descendants of former Jedi. I have come here to ask"—he turned to gesture toward Mon Mothma, swept his hands across the people gathered there in the chamber—"for two things.

"First, that the New Republic officially sanction my search for those with a hidden talent for the Force, to seek them out and try to bring them to our service. For this I will need some help."

Admiral Ackbar interrupted, blinking his huge fish eyes and turning his head. "But if you yourself did not know your power when you were young, how will these other people know? How will you find them, Jedi Skywalker?"

Luke folded his hands in front of him. "Several ways. First, with the help of two dedicated droids who will spend their days searching through the Imperial City databases, we may find likely candidates, people who have experienced miraculous strokes of luck, whose lives seem filled with incredible coincidences. We could look for people who seem unusually charismatic or those whom legend credits with working miracles. These could all be unconscious manifestations of a skill with the Force."

Luke held up another finger. "As well, the droids could search the database for forgotten descendants of known Jedi

Knights from the Old Republic days. We should turn up a few leads."

"And what will you yourself be doing?" Mon Mothma asked, shifting in her robes.

"I've already found several candidates I wish to investigate. All I ask right now is that you agree this is something we should pursue, that the search for Jedi be conducted by others and not just myself."

Mon Mothma sat up straighter in her central sea. "I think we can agree to that without further discussion." She looked around to the other senators, seeing them now agreement. "Tell us your second request."

Luke stood taller. This was most important to him. He saw Leia stiffen.

"If sufficient candidates are found who have potential for using the Force, I wish to be allowed—with the New Republic's blessing—to establish in some appropriate place an intensive training center, a Jedi academy, if you will. Under my direction we can help these students discover their abilities, to focus and strengthen their power. Ultimately, this academy would provide a core group that could allow us to restore the Jedi Knights as protectors of the New Republic."

CHILDREN OF THE JEDI
by Barbara Hambly
Setting: Eight years after *Return of the Jedi*

The Star Wars *characters face a menace from the glory days of the Empire when a thirty-year-old automated Imperial Dreadnaught comes to life and begins its grim mission: to gather forces and annihilate a long-forgotten stronghold of Jedi children. When Luke is whisked onboard, he begins to communicate with the brave Jedi Knight who paralyzed the ship decades ago, and gave her life in the process. Now she is part of the vessel, existing in its artificial intelligence core, and guiding Luke through one of the most unusual adventures he has ever had.*

In this scene, Luke discovers that an evil presence is gathering, one that will force him to join the battle:

Like See-Threepio, Nichos Marr sat in the outer room of the suite to which Cray had been assigned, in the power-down mode that was the droid equivalent of rest. Like Threepio, at the sound of Luke's almost noiseless tread he turned his head, aware of his presence.

"Luke?" Cray had equipped him with the most sensitive vocal modulators, and the word was calibrated to a whisper no louder than the rustle of the blueleafs massed outside the windows. He rose, and crossed to where Luke stood, the dull silver of his arms and shoulders a phantom gleam in the stray flickers of light. "What is it?"

"I don't know." They retreated to the small dining area where Luke had earlier probed his mind, and Luke stretched up to pin back a corner of the lamp-sheathe, letting a slim triangle of butter-colored light fall on the purple of the vulwood tabletop. "A dream. A premonition, maybe." It was on his lips to ask, *Do you dream?* but he remembered the ghastly, imageless darkness in Nichos's mind, and didn't. He wasn't sure if his pupil was aware of the difference from his human perception and knowledge, aware of just exactly what he'd lost when his consciousness, his self, had been transferred.

In the morning Luke excused himself from the expedition Tomla El had organized with Nichos and Cray to the Falls of Dessiar, one of the places on Ithor most renowned for its beauty and peace. When they left he sought out Umwaw Moolis, and the tall herd leader listened gravely to his less than logical request and promised to put matters in train to fulfill it. Then Luke descended to the House of the Healers, where Drub McKumb lay, sedated far beyond pain but with all the perceptions of agony and nightmare still howling in his mind.

"Kill you!" He heaved himself at the restraints, blue eyes glaring furiously as he groped and scrabbled at Luke with his clawed hands. "It's all poison! I see you! I see the dark light all around you! You're him! You're him!" His back bent like a bow; the sound of his shrieking was like something being ground out of him by an infernal mangle.

Luke had been through the darkest places of the universe and of his own mind, had done and experienced greater evil than perhaps any man had known on the road the Force had dragged him . . . Still, it was hard not to turn away.

"We even tried yarrock on him last night," explained the Healer in charge, a slightly built Ithorian beautifully tabby-striped green and yellow under her simple tabard of purple linen. "But apparently the earlier doses that brought him enough lucidity to reach here from his point of origin oversensitized his system. We'll try again in four or five days."

Luke gazed down into the contorted, grimacing face.

"As you can see," the Healer said, "the internal perception of pain and fear is slowly lessening. It's down to ninety-three percent of what it was when he was first brought in. Not much, I know, but something."

"Him! *Him! HIM!*" Foam spattered the old man's stained gray beard.

Who?

"I wouldn't advise attempting any kind of mindlink until it's at least down to fifty percent, Master Skywalker."

"No," said Luke softly.

Kill you all. And, *They are gathering . . .*

"Do you have recordings of everything he's said?"

"Oh, yes." The big coppery eyes blinked assent. "The transcript is available through the monitor cubicle down the hall. We could make nothing of them. Perhaps they will mean something to you."

They didn't. Luke listened to them all, the incoherent groans and screams, the chewed fragments of words that could be only guessed at, and now and again the clear disjointed cries: "Solo! Solo! Can you hear me? Children . . . Evil . . . Gathering here . . . Kill you all!"

THE CRYSTAL STAR
by Vonda N. McIntyre
Setting: Ten years after *Return of the Jedi*

Leia's three children have been kidnapped. That horrible fact is made worse by Leia's realization that she can no longer sense her children through the Force! While she, Artoo-Detoo, and Chewbacca trail the kidnappers, Luke and Han discover a planet that is suffering strange quantum effects from a nearby star. Slowly freezing into a perfect crystal and disrupting the Force, the star is blunting Luke's power and crippling the Millennium Falcon. *These strands converge in an apocalyptic threat not only to the fate of the New Republic, but to the universe itself.*

Here is Luke and Han's initial approach to the crystal star:

Han piloted the *Millennium Falcon* through the strangest star system he had ever approached. An ancient, dying, crystallizing white dwarf star orbited a black hole in a wildly eccentric elliptical path.

Eons ago, in this place, a small and ordinary yellow star peacefully orbited an immense blue-white supergiant. The blue star aged, and collapsed.

The blue star went supernova, blasting light and radiation and debris out into space.

Its light still traveled through the universe, a furious explosion visible from distant galaxies.

Over time, the remains of the supergiant's core collapsed under the force of its own gravity. The result was degenerate mass: a black hole.

The violence of the supernova disrupted the orbit of the nova's companion, the yellow star. Over time, the yellow star's orbit decayed.

The yellow star fell toward the unimaginably dense body of the black hole. The black hole sucked up anything, even light, that came within its grasp. And when it captured matter —even an entire yellow star—it ripped the atoms apart into a glowing accretion disk. Subatomic particles imploded downward into the singularity's equator, emitting great bursts of radiation. The accretion disk spun at a fantastic speed, glowing with fantastic heat, creating a funeral pyre for the destroyed yellow companion.

The plasma spiraled in a raging pinwheel, circling so fast and heating so intensely that it blasted X rays out into space. Then, finally, the glowing gas fell toward the invisible black hole, approaching it closer and closer, appearing to fall more and more slowly as relativity influenced it.

It was lost forever to this universe.

That was the fate of the small yellow star.

The system contained a third star: the dying white dwarf, which shone with ancient heat even as it froze into a quantum crystal. Now, as the *Millennium Falcon* entered the system, the white dwarf was falling toward the black hole, on the inward curve of its eccentric elliptical orbit.

"Will you look at that," Han said. "Quite a show."

"Indeed it is, Master Han," Threepio said, "but it is merely a shadow of what will occur when the black hole captures the crystal star."

Luke gazed silently into the maelstrom of the black hole. Han waited.

"Hey, kid! Snap out of it."

Luke started. "What?"

"I don't know where you were, but you weren't here."

"Just thinking about the Jedi Academy. I hate to leave my students, even for a few days. But if I *do* find other trained Jedi, it'll make a big difference. To the Academy. To the New Republic . . ."

"I think we're getting along pretty well already," Han said, irked. He had spent years maintaining the peace with ordinary people. In his opinion, Jedi Knights could cause more trouble than they were worth. "And what if these are all using the dark side?"

Luke did not reply.

Han seldom admitted his nightmares, but he had nightmares about what could happen to his children if they were tempted to the dark side.

Right now they were safe, with Leia on a planetary tour of remote and peaceful worlds of the New Republic. By this time they must have reached Munto Codru. They would be visiting the beautiful mountains of the world's temperate zone. Han smiled, imagining his princess and his children being welcomed to one of Munto Codru's mysterious, ancient, fairy-tale castles.

Solar prominences flared from the white dwarf's surface. The *Falcon* passed it, heading toward the more perilous region of the black hole.

The Corellian Trilogy:
AMBUSH AT CORELLIA
ASSAULT AT SELONIA
SHOWDOWN AT CENTERPOINT
by Roger MacBride Allen
Setting: Fourteen years after *Return of the Jedi*

This trilogy takes us to Corellia, Han Solo's home world, which Han has not visited in quite some time. A trade summit brings Han, Leia, and the children—now developing their own clear personalities and instinctively learning more about their innate skills in the Force—into the middle of a situation that most closely resembles a burning fuse. The Corellian system is on the brink of civil war, there are New Republic intelligence agents on a mysterious mission which even Han does not understand, and worst of all, a fanatical rebel leader has his hands on a superweapon of unimaginable power—and just wait until you find out who that leader is!

Here is an early scene from Ambush *that gives you a wonderful look at the growing Solo children (the twins are Jacen and Jaina, and their little brother is Anakin):*

Anakin plugged the board into the innards of the droid and pressed a button. The droid's black, boxy body shuddered awake, it drew in its wheels to stand up a bit taller, its status lights lit, and it made a sort of triple beep. "That's good," he said, and pushed the button again. The droid's status lights went out, and its body slumped down again. Anakin picked up the next piece, a motivation actuator. He frowned at it as he turned it over in his hands. He shook his head. "That's *not* good," he announced.

"What's not good?" Jaina asked.

"This thing," Anakin said, handing her the actuator. "Can't you *tell?* The insides part is all melty."

Jaina and Jacen exchanged a look. "The outside looks okay," Jaina said, giving the part to her brother. "How can he tell what the *inside* of it looks like? It's sealed shut when they make it."

Jacen shrugged. "How can he do any of this stuff? But we need that actuator. That was the toughest part to dig up. I must have gone around half the city looking for one that would fit this droid." He turned toward his little brother. "Anakin, we don't have another one of these. Can you make it better? Can you make the insides less melty?"

Anakin frowned. "I can make it *some* better. Not all the way better. A *little* less melty. *Maybe* it'll be okay."

Jacen handed the actuator back to Anakin. "Okay, try it."

Anakin, still sitting on the floor, took the device from his brother and frowned at it again. He turned it over and over in his hands, and then held it over his head and looked at it as if he were holding it up to the light. "There," he said, pointing a chubby finger at one point on the unmarked surface. "In there is the bad part." He rearranged himself to sit cross-legged, put the actuator in his lap, and put his right index finger over the "bad" part. "Fix," he said. "Fix." The dark brown outer case of the actuator seemed to glow for a second with an odd blue-red light, but then the glow sputtered out and Anakin pulled his finger away quickly and stuck it in his mouth, as if he had burned it on something.

"Better now?" Jaina asked.

"Some better," Anakin said, pulling his finger out of his mouth. "Not *all* better." He took the actuator in his hand and

stood up. He opened the access panel on the broken droid and plugged in the actuator. He closed the door and looked expectantly at his older brother and sister.

"Done?" Jaina asked.

"Done," Anakin agreed. "But *I'm* not going to push the button." He backed well away from the droid, sat down on the floor, and folded his arms.

Jacen looked at his sister.

"Not me," she said. "This was your idea."

Jacen stepped forward to the droid, reached out to push the power button from as far away as he could, and then stepped hurriedly back.

Once again, the droid shuddered awake, rattling a bit this time as it did so. It pulled its wheels in, lit its panel lights, and made the same triple beep. But then its camera eye viewlens wobbled back and forth, and its panel lights dimmed and flared. It rolled backward just a bit, and then recovered itself.

"Good morning, young mistress and masters," it said. "How may I surge you?"

Well, one word wrong, but so what? Jacen grinned and clapped his hands and rubbed them together eagerly. "Good day, droid," he said. They had done it! But what to ask for first? "First tidy up this room," he said. A simple task, and one that ought to serve as a good test of what this droid could do.

Suddenly the droid's overhead access door blew off and there was a flash of light from its interior. A thin plume of smoke drifted out of the droid. Its panel lights flared again, and then the work arm sagged downward. The droid's body, softened by heat, sagged in on itself and drooped to the floor. The floor and walls and ceilings of the playroom were supposed to be fireproof, but nonetheless the floor under the droid darkened a bit, and the ceiling turned black. The ventilators kicked on high automatically, and drew the smoke out of the room. After a moment they shut themselves off, and the room was silent.

The three children stood, every bit as frozen to the spot as the droid was, absolutely stunned. It was Anakin who recovered first. He walked cautiously toward the droid and looked at it carefully, being sure not to get too close or touch it. *"Really* melty now," he announced, and then wandered off to the other side of the room to play with his blocks.

The twins looked at the droid, and then at each other.

"We're dead," Jacen announced, surveying the wreckage.